# THE CHEMISTRY OF CHRISTMAS

*Shiloh Ridge Ranch in Three Rivers, Book 6*

LIZ ISAACSON

ISBN-13: 978-1-953506-35-1

## Get free books!

Join Liz's newsletter to stay updated with new releases, get access to exclusive bonus content, and more!

Join Liz's newsletter here. Get two free books!

Tap here to see all of Liz's books.

Join Liz's Reader Group on Facebook. We play games, have Book Clubs, and have lots of fun interactions! Come join us!

# The Glover Family

Welcome to Shiloh Ridge Ranch! The Glover family is BIG, and sometimes it can be hard to keep track of everyone.

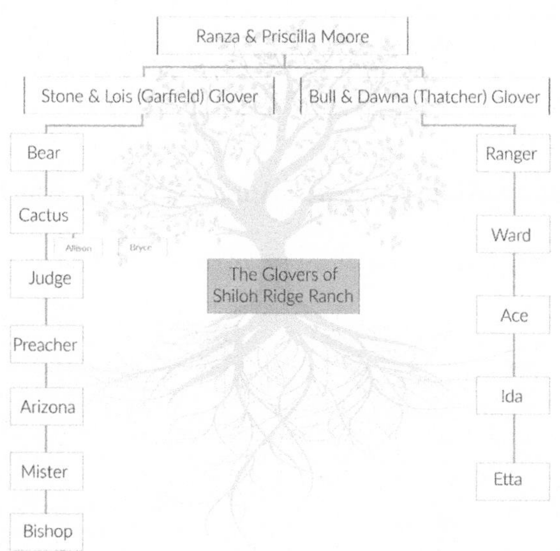

**There is a more detailed graphic here, on my website.** (But it has spoilers! I made it as the family started to get really big, which happens fairly quickly, actually. It has all the couples (some you won't see for many more books), as well as a lot of the children they have or will have, through about Book 6. It might be easier for you to visualize, though.)

HERE'S HOW THINGS ARE RIGHT NOW:

**Lois & Stone (deceased) Glover, 7 children, in age-order:** (Lois is engaged to Donald Parker)

1. Bear (Sammy, wife / Lincoln (9), step-son, Stetson (newborn), son)
2. Cactus (Allison, ex-wife / Bryce, son (deceased) // Willa, wife / Mitch (10), step-son)
3. Judge
4. Preacher
5. Arizona (Duke Rhinehart, husband, living at the Rhinehart Ranch, just south of Shiloh Ridge)
6. Mister
7. Bishop (Montana, wife / Aurora (17), step-daughter)

**Dawna & Bull (deceased) Glover, 5 children, in age-order:**

1. Ranger (Oakley, wife)
2. Ward
3. Ace (Holly Ann, wife)
4. Etta (Noah Johnson, fiancé)
5. Ida (Brady Burton, husband)

Bull and Stone Glover were brothers, so their children are cousins. Ranger and Bear, for example, are cousins, and each the oldest sibling in their families.

THE GLOVERS KNOW AND INTERACT WITH THE WALKERS of Seven Sons Ranch. There's a lot of them too! Here's a little cheat sheet for you for the Walkers.

**MOMMA & DADDY: PENNY AND GIDEON WALKER**

1. RHETT & EVELYN WALKER
Son: Conrad
Triplets: Austin, Elaine, and Easton

2. JEREMIAH & WHITNEY WALKER
Son: Jonah Jeremiah (JJ)
Daughter: Clara Jean
Son: Jason

3. LIAM & CALLIE WALKER
Daughter: Denise
Daughter: Ginger

4. TRIPP & IVORY WALKER
Son: Oliver
Son: Isaac

5. WYATT & MARCY WALKER
Son: Warren
Son: Cole

Son: Harrison

6. Skyler & Mallery Walker
Daughter: Camila

7. Micah & Simone Walker
Son: Travis (Trap)

THE GLOVERS KNOW AND INTERACT WITH THE SEVERAL of the cowboys and their families at Three Rivers Ranch too... There's a lot going on in Three Rivers!

You'll see:

1. Squire and Kelly Ackerman

Mother / Father: Heidi (owns Ackermans bakery) / Frank

Son: Finn

Daughter: Libby

Son: Michael

Son: Samuel

2. PETE AND CHELSEA MARSHALL (CHELSEA IS SQUIRE'S sister)

4 sons: Paul, Henry, John, Rich

3. REESE AND CARLY SANDERS: THEY'RE THE ADMINS FOR Courage Reins, Pete and Chelsea's equine therapy unit at Three Rivers Ranch.

# Chapter One

Preacher Glover yawned, but he kept his horse moving. Sidewinder plodded along, keeping the cattle going where they needed to go. He'd spent hours moving herds today, as he did most other days.

Today felt a little different, sure, because Cactus had just tied the knot mere hours ago. Preacher still wore his suit, in fact, but the work around the ranch didn't stop because two people said I do.

He'd gotten out of cleaning up in True Blue in favor of getting outside to move the last of the herd, and he signaled to Mister, who rode a couple hundred yards to his right. The two of them had plans to get online later, but Ace wouldn't be joining them. He and Holly Ann would be down in town, eating with her family. Duke and Zona had agreed to a game night at the Rhinehart Ranch, and Beau had said something about a date with a new woman who he wouldn't name.

Preacher had texted Charlie about the gaming, but she hadn't answered yet. His mind caught on the blonde woman, and he could picture her easily though they hadn't spent a lot of in-person time together. She came on their Chatty feed all the time, and he had yet to beat her at a game of Solitary Ops.

The woman had amazing gaming skills, and Preacher would like her just for that. She sometimes texted only him, in a private Chatty room, and sometimes the messages simply came on his phone. He hadn't asked her out, because she didn't seem too keen on dating, and he'd rather have her in his life as a friend than not at all.

He couldn't help thinking about her in a romantic way though. She was smart and funny, absolutely gorgeous, and Preacher had liked her from the moment he'd seen her making ice cream with liquid nitrogen at his cousin's wedding.

He didn't have hundreds with his name and number written on them, despite what she'd originally believed. He'd barely dated at all, thank you very much. He hadn't told anyone about his feelings for Charlie, but the men he spent time with had to know. Duke had said something a few weeks ago, and Preacher hadn't denied anything.

He hadn't confirmed anything either, and Mister had answered for Preacher, saying he didn't want to ruin things with Charlie because she was the best gamer they'd met in years.

Preacher had laughed, as if that was the reason why.

"Ho there," he called, and the cow trying to go left when he should stay right got back in line. Moving the herd didn't take many brain cells, so Preacher had plenty of time to obsess over Charlie.

He'd considered asking her to be his date to Mother's wedding, and he said the words out loud. "Maybe you'd like to come up to the ranch for my mom's wedding. I'm not a bad dancer."

Charlie would say, "Like as your date?" with plenty of bite in her voice, as if dating him was incomprehensible.

"As friends," he said, contributing his half of the conversation out loud. Only cows could judge him—and Sidewinder, though the horse was used to listening to Preacher talk to himself. "I just don't want to go to another wedding alone, especially my mother's."

Having Mother get remarried was weird enough, and Preacher just wanted the day to come and go. Sixteen more days, and it would be done. The year of weddings, where literally six Glovers had tied the knot, would be over.

Etta still had a wedding coming up, but not for another four or five months, and Preacher wouldn't have to be so central to that one. "Still have to wear a tie," he muttered. It wasn't the white shirt and tie he didn't like, because he wore one of those every week when he went to church. It was the ceremony of things. The way he showed up and no one looked at him or even noticed if he was there or not.

His phone chimed, and he reached back and pulled it from his pocket. His pulse picked up when he saw Charlie's name, and not in the Chatty where he'd invited her to play later.

*Are you done with the wedding?* she'd asked. *I just got something I want to show you.*

He could ride a horse hands-free, so he used both hands to tap out, *Done with the wedding, but I'm out moving cattle. Last herd. Should be finished in about twenty minutes.*

*I can video call*, she said before he could send the message. *It'll be fast.*

He sent his first message, and then added, *Sure, call.*

His phone rang in a strange up and down tone, indicating the video chat. He swiped up to answer it, and a couple of seconds later, she came up on his screen. "There you are," she said, smiling at him. "I wasn't sure you'd have service out there."

"We're fairly close to the epicenter of the ranch," he said, grinning back at her. She wore her sandy, streaked blonde hair in two braids, one falling over each shoulder. "Just moving a herd from one pasture to another."

"Sounds exciting."

"I can do it while on a video chat," he said dryly. "So no, it's not exciting." He didn't even have to watch the cattle. Sidewinder would keep them in line if they started to stray. He did look out over the land, and the sun had started to set, bringing with it gold and purple—and a newfound cold.

"I can game later," she said. "You'll shower and stuff first, right?"

"Yep."

"That'll give me time to eat," she said. "But I wanted to show you this new flight simulator I got."

"Oh, sweet," he said.

"I'm going to switch you around," she said. "Don't get

dizzy." She moved the phone before he could look away, and it was disorienting.

He groaned, and she giggled, and Preacher definitely had to ask her to come to Mother's wedding with him. The screen settled, showing her massive monitor, which had the best video card and sound system installed.

"Look how I can take off from that airport in Greece," she said, and of course, she did it flawlessly. The excitement in her voice infected him, and he laughed at her.

"That's great, Charlie," he said. "But can you land?"

"I've blown up twice," she admitted. "But the third time's the charm, right?"

"Sure," he said. "Let's see it."

"I can't just turn around and land," she said. "My flight plan is taking me to Paris."

"Of course," he said dryly. He didn't hate flight simulators, but they weren't his favorite. Charlie loved them though, and she'd told him in one of their private chats that if she hadn't become a chemist, she'd like to be a pilot. Her father was a pilot, and Charlie loved planes.

"I won't bore you with the flight," she said. "Hit me when you get on tonight."

"Okay," he said, and he knew she was about to end the call. "Charlie," he practically yelled.

She swung the phone back around, leaning it against the monitor so it angled up at her face. She didn't look at it, but kept her attention on the flight simulator as she said, "Yeah?"

"My mother's wedding is coming up, and I'm not a bad

dancer, and I...." He trailed off, because all the words were in the wrong order. "She loves dancing."

"Okay," Charlie said, glancing down at the phone.

"Would you come to the wedding with me?"

"As a date?"

At least he'd pegged her response with near one hundred percent accuracy. She picked up the phone and held it at eye level.

"No," Preacher said. "Just as my friend. I just don't want to stand there like a loser against the wall during the dancing. Mother's hinted she wants us all to dance." He'd spent plenty of time in junior high against the wall at dances. In high school, he'd stopped going to save himself the humiliation, but he couldn't skip out on his mother's wedding.

"I don't own a dress," she said.

"Sure you do," he said. "I've seen you on Sundays in church clothes."

"Those are skirts," she said. "Not dresses." She gave him a wide smile. "I've never owned or worn anything like the last woman you went to a wedding with. That things was...bright."

They laughed together, and Preacher actually found the action cleansing. He loved the bell-like sound of Charlie's laugh, and he shook his head. "We all make mistakes, and if you'd ever tell me about the last guy you went out with, I'm sure I could find something to tease you about."

She shook her head and mimed zipping her lips.

"It's not like I chose that dress for her, you know," he said.

"But you chose her, and a woman like her chooses dresses like that."

He'd seen Charlie in black skirts and white blouses, and he didn't mind those at all. She wore makeup to church, as far as he could tell, and her hair had always looked curled and cute on the Sabbath. "We all make mistakes," he said. "If that's my biggest one, I'll take it."

She grinned at him. "I don't know how to dance."

"You don't need to," he said. "It's the man's job to lead the woman in a dance. You just follow me, and we'll be fine."

She looked dubious, though the playful glint in her eye hadn't gone out yet. She could go from hot to cold in less time than it took to blink, and Preacher had seen her do it several times. Then she'd sign off the Chatty, and he'd pretend like he didn't care.

"I think I'm going to have to see your dancing skills before I agree. You're talking a shopping trip, Preach. And I don't do that unless absolutely necessary."

He chuckled, but Charlie was dead serious. She hadn't set up a kiosk in the mall, but she had told him she worked at HealNow, the new company in town that had gone into one of the tall buildings Preacher hated.

She seemed available for gaming almost all the time, and she'd only mentioned one friend in their couple of months of playing and talking. A woman named Shoshana, and Preacher assumed she worked with Charlie.

"Tell me when you can get together," he said, every cell in his body rejoicing at the very idea. And if they danced, he'd get to touch her, and breathe in the scent of her skin.

He imagined her to smell like peaches and cotton, but he didn't actually know, because they'd spent very little time together.

"No, you tell me," she said. "You're the busy one."

"We're operating on a holiday schedule until the New Year," he said. "So we're doing essentials only."

"You're moving cattle on your brother's wedding day," she said, cocking her head. "You'll still work eight hours a day."

He grinned and conceded the point with, "But it's not twelve hours."

"So...tomorrow?"

"Tomorrow's fine," he said, thrilled with the possibility of seeing her tomorrow. Touching her tomorrow. Being with her tomorrow. "Tell me what you like to eat, and I'll pick it up on my way in. Unless you want to go out to dance? We only need like five square feet."

She looked away from the camera and then quickly back. "My place is fine. I'll have to clean it up a little, but I should have time."

"I don't care if it's clean or not."

She only smiled and said, "I'll text you a place to get food, okay? I have to go."

"Oh, all right," he said. "Talk to you later."

"Yep. Bye." She was gone just like that, and Preacher frowned at his phone. Looking away from the device left him night-blind for a few seconds, and he nearly dropped his phone when Mister yelled at him.

"Yep," he yelled back, though he wasn't sure what his brother had even said.

It didn't matter. Preacher had a date with Charlie Perkins.

---

PREACHER PEERED THROUGH THE WINDSHIELD ON THE right, sure Charlie had missed a number or something in her address. The houses out here were massive and all brand-new. No one lived behind a coded gate in Three Rivers except for those who'd bought the luxury homes out in the subdivision northeast of town.

He'd been driving for what felt like hours, and the food he'd picked up twenty-five minutes ago would surely be cold. He'd texted her when he'd left Down Under, the barbecue place in town that Preacher actually liked.

Ranger had told him about it, and they'd gone together a couple of times in the past couple of years. Charlie apparently liked Texas barbecue, and she'd ordered a lot of meat and a lot of bread to go with it.

Preacher turned another corner, and only three homes sat on this street. They all hulked in the night, with huge dark shapes against the moonlight, as well as the lights coming from the buildings themselves.

The one with the numbers she'd sent him had lights under every window, all illuminated. Not only that, but bright, colorful Christmas lights hung along every perfectly straight eave, indicating the lines of the roof.

There were a ton of those on the two-story house with the three-car garage.

"This is incredible," he said to himself, wondering what

in the world Charlie did to be able to afford a place like this. He knew people like Wyatt Walker lived out here, and the dude was a billionaire rodeo champion.

Could Charlie be one too?

He hardly knew her, and Preacher's heartbeat boomed again and then again as he put his somewhat rickety pickup in park. He hadn't bought a new vehicle for something like eight or nine years, because he didn't need one. He could use this one until the day it decided to stop, his family's frugalness embedded inside him.

He reminded himself that he had plenty of money too as he picked up the box with all the food in it and headed for the front door.

Charlie opened it as he put his boot on the top step, and she stole his breath straight from his lungs, causing him to gasp.

"Hey," she said, everything about her feminine and soft. She had one hand curled around the back of the door, and she wore an oversized gray sweatshirt with a sports brand on the front of it, a pair of baggy jeans, and slippers. Legit slippers the color of sheep's wool.

"Look at you," he said, drawing his eyes down the length of her body and back up. "The wedding will be a little more formal than this." He was surprised he'd gotten so many words out, and he hoped he wouldn't say something tonight to drive Charlie away.

He'd considered talking to Ace and Bishop before the date, but had vetoed the idea every time it had come up. He'd told exactly one person where he'd be tonight—Judge

—and his brother had only looked at him with arched brows and said, "Okay, drive safe."

That was it.

Preacher could actually do with a bit more meddling.

Charlie smiled at him and tucked her loose curls behind her ears. "I didn't go to work today."

"No?'

"Didn't feel like it."

"Wow, I wish I could stay home when I felt like it." He looked up at the ceiling that stretched above him. "This place is incredible."

"Thanks," she said, closing the door behind him. "I've only been here about six months or so, so it's still pretty sterile."

Art hung on the walls in silver and gold frames, and Preacher was no expert, but they looked like professional paintings. She'd put a rug down in front of the door that led back into the house, but he waited for her to go first. She went behind the staircase that led up and into a living room filled with dark gray couches that looked like he could sink into them and never get out.

No TV in the room, but a crackling fireplace, plenty of potted plants, and wide open blinds on the windows. He did not like that, and he looked away from the darkness beyond the glass.

She passed a dining room table that could seat at least ten and led him into the kitchen. He could only stand and gape. Holly Ann would die here, and then she'd bustle around, making desserts and meals happily until the day she died.

Dark gray granite countertops sat atop lighter gray cabinets, and all of the appliances were black. The bar seated eight along its length, and he couldn't find a dish or a glass or a single thing out of place.

He looked at Charlie and scoffed, the only sound he could come up with. He felt like he barely knew her, and he told himself that was what he was doing there. Getting to know her.

"You're surprised by the house."

He put the box of food on the counter, almost feeling bad for dirtying it. "Yes," he said, kicking himself for being so blunt. He should've said, "A little," or "Not at all. I live in a huge mansion myself."

Bishop had remodeled the Ranch House a couple of years ago, and it was much more spacious, with an updated layout that made sense. They had new appliances and furniture too, but nothing like this. He couldn't even fathom why someone would ever need a house this nice, especially on a ranch.

The stuff he tracked in on his boots would ruin the stark white floor in her kitchen in a single day.

"Do you live here alone?" he asked.

"Of course not," she said, and he relaxed a little. She had roommates. Of course. That was how she could afford somewhere like this. "David Archuleta and Paul McCartney live here with me."

She flashed him a grin and started unpacking the food.

Preacher frowned, his mind racing at the names of the two celebrities. "What?"

"Archie and Paulie," she said. As if on cue, two cats

entered the kitchen. They jumped up onto the counter, one right after the other, and padded toward the food. "No," Charlie said, holding out her hand. "No. Get down."

The cats ignored her, but they did stop just shy of the box of food. Charlie took it and the bag of sauces she'd already taken from it around the counter, the cats—and Preacher—tracking her every move.

Preacher finally decided to act like he came to houses like this all the time. He shed his jacket and draped it over the back of one of the chairs at the dining room table, turning back to Charlie. She'd watched him, and she quickly looked away when his eyes met hers for a brief moment.

"I'll get out plates," she said, clearing her throat.

Preacher joined her in the kitchen as she did, and they scooped food onto their plates. She took hers to the huge table, and he followed, not sure what to say or do next. They ate for a few moments, and then Charlie sighed.

"I suppose you want to know a few things."

"I suppose I have a few questions."

"Lay 'em on me, cowboy."

"So you own this company called Below Zero, but as far as I can tell, you don't—aren't in business. You don't make money from that."

"Only for special occasions," she said. "Weddings and summer fairs."

"Okay," he said, glad that he'd worked that out correctly. "And you work at HealNow regularly."

"Yes," she said.

"Full time?"

Charlie shot him a glance. "Not full time, actually."

Preacher looked at her, his fork full of brisket only halfway to his mouth. "So you work part-time at HealNow, make ice cream for a wedding here and there, and live in a house like this?" He took the bite of food, his mind whirring. He swallowed quickly, so she wouldn't answer.

"I'm sorry," he said. "This is none of my business. I'm basically asking you how much you make, and that's rude." He gave her a smile. "I don't care." He had way more money than most cowboys, and he'd hate all the questions and gaping stares if he chose to buy a place like this one—which he could easily do.

Charlie blinked at him, clear surprise in her expression.

"What?" he finally asked when she kept quiet.

"You just—most people needle at me until they get the answers they want."

"I don't want to be rude," he said. "It doesn't matter to me what you do or how you got your money. It's not my business." He focused on his plate, wishing he'd ordered the spicy barbecue sauce. It hadn't been on her list, and he'd just forgotten.

He seemed to forget his own name when it came to Charlie Perkins, that was for dang sure.

"Okay, come with me," she said, standing up.

He hadn't finished eating yet, and he looked from his plate to hers. She hadn't either. "Where are we going?"

"Just into my office," she said. "It'll be two minutes." She picked up one cat and told the other to come with her. She walked away, and Preacher scrambled to his feet to follow her.

The office sat on the other side of the living room, through a doorway that branched left and right. On the left sat a bathroom, and she paused at the right-side door, her hand on the doorknob.

She looked over her shoulder at him, and then pushed into the room.

Preacher drew a deep breath and followed her.

The front window sat straight in front of him, with a couch to his right and an armchair nearly in front of the windows. The wall to his left held a long, built-in desk with no less than four monitors, three of which were on and showing various things. Email, a video, and some forum or something. Chat room, maybe.

The room continued to the left after a fireplace broke up the desk, and Charlie had put another desk over there that fit into the corner. Two more monitors sat there, and then on the other L-side of the desk sat a huge, flat-screen television. All of those were dark.

"Wow," he said.

"I work for HealNow a few days a week," she said. "Because I like what they stand for and what they're working to achieve. Plus, I'm the only one authorized to work in the veterinary department in this branch, so they need me to come in. I do the Below Zero ice cream, because it's fun for me, and I like seeing people's reaction to the liquid nitrogen."

She gestured to the screens, the desks, the whole set up. "But this is what I really do."

Preacher looked back and forth, his eyes finally coming back to the pretty woman who'd bitten him with her high ponytail and that cloud of liquid nitrogen. "What is this, exactly?"

"Have you heard of Nexus?" she asked.

"Yeah, of course, everyone's heard of...." He trailed off, his eyes widening. He saw the cameras on each monitor now. He saw the different controllers, each of them sitting benignly on a shelf, as if someone had put them there for display.

"I'm the top female gamer on Nexus," she said. "I have almost forty thousand subscribers, and I just signed a new sponsorship with SlimDown, because I drink one every morning during my breakfast broadcast."

Preacher looked back at her, new appreciation filling him. If he hadn't been smitten by her before, he certainly would've been with this new information.

"Forty thousand subs?" he asked. To subscribe to a gamer's feed on Nexus, it cost five dollars per month. Five time forty thousand was two hundred thousand dollars per month, and that money was Charlie's.

"How much are the fees on Nexus?" he asked. "Never mind. That was rude."

She grinned at him and stepped toward him. She hesitated, the physical barrier between them rigidly intact.

She broke it, putting her hand on his chest, which allowed him to slide his hand along her waist. "I get about six million views each day, cowboy. I'm very, very wealthy, and I earn all that money playing video games."

He swayed with her, thinking this was pretty easy dancing. He took a long breath, leaning down and getting that soft cotton he expected, along with barbecue sauce and... cherry. Not peach.

*Still amazing*, he thought.

"No wonder I can't beat you at Solitary Ops," he whispered.

She giggled, the sound burrowing right into his cowboy heart and implanting itself, and whether that was a good thing or not, Preacher wasn't sure.

## Chapter Two

Charlie Perkins couldn't believe what she'd revealed to the handsome cowboy. She couldn't believe he stood in her office. Of course, she wasn't aiming to keep her identity a secret. Most of her friends at HealNow knew she gamed, and the information about her was readily available online.

She had bought this house behind the gate for a bit of privacy and security, and she'd moved to Three Rivers for a slower pace of life—and her job had relocated her without costing her a dime. She did love working for HealNow, and she wanted to stay current in the world of chemistry, because she consulted with Sanderton Games on the science they used in several of their titles.

Everything she'd told Preacher about herself and her jobs was absolutely true, as the man had a way of making her want to be pure and clean and wholesome for him.

"Brands and saddles," he said suddenly, stepping back.

"You must think we're the biggest bunch of idiots on the planet." He wore horror in those blue eyes that had captured her from the very beginning.

"Of course not," she said. "Playing with you and your friends is...refreshing. It's fun."

"Have we been on the live-stream?"

"Of course not," she said. "You think I'd record without telling you?" She shook her head. "No. Of course not."

Nexus was a second home for Charlie, and she felt like she knew some of her online fans as personal friends. It made having in-person friends a bit hard, if she were being honest, because she never fought with the guys online.

She could get on and watch others play video games, or she could live-stream when she played, get donations and more subscribers, and enjoy chatting for an hour or two. She hadn't joined Nexus eight years ago with the intent to build the account to the level where it currently sat, but she wasn't complaining either.

In fact, every morning and every night when she knelt in prayer, she thanked the Lord for His goodness in blessing her with the success she'd had on Nexus. She happened to be very good at puzzles and games, and her natural ability to play video games had turned into a full-time career, almost by accident.

She wanted Preacher's arm around her again, and this time, she wished he'd use both of them when he held her to dance. She did miss the physical touch of another human being, especially a strong, sexy man.

"I did tell everyone this morning that I was having

someone over tonight," she said, smiling up at him. "A fellow gamer, but also this guy I'd met a while back...."

Preacher's eyes only got wider.

"Have you been on Nexus?" she asked.

He nodded, his mouth pressing into a thin line. He rubbed his lips together and settled his face into a normal look, and Charlie's head seemed to heat by ten degrees. The man was pure deliciousness, and he didn't even know it.

Maybe she liked him more because he wasn't a gamer. Maybe she liked him more now than when they'd first met, because she knew her assumptions about him had been completely false. He would never carry around bills with his name and number on them. They'd been friends for two months now, and he hadn't even asked her out, despite some of her best flirting attempts.

She was still searching for the game he liked best, and she'd thought she'd had him with flight simulators. But no, he'd listened to her talk about them, but in the end, he hadn't been too keen to play all the time.

She'd find his kryptonite one day, she was sure. Every gamer had one.

"So you know that sometimes my fans and I...we chat. They can type things in, and I read them out while I'm playing. That kind of thing."

"Yes," he said.

"Well, they suggested we play together tonight while you were here. I said I'd feel you out and see what you thought."

Preacher did not look happy about that. "I thought we

were dancing tonight. And eating. I think I took three bites."

"Let's go eat and dance," she said, gesturing for him to go first.

He did, spinning right on that cowboy booted heel and striding out of the room. Charlie sighed, because this was about how all of her relationships went. Men liked her because she was cute. Being on Nexus, she was well-aware of this. She had men commenting on her feed all the time about how she was the only one they subbed to, and it was because she was blonde and "cute."

Charlie didn't want to be *cute*. She wanted to feel beautiful and cherished—and not because of some move she could do on a first-person shooting game. Not because of anything to do with video games at all.

*You also don't have a relationship with Preacher*, she told herself. *It's a friendship, and those are two totally different things.*

By the time she arrived at the table, he'd already retaken his seat. She did too, and the distance between them felt eternal. She sighed. "You're mad."

"I'm not," he said, because Preacher never said more than absolutely necessary. It was "I'm not," not "I'm not mad." That would require an extra word.

"You seem mad."

"I'm processing." He put a very large bite of baked beans in his mouth. "I'm trying to decide if I want to be on the live-stream with you."

"It would be easy," she said. "Casual. I showed everyone the new simulator this morning, and the joystick. I talked about you, and how I'd have to learn to dance, and I got a ton of men offering to teach me." She kicked a smile in his direction, but he only looked even more disgusted. "I told them all no, of course." Charlie wished she could stop talking, but she'd started this ball rolling, and it had to go all the way down the hill.

Her mama had taught her that. *Don't push the boulder if you don't want to get to the bottom of things, Charlie.*

"I laugh them off, Preach. I said there was this guy who'd asked me to go to his mother's wedding, and that he'd teach me to dance, and that you were coming over tonight. That's it."

"And they suggested you have me on the feed."

"Yes."

He nodded and finished his beans. He then swiped up a bite of mashed potatoes and brisket, dunked it all in barbecue sauce, and ate it. As soon as he swallowed, he said, "There's a couple of things in my head. One, I'm thirty-eight years old. I'm not a guy. I'm a cowboy, or I'm a man."

Yes, he definitely was both of those.

She nodded, willing to correct her terminology if it would make him happy. "Okay."

"Second, if you're calling me a guy, I'm worried you're way too young for me." He shook his head. "Which is stupid, because we're just friends, and it doesn't matter how old you are. But see, in my head, I'm thinking I'd like to take you out dancing again, and to dinner, and to a movie, and all kinds of other things, and get to know you better. And that sounds like dating, in which case, it definitely *does* matter how old you are."

He took a giant breath and ducked his head. "It's a circular second thought."

Charlie giggled, unable to hold back the sound. "I can see that."

He wouldn't look at her, and Charlie finished her pulled pork and slathered cinnamon butter on her roll. "I won't call you a guy again," she said. "I'm thirty-seven, Preach. It's just video game talk. Most of my followers are in their early twenties, and I look young, so I don't disclose my age online."

He nodded, and she knew there were more thoughts swirling behind those beautiful eyes. "That addresses your two thoughts."

"Kind of," he said.

"Kind of?" she teased, knowing full-well what she didn't address.

"There's the middle of that second thought," he mumbled. "The part about us goin' out."

"That," she said, hitting the T hard. "Depends on how the dancing lesson goes tonight."

Preacher looked at her, the moment playful and fun, and his stoic face finally broke into a grin. "I'm a good dancer."

"But are you a good *teacher* of dance?" she asked, pushing her smoked turkey around her plate. "That's the real question."

"Let's find out," he said, pushing away from the table. "You ready?"

"I've taken maybe three bites," she teased, and Preacher

laughed. She took one more bite of turkey and stood up. "Okay, I'm ready."

"Praise the heavens," he said dryly, and she'd come to know his mannerisms of speech over the past couple of months. *Brands and saddles* was how he swore, and he was always praising the heavens. He did it when he did a great move during a game, or when his sarcasm came out.

"Right here?" she asked, looking down at her stocking feet. "I guess you did say we only need five feet."

"Right." He cleared his throat. "So at the wedding, there will be some slow dances. Those are pretty easy." He took a small step toward her, and then back. Then he sort of lunged at her, and put his right hand on her waist, and his left took hers.

Pops and zings shot through Charlie, and she couldn't stop the smile that spread across her face. He smelled like cedar and oranges, barbecue sauce, and something even spicier and pinier and more male under that. No matter what it was, it tickled her nose and made her want to lean in even farther.

She stepped a bit closer, and his hand tightened on her waist. "It's my mother's wedding," he said. "So we won't be super intimate. One hand out at all times. It's how my father taught us boys to dance when we started junior high." He smiled down at her, and with that cowboy hat tipped down, a little pocket of very intimate space was born.

They wouldn't be super intimate, her left eye. This was the most intimate she'd been with a man in five years. Her pulse seemed to know it as it raced from all the extra adrenaline.

"You put your hand on my shoulder. Yep, like that." He stepped in again, as she wasn't nearly as tall as he was, and the closer he got, the less she had to reach for him. "And we move back and forth like so." He started to sway with her, but it was more than that. He moved his feet, like, actually moved them.

"You move your feet," he said, his voice a near whisper. "It's not a sway. And you go with me, Charlie. I'll take us forward and back, left and right, all with little steps."

Charlie could barely hear him over the pounding of her heartbeat in her ears. "Like, we could go into the kitchen?"

"Mm hm." He moved a step right, taking her with him. She expected his feet to come down on hers, or hers on his, but it never happened. "My right foot is always on the outside," he said. "Yours is too. See?"

She could not see, because she could not look down. She could curl into his chest and press her cheek to his heartbeat, or she could look past his shoulder to the right. She supposed she could lean into him and press her left cheek to his chest and look away from him too, but she didn't know why she'd ever do that.

She wanted to be enclosed in the safety of his arms and feel the warmth of his breath as it wafted across her face. Thoughts of kissing him danced through her mind, which was absolutely ridiculous, as she didn't even know the man's real name.

"What's your Nexus handle?" he asked, his voice low and oh-so-sexy.

"The Chemist," she said. "I'm not hard to find. I use my real picture and everything."

"Hm. I noticed you didn't eat any barbecue sauce. Is that because you don't like it?"

"I like the spicy stuff, and I forgot to mention it to you."

"I love the spicy kind too," he said, and he wore a smile in his voice. Charlie didn't dare look at his face for fear of breaking this moment, and it was one of the better ones of her life. "How long have you worked at HealNow?"

"Thirteen years."

"And when did you found Below Zero?"

"Four years ago."

She could honestly answer his questions all day and all night, as long as he'd keep dancing with her.

"Here we are," he said, and Charlie pulled away slightly and looked around.

"Holy brands and saddles," she said, somewhat stunned. "You danced us into the kitchen." She met his eye then, and oh, that was a mistake. The man had complete power over her with those eyes, and he had to know that.

He grinned at her, and she grinned back up at him. "What do you think? Decent dancer? Good enough teacher to earn myself another date?"

Another date, yes. She should start there instead of grabbing onto the man's lapels and pulling him in for a kiss. "Yeah," she said. "I think I can stand to see you again."

"Inside this house or outside?" he said. "I'd invite you up to the ranch, but I live with my brother." Something shuttered over his expression too, and Charlie had the feeling he wouldn't be telling anyone in his family about tonight—or any future dates—for a long time.

"Here or wherever," she said. "There's a new place that went in the building next door to HealNow. It's a Tepanyaki restaurant. Have you been to one of those before?"

"I...no," he said, even more of his face closing off. He stepped back, breaking the dance. "I try to support the local restaurants that have been in Three Rivers for generations. You know, the mom-and-pop type of things."

"Oh," Charlie said, taken aback by his statement. "I'm sure that's fine too."

"Do you normally stream in the evenings?" he asked.

"Yes," she said. "Here and there. I publish a schedule every week, so people know when to tune in. I didn't specifically put anything on the schedule for tonight, though."

"I'll get on with you, if you want," he said. "I'd kind of like to see how you do it."

Relief streamed through Charlie, because she hadn't driven Preacher away with her talk of subscribers, younger men hitting on her, or her poor dancing skills. She'd flirted with him successfully, and he'd rewarded her with a slow, close dance that still had her skin buzzing.

"All right," she said. "We'll play Journeyman, how 'bout that?"

"My favorite," he quipped, and Charlie laughed.

"I'm going to figure out which game is your favorite," she said. "I really am."

He chuckled too, gently lacing his fingers through hers. "This is okay?"

More than okay, but Charlie only nodded.

"Okay," he said, starting toward the living room and then the office. "I'm at least decent at Journeyman."

"We'll be on the same team," Charlie said, thinking that would take some of the pressure off him. "It'll be super fun."

"Oh, okay," he said with that classic Preacher sarcasm. "Super fun. Can't wait for that."

Charlie sat in front of the ultra-wide monitor and tapped to get everything awake and ready. "You have to get in close here, Preach, or you won't be on the screen. See where the camera is?" She reached up and pressed a button. "You know what? I think I can make the zoom wider...yep. There we go."

She and Preacher fit in the frame easily, and she clicked to get Journeyman up and going. "I talk during the livestreams," she said. "You can too, or just say hello. Whatever."

"I've seen a few feeds on Nexus," he said, but his nerves poured from him in waves. Charlie's stomach clenched around her dinner, because she'd never had anyone on her livestream with her before.

She looked at him, again fighting the intense urge to kiss him, and asked, "Are you ready for this?"

"Hit play, sugar," he drawled, and Charlie thought she should totally get him to be as cowboy country as possible on the feed. She could get female gamers to come over then, and she'd get every man who'd ever heard of Nexus subscribing if they felt like one of their own would be on-screen.

Instead of responding, she clicked on the screen where Nexus sat, tapped GO LIVE, and said, "Hey, hey, everyone out there in the Nexus. It's ya'girl Charlie here tonight, and I have that friend I talked about this morning with me." She looked at Preacher then, wondering what he thought of her ridiculous intro.

He beamed with the brightness of two suns, that was what.

She giggled at him and swatted at his bicep. Chats started popping up on the side of her forum before she'd even faced the screen again. The ones with the bright orange slugs next to them were paying subscribers, and her face heated at the comments flying by.

*Holy hotness* went by, as did *He's a cowboy?! Wow, Char, you've been holding out on us!* among other things.

"Let's give people a minute to get over here," she said, working incredibly hard not to clear her throat. "And then I'll do the formal introduction of this fine man sitting next to me, and we'll be playing a two-player game of Journeyman." She clicked to start the timer, which would literally count down from sixty, and she muted her mic.

Turning to Preacher, she said, "Sometimes the comments aren't G-rated."

"I'm thirty-eight, baby," he said. "I can handle some comments."

"I can mute everyone who's not a subscriber, and I can tell them to behave when the sixty seconds are up." She wiped her hands nervously on her jeans. Preacher saw the movement and brought his eyes back to hers.

"I'm fine, Charlie."

"Sometimes I have to act a little fake," she said.

"Then I'll know who you really are." He smiled at her, reached out, and tucked her hair behind her ear. "Don't worry so much."

"I think this is a bad idea." What planet had she been on when she'd thought having him join her live on Nexus would be a *good* idea? Obviously not this one.

"We're live already," he said.

Before she could decide if she should cause a system-wide failure, or "accidentally" trip the Internet, the timer started to chime at her.

She turned back to the screen. Nine, eight, seven....

She unmuted herself and put a smile on her face. *Nothing for it now*, she thought.

"All right, everyone. Wow, look how many of you there are tonight." She grinned at the camera in front of her. I told you I might have a friend on with me tonight, and it happened! My first friend livestream, and you're all here for it. Now, this handsome man's name is Preacher, and that right there should tell you what kind of comments I'm expecting to see tonight."

Preacher lifted his hand in a wave, his smile wide and stunning.

"That's right, Dollface," she said, reading the comment at the top of the stream. "He is gorgeous, isn't he?" She turned and smiled at Preacher. "Yes, we're just friends right now. I've been playing with him and his friends for a couple of months."

She scanned a few more comments. "We've got Tiny-Twinkle, NinjaMonkey, Thimble, Fireball, and about fifty more of you who want to know if he's my boyfriend." She grinned at Preacher again, noticing that his smile had definitely slipped.

She leaned closer to the screen and lowered her voice to a mock whisper. "Not yet, you guys, and you're making this awkward for me, okay? He's the first man I've liked even a little bit in years, so can you just stop?" She grinned at the screen, because this was how she made her money, after all.

She hadn't lied though. Not even a little bit.

The comments flew, positively flew, and Charlie could barely see them before they were gone.

"Y'all are lively tonight," she said. "I see Unicorns-and-Sunshine, Hailey's Comet, and Talksalot saying they won't ask any more questions about the boyfriend-status of Preacher and I. Thank you, guys. All right, I'm going to switch us over to in-window mode, and we'll get started with Journeyman. You ready, Preach?"

"So ready," he said, and he gripped the controller like he might need to strangle it to stay sane.

*That voice—I'm fanning myself*, someone commented, and one of her subscribers—Winnie the Pooh—made a similar comment.

*What have I done?* Charlie thought, but she acted like she was thrilled to be online with Preacher, playing Journeyman, and she hoped she could give him a proper apology and any explanations he needed once the stream finished.

## Chapter Three

Preacher yelped as he hit the last enemy in the tower, and Charlie cheered for him. She turned to him and he gave her five when she held up her hand. "Nice one, Preach." She put her controller down, her smile wider than the Mississippi as she leaned toward the screen.

Preacher felt a thin sheen of sweat covering his whole body, and he had no idea what time it was. *Time to get on home*, he thought. Charlie lived at least an hour from Shiloh Ridge, and Preacher stifled a yawn. Couldn't do that while the camera still rolled.

"Thanks to everyone who joined tonight, and we hope y'all had a good time watchin' us play. Be sure to subscribe with the blue button over there on the right if you haven't already, and if you have, thanks to all my orange slugs."

Preacher marveled at this woman, who was everything he hadn't even known he wanted. He kept his smile hitched in place as she finished with, "Slug army unite!" and lifted her right fist up over her head.

Comments flew up the side of the screen, and Charlie set another timer for thirty seconds to capture ending comments, which she'd already promised everyone she would read and respond to during her "breakfast broadcast" the following morning.

Then, the camera shut off, and Charlie leaned back in her chair.

The buzz in the air didn't lessen though, and Preacher found he couldn't sit still for another moment. He burst to his feet and paced toward the dark television on his left. "Wow," he said.

"You did great in the game, Preach," she said, her voice right on back to normal. "Great online too. My people *loved* you."

Preacher had tried to forget about the scads of people watching, how many of them were men, and what they were saying about him, specifically.

Charlie had helped a lot by choosing one of the easier maps in Journeyman, and just like she sat about half a foot in front of him during the livestream, he'd followed a half-step behind her in the game.

He turned back to her, not sure what to say next. The dancing had been spectacular. The best dancing he'd experienced in years. His phone buzzed from where he'd put it on her desk, and she looked at it at the same time he did.

She stood closer to it, so she picked it up, her eyes dropping to it. She started to extend it toward him, but the movement stuttered. "Who's Mindi?"

Preacher's heart dropped all the way to his cowboy boots, and his first inclination was to grab the phone and throw it through the window. A frown furrowed his brow. "Did she seriously just text me?"

"She seriously did." Charlie shook the phone at him, but Preacher didn't want to take it.

He did anyway, his pulse doing weird things tonight. "She's this woman who...." How did he explain this? "What did she say?"

"She wanted to know what you were doing tomorrow night." Charlie turned her attention to her computer screen, turning off the double-wide one and putting their controllers back on the shelf where they belonged.

"I can see that," Preacher growled, reading Mindi's message. *Hey stranger, what are you up to tomorrow night?*

His brain whirred. Preacher thought of his workload at the ranch tomorrow, and because they were still operating on a holiday schedule, he could make the drive to town again.

He shoved his phone in his pocket and looked at Charlie. "I was thinking you and I would go to the Country Christmas wagon ride out at the Bellamore Ranch," he said. "It's actually the Southern Belle Ranch, but Bellamore is their last name."

He told himself to stop talking.

"Christmas was a few days ago," Charlie said.

"They're doing the wagon rides and chuckwagon dinner through New Year's," he said. "It's pretty fun. Dinner. Christmas lights. Wagon ride with these huge Clydesdale horses." He cleared his throat as Charlie finally stopped fiddling with her gaming gear.

She looked at him, her blue eyes clear and bright and wide. "What about Mindi?"

Preacher stuck his hands in his pockets. "Uh, Mindi is this woman who uses me whenever her boyfriend treats her like garbage."

Charlie opened her mouth, then promptly closed it again.

Embarrassment squirreled up Preacher's spine. "I'm gonna go." He turned toward the exit, glad he had such long legs so he could get out of there quickly.

"Preach," she said behind him, but Preacher would rather end this night on a high note.

*Too late for that*, he told himself as he rounded the corner. He put his hand on the doorknob and opened the door, the chilly night air clearing his thoughts. Or making his thoughts clearer.

He'd let Mindi Adams *use* him for over a year. How pathetic was that?

He'd just reached the bottom of the steps outside when Charlie called, "Will you stop, please?"

Preacher stopped. She'd said please.

He tipped his head up to the stars, which he'd always loved. The moon hung low on the horizon, and he sure did love that bright orb too.

Charlie's footsteps came down her front steps, and she stepped to his side. She said nothing, and Preacher didn't think two people who didn't want to start a conversation should really be together.

"I'll chat you next time we play," he said, making his voice quiet so it wouldn't disturb the peacefulness of the sky. He took a step to leave, wondering if he'd ever be able to stand in her presence again.

Her hand shot out and latched onto his, and she said, "Don't go."

"It's over an hour back to my house," he said. "I have to be up at six to feed horses."

"Five minutes," she said, and because Preacher could stand in the cold, midnight sky with her for hours, he didn't move.

He swallowed, but he had nothing else to say.

"I'd love to go to the Country Christmas thing with you tomorrow," she finally said.

"Really?" Preacher looked down at her, and she looked up at him. She absolutely mesmerized him, and his brain turned foggy for a moment. "I'm not seeing Mindi. I told her months ago that I wasn't interested in being her little pet."

"I'm sorry," she whispered. "It's no fun being used like that."

Preacher's pulse thumped excessively, especially when Charlie lifted up onto her slippered toes and pressed her lips to his cheek. "Thank you for dinner. Thank you for not caring about my money. Thank you for gaming with me."

His whole head had burst into flames, the origin where her mouth had touched him. He couldn't speak, so he just nodded.

"You'll pick me up at what? Five?"

Preacher cleared his throat. "Five's good."

She smiled at him, and how she could be so relaxed after the tension they'd just been through, he wasn't sure. He'd never been good at managing conflict, choosing to shut down and go silent when problems arose. The lines from his father's letter ran through his mind again, and he honestly felt like his dad didn't know him at all.

He didn't unite anyone, and he was still trying to figure out how to live up to his name. He ducked his head, a smile touching his lips. "See you tomorrow, sugar."

Her smile brightened, and she nodded, tucked her hair, and released his hand. He tipped his hat at her and headed for his truck. After he backed out of her driveway, he glanced up to her front porch, but she'd gone back inside and closed the door already.

"Hey, you got another date," he muttered to himself. Now he just needed to get back to the ranch before he nodded off—and then buy tickets to the Country Christmas wagon ride for tomorrow night.

---

Preacher woke only a few seconds before his alarm, and he groaned as he rolled over. His back hurt in a new way, and he realized it was from sitting in front of Charlie's computer last night. He'd leaned so far forward, hunched at the shoulders, and he carried too many years in his bones to do that.

He sat up and stretched his arms right up above his head. He took these calm, quiet moments before the whole world rushed at him to think through his day. He reflected on the previous day and what he'd like to do differently today.

He wanted to be kinder to Judge. He wanted to continue to rebuild the bridge between him and Mister. He wanted to be more confident when he saw Charlie that evening.

He'd gotten tickets to the wagon ride and light display the moment he'd returned to the Ranch House, and he'd been so late that Judge had already gone to bed. Preacher didn't mind, because he didn't want to explain anything to anyone.

When Preacher and Judge spent time just the two of them, they got along great. Neither of them was trying to put on a show or get the most attention. It was only when they got together with even one other member of the family that Judge turned into a different person. He had a good heart, because Preacher had seen it. He worked hard around the ranch, and he held all of the same family beliefs as the other Glovers.

So he liked to laugh and joke. Sometimes his teasing went too far, and Preacher was definitely growing tired of the practical jokes. Since Ace had gotten angry about Judge hiding his truck, Judge had backed off on the tricks. Thankfully.

"Preach," Judge yelled now, and Preacher got to his feet and turned toward the door.

"Yep."

His brother walked in, and he was already fully dressed, right down to his cowboy boots. "Zona's here to move the Corvette."

Preacher's panic roared through him. "I forgot."

"She brought Duke's truck. She said she doesn't need your help."

"Don't let her leave before I get out there." He quickly stepped over to the weight bench in the corner and grabbed one of the T-shirts draped there. Judge left, and Preacher dressed as fast as he could and took his boots with him into the living room.

Zona sat at the dining room table with Duke and Judge, and all three of them nursed cups of coffee. He relaxed and took his time putting on his socks and cowboy boots before he joined them. "Sorry," he said, still barely awake. The day hadn't lifted its head yet either, and darkness yawned at them beyond the back windows that filled the kitchen with light in the summertime.

"You're not usually late," Zona said.

Preacher tossed her a look as he flipped over the last mug on the counter and poured himself a cup of coffee. He added a splash of cream and a healthy amount of sugar before joining everyone at the table.

He met Duke's eyes and gave him a smile. "I saw you land Hong Kong."

"Not live," Duke said, his question obvious.

"No," Preacher said, not volunteering any further information. "But it looked good."

"I'm getting better."

"He spends too much time on those games," Zona said, giving her husband a look as she stood up. "Let's get this car home, baby. We have a ton to do today, and if Preacher's not going to tell us why he was late getting up or why he couldn't watch you land live, we might as well get out of his hair."

Preacher lifted his coffee mug, not about to say where he'd been last night. To his great surprise, Judge didn't rat him out either, and he took one more swallow of coffee before following Zona and Duke out to the garage.

Dad's Corvette sat in the third spot from the door, where it had been for over a decade. Preacher had loved the car as much as his father, but not as much as Arizona. He'd told her for years he was going to restore it, get it running again, and bring back the rumbling, chugging engine to Shiloh Ridge that Dad had first done.

He didn't spend much money on very many things, but he'd loved Corvettes his whole life. When one had come up on the used car lot, Dad had bought it and brought it back to the ranch. Preacher could still remember the very first time he'd driven it under the arch that marked the entrance to Shiloh Ridge.

He'd been sixteen years old, and he'd just gotten his driver's license. He'd been driving around the ranch for a couple of years, though, and Daddy let everyone who had proper license drive the Corvette.

Every time Daddy left the homestead to go "tinker" with his beloved Corvette, Preacher joined him. It didn't matter if he needed sleep or if he had a metric ton of homework. He'd wanted to be with his father, and he'd inherited his love of vehicles from him.

He had a storage unit in downtown Three Rivers with two Ford Mustangs that he drove all summer long, and he'd only told a few people that the cars actually had names. In his opinion, there was nothing better than a long, straight road, warm sunshine, and an old convertible with a big, growly engine.

He gazed at the bright red Corvette, which he'd never had time to work on. It had broken down seven or eight years ago, and Preacher had liked looking at it enough to keep it. Zona could fix it up though. She had more time than him since she'd pulled back on her tasks here and moved some of them to the Rhinehart Ranch, which sat just south of Shiloh Ridge.

Zona got behind the wheel and tried to start the engine, but it refused to turn over. It sputtered and groaned, but she had no more luck than he had. She got out, a bit of dismay on her face. "Hook 'er up, baby," she said to Duke, and he started to put the tow rope on the back fender.

Zona tucked her hands in her back pockets and faced Preacher. He smiled at her, and all of the healing that had started a couple of weeks ago still bloomed between them. "You have a plan already, don't you?"

Zona smiled back at him and lifted one shoulder in a shrug. She had lighter hair like Bishop, and the bright, blazing blue eyes that sat on Bear's face. She almost always wore her hair in a ponytail right on the back of her head, and Preacher never saw her wear anything but jeans and work boots—except for when she went to church.

"Thank you, Preacher."

He went down the few steps to the garage floor. He hugged her and said, "Maybe you'll let me drive her when she's running again."

"You got it." Zona hugged him back, and it sure did feel nice. "Will you carve me something to hang from the mirror?"

"Sure," he said, wishing he'd thought of that. He hadn't spent much time with a knife in his hand lately, and once he started as the second foreman here, he'd have even less time.

He thought of Charlie and how far away she lived, but he wouldn't remove her from his life either. Not if she wanted to be there.

"You're not going to tell me what's going on with you?" she asked.

Preacher pulled away from Zona and looked down at her. He could still see and hear Ace going ballistic and saying everyone's secrets, and he didn't want anyone to know his yet.

"I'm not quite ready," he said.

"Okay," Zona said, her voice pitching up. "Just tell me this: Is this a work thing or a woman thing?"

Preacher grinned at her. "Both."

# Chapter Four

Charlie hadn't been on a proper date with a man in a very long time. Far, far too long. She took off the jeans she'd chosen and switched them out for a pair of the black slacks she wore to the lab.

"Nope." She peeled those off and tossed them onto her bed. Back in the closet, she found a black and white buffalo checkered pair of pants she hadn't worn in many a moon. They finally felt right, and she started flipping through the hangers in her closet to find a blouse to pair with the pants.

"Something bright," she muttered to herself, knowing full well she looked good in blue and green. Red would be okay too, and probably pretty festive for a wagon ride around a ranch to look at Christmas lights.

In the end, she chose a bright blue blouse with white butterflies on it, and she stepped into a pair of sandals. As she studied herself in the full-length mirror, she reminded herself that she and Preacher would be spending most of the night outside. At the end of December.

The whole outfit came off, and Charlie hissed out a sigh and picked up her phone. Her sister's phone rang a few times before it went to voicemail, and Charlie's frustration poured through her, staining her voice as she said, "Davie, I need your help. You won't believe it, but I have a date with a man—yes, a real man—and I have nothing to wear. I need your help." She hung up and rolled onto her back.

Staring at the ceiling, she could see the perfect date with Preacher. They'd walk along the dirt road at the ranch, hand-in-hand. He'd be wearing a dark brown leather jacket, jeans, his cowboy boots and hat, and a smile.

In her mind, she wore a blue sweater with jeans and her cowgirl boots that she very rarely got the opportunity to wear. She wore her hair down, curled, and Charlie scooted to the edge of her bed.

She was nowhere near ready to step into that vision, and she hurried into the bathroom to plug in her curling iron. "Lord," she said. "Make him a little bit late, okay? If at all possible. I just need maybe ten extra minutes."

Her phone rang, and she darted back to the bed to swipe on Davie's call.

"A man?" her sister asked instead of saying hello. "Char, you tell me right now if it's that super hot cowboy from your stream last night. Right now, Char!"

Charlie giggled, which should've been good enough for a yes for Davie. She still said, "It's him."

"Oh, I'm fanning myself," Davie said breathlessly. "You two were so cute together. I'm so glad you're going out with him. As for clothes, you need something flirty and fun."

"It's cold here," she said.

"Wait. You're still in Texas, right?"

Charlie smiled and shook her head. "Yes, Davie, but the Panhandle gets cold. It snows here and everything."

"Just another reason never to visit," she said, her tone full of darkness.

Charlie wasn't going to argue with her about her move to Three Rivers. No, they'd never lived more than ten minutes from one another. Never more than five miles.

But now, hundreds and hundreds of miles stood between them, and Charlie stuffed everything away so she wouldn't say something she'd regret the moment it left her mouth.

"So a sweater," Davie said. "You have to have something in blue or purple. Oh, go with purple, Charlie. Wear your hair down and don't overdo it with the makeup. You tend to do that when you're excited."

Charlie returned to her closet and started looking through her built-in drawers. "I do have a purple sweater," she said, pulling it out. "It has a giant white star on the front." She looked down at it. "Is that okay?"

"Of course," Davie said. "Every Texan worth his salt loves the star."

Charlie grinned, because nothing could be truer. "Jeans?"

"If you have anything wider in the leg, I'd do that."

"Wide leg?" Charlie asked. "Really?"

"They make you look older," Davie said. "More refined."

Charlie would've never picked her wide leg pants. She'd been wearing them for years, even before they were in fashion, because she didn't like things that hugged too close to her skin. She pulled out a dark pair of the wide leg pants and stepped into them. She pulled a white undershirt on and then the sweater before heading into the bathroom to do her makeup and get her hair at least a little wavy.

She let Davie talk about her job, about how Mom really needed a boyfriend of her own so she'd stop asking Davie if she'd found one yet, and how things had been at Dad's for the holidays.

Charlie hadn't left Three Rivers, and she'd gone down the street to Judy Bell's for Christmas dinner. The older woman had taken Charlie under her wing from the moment she'd moved to town, and while Judy was twice her age, Charlie had felt a kinship with her instantly.

She always felt like that with older women. Mama had always told her she possessed an old soul in a young body, and as Charlie had grown close to more and more women older than her, she'd believed her mother.

She'd just unplugged the curling iron and capped her tube of mascara when the doorbell rang. Archie mewed from his position on the bathroom counter, where he always sat to watch Charlie get ready.

She picked him up and gave him a quick squeeze. "Wish me luck."

The cat meowed again, and Davie said, "Good luck, Charlie. I wish you could put me on video!"

That was the last thing—the very last thing—Charlie would ever do. She'd rather not have an audience for the embarrassing blunders she always committed on dates.

Her mouth turned dry, and she paused before going down the hall to answer the door. "Lord, one more thing. If Thou could help me not to make a fool of myself tonight, that would be epic."

She smoothed her hands down her body and continued toward the front of the house. She'd disliked Preacher's reaction to it, but she'd expected it. She'd bought the house, and she knew what her life looked like on the outside.

What she couldn't believe was that she was going to let Preacher see what it really looked like on the inside.

She opened the door, and he stood there holding a bouquet of roses. The most perfect bundle of red roses. A smile. A sexy pair of jeans that stretched down his long, long legs to a pair of dark brown cowboy boots.

He'd donned the leather jacket in the precise shade Charlie had fantasized about, but the garment was unzipped to reveal a red, green, and white checkered shirt. His trademark ivory cowboy hat sat just-so on his head, with his dark hair peeking out a little behind his ears.

"Oh, my," she said, sagging into the doorframe. It took her a few seconds to realize she'd said the words out loud. And that she'd gone soft at the mere sight of him.

"Aren't you beautiful?" he asked, his soulful blue eyes leaving hers to slide down her body to her feet. When he returned his gaze to her face, Charlie felt as if he'd doused her in gasoline and tossed a match in her direction. Fire licked along her skin and through her veins, and she really wanted this date to go well.

*Watch your mouth*, she told herself as Preacher's smile cocked up a little on the right side. Oh, he'd surely broken a fair few hearts with that crooked smile. It was the only imperfect thing about him, and it somehow made him even more perfect.

"Come in," Charlie said, backing up a step. "Do we have a minute for me to put those in water?" She nodded to the roses, and Preacher looked at them as if just now realizing he held them.

"Yes." His voice sounded like he'd swallowed thorns, and while Charlie had been out of the real-life dating game for a while, she knew the effect her curled hair and makeup had had on the handsome cowboy.

He stepped into her house, and because she barely gave him any room to do so, he slid his free hand along her waist as he nudged the door closed with his foot. The scent of the petally roses filled the air between them, which was only a narrow alley of about four inches.

"You are beautiful," he said in a near-whisper. "I'm glad you said yes to this."

Charlie could barely breathe, let alone think. "Thank you, Preach," she managed to say. "You look real nice yourself."

He nodded and handed her the flowers. Charlie leaned over to smell them fully, her heartbeat tipping up a few notches for some reason. Could she kiss him before they even went out? What would that make her?

They'd been playing video games for a couple of

months now. She knew him a little bit. They'd been texting a lot lately, and Charlie looked up from the roses and into Preacher's eyes, which hadn't left her face.

Davie would go absolutely insane if Charlie called in a few hours and said she'd kissed the hot cowboy she'd had on her livestream.

Fear clenched in her stomach. Kissing a man took him to a new place in her life, and she hadn't had anyone in that spot in such a long time. The last man who'd been there had tried to take her heart with him when she'd finally ended things with him. It had been a fight to keep it, and even then, he'd thrown it back at her in a thousand pieces.

Sometimes she still felt like she was trying to get them all in the right place again.

Preacher cleared his throat, dropped his hand, and put a good two feet between them. "Go on, now," he said. "We don't have all night to stand in the foyer." A smile accompanied the words, and Charlie quickly scampered away from him.

With the roses in a vase of fresh water and a stern warning to Archie and Paulie not to touch the flowers, Charlie rejoined Preacher near the front door. She opened the closet and pulled out her dress coat, and as the perfect Texas gentleman that he was, Preacher helped her into it.

"Ready?" he asked.

She could only nod.

Outside on the front porch, Preacher took her hand after she'd closed the door behind them, and they went down the steps and sidewalk to his truck together.

"Anything exciting happen online today?" he asked as he opened her door.

She glanced up at him, suddenly so much to say. "Not online, but yes, I had something exciting happen today."

He grinned and let his hand linger on the small of her back as she got into his pickup. "Can't wait to hear about it."

As he went around the front of the truck, Charlie took stock of the cab. The bench seat meant she could slide over and sit right next to him. She'd had a few cowboy boyfriends in her teens and early twenties with trucks like this, and nostalgia at the comforting memories of sitting right beside them as they drove through the Texas countryside tugged at her heartstrings.

The radio had been replaced with something much newer and more advanced, and the scent of clean, crisp linen meant he'd sprayed something in here to drive away anything foul that might have existed.

He opened his door and got behind the wheel. She couldn't read the quick glance he gave her, and the truck started smoothly, the heater blowing out warm air and the radio blasting a Chris Ledoux song Charlie knew by heart.

Preacher hastened to adjust the volume. "Sorry," he muttered, flipping the truck into reverse to get out of her massive driveway.

"I love Chris Ledoux," she said.

The surprise in his expression wasn't hard to find when he looked at her this time. "Is that so?"

She giggled and shook her head. "Don't act so surprised."

"I think I have a right to be surprised," he said. "You're a chemist who makes millions playing video games. That's about as far from Chris Ledoux as a person gets."

"I was born and raised in the great state of Texas, cowboy," she said. "I know—and love—country music." She turned toward him. "*Real* country music. None of this Taylor Swift stuff."

Preacher nodded, the subject of country music obviously extremely important to him. "Who else do you like?"

"The queen," she said. "Dolly Parton. Willie Nelson. I tried Johnny Cash, but I just don't get it."

Preacher chuckled, and Charlie felt like she'd achieved some great victory. The man could be hard to crack sometimes, especially when nervous. She reminded herself that she'd kept him in the friendship box, and that she was nervous too. People dated to get over the nerves and learn to be comfortable with one another.

"What about you?" she asked.

"Reba," he said. "Of course. George Strait. And I even really like Miranda Lambert. She's not as country, but she sure has a nice voice."

"I can get on board with those selections," Charlie said coolly, hoping he'd hear the teasing quality in her voice.

"I'm glad you approve," he said dryly, and they laughed together. Charlie relaxed with every moment and every mile that passed. "Tell me your exciting, offline news." He glanced at her as they came down the last stretch of highway to Three Rivers.

"Oh, right." Charlie shifted in her seat. "I talked to a curriculum coordinator at the school district today. They want me to go into classrooms and do chemistry experiments with the kids."

Preacher glanced at her before making the left turn to take the road that went around town. "Chemistry experiments. That sounds fun." His eyebrows went up, asking the question that hadn't been in his voice.

"Yeah," she said. "I want to do it. I'm not sure how to make it work with HealNow, though." Her mind churned, and she needed to get the mess out and try to make sense of it. "Maybe you could help me with something."

"Shoot."

"I don't hate my job at HealNow. They're really flexible with me most of the time. I'm the only one that can work with their veterinary pharmaceuticals—at least here—and I know they won't want to lose me."

"Veterinary pharmaceuticals," he repeated. "I can barely say that."

Charlie only smiled. "It simply means I work on developing new medicines for animals," she said. "It's not that exciting." Though she did love it.... She'd always loved animals, but she'd never felt the calling to be a vet.

She'd adored science growing up, and she sighed as she remembered the first chemistry set her father had brought home. "My dad got me into chemistry," she said, taking a huge tangent from her current problem at hand. "He brought home this set that someone at his work didn't want anymore. I guess they'd bought it for their son, who wasn't interested. I was bitten the moment I opened the kit and smelled all the chemicals."

"That's...weird," Preacher said.

Charlie laughed. "That came out wrong." She leaned her head back against the rest, wishing she'd slid all the way over next to him so she could hold his hand. The bench seats in these older trucks were so wide. "I don't inhale chemicals."

"Good to know." He grinned at her and nodded to the spot next to him. "You want to slide on over here?"

Charlie didn't need to be asked twice. She unbuckled her seat belt and made the move in less time than it took to inhale. With the middle belt on, she reached for Preacher's hand.

He lifted hers to his lips and kissed the inside of her wrist. Sparks shot up her arm and into her head, erasing everything she'd been thinking.

"That's better," he murmured, settling their joined hands on his thigh. "Go on with your story."

Charlie had to think so hard to find the thread she'd lost. "Uh, anyway. I like my job. But I've been thinking more and more about really opening up Below Zero. There are ice cream shops here, but nothing like liquid nitrogen. I could do that and do the elementary classes."

"Is the district going to pay you?"

"Yes," she said. "I just talked to them today. I guess with the state crime lab coming here, and HealNow here, they want more emphasis on the sciences—especially chemistry—in their schools."

Preacher nodded, his fingers tightening in hers for a moment. Charlie looked at him, and all the tension that had suddenly appeared dissipated.

"What do you want to do?" he asked.

Charlie lifted her free hand and swept it in front of her body, indicating the whole world. "I want to do everything." She sighed, and it wasn't a happy, blissful sound. "My mama told me my desire to have all the cake in the whole world and eat it too would sneak up on me and bite me. But I can't help it. I want it all."

"Money, fame, and chemistry experiments," he said.

She smiled, because he made the world and all the cake in it sound so easy. "Time to play video games," she added. "I want to travel. I want to taste a lot of different types of foods. I want to open a dedicated storefront for Below Zero. I want to help animals." Another sigh. "I want it all."

She looked away from him, because the threads of unhappiness that always came when Charlie thought about what she wanted and what she hadn't achieved yet bound her so tight. She hated feeling like this, and she started mentally listing her blessings.

She always had to come back to gratitude when the "all" she hadn't gotten yet crept into her mind.

*You shouldn't have said any of that*, she chastised herself. So much for watching her mouth.

## Chapter Five

"I lost you," Preacher said, watching Charlie wage some battle with herself.

She finally looked at him, a vein of displeasure in those pretty blue eyes. "Sorry," she said. "What was I saying?"

"That you wanted it all," he said. "And I said you should be able to have it. You're only thirty-seven, and you've got plenty of life left to live."

She nodded. "Sorry I said that."

"Why would you be sorry about that?" He frowned at her and moved his eyes back to the road.

"My mama says I should be content with what the Lord has given me."

"Mm, your mama sounds like my daddy." He smiled now, the memories of his father so strong and so good. "I think...I think it's okay to want bigger and better things," he said. "As long as there are checkpoints along the way to make sure you're still on the path God wants you to be on."

The weight of Charlie's gaze landed on the side of his face again. Preacher wasn't used to being looked at quite so much, and he could barely hold it.

"That's a really good point," she said.

"Do you feel Him tugging you in any one direction?" Preacher asked. She'd asked him to help her with this problem, but he didn't want to give advice that wouldn't ring true for her.

"I think I need to talk to my boss at HealNow," Charlie said. "I'd love to work with kids, and I could do morning classes at the schools and open my ice cream shop in the afternoons and evenings."

"And The Chemist?" he asked.

"She can still broadcast at breakfast and do a few nightly things."

Preacher smiled at her third-person use of "she," as if The Chemist was someone different than Charlie herself. After watching her game live, Preacher knew she was. Charlie was both people, but The Chemist definitely had walls up to keep fans on one side and her private, personal life on the other.

He sure did like that. He liked both Charlie and The Chemist, far more than he should after a couple of months of friendly texting and one dinner together.

*Tonight makes two*, he thought, reminding himself that everyone started somewhere. Every relationship had a beginning.

"Maybe you could consult with HealNow," he said. "That way, you wouldn't have to go in all the time, but you could work on your own schedule." He glanced at her.

"Like when you aren't doing school assemblies or whatever, you could go into HealNow."

"That's a really good idea," she said slowly. "Thanks, Preacher." Her fingers tightened in his as she adjusted her hand. She leaned her head against his bicep, and a whole new level of satisfaction moved through Preacher.

He'd dang near kissed her standing in her foyer, and it had taken every ounce of self-control he had to step away. He wanted to kiss Charlie with the strength of gravity, but he didn't want to rush things. He'd rushed things in other relationships, and that had never worked to his advantage.

He'd bided his time over the past couple of months of playing video games with her. He could wait to kiss her until they'd been out a few times. Until he was sure she wasn't going to disappear the moment someone better came along.

Familiar bitterness surged up his throat, but surprisingly, it wasn't for Mindi. But for himself for allowing her to treat him as she had. Foolishness and humiliation swirled within him, and he hated that they reared up so quickly and would stay so long.

He cleared his throat again, as if that would settle the emotions right on down. It never did, and he wished he'd brought something to drink with him.

"Tell me about your family," he said to get her to keep talking. If she talked, then he didn't have to.

"I have a twin sister," Charlie said. "Her name is Davie. Two younger brothers, Mack and Ian. They all live down in the big cities. Dallas, Houston, or San Antonio."

"And you came from Dallas."

"Yes, sir."

"Who's older? You or Davie?"

"Me."

He nodded. "Any of them married?"

"No, sir. My mom and dad are divorced, and it wasn't real pleasant, so I don't think any of us—" She cut off, and Preacher glanced at her. Her eyes rounded, and she looked at him with panic pouring from them. "I want to get married," she blurted out. "I do. I just...I need to be sure before I take that step."

Preacher couldn't believe they were talking about marriage right now, even if this was their second date and they'd talked a lot over the months. He honestly couldn't recall his name at the moment.

The atmosphere turned tense. Preacher kept on driving, finally seeing the lights from the Bellamore Ranch up ahead. "There it is," he murmured.

"I see it."

They arrived at the ranch and followed the cowhand's directions for where to park. In the truck, he paused and turned slightly toward Charlie. "Hey, we're not going to—I mean." He ground his voice through his throat, needing that blasted mic in his ear, with Bishop on the other end. Or Ace. Someone to tell him what to say.

"We can go as slow as you want," he said. "I want to go kind of slow anyway. I, uh." He cleared his throat, and if he did that one more time, he was going to seriously kick himself in the teeth. "I haven't had a real girlfriend for a while. Mindi was...."

He looked away, not sure how to explain the situation.

"She wasn't good for me," he finally said, and talking was easier when he didn't have to look into Charlie's eyes. "She hurt me in a lot of ways, and I didn't even know it." He nodded, like that explained everything. "I'm not saying we'll get married, because I don't know that, but I'd sure like to keep seeing you and getting to know you."

"I'd like that too," Charlie said, and her soft, emotion-filled voice got him to look at her again.

He nodded. "Okay. Should we go eat and see these lights? No more talk of heavy things tonight, okay?"

She grinned at him. "You've got yourself a deal, cowboy."

He smiled back and got out of the truck. He turned to help her, asking, "Am I going to be The Cowboy on your livestream?"

"Oh, that's a great idea," she said. "What's your handle on Nexus right now?"

"Preacher," he said. "So boring, I know."

"Hey, it sounds like it fits in with everyone else there."

"Yeah, like Dollface and Scars and Savage." He chuckled and took her hand in his again.

"What's your real name?" she asked. "I'm assuming it's not Preacher."

"Why wouldn't it be Preacher?"

"I don't...know." She shrugged. "I guess I got the feeling it wasn't?"

Charlie was far too smart for Preacher, but he kept that to himself for right now. She'd see all of his faults soon enough, and he didn't need to go displaying them for her so soon.

"It's Paul," he said. "Most everyone in my family has a different name than their legal, given one."

"Fascinating," she said. "It's like you guys have your own Nexus up there at that ranch. It's just not online."

Preacher burst out laughing, because she was so right. The scent of steak and salt filled the air, and with the glow of the cheery Christmas lights, Preacher thought he'd found a version of heaven with the pretty blonde at his side.

*But you're not going to kiss her tonight*, he told himself. All he had to do was remember that anxiety in her eyes and his hormones calmed right on down.

"Preacher," a man said, and he turned toward his name. Brit Bellamore stood there, and he grinned at the man. "It is you."

"Hey, Brit." Preacher released Charlie's hand to shake Brit's. He had a couple of decades on Preacher, and he mostly dealt with Bear or Ranger if the two ranches needed to coordinate for some reason. All of the ranchers helped one another around Three Rivers, especially in difficult times, and Preacher had been to this ranch to clean it up after a few tornadoes had touched down a few years ago.

"Brit, this is Charlie," he said. "Charlie, Brit owns this place."

"It's beautiful," she said. "How long does it take you to put up the lights?"

"Oh, the girls do that," Brit said, looking around. "Liberty spearheads all of it. She probably works on it for a month or so." He grinned at Charlie and Preacher. "Glad y'all came out. There's Libby right there, and she'll take your tickets."

"Thanks," Preacher said, turning to the sandy-haired woman.

Libby wore a smile in her dark eyes, and she took Preacher's tickets with a, "Hey, Preach."

"Heya, Libby."

"You guys have the all-access pass," she said, picking up a brochure. "Here's a map of the ranch, with all of the activities and events we have going on tonight. Dinner is in the Bell Barn, and it's pretty dang hard to miss." She continued to explain things to them, and then put a stamp on each of their hands.

"Your dinner ticket starts in fifteen minutes," she said. "But you have an hour to come and go, so no rush."

"Thanks, Libby," Preacher said, handing the brochure to Charlie, who immediately started leafing through it. He started to move past Libby when she put her hand on his forearm. He looked at it and then back into her eyes.

Plenty of nerves vibrated there now. "Uh, how's Mister?" she asked, swallowing. She glanced to the people behind him in line.

"Mister?" Preacher asked.

"Forget about it." She dropped her hand and looked to the next customers. "Tickets, please."

Preacher had to move out of the way, but he turned back to look at Libby again. Mister? Why would she be asking about Mister?

"You comin'?" Charlie asked from down the path, and Preacher pulled out his phone to text his brother.

"Yep," he said. "Give me one...minute...." He sent the quick message and shoved his phone in his back pocket again. Mister would probably ignore the text, because if there was someone even more tight-lipped about his relationships than Preacher, it was Mister.

He pushed his brother from his mind, because he could talk to Mister tomorrow. Tonight, he wanted to spend time with Charlie. Learn more about Charlie. Talk to Charlie. Focus on Charlie.

He wanted to find out if he could get his heart back to a place of normalcy, and if he could fall for a woman in the right way. *Help me*, he prayed. *I want to do what's right, and I don't want to be alone forever. Lead me. Guide me. I'll do what You want me to do. I'll go where You want me to go.*

Satisfied that he'd do the will of the Lord, Preacher put a smile on his face and slipped his arm around Charlie's waist. "All right, little lady. Where to first?"

---

PREACHER FINALLY STEPPED INTO THE RANCH HOUSE, pure exhaustion pulling through him. It drowned him, threatening to pull him all the way under the surface of sanity.

"Hey," Judge said.

He continued kicking off his boots by the back door. "Hey." That job done, he turned to the kitchen, which was open now and much nicer than before. Judge had set the table with six places, and Preacher's pulse jumped. "What's going on?"

"I knew you'd forget," he said, looking anxious.

"I forgot," Preacher admitted. "Who's coming over?"

"Bear and his family. And Ward." Judge adjusted one of the plates to make room for a highchair. Preacher had no idea where he'd gotten it from. "They want to go over all the foreman stuff."

Preacher swallowed, his throat already dry from the straw he'd been stacking in the barn. "Oh, right." He skated his gaze past his older brother. "Are you really okay with it?"

"I don't want more responsibility around here," Judge said, and his voice sounded perfectly normal. "Don't worry about me, Preach."

"I can't help it," Preacher muttered. "I just...." He stepped over to the sink and turned the water on cold. He bent to drink straight out of the faucet, then washed his hands. "No one worries about us, Judge. I feel like I have to, so you know someone cares about you."

"I know people care about me," Judge said. "It's you who bears that chip on your shoulder." He stepped next to Preacher. "Which is stupid, by the way. They obviously see you, Preach, or they wouldn't have asked you to be foreman."

Preacher rinsed his hands and then cupped them to hold the water. He splashed it on his face, his breath sucking in involuntarily at the chill. He removed his hat and washed his face and ran water through his hair.

Judge handed him a towel, and as he dried off, he said, "It smells good in here."

"That's because I had Holly Ann make dinner." Judge

grinned and picked up the towel from where Preacher tossed it on the kitchen counter. "I'm just warming it up."

"Still takes effort," Preacher said. "More than I did today."

"You're just going to ignore what I said." Judge shook his head.

Preacher couldn't quite meet his eye. Things had been so peaceful since Mister had moved out of the Ranch House, though Preacher missed his brother. Mister had taken some time to himself, and Preacher had worried about him up in those cabins along the top of the ranch, all alone.

Turned out, he hadn't been up there for very long, but right down the lane from the homestead, at Bull House. Preacher still couldn't describe the relief he'd felt when he'd learned that. He hated the contention between Judge and Mister, but he hadn't figured out a way to bridge it.

Mister felt even more alone than Preacher did, because Preacher had "taken Judge's side." He hadn't; not really. Judge knew it, and Preacher was slowly working on making sure Mister did too.

"I know people see me," he said. "I know Bear and Ranger appreciate what I do around here."

"Everyone does," Judge said. "I know we've always been on the outside of the family, but sometimes I wonder if that's just something we tell ourselves."

"Maybe," Preacher admitted. He was never not invited to do something with the family. He had a good friendship with Bear, his oldest brother. Maybe not the same special tight bond that Bishop seemed to have with him, but they got along great. He wasn't intimidated by the man, though he could have a very loud growl.

Getting married and having kids had changed Bear a lot, and in Preacher's opinion, for the better. He liked Sammy as much as anyone could like a woman and not be in love with her, because she was level-headed and rational. She owned her own business, and she'd taken on the responsibility of raising her sister's son after a tragic accident had left Lincoln an orphan.

Preacher admired a lot about Sammy, including the way she'd worked really hard to get to know him personally. She had a gift when it came to people, and she didn't even have to say a lot to do it.

She reminded him of...Charlie.

His pulse thumped, and he swallowed. "Listen, I don't —you don't need to say anything about Charlie Perkins, okay?"

"Why would I?" Judge asked.

"You know Sammy will ask." Preacher grinned. "So you better have your answer for who you're seeing prepped. I'm surprised you don't."

"I do," Judge said with a smile. "You're not going to tell them about Charlie?" He turned toward a drawer and got out the oven mitts.

Preacher shrugged and said, "Not much to tell. We chat and play games. That's about it."

"But you went out with her over the holidays."

"Yeah." Preacher turned away as Judge bent to get out a tray of roasted potatoes. The date at the Bellamore Ranch had been amazing. By far the best date Preacher had been on in years. He'd enjoyed himself immensely and talking to Charlie had gotten easier and easier with every sentence he said.

True to his word, he hadn't kissed her, and they'd talked every day since. But life had gone back to normal at Shiloh Ridge, and Charlie had been making a lot of big changes in her life too.

She'd talked to her boss at HealNow, and she'd been meeting with the curriculum team at the district office to develop some chemistry lessons, demonstrations, and experiments for every grade level, kindergarten through twelfth grade.

That project had taken on a scope she hadn't been anticipating, and since she lived literally an hour from the ranch, Preacher hadn't gone down to town in a couple of weeks now.

He missed the scent of her. The feel of her skin against his. He got to hear her voice on the chats, and they were definitely still flirting in their private feeds.

He simply wanted more. He suspected she did too, but she hadn't suggested she could come up to the ranch to see him, nor had she asked him to come stream with her or bring dinner or anything of the sort.

"Nothing to tell," he said to Judge. "We're friends, and I certainly don't need Sammy making a big deal of it."

"Okay," Judge said, holding up his mitted hands as if in surrender. "Fine by me."

"What's your story going to be?" Preacher asked, turning to the table. He picked up a couple of glasses and went to the fridge to fill them with ice and water.

"I met someone on Three Rivers Singles Central," Judge said.

Preacher dang near dropped the glass. It stumbled over the lever he needed to press to get ice, and he gripped it tighter. "Really?"

Judge laughed. "No, Preach. It's a *story*." He lifted his head and bobbled it a little bit. "And things are still so new, and I don't want to jinx anything." He grinned like he'd just gotten a huge present for his birthday.

Preacher laughed with his brother, but he wondered if Judge really would like to meet someone. He set the two glasses down on the table and picked up two more. "Maybe you should try Singles Central," he said causally. A little too casually.

"I'm not interested in finding someone new." Judge didn't look at Preacher, and he heard all the underlying messages in those few words. He'd found someone he was interested in, and he'd even started dating Juniper Nichols, back when Bear and Sammy were dating. Preacher could hardly believe it had been over two years ago. Three, come summertime.

He opened his mouth to say something about June, but quickly decided against it. Judge still saw her occasionally, but theirs was a friendship, just like him and Charlie. He had no idea if Judge had ever held June's hand or kissed her, because they were grown men and didn't gossip about their love lives.

"How's Lucy Mae?" he asked instead.

Judge inhaled sharply. "She's almost sixteen," he said, as

if that explained everything about June's daughter. Preacher didn't understand, but he nodded anyway.

"Knock, knock," Sammy said, and the whole crew came in the back door. Lincoln dashed in while she held the door, and Bear followed with baby Stetson in his arms. The baby was ten months old now, and his face lit up when he saw Judge.

Judge cooed at the child and took him from Bear, all smiles now. Preacher wouldn't mention June, and he'd act like he knew who this mysterious woman on the singles site was so he wouldn't blow his brother's cover.

Benny trotted inside, and Preacher related more to the dog than the people. He bent down and patted him, scratching behind his ears and getting the scent of dirt and mud from the dog's fur.

"Heya, Bear," he said, standing to embrace his brother.

"Preach." They hugged, Bear clapping him hard on the shoulder. "You ready for this?"

"I suppose so."

Ward entered the house last, his phone pressed to his ear. He wore a smile from ear to ear, and he said, "Okay, I'm at my cousin's, and I have to go. Can I call you later?" A pause, and then he said, "Great, bye."

He hung up, pocketed his phone, and stepped over to Preacher too. Another hug. Another round of smiles. "You look tired, Preacher," Ward said.

"It's been a long day," he admitted.

"Well, they're about to get longer," Ward said, and he looked absolutely gleeful about it. He spotted the food. "Oh, thank you, Lord. Holly Ann made dinner."

# Chapter Six

Judge Glover hated his weeping heart. He hated that he'd inherited all of Dad's emotional genes. All the ones that made him cry at sad movies. Heck, happy movies. Romantic movies. Action-adventure movies with a romance subplot. Anything where people had to overcome something, win, and then live a great life together.

He hated his emotions. He let them get the best of him sometimes, and that always caused him trouble. His frustration and anger had put a massive divide between him and Mister, and that was the biggest regret of his forty years on this planet so far.

His attachment to his family made him into a prankster. That way, no one would know how much he desperately loved them. The only person who might actually know was Cactus. Maybe Preacher. He'd been the most real with them, and he'd had the most honest, open, heartfelt conversations with the two of them.

Separately, of course. Judge didn't do well in crowds.

So standing in True Blue, all dressed up for his mother's wedding, Judge definitely had the strong urge to flee into the night.

Ace and Preacher had done that once. Packed bags. Got in a truck. Drove away. Judge had been so, so angry when he'd found out. He'd have liked to have gone too, and he'd almost packed his own bag and driven off Shiloh Ridge alone. The reason he hadn't?

Mother.

Everything came back to his mother.

She would be disappointed and heartbroken if she knew her children didn't feel loved and wanted. She already disliked the contention between them, and she'd been talking to Judge about setting things right with Mister since the holidays, when Preacher had given Arizona that Corvette.

Judge glanced around for his sister, though he wasn't sure why. He and Zona had been good friends growing up, and he'd always taken her side when she had issues with Preacher. He could always count on Arizona to come to his side.

But tonight, she sat with her husband. Of course that was where she would be. Her new normal was at Duke Rhinehart's side, and Judge's throat tightened with the keen sense of abandonment.

It made no sense. His sister had not abandoned him by falling in love and getting married. Just like Bear hadn't, and Bishop hadn't. It was called life, and Judge wanted to live his more fully.

What he really wanted was another chance with June Nichols. He hadn't talked to her in a while, but he knew where she worked, and he could easily stop in at Nichols Networking and say he was having a problem with his WiFi. At the same time, he didn't want to do that, because it would sting when June sent someone else to look at it.

In the few months they'd started seeing each other, she came to Shiloh Ridge if he needed help. She'd come to make sure his network could handle the Christmas lights, and every year, he had to call her to come upgrade it.

But maybe that was his way back into her life....

Ward had been doing massive groundskeeping projects, and he could certainly have clipped something while putting in the new road that led out to the Edge Cabin. Surely June herself would have to come see what had happened and how to get the Ranch House back online.

All of the landscaping had been redone at the Ranch House when Bishop had exterminated the termites, then rebuilt the house to expand the living area and kitchen, put things in a more functional layout, and remodel everything to bring it into the current century.

Of course, June had come then and Judge hadn't had a problem with his network since. Still...there had to be something he could do to casually get himself back in June's life.

He pulled at his tie, wishing this wedding was over so he could take it off. The ceremony hadn't even begun yet, and then there would be dinner and dancing.

"Get yourself together," he muttered to himself. "You're marrying your mother in fifteen minutes."

Mother had included everyone in the wedding. Judge had gone to the seminary for a little bit, then taken a few psychology classes for a year or two in college, and then he'd become a legal representative of Texas, able and willing to bind two people in holy matrimony.

Besides all of that, he mostly just played a cowboy, working around the family ranch on whatever someone with more authority asked him to do.

And today, Mother had asked him to marry her and Donald Parker, the fire chief in Three Rivers. He'd be retiring at the end of June, and Mother said they'd be "traveling the world" for a while, and that none of her kids could get married or have babies while she was gone.

No problems there for Judge. In fact, he had half a mind to pull out his phone and text June right now.

His eyes caught on movement across from him. Mister had just arrived, and he had a stunning blonde on his arm and a near-blinding smile on his face.

Judge's heart dropped to the tips of his boots.

Mister had brought a date.

Bear had Sammy. Ranger had Oakley. Bishop had Montana. Ace had Holly Ann. Cactus had Willa. Arizona had Duke. Ida had Brady. Etta had Noah.

Preacher wasn't there yet, because he'd gone down to town to pick up Charlie, so he'd have a date too.

Judge had no one.

*Ward.*

He seized onto his cousin's name, because Ward wasn't dating anyone either. Surely he wouldn't have a date for the wedding, and Judge wouldn't be the only one there alone.

A few minutes later, Ward entered the great hall in the remodeled barn, his elderly mother on his arm. Relief poured through Judge, who hadn't moved from his position holding up the wall near the kitchen entrance.

Mother had hired a catering company to feed the Glover clan, despite Holly Ann's insistence that she could do it. Mother loved Holly Ann's food—everyone did—but she just wanted her to be able to relax and enjoy the wedding.

Plus, one of Donald's fireman owned a catering company called Firehouse Food, and Judge had seen the menu. His mouth watered just thinking about the baby back ribs and cheesy potatoes on tonight's menu.

His appetite fled as he watched Ward turn back to the entrance and extend his hand toward someone. A woman slipped her fingers into Ward's as she looked at him with stars in her eyes. A small, shy smile sat on her face, and she looked like Ward walked on water.

Judge had no idea who she was, but Ward had been out with several women in the past few years. It wasn't anyone he'd gone out with before, and Judge wondered how in the world he managed to meet these women.

This one had plain brown hair she'd swept up into a curly up-do, and she wore a dress that was mostly made of gauzy, white fabric for the skirt. The top hugged her shoulders and bodice, and boasted a blue flowered print over white fabric. With long, dangling diamonds at her ears, she definitely looked ready for a wedding.

Maybe not a cowboy wedding, but a wedding nonetheless. She held Ward's right hand while he slipped his left arm through his mother's again. He guided them both to a row near the front, and he ended up sitting right behind where Mister had sat with his date.

Whoever she was, she spoke with Mister in an easy way, her eyes bright and her smile quick. She sure seemed to like Mister, and Judge couldn't take his eyes from the pair of them. He wanted his brother to be happy. Of course he did. Just because they'd had a few arguments in the past didn't mean he wished bad things for Mister.

*You've got to forgive him*, Judge thought. *And yourself.*

Preacher arrived, barely beating the music to his seat with a stunning Charlie Perkins. If he'd thought he could keep the gorgeous blonde a secret, he was sorely mistaken. Or he shouldn't have brought her to Mother's wedding.

Every Glover eye seemed to zero in on them, despite the late entrance. Maybe because of it.

The moment he sat down, the music changed, and Judge needed to get over to the altar. Mother had asked Bear to walk her down the aisle, of course. Cactus had chosen the ties and cowboy hats for all the men, right down to Stetson's bow tie and Mitch's and Lincoln's matching suspenders.

Arizona had selected the colors for the flowers, the decorations, and the bridesmaid dresses. She, Ida, Etta, Sammy, Oakley, Montana, Aurora, Holly Ann, and Willa wore gowns the color of pale, ripe peaches, with pearls and jewels in their hair.

Preacher had written Mother's vows for her, as well as Donald's for him. They'd collaborated last night for over an hour when the couple had come to the Ranch House for final preparations. Judge had then practiced with them, and if he could make it through the next fifteen minutes, the most important part of today would be over.

Maybe then he could leave.

Just slip out the back door and walk through the darkness back to the Ranch House.

Tension filled his lungs as he took his place behind the altar. He hadn't married anyone in years, but he knew what to say. He'd practiced it in front of the mirror again this morning. Looking out at the sea of people who'd come to the ranch for this wedding, the very real urge to throw up tugged in his throat.

He swallowed and reached for the bottle of water he'd put there. He really didn't want to get emotional in front of all of these people. It was bad enough that he sometimes showed his weakness to his brothers and cousins. He could barely pray over a meal without his voice breaking, and he really had no idea why he'd agreed to do this.

He took a drink and set the water back on the shelf. Bishop had carved the altar from one of the trees that had stood tall and proud in front of the original homestead here at Shiloh Ridge. Mother and Daddy had raised their loud, boisterous family of seven children in that house, with those trees watching over them.

Judge's chest tightened as his eyes filled with tears. *Dear God*, he thought. *Please, please help me be strong.*

He couldn't help thinking of his father as Donald Parker appeared opposite of Judge, in the doorway at the back of the barn. Down the hall to the right sat all the dressing rooms for the bride and groom, or storage rooms for other parties. Bishop had done an amazing job designing this barn to be party central, and Judge could admit he'd very much like to get married here.

He closed his eyes and breathed in through his nose, and in that brief span of time, he could see himself on the other side of this altar, waiting for his bride to make her way toward him.

That bride was Juniper Nichols, and her daughter would be the one to escort her toward Judge. They'd be a family, and it wouldn't matter that June couldn't have more children and Judge would never be a biological father to a child.

He opened his eyes, his fantasy wedding disintegrating from right before his eyes. Donald had almost reached him, and when their eyes met, they both smiled.

Judge shook the man's hand, and Donald turned to wait for Mother to appear. The whole barn held its breath, and then Bear stepped out of the hallway and faced the crowd. He extended his hand back toward the hall, and Mother appeared.

Judge pulled in a breath, hearing Donald do the same. His gratitude that Mother had found someone who loved her so completely filled him, and that only caused more blasted tears to prick his eyes and choke his voice way down inside his chest.

*Get it together*, he commanded himself, because it seemed like the Lord had taken a vacation today and Judge would be on his own to control his emotions. He hadn't been able to do it for the past four decades, so he didn't have much hope for today.

Mother filled the doorway, both fists holding up the skirts of her dress. She released them and fluffed the fabric out, making sure it lay right, and then she laced her arm through Bear's as she looked up at her oldest son.

Judge snapped a mental picture of the two of them looking at one another like that, and he could see Daddy right there in Bear's face when he looked toward the front of the hall. Did Mother see her late husband every time she looked at Bear?

Probably, and Judge decided right then and there he was going to lose the battle against his emotions, so he might as well let them rage.

He didn't have a date here to impress anyway. He was the only one who didn't have someone to dance with later, and he wondered what memo he'd missed that had said to get a date for this particular event.

He reached up to wipe his eyes while everyone still trained their attention on Bear and Mother, now steadily making their way toward Donald and Judge.

She arrived, and she swept a kiss across Bear's face before he turned to sit with his family. She took both of Judge's hands in both of hers across the altar, and he leaned toward her so she could kiss his cheek too. She kissed both of his, and he did the same to her, his feelings swelling and growing past the point where he could contain them.

Mother looked at Donald, and the love shining from her face would've undone Judge had he been able to lace everything together. Since he hadn't, he let the moment fill the entirety of the barn, and he let himself weep with the joy and tenderness between these two older people.

Finally, he cinched everything tight and said, "Welcome, everyone, to the marriage ceremony of Lois Darla Glover to Donald Louis Parker."

They both looked at him, and he gazed back at them. "I had a script for this," he said. "Preacher helped me write it, and we went over it with everyone last night." He looked out at everyone watching him, and thankfully, Mother and Donald blocked some of their faces. Less eyes on him, and Judge inhaled some strength into his chest.

"But I feel impressed to say something else. I hope Mother will forgive me." She nodded at him, and Judge opened his mouth again. "I can feel Daddy here, and he is so happy. Happy is not a big enough word for how he feels right now. He loved Mother with every fiber of his whole soul, and I'm not sure I ever realized that until right this moment."

He paused, because his throat had narrowed to the size of a drinking straw. As it opened, he continued. "When I saw Bear and Mother looking at one another, I felt like I'd been present when Daddy and Mother had said I-do so many years ago. Their love was written in the stars, and while I'm sure Mother didn't anticipate losing him so soon, her faith in God's plan for her has shown me personally how to be a better man. A better follower of Christ."

She beamed at him, and Judge hoped this deviation from his planned speech wouldn't ruin her wedding day.

"I don't know what Daddy told Mother before he died, and I have no idea what she went through to lose a spouse so young. What I know is that the Lord has a special way of blessing His children, no matter how old they are, with the people and situations they need to heal. With the people and situations they need to find happiness. With the people and situations they need to experience love on a level they've never experienced it before." He took a long breath. "These past few years have seen a lot of changes and additions to the Glover family. As someone who hasn't changed, who's been standing still and seeing it all happen around him, I can attest to the fact that there is more love here at Shiloh Ridge than there was even a couple of years ago."

He couldn't see Sammy, praise the stars, but he knew a lot of the changes had to do with her.

"I love how much we love each other, and I love all of those people who have joined us. My siblings' spouses and children, their parents, aunts, uncles, and anyone else they know." He swallowed, his voice teetering on the very edge of his emotion. "I love them, and I love my siblings for bringing them into my life. I'm grateful for Don—" His voice gave out on him then, but he powered through.

"For loving Mother so much, and for being so willing to accept all of us into his life too." He swallowed, his heart pounding in his throat and making his eardrums throb.

"Let's get this deed done, because I can practically hear Bishop's stomach growling." That got a few twitters, and as Judge looked out into the audience he could see past Mother and Donald, he saw several people wiping their eyes too.

He wasn't weak for having emotions, or for letting them show, and relief filled Judge from top to bottom. He was so tired of feeling weak. Even Preacher was stronger than him in every way, and the fact that Bear had bypassed Judge in favor of his younger brother for foreman proved it.

"I believe Mother is going to read her vows first." He nodded at her, glad he would get a break for a few minutes. Donald and Mother read their speeches Preacher had written for them, and then they turned back to Judge.

"Lois Darla Glover," he said. "Do you give yourself to Donald Louis Parker, to be his legally and lawfully wedded wife, to experience and share the good and the bad, the easy and the hard, as long as you both shall live?"

"I do," she said.

"Donald Louis Parker, do you give yourself to Lois Darla Glover." He paused to clear his throat, his emotion rearing up again and his voice cracking on his surname. "To be her legally and lawfully wedded husband, to experience and share the good and the bad, the easy and the hard, as long as you both shall live?"

"I do," he said in a strong, bass voice.

"By the power vested in my by the great state of Texas, I now pronounce you, Donald Louis Parker and Lois Darla Glover, husband and wife." He grinned at them through his tears. "You may share your first kiss as husband and wife."

Someone started clapping, and then the Glovers came to life, cheering and applauding as Donald turned to Mother. Both of them smiled with everything they had, and Judge added his catcall to others as they kissed.

Mother didn't let that go on too long, and she ducked her head to Donald's shoulder after only a moment or two. Judge could see her when the rest of the crowd couldn't, and she was angelic with her laughter and smile and the way she clung to Donald.

Bear and Cactus arrived at the altar to hug everyone, and surprisingly, Arizona stepped around the altar to Judge first. "That was so beautiful," she said, not bothering to hide her tears. "We should've had you officiate our wedding."

"Thank you," Judge said, hugging her. He joined the group and hugged his siblings—all but Mister.

He and his brother seemed to know how to rotate around each other without knocking into one another. It was quite the delicate dance, and finally, Bear yelled, "Everyone help with the tables so we can eat."

Everyone did as he said, because nothing motivated the Glover family quite like food. Judge moved chairs and spread tablecloths with everyone else, and soon enough, he sat next to Preacher and Charlie, who'd sat with Ace and Holly Ann, and Mister and his mystery date.

"Who is she?" Judge asked, leaning close to Preacher so Mister wouldn't overhear him. He sat almost directly across from Judge, and with the tall vase of flowers, he wouldn't have to look directly at him or speak to him. Beside the flowers sat a painting of the old homestead, and that was Mister's contribution to the wedding—the art on the tables. He'd painted all of them, and each depicted a different aspect of Shiloh Ridge Ranch.

"Her name is Claudia," Preacher said. "She's a friend of Holly Ann's. She offered to set them up last Christmas, and she finally did it."

"Mm." Judge looked away as Claudia looked toward

him. He noted the empty seat next to him, the seventh wheel at a table for eight. "Who's Ward with?"

"Dunno," Preacher said, looking over his shoulder toward the couple. "I think he took her to dinner last week, though. Miranda, maybe? Meredith?"

"Her name is Brenda," Charlie said, and Preacher turned toward her.

"You sure?" he asked. "I swear it started with an M."

Charlie grinned at him. "You're way off, buddy. It's Brenda."

Preacher grinned right on back. "I think it's Miranda for sure."

Charlie giggled and shook her head, and Preacher put his arm around her and leaned in closer to say something else. Judge watched them flirt, and he knew there was so much more than friends on the label of their relationship.

"I'm going to go find out," Preacher said, standing up. "If I win, you owe me dinner." With that, he walked away, and both Judge and Charlie watched him.

Their eyes met, and Judge stuck out his hand. "I'm Preacher's brother. Just older than him. Judge."

"Charlie," she said, shaking his hand. "You live with him too, right?"

"Yes, ma'am." He smiled at her, and she was exactly Preacher's type. "What do you do, Charlie?"

Surprise blinked across her expression. "Preacher hasn't told you?"

"Let me tell you something about Preacher," Judge said, sliding over one chair. Mister came into view, but Judge simply didn't look at him. "He is a complex, *complex* man.

He's smart and thinks a lot. He feels things deeply, even if he doesn't show it. You'll never know, though, because he is so quiet. So no, dear Charlie, he has not breathed a word about you to me."

Judge grinned at her. "So tell me: What are your intentions with my dear brother?"

# Chapter Seven

Charlie didn't know how to answer Judge Glover.

"What's going on here?" Preacher asked, arriving. "Move on over, Judge."

His brother did, his smile never wavering, and Charlie looked away from him to Preacher. They looked a lot alike, though Preacher had a straighter, longer nose and he simply seemed more refined than Judge.

Judge's hair was a bit lighter, and the blue in his eyes was more washed out than Preacher's. He seemed like he existed behind a layer of waxed paper, where everything was simply more muted than his brother. Or maybe Charlie just had an emotional connection to Preacher she didn't with Judge.

He wore a cowboy hat too, identical to Preacher's. It wasn't ivory, and that color deviation had been enough to make Charlie swoon all over again.

She'd tried to tell Preacher she could drive up here for

the wedding, but he'd insisted on coming to get her. He'd driven an hour to her house, complimented her on her gown, and turned right around and drove back. He'd do it all again in a couple of hours, and Charlie's guilt pricked at her heart.

"Do you have your cards?" a man asked, and Charlie looked up at him.

"I've got 'em," Preacher said, reaching into his jacket pocket and pulling out a couple of cards. He set one on Charlie's plate, and she caught filet mignon on it before the waiter picked it up.

She unconsciously leaned toward the body heat coming from Preacher, and he put his arm on the back of her chair again. "What was her name?" she asked.

"I was hopin' you'd forget." He sighed.

"Must've been Brenda," Charlie teased.

"It wasn't Miranda," he said, refusing to say she was right. Charlie giggled, and she looked at the beautiful brunette next to Ace Glover. His wife, Holly Ann, was watching her, and Charlie gave her a smile.

"You're Charlie," she said.

"Yes." She leaned forward to shake her hand. "You're Ace's wife, Holly Ann."

She glanced at her husband. "That's right. Nice to meet you finally. Ace talks about you all the time."

Charlie had heard words like that before, and they weren't good. Ever. Ace looked back and forth between them, saying, "She's the best at Aces High."

"The flying game?" Holly Ann asked.

"Yeah," he said. "You should see her fly. Wait. You were

there the other day. She was the one who hit all those rings I literally can't get to." He looked at Charlie. "I still don't know how you did it."

Charlie knew how she did it, and she smiled at Ace. "You need the Activation controller," she said. "It's impossible otherwise."

"That's so stupid," he said. "You should be able to pass the levels without having to buy the name-brand controller. Or an extra one. If you need that one to play the game, it should come with the game."

Charlie had heard all of this before. Not from Ace, but from plenty of others. Video game companies wanted to make money, and they often sold things separately in order to do that. "Preaching to the choir, Ace," she said.

"Preacher can do it without the Activation," he said, nodding to the man beside her. "I don't know how he does it either. Must be the fancy controller he uses for his basketball games."

Charlie nearly got whiplash she turned toward Ace so fast. "Basketball games?"

"Thanks, Ace," Preacher said dryly. His eyes met Charlie's, and she promised herself for the fifth time since he'd picked her up not to let more than a few days go by without seeing him in person. Almost three weeks had passed since their date on the wagon, and she hadn't realized how big of a hole he'd left in her life until he'd stepped back into it.

"You like *sports* games," she said, all kinds of dots firing at her now. "How did I miss this?"

He cocked his head as he shrugged. "You might know

chemical compounds, but you missed what almost all men like."

"Food," Holly Ann said, grinning at Preacher.

"Horses," Ace said, joining in. "Wait. For Preach, it's dogs."

"Dogs?" Charlie asked, her eyebrows sky high. "I have two cats."

"No wonder y'all are just friends," Ace said, but his blue eyes held a sparkle in them that said he knew Charlie and Preacher were more than friends.

She knew it when she was with him. Apart, she sometimes forgot. She wasn't sure if that was a good thing or not—shouldn't she be friends with him too? Shouldn't she want to share things with him in a friendly way?

She'd never been an overly emotional woman, though Judge's speech had moved her and made her sigh in happiness. She normally didn't like the sappiness of weddings, nor the way they made her feel so alone. Today, though, she'd enjoyed the spirit she'd felt as Preacher's oldest brother walked their mother down the aisle to a man who clearly adored her.

She'd appreciated Judge's speech, and she did feel welcome here, almost like because she'd arrived with a Glover, she could stay as long as she'd like. She could come back any time too, and they'd all open their hearts and let her in.

Waiters arrived at their table, plates of food getting set in front of the seven of them. Charlie looked down at her steak, which had been wrapped in bacon and paired with green beans, asparagus, and creamy mashed potatoes. A dark au jus sauce slathered the steak and dripped onto the potatoes.

Her mouth watered, and Charlie couldn't wait to taste this food. She also knew money when she saw it, and this family had money. She'd commented on it when Preacher had pulled up to the barn, but he'd simply said. "You've been here before," as if that addressed her comment of, "Wow, this place is really nice."

She could talk to him about it while they danced, just like she'd be grilling him about which basketball game he liked best while he moved them around the dance floor. Right now, she was going to eat.

The first bite of food was savory and salty, rich and tangy. She groaned and looked at Preacher. "This is incredible."

"Firemen know how to cook," he said, slicing off another bite of steak. The conversation at the table focused on the work they did here at the ranch, as most of the people contributing were the Glover men. Charlie knew nothing about ranching, cattle, farming, or rotating pastures, so she kept quiet. Preacher didn't say a whole lot either, which surprised her somewhat, because he was going to start as foreman in a couple more weeks.

Just when the conversation lulled, someone stepped up to the microphone and said, "Lois loves dancing, so she wanted to have a big dance party at her wedding."

At the table in front of theirs, Charlie saw a man with an identical cowboy hat and tie to Preacher's signing to a little boy. That intrigued her, and she couldn't look away from the cowboy's hands as he translated what the woman at the mic said.

"Who was that?" Charlie asked once she'd stopped talking.

Before he could answer, deafening music blasted into the hall. She wasn't the only one who yelped and covered their ears, and the music got adjusted quickly. "Sorry," the woman said. "But come on, everyone. Everyone has to dance. It's part of the requirement to be here at this wedding."

"I'm out," Judge said, standing. He walked away from the table before anyone could say anything to him.

Preacher stood up and buttoned his suit coat. "You said you could dance in that dress," he said. "Let's see it, sugar." He extended his hand toward her with a smile, and Charlie hoped her legs could hold her.

She put her hand in his and stood, though it was a bit hard in the gown. She wasn't sure she could wear black to a wedding, but the boutique attendant had insisted the satin flowers woven through the dress's fabric made it okay.

She'd taken a picture of herself in the dress and sent it to Preacher, who'd called instantly. She could still hear his words. *That is the sexiest dress I've ever seen.*

Charlie felt sexy in it, and she never felt that way. Wearing jeans and a lab coat didn't make one feel like a head-turner. When she live-streamed, she usually wore sweats and a blouse, as people only saw her from the chest up.

She'd curled her hair again, and she'd put on eye makeup and lipstick for this wedding.

"I can dance in this dress,' she said. "I practiced and everything."

Preacher's hand slid easily along the slick fabric at her waist. "Wish I could've been there." He led her past the last table and onto the dance floor, where several other couples had already started swaying together.

She melted right into the strength and comfort of his arms, wondering if he'd kiss her when he dropped her off that evening. He smelled like pine trees and leather, money and steak, butter and a hint of musk. She loved the scent of him, and she breathed him in as he moved them around the floor.

He didn't hold her too close, just as he'd said he wouldn't, but Charlie wouldn't object if he did.

"When are you meeting with the mall manager?" he asked, his mouth at her ear.

She shivered, kneading him closer to her until their shoulders touched on her left side. "Tuesday," she said. "Can you still come and help me go through all of my supplies?"

"Sure thing," he drawled. "Monday night?"

"If you can."

"I can." He touched his cheek to hers, and Charlie sank into the comforting place where she and Preacher danced the night away, falling more and more in love with every song.

Normally, she'd be scared out of her mind to be in this position—dancing and thinking she was falling for the man who held her right where he wanted her. After all, the last time she'd been here, her heart had been stomped on, pureed, and left for her to put back together.

It beat swiftly through her body now, reminding her that it wasn't quite whole, but she soothed it by reminding herself that Preacher had said they could go slow.

*He might reconsider once he knows who you really are*, she thought. But for tonight, Charlie was going to keep her secrets and enjoy the dance.

# Chapter Eight

Preacher pulled into the parking lot at the storage facility Charlie had specified. He didn't see her car, but then he realized he had no idea what kind of car she drove. He recited the unit number she'd given him, and he turned a corner to find the unit door up, a motorcycle parked out front.

"She drives a motorcycle," he said to himself. "Of course she does." As if he needed another reason to be unreasonably attracted to her. The inferiority he felt doubled as he parked his ancient truck behind the shiny bike.

He got out as she exited the unit. She smiled and dusted her hands down the front of her leggings. "Hey, Preach."

"Hey, Chemist." He grinned at her, but she just giggled and shook her head. He took her right into his arms, because he wanted to. He wanted to breathe in the scent of her hair and skin, and he wanted to be close to her physically.

She hugged him back, and he got a nose full of strawberries, dust, and something that smelled quite chemically. He liked it, and he hoped he didn't smell too much like cattle, as he'd been wrestling with them a lot today.

"You ride a motorcycle?" he asked as he stepped back.

"From time to time," she said, looking at it. "Today felt like a day where I wanted the wind in my hair."

"It's freezing," he said, actually tucking his hands in his jacket pockets.

"I've got leather inside," she said, looking over her shoulder. "Let's go through this, and then I'll take you to dinner." She flashed a smile in his direction, and Preacher followed her into the wide storage unit.

She could've easily parked two cars inside, side by side. It extended back a ways too, and she went to the cart he'd seen at Ida's wedding, sighing as she came to stop. "Okay," she said. "I've got this that I haul to fairs and things like that."

"You won't need that if you have a store," he said.

"No," she said. "I just need my machines." She indicated those, which rested on a long, chest-high stainless-steel table. "I only have two of those."

"How many do you need for a storefront?"

"The big stores have a dozen or more."

"Wow." Preacher looked at the machines, which had tubes extending straight up from the bowl mixers they were attached to. "You don't need a big store, maybe?"

"Honestly, I still think a kiosk is a good idea." She

looked at him and back to her machines. "I'll talk to the manager tomorrow and see what she says. Maybe she'll have some idea of how many people come to the mall for ice cream."

"Well, what's already there?" he asked. "There's Scooped!, right?"

"Don't even get me started on other ice cream places," she said, rolling those pretty eyes. "My ice cream is ten times better. It's smooth and creamy, and it doesn't melt nearly as fast."

"Hey, I'm sold," he said. "I was just brainstorming the competition."

"How much time do you spend in the mall?" she asked, clearly teasing him.

"A bit," he said. "We go there to get games."

She flipped the lapels on his plaid jacket. "You didn't get this there."

"No, ma'am, I did not." He kept his hands in his pockets so he wouldn't grab onto her and kiss her.

"Oh, you're going to make me work for it." She shook her head, her ponytail up on the crown again tonight. "Okay, I'll bite, Mister Glover. Where did you get your jacket?"

"There's a great online store for ranchers," he said. "They have phenomenal outdoor gear. Boots. Pants. Jackets. Hats. All of it."

"Do you wear other types of hats?" Her eyes moved up to the standard ivory cowboy hat he couldn't leave the house without. "I'd really like to see that."

"Would you now?" he asked, grinning at her. "If it's real

cold, I'll switch out this for a beanie. Something to keep my ears warm."

"Mm, fascinating."

Preacher found her fascinating too, and he wondered how he could say such a thing. He and Charlie were really good at flirting with one another. The physical barrier between them had been broken, and he could call or text her whenever he wanted.

What he wasn't great at was saying the things in his heart. He'd never told a woman he loved her, because he'd never been in love before. He swallowed just thinking about letting something so intimate come out of his mouth.

"What's the name of the online store?" she asked.

"Western Cardigan," he said. "That's where Cactus got all of the wedding garb."

"That was such an *amazing* wedding," Charlie said with a sigh, this one filled with happiness and the femininity Preacher was used to in the women he dated.

He wasn't used to someone as strong and smart at Charlie. Today, she wore a dark purple hoodie with two beakers of chemical compounds on the front of it. They had cartoon eyes and mouths, and the red one boiled over, his eyes angry as he cried about something.

Next to him, a beaker with cool blue liquid simply looked at his friend, the conversation bubble above his head saying, "You're overreacting."

He grinned at it and pointed to the sweatshirt. "I like this shirt. Where'd you get it?"

She looked down at herself and back to him. "I have a

ton of stuff like this." She looked at him with wide, open eyes. "You really like it?"

"It's funny." He chuckled, and Charlie gazed at him as if she'd never seen anything quite like him. He quieted quickly, coaching himself not to clear his throat.

He'd done way too much of that with this woman, and he needed to start acting a little more confident around her. He was smart too. He was strong too.

"I have one with the periodic table on it," Charlie said. "It says 'I wear this shirt periodically.'"

"Nice." Preacher looked around the storage unit. "What else do we need to do here?"

"I have these signs," she said, stepping over to a couple of sandwich signs one would set out on a sidewalk to direct people to her cart.

"I don't think you'll need those for a kiosk or a storefront."

"I need all new signage," she said, picking up a clipboard from the countertop. "I've made a list here." She handed him the clipboard, and he looked at her list.

"New signs," he said. "A marketing plan. Updated menu. Additional mixers, maybe six to start, depending."

"Depending on what kind of shop it'll be," she said.

"If you go into the food court, you'd have more room," he said. "And people would have a place to enjoy their ice cream."

She nodded, her lips pressed together. Preacher went back to the list. "Aprons. Maybe a new logo." His head started to spin. "This is a lot, Charlie."

"I hate my logo," she said.

Preacher looked up to her cart, and he didn't hate it. A zero with a degree sign next to it sat above the word "below," and he actually thought it was a clever way to say below zero. "Maybe something more trendy," he said. "I could talk to Mister about it. He does some design work."

She swung her attention back to him. "He does?"

Preacher nodded. "He's a good artist. Likes to draw and paint and all of that."

"Sure," she said. "You can ask him."

"Okay." Preacher went back to the list. The last thing on it said, "A well-defined business plan." He put the clipboard down, his mind spinning. "I don't even know how to write a business plan."

"I've started," she said. "It's been overwhelming. I just work on it a little bit each day." She reached up and took her ponytail in her hand and slid her fingers through it. He'd seen her do that on some of her livestreams too, and he realized it showed her nerves.

He reached out and took that hand in his, and he watched her visibly calm. Their eyes met, and Preacher had no idea what to say in a moment like this. He took a moment, the same way he did when he and Charlie texted, and then he said, "We can go over it during dinner, if you'd like."

Hope entered her expression, and the softness she hid from everyone else emerged. "You're amazing," she said, the words sticking in her throat. He heard the effort it took for her to say them, and he sure did appreciate it.

"Thanks," he said, his own voice stuck somewhere between his ribs. "I think you're amazing too."

She leaned toward him, but Preacher did not want their first kiss to be in a freezing storage unit. His heart pounded, because he wasn't sure where that kiss should happen, but it wasn't here.

"It's cold, cowboy," she said, her voice full of heat. "Let's go get warm somewhere."

"You wanted to try that veggie place," he said.

"I can go with my girlfriends," she said. "I doubt you'll even see men there."

"Sure you will," Preacher said, knowing exactly who'd be at The Garden.

"Yeah?" she challenged. "Who?"

"Well, sugar," he drawled, drawing her right back into his arms. They began to dance right there in the storage unit, and this time, Preacher put both hands on her waist and brought her flush against his chest. This was intimate dancing; none of this proper, formal stuff they'd done at Mother's wedding.

Her breath sank into the fabric of his shirt, and he could lose hours with this woman in his arms.

"You'll see every good man in Three Rivers at The Garden," he whispered. "Who wants his wife or girlfriend to be happy. That's who you'll see there."

"And you want me to get happy?" she asked.

"Yes," he whispered.

"Am I your girlfriend then?"

Preacher stumbled over his own feet, something that never happened while he danced. "Um." He didn't know how to answer that. "I don't know," he ended up saying, which he knew was the absolute wrong thing to say.

Quickly, he asked, "When do you know a man is your boyfriend?"

"When...well, when we decide we're exclusively seeing one another." She pulled away from him slightly, her expression masked but full of challenge too.

"I'm not seeing anyone else," he said. "I don't even want to see anyone else." He kept moving with her, wishing she'd say something similar so he'd know what they were to one another.

She said nothing, though she didn't look away from him for even a single heartbeat.

# Chapter Nine

Charlie's heart warred against her, and she couldn't get it to calm down. A storm waged its way across Preacher's face, and he slowed their dance to a stop and tried to pull away from her. She kept her grip on him and finally managed to say, "I'm not seeing anyone else either, Preacher."

Relief poured through his eyes, and he said, "So we're exclusive then."

"I would say so." She had so much more to say to him too. Only a couple of days ago, she'd wanted to keep her secrets forever. But if she dated him exclusively, that elevated them to a new level of friendship. The kind where she had to share personal things with him.

"Why do you look so unhappy about it?" he asked, and he could've made the question flirty if he'd smiled and added some playfulness to his tone. He did neither.

"Preacher, I—" She didn't know how to say the things

she needed to say. *Don't say all of them*, she told herself. *Just say one.*

"I'm not very nurturing," she said, actually surprised that she'd led with that. At least she hadn't started with children. They weren't ready to start talking about having a family together.

"I don't get it," Preacher said.

"I'm not a nurturer," she said. "I'm not good at telling people what I'm thinking or how I'm feeling about them. I'm not good at making sure they know I like them or appreciate them. I don't *nurture* things." She released him and stepped away, reaching up to pull her ponytail through her fingers.

"I'm not like other women. I don't talk about how I feel until I can't breathe. Sometimes I don't feel anything. I'm not crying into my coffee because I don't have a boyfriend, and I actually like spending time by myself."

Horror struck her behind her lungs, and she needed to clarify before he walked out and wished her well with her life. "I mean, I don't want to spend every day alone, or be alone forever, but yeah. I like my independence, and I do need to be alone to recharge most of the time." She sucked in a breath, because she'd said so much in such a small space.

"Charlie," he said, and she dropped her eyes to the concrete at her feet. "Sugar," he tried again, actually taking a step toward her. "You don't have to be—you don't have to tell me how you feel until you can't breathe."

"I'm more of a doer," she said. "If we're talking, I'm fine. If we're texting, we're fine. If we're gaming, we're fine." She lifted her eyes to meet his again, the ground beneath her shaking now. She honestly wished it would open up and suck her down, so she'd stop talking. "If there's not anything bothering me, I just don't say anything. It's fine."

He took a small step toward her. "But do you want 'fine,' Charlie?"

"You don't play fair," she said, though she certainly didn't mind her name in that savory voice of his.

"I'm sorry?"

"Saying *sugar* all sexy like that, and then my name in the same way. It's not fair."

"I'm not playing with you," he said, frowning. "This is how I talk."

Charlie found him absolutely adorable, but she'd never tell him that. "No," she said. "I don't want fine."

"I didn't think so." He reached for her, and she extended her hand toward him too. Familiar sparks raced through her when her skin met his, and she couldn't ignore that.

"You want the world," he whispered. "If I remember right."

Charlie nodded. "I do, Preacher. I wish I didn't, but I do."

"My world is right here in Three Rivers," he said. "Maybe I'm not the cowboy for you."

"Don't say that," she said. "You're an amazing man. I want more time with you before you decide you don't want me."

He looked at her, a scoff coming from his mouth.

"Charlie," he drawled. "I don't think it's going to be me who decides I don't want you. I'm worried I can't give you the world though, I'm not gonna lie about that."

"The world comes in many forms," she said, desperate to keep him for another day.

"I suppose so," he said. "Will you...I mean, could you tell me if I'm not good enough for you the moment you know?"

"Preacher, come on," she said. "You don't see yourself properly at all."

"Can we go to dinner?" he asked, backing away from her and from the conversation. "It's cold out here." He tugged gently on her hand, and she stepped forward with him. "Do you want to pull your bike inside or drive over and meet me?"

"I'll pull it in," she said. He got behind the wheel of his truck while she put her motorcycle in the storage unit and locked everything up. When she got in the vehicle, he had the heater going, and she slid all the way over beside him on the bench seat.

"Can I finish now?" she asked, holding her hands up to the heater vent. "It's warm in here."

"Go ahead," he said, and he didn't put the truck in drive.

"Why don't you see yourself as a sexy, smart, capable man?" she asked. "Because I guarantee you, that's how women see you. Your family. Everyone."

"It's a long story," he mumbled.

"Good thing we're exclusively dating then," she teased. "So I'll get to hear it."

He tilted his chin down and toward her, his eyes cutting out of the corners to look at her. "It's a dull story."

"I doubt that," she said, thinking of Mindi and how she probably played into his erroneous perception of himself.

"You're wrong about my family," he said. "They don't really see me the way you described."

"That's not true," she said. "Aren't you moving into a leadership position in a couple of weeks?"

He nodded and looked out his side window.

"Preacher, you're an *incredible* man," she said. "Open your eyes and look at yourself in the mirror next time you're standing in front of one. Your family wouldn't promote you to a leadership position if they didn't agree with me."

"I doubt they think I'm sexy," he said.

Charlie burst out laughing, and Preacher twisted to look at her again, a smile riding that mouth. Oh, that mouth. Charlie needed to taste it, and she panicked as she tried to remember the last thing she'd put in her mouth. Had she brushed her teeth before donning her helmet and riding down to the storage unit?

She grinned at him too, deciding it didn't matter. She needed to kiss him right here, right now. Then he'd know how she felt about him. Carefully, she reached up and ran her fingertips along his jawline, which caused his laughter to dry right on up.

He didn't wear a beard, and his skin was smooth and rugged at the same time. She curled her fingers around the back of his neck and tipped her head back, her invitation pretty dang clear in her book.

Preacher breathed in, his eyes blazing with blue fire, and then he took her face in both of his hands and kissed her.

Her cells rioted. A chemical reaction happened, with everything bubbling and boiling and foaming through her veins, her nerve endings, and her stomach.

And boy oh boy, the man knew how to kiss a woman. Just one more thing to add to the long list of his amazingness.

"I don't mind that you're not like other women," he whispered, removing his mouth from hers and touching it to her jaw.

Charlie's heartbeat nearly drowned out his voice. Tingles exploded across her skin wherever he touched, and she pushed her hands through his hair, enjoying the way it felt to be so close to another human being.

"You don't have to tell me how you feel," he said, lighting a string of kisses down her neck. "I'm fine with the doing."

"But do you want fine?" she whispered, taking his face in her hands and bringing it level with hers. Their eyes met in the semi-darkness, and she searched for an answer in the navy depths of his.

"No," he admitted. "I want the world."

"Loving wife," she whispered. "Big family. Probably those dogs your cousin mentioned."

"I'm fine with cats," he said with a smile. "And trust me, big families are overrated."

Charlie swallowed back her next confession. One was enough for tonight, and she certainly didn't want to ruin the magic of their first kiss. In fact, she wanted to kiss him again.

So she did.

---

"So I'd like to offer my services as a consultant," Charlie said, nearly done with her speech. Darrell Fitzpatrick had sat through the whole thing, the line between his eyebrows getting deeper and deeper with every sentence she said. "I can definitely still do some things here at HealNow, but my focus is going to be on growing my ice cream business and working with the school district to enhance their chemistry curriculum."

She had another meeting that afternoon at the mall, with the same woman she'd met with a few months ago. She still had the quotes for shop space and kiosk charges, but this meeting would be more than logistics. Charlie wanted data, so she could operate from a place of good business.

She and Preacher had gone over her business plan during dinner. Sort of. They'd talked about it for a few minutes, and then he'd told her a story about how he'd fallen out of a tree when he was nine years old. He apparently had an affinity for falling out of things or into them, and she'd enjoyed a fun, carefree dinner with him at The Garden.

He'd been right. The restaurant had been stuffed to the gills with couples, most of whom had women with shining eyes and men looking around shiftily lest anyone they knew see them there. Preacher hadn't acted like that, and he'd ordered the portobello burger with sweet potato fries like he ate such cuisine on a regular basis.

"We'll miss you," Darrell said. "Who knows how long it'll take to find someone with your skill set to replace you?" He sighed and opened a drawer on his side of the desk. "A while, I'm assuming. Of course we'll want to consult with you." He slid a piece of paper across the desk toward her. "This is the termination agreement. Two weeks notice, which puts you here until the twenty-eighth. If you finish out that week, you could go all the way to January thirty-first."

"I can do that," Charlie said. "I'm not starting in the schools until after President's Day. We're working on all the demos, the classes I'll be teaching, and the assemblies."

"Who are you working with over at the DO?" he asked, digging through his drawer for something else. "My wife works over there."

"Hayden Leonard," she said.

"Oh, of course. He does all the community outreach programs."

"Do they do a lot of them?" Charlie asked. "I've only met with him once, and we're sitting down together again this week."

"The school district partners with ranches," he said. "The apple orchards and cider mill. Local businesses and banks. They bring a lot of real-world, practical lessons to the students. In turn, the industries in town are fed with people who are interested in them." He smiled. "Hayden does an amazing job for the people in Three Rivers."

"That's good to know," Charlie said.

"This is our standard contract for consulting," he said, handing her a packet now. "You should read over it and fill it out. Turn it in to Clarice in human resources, and we'll go from there." He smiled and stood up. As they shook hands, he said, "I'm really going to miss you, Charlie. You've done so much for HealNow and the veterinary arm of our operation."

Charlie nodded, her voice stuck somewhere down in her throat. She needed to call Davie and tell her how this had gone. She hadn't mentioned kissing Preacher either, because she knew Davie would pick up on it just from Charlie's tone of voice when she said hello.

"Thank you, Darrell," she managed to say before leaving the man's office. She left the high-rise building in Three Rivers—one of only two—and headed to her SUV. She'd agreed to lunch with a couple of the girls from her lab, and she sat behind the wheel of her car to wait for them.

"Call Davie," she said to the infotainment system, and the radio stopped playing. A cool, male voice came back with, "Calling Davie," and a few moments later, the line began to ring.

"Heya, Charlie," her sister chirped. "How do you always know right when I go on break?" She twittered with laughter, and Charlie smiled too.

"Twin thing," she said.

"Oh, mine is buzzing," Davie said, holding out the Z's. "What's going on? What's happened? Tell me right now, Char."

Charlie smiled at her overly dramatic sister. Mama always said the twins had stolen from each other in the womb. Charlie had gotten all the brains while Davie got all the beauty. Charlie had reserved emotions while Davie was as dramatic as they came. Charlie had mad skills with games and puzzles, and Davie could charm the socks off of anyone, even a homeless man on a winter night.

"Charlie!" Davie demanded, and Charlie laughed.

"Guess," she said.

"You have so much going on," Davie said, a clear pout in her voice. "That's not fair. But okay, let's see... You kissed Preacher."

Charlie hesitated a moment too long, because if she hadn't kissed Preacher, she'd have scoffed and said, "Come on, Davie. We've only been seeing each other for a few weeks." Her silence said so much.

Davie squealed, and Charlie should've anticipated that. She hastened to reach for the volume knob so she wouldn't go deaf. The twins giggled together, and Davie said, "Okay, Char. All the details. Every last one."

"Ew, no," Charlie said. "I'm not doing that." The moment with Preacher had been special to her. Sacred. Intimate. She wasn't going to cheapen it by describing it to Davie. Her sister had no place in her relationship with Preacher.

"Fine," Davie said. "You're no fun."

"Yes, well, Preacher disagrees."

"Charlie," Davie said, pealing out another string of laughter. "My goodness, I've never heard you say anything like that." She kept giggling, and Charlie couldn't stop smiling. She and Preacher had no plans in the foreseeable future to see one another in person, but they were going to get on the livestream that night and play Solitary Ops on split screen. Of course, Ace, Mister, Duke, and Beau were joining them, and the six of them were doing a special group night on Nexus.

Charlie had been getting messages about it continuously since announcing it on Sunday morning.

She saw Shoshana and Mei coming her way, both of them wearing black slacks and white lab coats. "I have to go," she said. "My friends and I are going to lunch."

"Okay," Davie said. "Call me tonight, though, because I want to hear how it goes at the mall and what you decide to do."

"Okay," she said, ending the call by tapping the red phone icon on her radio's screen. Mei opened the front passenger door, letting in a gust of wind that tried to steal her shiny, black hair right off her head.

"Mother Nature is mad today," she quipped.

"Just like Riscinda," Shoshana said from the back seat. "Seriously, Charlie, you should hear that woman talk to us. She treats us like we don't know what $CO_2$ is." She shook her head, clearly disgruntled.

Charlie would not miss Riscinda's condescending tone, that was for sure. She didn't have to work with the supervisor very often, but the woman had a reputation at HealNow everyone knew about. "Maybe she's having a bad day," she said, because she genuinely wanted to believe the best about people.

"If so, it's more like a bad week," Mei said.

"A bad month."

"A year," Charlie said, and the three of them laughed together. As she pulled out of the parking lot, she added, "Listen, ladies, I have some news."

"Jason from accounting finally asked you out," Mei said.

"Girl, if that's true, I can't believe we didn't get a text immediately afterward," Shoshana said from the back seat. "Have you been holding out on us?" She ran her hand through her auburn hair and met Charlie's eyes in the rear view mirror.

"I'm not going out with Jason," she said. "Even if he did ask, which he didn't."

"Why not?" Mei asked. "He's good-looking. I'd go out with him in a heartbeat."

"Ditto," Shoshana said.

"Great," Charlie said. "You ladies do that."

"Can you imagine?" Mei said, twisting to look at Shoshana. "Sneaking off to the drab, boring accounting floor to sneak a kiss?" She giggled and fanned herself. "I'd do it."

"Heck, I'd say yes to anyone right now," Shoshana said. "It's been such a dry spell for me. Everyone in this town seems to be taken."

"That," Mei said as the downtown buildings started going by. "Or they're not asking."

"Or they're losers." Shoshana scoffed and shook her head.

Charlie stayed right on out of that conversation, because she had a new boyfriend she didn't want to talk about. She told herself it was because she didn't want to rub her friends' noses in the fact that she'd managed to find a spectacular man who wasn't taken, who was asking, and who wasn't a loser.

They'd grill her for the next hour to find out how she'd done it, and Charlie would rather stab a fork into her eye, thank you very much.

This was the part of women she didn't understand. The back and forth about the last time they'd had a date, and who they'd go out with if only he'd ask. Charlie had suggested to Mei once that she ask the man she'd been crushing on to get coffee with her, and Mei had actually pressed one palm to her pulse as if Charlie had suggested she cut out her own heart and eat it.

It took the whole fifteen-minute drive to Sweet and Saucy before Mei finally circled back to what Charlie had said to kick off the conversation. "What's your news?" she asked.

Charlie took her time pulling into a parking space. She put the SUV in park and looked at her friends. They'd all been working at HealNow together for the past eight years, when Sho had started there.

"I'm leaving HealNow," she said, a sudden lump in her throat. "My last day is January thirty-first." The weight of her decision to quit her job hit her squarely in the chest, and she pulled in a sharp breath.

What if she'd made a mistake?

"Oh, no," Mei said. "Why?"

"Yes, why?" Sho asked as she gathered her purse. The three of them got out of the car, and Charlie had always thought they made an interesting trio. She was petite and fair. Mei was Asian, with Chinese parents who still lived in China. She'd come to the United States for school, and she was currently working here on a work permit until her green card came through.

Sho was a tall woman, with dark brown hair and a slight slant to her eyes that suggested some Native American blood in her ancestry.

"I'm going to open my liquid nitrogen ice cream shop," she said. "And consult with HealNow, and develop a chemistry curriculum with the school district here in Three Rivers."

Mei and Sho simply looked at her as they walked toward the entrance to Sweet and Saucy. Finally, Sho said, "Wow, Charlie, that's such great news." She paused to hug her, and Charlie smiled as she embraced her friend.

"I'm going to miss you so much," Mei said when it was her turn to hug Charlie. "Promise me we'll still go to lunch."

"Yes," Charlie said. "We'll have to keep going to lunch. We made a pact to try every restaurant in Three Rivers, and we're only on like, the twentieth one." She snapped her fingers as they entered the restaurant none of them had been to before.

All three of them were transplants to Three Rivers, and that alone had bonded them as they struggled with how to fit into this small town in the Texas Panhandle. Three Rivers had such great traditions and customs, but some people here weren't pleased with the two new high-rises and all the development happening.

Some people didn't like that a state crime lab was going

into the building next to HealNow. They'd process the drugs for hundreds of legal cases across Texas and the Southwest region of the US, and Charlie had actually considered applying.

That crime lab wasn't open yet, though, and they wouldn't be for another ten months.

She was only thirty-seven. If she wanted to work at the crime lab, she still had time. Preacher had told her that.

"Oh," she said. "I ate at The Garden last night. *Very* good. *Highly* recommend." She might not understand the lamentation about not having a boyfriend, but she understood food.

"You went to The Garden?" Sho asked, holding up three fingers for the hostess. "With who?"

Charlie opened her mouth to say, then realized what a trap she'd set for herself. If she even mentioned a male name, her lunch hour would be shot. She couldn't lie to her friends, though.

"Preacher Glover," she mumbled.

Mei actually yelped, and Sho leaned in closer. None of them made a move to go with the hostess as she said, "You can follow me, ladies."

"I'm sorry," Sho said. "But it sounded like you said you went to The Garden—a vegetarian restaurant—with Preacher Glover."

Charlie lifted her chin and looked the taller woman in the eye. "I did."

"Monoxide molecules," Mei said, her voice coated in disbelief. "You had a date and you didn't tell us?" She swatted at Charlie's arm. "What is wrong with you? I'm pining away night after night, and you're off with some hot cowboy!"

Charlie finally started walking when the hostess returned to the podium. "Sorry," she said. "We're coming." Once they were in a booth, she picked up her menu so she could hide behind it. "First off, how did you know he was a cowboy?"

"Every man in Three Rivers is," Mei said matter-of-factly. "It was a guess."

"He could be a complete toad," Charlie said, looking at the appetizers. She needed something fried to get through this meal.

"Please," Sho said. "Everyone knows Ranger Glover developed the app everyone in this town uses. The Glovers are like royalty here."

"Royalty," Mei repeated, her voice awed.

Charlie rolled her eyes, though a new worry had started to nip at her. If the Glovers were royalty, what was Preacher doing with a woman like her?

"I heard they're all recluses up there at that ranch," Mei said.

"That's not true," Charlie said, though she'd only met a few of the Glovers, and very briefly at Lois's wedding.

"They're super rich," Sho said. "I know that."

"How do you know that?" Charlie challenged, though she'd been to the remodeled barn a few times, and there was definite money in that place.

"*Everyone* knows that," Sho said. "Plus, when I learned HealNow was moving here, I did a bunch of research on

Three Rivers. Shiloh Ridge—the Glovers own Shiloh Ridge Ranch, right?"

"Yep." Charlie nodded as the waitress set water in front of her. She reached for her glass, gulping it because of the turn in the conversation.

"Shiloh Ridge was named in more than one thing I read," Sho said as if discussing the weather and not telling Charlie something she didn't know about her own boyfriend. "Lots of money up there. I think they're the most profitable ranch in Texas."

"All of Texas?" Mei asked. "That can't be right. Do you *know* how many ranches there are in Texas?"

"Fifty-seven thousand," Sho said as if yes, indeed, she knew how many ranches there were in Texas.

Charlie laughed with her, but Mei simply scowled. "I'm going to look it up when I get back to the lab," she said.

"Go ahead." Sho waved as if she didn't care how many ranches there were in Texas.

Charlie did, and she suddenly needed to know if the one Preacher was about to become foreman of was really the most profitable ranch in the whole state of Texas.

She needed to learn more about his family history, stat.

## Chapter Ten

Preacher inhaled deeply and watched as Bear laughed with Ranger. They stood in the kitchen with the tray of sandwiches Etta had brought from town. The front door of the homestead opened—Preacher knew, because the change in pressure whipped the back door inward—and more voices filled the house.

Someone had put a chair in the back door so it wouldn't slam, and as Ida and Brady Burton entered the kitchen, Ace came through the back door, having climbed the steps to the deck on that side of the homestead.

Preacher swallowed against his nerves, hating that Bear had staged this massive family get-together simply to commemorate Preacher's first day as foreman.

Thankfully, Sunday came after Saturday, and they always took it easy on the Sabbath. Noon had arrived already, and Preacher only had to make it through half a day as foreman over animals and equipment before he'd be able to breathe properly again.

Ward acted as foreman over agriculture and physical facilities, and Bear and Ranger still managed all the personnel on the ranch, as well as all the finances. They made all the big picture decisions, and they had daily chores around the ranch as well.

Preacher would keep working with the horses and cattle, but his job would expand to handle all the scheduling for market day, something he'd never done before. It would include managing all the scheduling for vaccinations, and he'd work with Cactus a lot more closely than he had in the past.

He'd be responsible for everything that happened in the equipment shed, including maintenance and care of all of the machinery they used to prep fields, harvest, move cattle, garden, maintain roads, and more.

He swallowed again, his nerves tripling at the thought of his huge list of tasks. A lot of it was administrative—book work—and Preacher didn't necessarily excel at that kind of thing. He was extremely detailed, and Bear had been meeting with him daily to go over everything for the past month.

*You're ready*, he told himself. *It's not like they'll fire you anyway.*

He'd make mistakes and learn, just like he'd been doing his whole life. A thought from his father's letter to him popped into his mind, and Preacher seized onto it like a shield against the tide of people in the homestead.

*You're one of the smartest Glovers, Preacher. Don't underesti-*

*mate yourself. You may not be book smart, and you may not have gone to college, but your intelligence comes from somewhere else. It comes from your willingness to try and fail and try again.*

*Don't ever stop trying, son. Don't ever stop failing, learning, and picking yourself up to try again. You will achieve great things someday, and I only wish with the energy of my soul that I could be there to see them.*

Judge walked in with Ward, and that nearly completed the family. Sammy wasn't back from town with her parents yet, and she'd picked up all the salads from Wilde & Organic to go with the sandwich platter.

Preacher thought of Judge's speech during Mother's wedding, and he closed his eyes and tried to grasp the same feeling he'd had then. Judge had always been so close to the spirit, able to feel things Preacher never could. When he'd mentioned how strongly he could feel Dad, Preacher had actually felt the presence of his father too.

*Where are you?* he asked. *I need you here.*

He wasn't sure he could do this job without the strength and confidence of his father. The truth was, most of Daddy's supreme confidence and ability had gone to his very first son—Bear. Cactus had taken all of the knowledge Daddy had possessed, and Judge had gotten all of the emotional capacity.

By the time Preacher had been born, there wasn't much left. Bits and pieces of the powerhouse Stone Glover had been, and Preacher had never minded walking in the shadows of his older brothers.

Today, he had to step out into the light, and he wasn't sure he could do it by himself.

His thoughts stayed on his father as the noise increased, and he only opened his eyes when the couch next to him moved. He met Mister's eye and managed a smile.

"You're going to do great," he said, extending a slim, brown-paper-wrapped package toward Preacher. He smiled more fully, because it wasn't him who'd have to accept the applause and cheering in a few minutes. It wasn't him who'd have to hunker down behind a desk a couple of days a week and make sure all the moving parts on the ranch stayed greased and smoothly functioning.

It wasn't him who wouldn't have time for horseback riding and relaxing evenings with his girlfriend.

Preacher pictured Charlie Perkins in his mind, and his body heated instantly. He ignored his hormones and took the package from his younger brother. Mister had inherited Grandmother's affinity for creative things, including painting and art, as well as creative writing and thinking outside the box.

"You didn't have to get me anything."

"I saw them and thought of you," he said with a shrug.

Preacher slipped his fingers under the flap on the back of the package. "You still working on that novel?"

"Here and there," Mister said in a tone that indicated he didn't want to talk about his writing.

Preacher didn't push him. He removed the paper from the box to reveal a pair of lambskin gloves. The leather shone up at him in a deep, rich brown the color of freshly turned soil. The stitching along the back of them looked like three long slashes from a large cat, and they ran diagonally from the wrist up to between the knuckles of each finger.

Preacher's mouth dropped open. "Mister." He looked at his brother and took the gloves out of the unmarked box. His brother had made these. A distressed, dark nail head sat on either side of the wrist, and Mister had engraved a P onto each one. "These are incredible. Thank you so much."

He slung his arm around his brother and gave him a hug.

"Try them on," Mister said. "I borrowed a pair of your gloves from the barn to measure, but leather is finicky."

Preacher stuck his hands inside the first glove, noting the soft lining inside. He worked so much with his hands—hauling hay and straw, shoveling stalls, saddling horses, pulling fence line tight—that Preacher went through gloves like most normal people drank water.

"They're perfect," he said, lacing his fingers together and pressing the gloves right down into the creases between his fingers. "I love them so much." He smiled at Mister then, fully relaxed now.

"I'm glad." Mister glanced over to the kitchen as several men filled the air with laughter. Bishop had joined the fray, and he was the fun brother. The one everyone felt close to and confided in—and he did the same for them.

He currently laughed with Bear, Ranger, their wives, Ace, Ward, and Judge. Preacher wondered what would happen if he got up and crossed the room to them. If he just stepped into their circle. Would he fit there?

*Try it*, he thought, and he found himself getting up and

doing exactly what he'd thought about doing. He stepped next to Bishop and asked, "What's so funny?"

"Look at this comment on Two Cents." Bishop handed Preacher his phone, and he read what was on the screen. It was a comment on Holy Fritters, one of the best doughnut shops in Three Rivers. *Ridiculous that the name of this place is Holy Fritters, but the fritters don't have any holes. Would not come back here. Not that unique.*

Preacher laughed too and handed the phone back to Bishop. "They obviously don't understand what a fritter is."

"Right?" Bishop shook his head and pocketed his phone. "Let's get this party started. What are we waiting for?"

"Sammy's five minutes out," Bear said, glancing at him. He grinned at Preacher and practically shoved Bishop out of the way to engulf him in a hug. "How are you, brother? Ready?"

"Ready as I'll ever be," Preacher said, basking in the warmth and strength of his brother's personality.

"Sorry, my wife is always running late." Bear grinned as he stepped back and looked at the sandwiches. "It's actually Stetson's fault today, because he had an accident and she had to pull over to change him on the way back up."

"Oh, don't you blame that baby," Mother said, stepping up to Bear and giving him a hug too. She turned immediately to Preacher and took him into a hug too, and Preacher grinned widely at the love of his mother.

"You are a brilliant man," she said. "Don't forget it." She pulled away and kissed his cheek, and Preacher wondered if she'd collaborated with Daddy on his letters.

Before he could ask, the front door opened again and Sammy called for help.

Several cowboys went to help her, but Preacher stayed with Russ, Max, and Royce near the back of the couch. They all lived in the cowboy cabins in the center of the ranch, and Preacher worked with them a lot as they all had expertise and experience with cattle, horses, and pigs. Max's babies were the chickens, and Preacher had no problem letting the tall, lean cowboy coddle the birds into laying the best and most amount of eggs possible.

"You deserve this," Russ said, and he shook Preacher's hand. He felt like a politician, and he coached himself to smile and act grateful.

He *was* grateful. Bear and Ranger had literally a dozen choices for foreman, and they'd come to him. Sammy walked in with her baby in her arms, immediately passing him to Mother. Stetson looked like he'd been crying, which was unusual for the infant. He'd be a year old next month, and Preacher wasn't sure he'd ever seen the child cry.

"Oh, you poor thing," Mother said, turning to get a cold cloth from the sink. "Do you just feel terrible? Let's get you fed and to bed."

Preacher wished someone would feed him and put him to bed. Cowboy after cowboy brought in containers of salad, several pies, and dozens of two-liter bottles of soda pop. With everything on the counter, both Ranger and Bear got up on a couple of chairs.

As if Bear wasn't huge enough, he lifted both hands above his head and said, "All right, everyone. Quiet down."

It was more like a bellow, and Preacher grinned at his grizzly bear brother.

Preacher looked around the room as it quieted, almost seeing everyone with eyes that existed outside of his head. They'd all gathered here for him.

*Probably for the food, actually*, he thought dryly.

He watched Bishop take his wife's hand, grinning at her like a fool in love. Ace had his arm around Holly Ann, and she turned toward him and whispered something that made his whole face light up. Sammy and Oakley stood next to one another, both of them swaying as if they had a baby in their arms that needed soothing.

Arizona stood with Duke and Mister near the back door, and Judge had retreated with Ward and Cactus to the far side of the long picnic table, and Willa currently signed to Mitch and then herded her son and Lincoln over to Cactus.

He took both boys right onto his lap, settling one on each knee, and the joy radiating from him sparked something inside Preacher that spoke to his desire to have a family and be a father. He'd honestly never given that much thought to it before, but with the picture of it right before his eyes...he did.

Everyone there had their significant other with them, if they had one. Judge and Mister didn't. Ward hadn't invited the woman he'd brought to Mother's wedding. Preacher probably should've invited Charlie to come to the ranch. Had he been Bishop, he would have. Ace had brought Holly Ann to family parties like it was no big deal.

Ida had been bringing Brady long before they got

engaged or married. Etta had kept Noah Johnson away from the family for a while, but he'd been coming around for a while now—over a year—and they weren't married yet.

For some reason, Preacher wanted to keep Charlie to himself. Perhaps because of the way he'd seen Mister look at her. Perhaps because he liked having something separate that belonged only to him.

His lips tingled at the memory of that kiss in his truck. A moan almost escaped his mouth, and that would've been embarrassing, as everyone had quieted down now. He needed to get back down to Three Rivers and that mansion where Charlie lived. He hadn't been with her in the flesh since that night, and texts and chats and video games weren't enough.

*Tonight*, he told himself. *Maybe tomorrow*.

He looked at Bear in an attempt to focus on the here-and-now so he wouldn't miss his own party as he fantasized about kissing Charlie again.

"Range?" Bear asked.

"Thanks for coming, everyone," Ranger said, beaming out at everyone gathered in the massive kitchen, dining room, and living room. "We don't get together like this often enough." He glanced at Bear. "It's nice."

Bear nodded, and Preacher noticed several others did too. He thought they had Sabbath Day dinners together every week. The cowboys usually didn't come to that, though. The feeling that prevailed in the homestead at the moment wasn't usually there either.

All at once, Preacher knew exactly what that feeling was.

Daddy.

Relief and gratitude filled him, and he took a page from Judge's book and let the emotion choke him as Ranger said, "We're celebrating the promotion of Preacher, who will be foreman over all activity dealing with our animals here on the ranch, all equipment maintenance, issues, and replacement, and all scheduling. Ward will continue to maintain his role over the agriculture and all the rotational ranching practices here, as well as all the physical facilities—which, by the way, don't the roads look great?"

A cheer went up, and Preacher joined in along with everyone else. For the first time in a while, he felt like a Glover and all that the name entailed. He physically felt like his father stood next to him, and he'd just lifted his arm and settled it around Preacher's shoulders.

*You're a good man, son*, Preacher heard in his mind, and he wished with all the power of his heart that he could hug his father and say thank you.

*Thank you for teaching me.*

*Thank you for never overlooking me.*

*Thank you for being a good father.*

"Preacher is the perfect man for this job," Bear said. "No one knows the day-to-day operations of the ranch better than him, and no one has his level of expertise and attention to detail."

That wasn't entirely true, because both Bear and Ranger had more experience than Preacher, and they knew every in and every out of Shiloh Ridge, same as him.

"So help me welcome him to our leadership team with a big *yeehaw!*" Bear said.

Preacher didn't have time to blink before every man, woman, and child yelled, "Yeeee-haw!" together.

Laughter broke out, especially when Stetson, the youngest of them all yelled something that sounded suspiciously like "haw!"

"Okay, we have sandwiches, potato salad, egg salad, deviled eggs." Bear looked down at the counter. "It's food. You can look at it and know what it is."

"Praise the heavens," Preacher said, though he knew Ida and Etta wouldn't like the fact that every dish hadn't been detailed to death.

Ranger and Bear got off the chairs, and the crowd swarmed toward the island holding the food. As usual, Preacher held back, and this time, instead of others just walking by him to get their food, he accepted their congratulations, handshakes, and hugs.

He basked in the limelight instead of shying away from it, and he did it all with his father at his side.

"No Charlie today?" Cactus asked as he stepped back out of his embrace with Preacher.

"Should I have invited her?" Preacher asked.

Cactus blinked, his dark features turning a blip darker. "I don't know," he said. "You brought her to Mother's wedding. I thought maybe you two were getting serious."

"It's been a month. Do people get serious after a month?"

Cactus glanced at Oakley, who'd just joined them. "I think Ranger and Oakley were engaged after only a month," Cactus said with a smile, and Oakley swatted at him.

"It was *two* months, thank you very much," she said. "And several before that while I tried to get Ranger to go out with me."

"I feel that," Cactus said as Willa slipped her hand into his. He gazed down at her with pure love in his eyes. "I waited months for this one to go out with me."

"And it was worth it, wasn't it?" Willa teased, giggling.

Cactus leaned down and kissed her, and Preacher supposed that yes, she was worth the wait.

"You didn't bring Charlie." Oakley looked at Preacher out of the corner of her eye. "Are you two still seeing each other?"

"We game," Preacher said evasively.

"He's seeing her," Willa said after breaking her kiss with Cactus.

"How do you know?" he asked.

"I have a unique view point from the pulpit," she said with a knowing smile.

"We don't even sit by one another at church." Preacher shook his head. "She wasn't even there last week."

Willa exchanged a glance with Cactus and then Oakley before moving her eyes back to Preacher. "And the fact that you noticed is how I know you're still seeing her." She stepped away, tugging Cactus with her. "Come on, baby. I want one of those pecan bars, and I just saw Ward take a plate to Dawna with four on it."

After they'd moved away, Oakley leaned in closer to

Preacher. "If you need help with Charlie, Preach, you let me know."

"Why would I need help with her?"

"She's a lot like me," Oakley said. "At least it feels like it. She's isolated, a bit standoffish. A woman in a male-dominated career. She feels like she has some walls up."

Preacher's first thought was to defend Charlie. He thought slow enough that a few seconds went by and he could see past that initial reaction. "She has some walls up," he admitted.

"Don't worry, Preach," she said. "The right man will break those down faster than she can blink."

"You think so?"

She glanced over to Ranger, who finished putting food on a plate and started toward his mother. "I know so." She grinned at her husband as he served his mother, nodded to Preacher, and went to get in line with Ranger so they could get their own food.

Preacher still didn't know if he should've invited Charlie to this celebration or not, but he hoped he could continue to break down her walls and find out if he was the right man for her or not.

# Chapter Eleven

Charlie glanced at the analog clock above the cash register, sure Preacher would walk in at any moment. She'd been sitting at a table for two by herself for twenty minutes, and that was after waiting twenty past the time he'd said he'd meet her for dinner.

She'd insisted they meet at the quaint bistro on the south side of downtown. It shaved thirty minutes from his drive, and she had a number of vehicles to choose from. He'd texted when he'd left the ranch, and he'd been late then.

He'd texted when he'd arrived in town to say there was more traffic than he'd ever seen on a Saturday night before. He'd said he'd be at The Lacy Bonnet in ten minutes, and that had been ten minutes ago.

"Still waiting?" The waitress picked up the Diet Coke Charlie had ordered for Preacher, because all the ice had melted. "Let me get another one of these."

"He should be here any second." Charlie watched sympathy roll across the woman's face. She clearly didn't believe anyone would be meeting Charlie that night for dinner. With the long wait, Charlie honestly wasn't sure either.

"I'll be right back." She walked away, and Charlie's eyes went right back to the entrance.

The door opened, and Preacher walked in. She nearly exploded to her feet, her hand already in the air. He said something to the hostess, his eyes roaming the restaurant. He caught sight of her, nodded toward her, and the hostess looked her way too. Preacher came toward her, weaving through the tables to get to the one situated against the wall.

"I am so sorry," he said, taking her into his arms. He pressed a kiss to the sensitive spot right behind and below her ear, sending fireworks through her bloodstream. "You would not believe the traffic out there."

"HealNow is having a company party tonight," she said. "Food trucks in their parking lot, games for the kids, the whole nine yards." She stepped away from Preacher and gazed up at him. Would it be inappropriate to kiss him right here in the restaurant? With other people watching?

If she kissed him the way she had in his truck a couple of weeks ago, yes. But a quick peck should be okay. She just wanted to kiss him. She'd thought of little else since sitting in his truck with his lips stroking hers.

Fine, she'd thought of plenty of other things in the weeks since then. Namely, how they didn't see each other very often. How much curriculum she had to develop. How she'd put a deposit on a small food service booth to be custom-built for a kiosk in the mall.

He wore a dark look on his face as he met her eyes. "HealNow." He shook his head.

"What does that mean?"

"It means I hate those huge buildings." He pulled out his chair and sat down, leaving Charlie to slide onto the bench seat across the table from him.

"You hate HealNow?"

"Not them specifically," he said, picking up his menu. "Just the building. I don't...." He looked over the top of his menu. "It doesn't fit here. Three Rivers is a small town."

Charlie didn't know what to say. "I disagree completely. There are thirty thousand people who live here."

"I know," he said, his voice disgruntled. "I don't like it. Only five or six years ago, there were half that many. We're losing the culture of our ranch town."

Charlie sat back against the padded booth. "I wouldn't be here if not for that building."

Preacher's face changed in an instant. "I...."

"You don't like cities," she said.

He shook his head. "I can't say that I do."

"Or people."

"I like people just fine," he said. "In small groups."

Charlie didn't know what to say or do. She didn't mind the crowds, and sometimes she thrived on a big party. She always needed to rejuvenate in a quiet, dark room. Just her, the cats, and some music. She didn't even play video games to find the very center of herself and recharge for whatever came next.

"I think Three Rivers is ripe for a huge boom of growth," she said. "It's not going to go away."

"I signed the petition to limit the height of buildings," he said, lowering his menu completely. "And the growth. It should be done in a thoughtful, controlled way, so our existing local businesses don't lose everything to huge corporations." He leaned his forearms on the table and tilted his head to the side. "Places like this, that are owned by a single family would disappear. I don't want that. It's the uniqueness of Three Rivers that makes this place so great."

"I can agree with that."

"You just want huge shopping malls and skyscrapers," he said, not bothering to form it as a question.

Charlie supposed she hadn't phrased anything she'd said as a question either. "I don't hate them," she said.

"Well, I do," he said, picking up his menu again. "Just the two we've got have completely changed the view."

"The view?" She scoffed, though she didn't entirely mean to. Mama would say she hadn't meant *not* to, and that was as good as meaning to. "What view?"

Preacher's gaze held razor blades as it met hers. "The view from my front porch. The whole city skyline is changed now. I don't like it."

Charlie nodded, because she didn't need to ruin everything between them over a couple of tall buildings she didn't really care about. "Interesting. I'm sorry your town has changed."

The sharpness in his eyes smoothed out, and he accepted her statement with a nod. "I suppose I'm just grouchy tonight."

"Why?" she asked, reaching for her glass of iced tea. "I ordered you a Diet Coke. She took the first one, because the ice was all melted, but she said she'd bring you another one."

"Thank you," he murmured, a hefty sigh following the soft words. "I don't like being late. I don't like that I wasted the little time we have together stuck in traffic." He reached across the table and took both of her hands in both of his. "I didn't get to kiss you hello." His expression danced with delight now, and the warmth there shot through her.

"Mm, so you took it out on HealNow and the skyscrapers. I see how you are."

He chuckled, and the mood between them lightened a little bit. He'd still spoken from a place of truth though, and he did not like the growth and change transforming Three Rivers from a place he knew and loved to something else.

She could understand that, she supposed.

"Ah, you came." The waitress appeared and set his fresh glass of Diet Coke on the table. "Have you had a chance to look at the menu?"

"Yep," he said. "And we want this to go. Is that possible?"

Surprise crossed her face, and Charlie felt it zooming through her too. "I can do that," she said. "What did you want, sugar?"

"Anything equivalent to a bacon cheeseburger," he said.

"We have three bacon cheeseburgers," she said, reaching down to point at the menu he'd set on the table. "Our Texas comes with house barbecue sauce and hand-cut onion straws. One with provolone and avocado. That's our California. And we have a New Yorker with full onion rings, double mayo, and grilled apples."

"Brands and saddles," he said, which made Charlie laugh. He met her eye and looked at the waitress. "I'll take the Texas one."

"Rosemary fries, sweet potato, curly, tots, or regular?"

Charlie covered her mouth to stifle her laughter this time, because Preacher looked like he might commit some sort of waitress homicide. "Regular," he said.

The waitress looked at Charlie, who said, "I'll have that roast chicken dinner, please."

"You got it. Give me ten minutes or so." She picked up the menus and walked away, leaving Charlie to laugh at Preacher's incredulity in private.

"Rosemary fries?" he asked, glancing around. "What kind of place is this?"

"This is one of your precious small-town hotspots," she teased.

"It feels uppity," he mumbled, returning his attention to her. "I think I'm the only one in here wearing a cowboy hat."

"Mm," Charlie said, watching him reach up and take off that sexy hat. "Oh, don't take it off."

Preacher froze, the hat halfway from his head to the table. "No?"

Charlie could only grin at him. He did look different without the hat on, and the front of his hair had been smashed back. He was still easily the most handsome man Charlie had ever spoken with, and she couldn't believe she'd somehow captured his attention while wearing an apron and jeans and making ice cream at a wedding.

"I like you either way," she said. "But the hat is definitely sexy."

"Sexy?" Preacher asked as if he didn't know the meaning of the word.

Charlie shook her head. "This is another one of those times where you don't see yourself properly."

He cleared his throat, frowned, and put his cowboy hat back on his head. "How was your last day?"

"It was good." Charlie sighed and sat back in the half-booth again. "They had a big cake and we did this big explosion experiment thing." She grinned, remembering the party that had taken up most of yesterday afternoon. "I'm going to miss everyone there, but I got all the paperwork signed for consulting."

"And your first demo is the day after President's Day."

"Yes. You can still come help me set up?" She'd already asked him this, and he'd already put it on his calendar. "I just don't know how long it will take, because I've never done it."

"I'm good," he said. "Unless we have a ton of cows go into labor that day, at which point, I'll call you."

"Is that normal?"

"Cows seem to do the most inconvenient things at the

most inconvenient times," he said dryly. "But there are other men I can call on if I need help. I'll be here, Charlie."

"Okay," she said, nervous about taking her work into the schools for some reason. The opportunity had seemed so good, and she'd been excited about it. She still was. She was just nervous too.

The waitress appeared with their food already bagged up, as well as two to-go cups with their drinks.

"Thank you," Preacher said, standing and pulling his wallet from his back pocket. He tossed a hundred-dollar bill on the table, and Charlie snatched it.

"Let me see that."

"Oh, jeez," he said, rolling his eyes.

Charlie examined the bill anyway, looking for his name and number. It wasn't there, and she hadn't truly expected it to be. She grinned at him and handed the money to the waitress. "Thanks for keeping my sweet tea full."

"You're welcome, honey," she said, taking the money with wide eyes. "You know the food is only like twenty-five dollars, right?" She looked from the Charlie to Preacher, who stood there kind of frozen.

"He's super rich," Charlie said, smiling. "Don't worry about it."

The waitress looked at Preacher and said, "Thank you."

He tipped his hat to her and said, "You have a good night now." He waited until they'd left the bistro to ask, "I'm super rich?"

"Aren't you?" Charlie looked at him, the orange streetlights making his cowboy hat glow with a peachy light. The scent of his burger lifted from the bag, and her stomach roared for more than sugary tea.

Preacher didn't say anything as he continued down the sidewalk. She looped her arm through his, because she wanted to be close to him, and he was carrying the food. He relaxed slightly, but he didn't ask if she'd go with him. She did, and willingly, and he held her door for her while she climbed into his truck.

Instead of going around to his side, he crowded into the doorway and handed her the bag of food. "I thought maybe we could drive out to this wishing well I know about."

"Sounds fantastic," she said, about level with him now that she sat up in the truck and he still stood outside it. She lifted her hand to the side of his face and whispered, "I'll take my kiss now."

"You will, huh?" He grinned at her, lowered his head, and touched his mouth to hers. Instant fire flowed through her like liquid lava, but Preacher kept the kiss slow this time. Almost methodical, and wow, Charlie liked that as much as the passionate, almost frantic kissing from a couple of weeks ago.

"You looked up Shiloh Ridge, didn't you?" he asked, his lips moving to her earlobe. He held very still there, and Charlie tensed in his arms.

"I went to lunch with a couple of my girlfriends a few weeks ago," she said. "I may have mentioned that we'd been out, and one of them said Shiloh Ridge was the most profitable ranch in the state."

"Not true," he whispered.

"No," she whispered back. "But it's the most profitable in the Texas Panhandle. In fact, I think the website I read said it was the most successful ranch north of San Antonio."

"Do you believe everything you read on the Internet?"

"When my handsome cowboy boyfriend shows up looking like a million bucks every time I see him, has all the newest, nicest gaming gear, and throws hundred-dollar bills around like they're confetti?" Charlie pulled back, though she mourned the loss of his body heat next to hers. "Yes, I believed it. Am I wrong?"

He didn't immediately say that of course she was wrong, which meant she wasn't wrong. "My income is not the same as the ranch's," he said. "I have eleven siblings and cousins, remember?"

"I'd actually forgotten," she said. "I haven't seen any of them for a while."

"All you have to do is show up to church, sugar." He grinned at her, and wow, he shouldn't do that in such beautiful moonlight. Or maybe he should. All she knew was the moment between them was soft and full, and she wanted to exist inside this level of comfort and acceptance for a long, long time.

"Shoot straight with me, cowboy," she said. "I told you. How much money do you have?"

Emotion sprang across his face, and it was clear he wasn't sure about telling her. "More than you."

Charlie had been shocked sitting in front of her

computer in her office, but she'd had time to process his assumed wealth. "How much more?"

"Do you want dollars and cents?"

"Ballpark," she said.

Preacher fell back a couple of steps and gave her a smile as he closed her door. He went around the back of the truck instead of the front, as he'd parked right up against the building. When he got behind the wheel, she'd taken her spot immediately against his hip, and she took his phone when he handed it to her.

"Dollars and cents," he said.

She peered down at the phone, which had Three Rivers National Bank along the top. He'd logged in to his account, and the number in his balance had ten figures.

Ten. Figures.

Charlie sucked in a breath and said, "Barrels and buckets."

Preacher burst out laughing, but Charlie was still staring at all those numbers. The first one was a three—he had three billion dollars in the bank.

"This is way more than me," she said, swallowing.

"It's *brands and saddles*," he said, taking his phone from her. "Not barrels and buckets." Their eyes met, and Charlie couldn't believe he was correcting her cowboy swearing at a time like this.

"Why do you look like you're going to throw up?" he asked. "I made you wait too long to eat, didn't I? We can eat right here, baby. The wishing well is at least twenty more minutes."

"You're a billionaire," she blurted out.

He nodded. "It's a burden I've been bearing for a while now." He sounded quite forlorn about it too, and it took Charlie a moment to realize he was kidding. She elbowed him about the time a smile burst onto his face, and that seemed to break the ice that had formed between them.

They laughed together, and Charlie actually experienced a measure of relief. He put the truck in gear and backed out of the stall, still chuckling.

Charlie let her laughter die too, recognizing how happy she felt in that moment. She liked being with Preacher so much, and she hadn't had a relationship like that in a long time. Maybe it was time to tell him.

She pushed against the words and said instead, "I've never dated anyone with more money than me."

"Is that a problem for you?" he asked quietly. Everything about Preacher focused on his quiet strength.

"Not at all," she said. "I was just—you seemed so surprised that I had money."

"Yeah, because I thought you owned an ice cream shop that was never open." He cut a glance at her and started toward a road she'd never been on. It led west, into the night, and a shiver of anticipation ran up Charlie's arms.

"I ordered the custom booth," she said. "That was my big news for tonight. It should be ready in six to eight weeks, and then it has to be installed in the mall. I rented the spot in the hub right outside the food court, where the holiday nut mixes go."

"That's amazing, Charlie," he said. "I can't wait to come get some more ice cream."

She sighed under the new weight of all she was changing this year. She'd wanted new things in her life, but it felt like she was making a lot of changes at the same time. New job. Really amping up her business. Maintaining her Nexus work. Dating Preacher.

"I wanted to—I hate that we see each other once a month," she said.

Preacher turned his head fully and looked at her. "I don't like it much either."

"I get we're busy, and I'm willing to come to you. I'd love to sit with you on your porch and see the view."

Preacher kept quiet for a moment, and then he said, "You could come for breakfast on Sunday sometime." He shook his head. "Not tomorrow. Ward—he's one of my cousins—wants to meet tomorrow before church."

"He's the other foreman." Charlie wouldn't know him if she saw him, but Preacher had talked about Ward during their chats enough for her to know a few things.

"Yes."

She thought about asking him to sit with her at church, but she wasn't sure how far that would advance their relationship. He sat on the rows near the front with his family, and Charlie had been sitting on the right side, near the back, for months. If she went to church at all.

Sometimes she did, and sometimes she didn't. Lately, she'd been overwhelmed with trying new ice cream recipes, developing chemistry curriculum, and live-streaming that her Sabbath Days were as full as her weekdays.

Mama would tell her that when she was busiest was

when she needed the Lord more. Not less. "*More*, Char. So get on your knees and get up in the morning on Sundays."

Mama was right, and Charlie reminded herself to call her mother in the morning, as it was her birthday tomorrow. In fact, she pulled out her phone and set an alarm so she wouldn't forget.

"What's that for?" Preacher asked.

"My mom's birthday is tomorrow."

"When's your birthday?" he asked.

Charlie swallowed, feeling their relationship turn more serious as they went deeper into what they knew about one another. As they shared more and more experiences together. "End of May," she said. "What about you?"

"November," he said. "We're super busy on the ranch in November, and we do a ton for Christmas in my family. It gets overlooked a lot."

"Not this year," she said.

That got Preacher to look fully at her again. "You think we'll be together in November?"

Charlie blinked, because she hadn't thought they wouldn't be. This man had somehow caused all of her defenses to crumble, and she hadn't even known when that had happened.

"I don't know," she said. "I can't see the future, but I sure like you, Preacher." Her voice caught in her throat. "I don't want to break up or anything."

He reached over and took her hand, lifting her wrist to his lips. "I like you too, Charlie."

Those words sustained her through the next week. She

heard them when she woke in the morning and as she laid down at night.

She reminded herself of them as another week passed, and Preacher couldn't get away from the ranch. He didn't invite her up to it either, and Charlie's frustration grew—until she heard those words in her mind.

*I like you too, Charlie.*

She saw Preacher online. They texted and talked and chatted in their private forum. They'd made plans a few times, and his cattle prevented him from coming down from that ranch in the hills to take her to dinner or be on her livestream. Her subscribers had started asking—some of them had never stopped actually—if she'd ever have him on her feed again.

*I'm trying to get him here*, she'd told them with the brightest smile, in her most chipper voice. *He's a rancher, you guys. He's really busy.*

She'd talked more and more about her chemistry experience, and she had a call with an executive at SkullSkills, an online gaming company that specialized in realistic, science-based gameplay, on Monday morning.

They, apparently, didn't take holidays off.

Preacher didn't either, but Charlie couldn't help texting him to find out if she could bring him lunch on Monday. He didn't answer, and she sighed as she looked up at the ceiling in her bedroom. The space suddenly felt so cavernous, and Preacher had never felt so out of her reach.

She got up and stepped into the shower. After feeding her cats and doing a super-fast breakfast broadcast in her church clothes, Charlie got behind the wheel of her tiny, sporty Mini-Cooper and drove to church.

She'd come the day after Preacher had told her that if she'd come, she'd get to see his family. She'd seen them, all right. Loads and loads of them, and they all arrived in stages. They seemed to have specific places they all sat, and they brought an insatiable energy with them that Charlie really liked.

So much energy that they repelled her courage. She had no idea how to break into their midst and claim a spot at Preacher's side. Not only that, but he didn't invite her to do so. He'd never mentioned sitting by her at church, and though he'd seen her that day and tipped his hat to her, he didn't even come over to talk to her.

She'd left feeling confused and frustrated. So much so that she didn't go back last week, choosing instead to lay in bed and watch her favorite movie, set up the demo for the seventh graders she'd been working to perfect, and bake a chocolate cake she'd then put half of in the trashcan a few days later.

"You're going to talk to him today," she said, gripping the steering wheel. "You're going to go sit right beside him, even if you have to crawl over six cowboys to do it." Even as she spoke the words, Charlie knew they were false. One look from any of the tall, dark, handsome Glover men, and Charlie would whimper, tuck her tail, and flee.

Still, she'd put on her black pencil skirt, because it made her legs look slim. She'd slipped her feet into a pair of heels the same color as the skirt, and she'd donned her best bra underneath a pale pink blouse. If that didn't scream Valentine's Day, she didn't know what did.

That holiday had been on Friday, and while Preacher had planned to take her to dinner—he'd texted her a copy of the email confirmation for Migliano's, one of the best restaurants in town—he'd had four cows go into labor about three o'clock that afternoon.

That meant no Valentine's Day dinner for him and Charlie. He'd sent flowers the next day, so he was trying.

Charlie knew he was trying.

She simply wanted more.

*What will life be like if you marry him?* she thought as she pulled into a parking spot at the church. "Different," she said out loud. He'd come home to her every night—and it wouldn't be an hour's drive one way to do so. She'd make him Valentine's Day dinner instead of planning a romantic night out. They'd go to church hand-in-hand, and she wouldn't have to fight a nest of angry vipers in her gut, telling her to go on home because Preacher didn't want her there.

"What if he doesn't want me?" she asked the slice of her reflection in the rearview mirror.

*I like you too, Charlie.*

He'd said he liked her. She did not think for one moment that a man could kiss her the way he had if he didn't mean it.

"Okay, Lord," she said, her voice dubious. Mama had talked like this so often in Charlie's youth. "If this is what I'm supposed to do, You better open some doors for me." She put on her bravest face and got out of the car. The wind blew today, stealing her breath and trying to lift her skirt. She pressed her palm against her thigh and hurried toward the little white church.

Inside, she ran her fingers through her hair, but re-fluffing it into something cute was now impossible. Behind her, the door opened again and a few more people came in. Charlie froze, because every single one of them looked like Preacher.

Or at least very close to him.

They hardly looked at her, their eyes skating right by.

Then there he was, exhaling as he made it out of the wind and adjusting his hat on his head. He too glanced in her direction, but he stopped. "Hey." He cast a worried look toward the rest of his family members, and that only set the snakes in Charlie's gut to hissing. Loudly.

"Hey." She stepped over to him and swept a kiss across his cheek. Threading her fingers through his, she added, "Boy, it's good to see you." She gave a nervous giggle, because the ground they stood on felt so fragile to her.

"You too, sugar," he said easily, his smile wide and genuine.

"Will you sit with me today?" she asked, glancing toward the entrance to the chapel. His family had all gone inside, and she wasn't sure if they'd looked over their shoulders for him or not.

"Sure, let's go."

She thought he'd take her down to those front middle rows, but he didn't. He veered to the right side and led her to a bench she'd probably sat on before. He kept his hand in hers, though, and while Charlie's attention span didn't really suit sermons, she made it through this one with flying colors.

"Did you get my text?" she asked as the congregation stood to sing the closing hymn. She wasn't much for singing, though she could appreciate good music. "About breakfast tomorrow?"

"I'll bring it to you," he said with a smile. "How about that?"

Charlie wanted to see him, and though her guilt tore at her for making him plan it, get the food, and bring it to her, she nodded. "If you're sure. I'm not even working tomorrow."

"I saw your schedule on Nexus," he said, leaning real close as an older gentleman turned around. They weren't even talking that loud—certainly not loud enough to be heard over all the voices singing *Lord, My Savior and King.*

"You're doing two broadcasts tomorrow."

"They're games," she whispered. "I have plenty of time to get breakfast and drive up to you." Did she sound desperate? Was she coming off as needy? Charlie had never felt like she was either of those things, but with Preacher, she was starting to.

"I'll plan to arrive right after your first broadcast," he said.

"You could come do it with me," she said.

Preacher looked at her, those gorgeous eyes searching hers. "I could do that."

A smile filled Charlie's whole face, her whole soul. "Awesome," she said. "I can make breakfast."

Preacher dipped his head toward her and touched his

lips to the side of her neck. "I've seen what you eat for breakfast, sugar. Leave it to me." With that, the song ended, and while Charlie's skin hummed and her blood warmed, he slipped out of the row and headed for the exit at the back of the chapel.

## Chapter Twelve

Preacher pulled up to Turner Elementary, peering through the windshield at the shiny rooftop. Mother Nature had been moody this winter, blowing wind across the Panhandle like she was trying to flatten everything in Texas to the same height.

She'd dropped snow three or four times, and the weather forecast currently called for rain by evening. Preacher would leave town long before then, though he had spent a large portion of yesterday at Charlie's house.

A sigh passed his lips, because yesterday had been an amazing day. Casual and light. He hadn't argued with her about the culture Three Rivers was losing, and he hadn't rushed off to get back to work on the ranch. He'd shown up with bagels, cream cheese, and orange juice only ten minutes before her first livestream was set to begin.

She'd eaten afterward, because she had a sponsorship

with SlimDown. She'd only taken a few sips that Preacher could tell, and she'd eaten two bagels with him while they sat on a comfortable piece of patio furniture and took in the view from her back porch.

She had more trees obstructing her view, but Preacher could still see the tops of those blasted skyscrapers, and he hated them.

They'd talked about other things, and Preacher sure did enjoy his time with the woman.

Today, he got out of his truck and went inside the elementary school, one of two here in Three Rivers. He'd gone to Clarkton Elementary, and Charlie would be there tomorrow. He couldn't come down and help her set up everyday, but he had wanted to be there for her inaugural assembly.

She'd do three of them this morning and be done by noon. She said that was perfect, because once she had her ice cream kiosk open, she could head over there for a few hours and whip up frozen treats in the afternoons.

He wondered what drove her, as the woman had plenty of money. She didn't have to spend almost two months creating and designing chemistry experiments for specific grade levels. She didn't have to figure out new ice cream recipes or work twelve hours a day to serve it to people. She could literally livestream for an hour a day and maintain her high-end lifestyle.

"Sir, you need a visitor badge," a woman said, and Preacher turned to look at her. "You get them in the office." She pointed back the way he'd come.

He retraced his steps to visit the main office to get his badge. The secretary guided him in the right direction to the gymnasium, and he arrived just in time to see Charlie struggling with an oversized blue bin and the heavy metal door.

"Hey, hey," he said, his pulse jumping around at the sight of her. "Let me." He jogged toward her and took the bin.

She exhaled and wiped her hair back. She hadn't pulled it into a ponytail today, and he thought she should've. In fact, she wasn't wearing clothes he normally saw her in. Of course, he usually saw her while she played video games or came to church, and those were two opposite ends of the spectrum.

Today, she wore a pair of black slacks that made her legs seem miles long. They certainly made him look twice. His mouth turned dry too.

"There's more in the truck," she said, using one of her heeled feet to guide a doorstop into position.

"I'll get it," he said, putting the bin he carried on the table in the middle of the gym. "You start unpacking." He walked toward her, unable to stop himself from reaching for her as they started to pass. "You look amazing, by the way."

"I'm sweating already," she said, plenty of fear in those light blue eyes.

"Take a minute then," he said, dropping his head to take in a deep breath of the scent of her skin. She smelled like soft, petal-scented soap, fresh cotton, and rosy perfume. No fruit today, and he really wanted to taste her lips, which she's painted a glossy pink.

With her black slacks, she wore an off-white sweater that looked like sheep's wool with a black pi sign stitched across the chest. It was both classy and funky at the same time.

"You should wear your hair up," he said. "It really completes the chemist look."

Her eyebrows shot up. "Oh? And what's the chemist look?"

"You know, this sort of sexy scientist look you've got going on." He released her and stepped back, letting his eyes drip down her body again. Yeah, she lit him on *fire*, and he honestly didn't know what to do about it. "Nice slacks. Heels. Funny yet sophisticated sweater. Your hair should be up, and then with the lab coat." He smacked his lips. "You'll have to make sure all the boys in high school know how old you are."

"Stop it." She grinned at him. "Go get my stuff, Mister."

"Mister is my brother," he said over his shoulder as he walked away.

She giggled behind him, and Preacher liked the sound of that. He'd been shocked when he'd seen her at church yesterday, and he wasn't even sure why. She came to church. No one in the family had even noticed her, and Preacher had been glad for that.

He'd enjoyed holding her hand during the sermon, but Judge had wanted to leave early so Pastor Summers couldn't ask him to run the church-sponsored Spring

Bazaar, and Preacher had left the moment the closing song had ended. Charlie hadn't said anything about his sudden departure, but his guilt still twisted in his stomach.

*I just want to keep her as mine for a little longer*, he thought. *Is that so wrong?*

He didn't want to share her with everyone, and if she came up to the ranch, he'd have to share her with Sammy and Oakley. Judge and Ward and Cactus. Willa would get her hooks into Charlie, and the next thing Preacher knew, he'd be on the sidelines again.

Guilt heaped onto his conscience, and he didn't know how to dig his way out. He reasoned that he and Charlie had only been dating for a couple of months, and lots and lots of people didn't take their girlfriends home to meet twenty or thirty people that soon.

Once he had all of her supplies in the building, he helped her unpack them. He noticed that she'd pulled her hair up into a ponytail, and his hormones once again kicked at him, as if he didn't already know how much he liked her.

Finally, students started to enter the gym, and this assembly was for third and fourth graders. Preacher did what he did best—he blended into the background. Charlie stood next to him off to the side while the children sat down, and then the principal got up in front of everyone.

"We have such a special guest with us today," she said, beaming out at the children. "It's important you stay in your seats. If Miss Perkins wants any volunteers, she'll call on you." She glanced down at a paper in her hand. "Charlie Perkins is a board-certified pharmaceutical chemist, with an emphasis in veterinary medicine. She spent fourteen years working in the labs at HealNow, a company that provides low-cost and low side-effect medications for humans and animals alike. Now a consultant for them, Miss Perkins goes around to schools to show that chemistry is a real-life science that anyone can do. In her spare time, she makes ice cream with liquid nitrogen for her company Below Zero and enjoys playing video games."

"Wow," Preacher said under his breath. "That sounds so professional."

"I'm going to puke," Charlie hissed.

Preacher squeezed her hand. "You're the smartest person in the room, baby. Remember that."

She looked up at him, stars in her eyes. Well, if he could see past all the terror, he thought she'd have stars in her eyes. "Thanks, Preach."

"You're on," he said as the principal and all the children started clapping and cheering for Charlie. She released his hand and walked confidently out onto the stage, her smile wide even from his profile view of her.

She took the mic from the principal, and Preacher simply marveled at the easy way she could charm adults and children alike. He was riveted to her experiment involving static electricity, and before he knew it, the forty-minute assembly had concluded.

She came toward him again, this time carrying a water bottle. She guzzled from it and asked, "How was it?" as she crunched the plastic in her bare hands.

Preacher gazed at her. "This is one of those times where you don't see yourself clearly at all."

Her eyes jerked to his. "What?"

"It was *incredible*," he said. "You could hear a pin drop out there. Everyone from the adults to the kids was engaged. *You* were incredible."

"Do you think they learned some chemistry?"

"I know I did." Preacher might have meant the kind that bubbled between him and Charlie, but that didn't matter. He took her in his arms and kissed her, whispering one more time, "You are incredible," right before the fifth and sixth graders started entering the gym.

He released her so she wouldn't be embarrassed, and he said, "I'll leave lunch at your place, okay? Then you can just go home after and relax."

"Thank you, Preach," she said, and he waved as he left the gym.

She'd been up late and then early, worrying over today. He adored that she wanted to do a good job. He liked her intelligence, and he sure did like the way she looked in those slacks, heels, and lab coat.

The chemistry between them had always been off the charts. On the way back to Shiloh Ridge after nearly getting his face clawed off by one of her overprotective cats, Preacher wondered if she'd ever be content to be a rancher's wife.

Somewhere, deep in the back of his mind, he knew the answer, and he didn't like it. After all, women who wanted the world didn't generally settle down in the Texas

Panhandle while their husbands worked sixteen hours each day.

What kind of world was that to provide for a woman like Charlie Perkins?

"Not good enough," he muttered. The problem was, that was the only world Preacher had to offer her.

# Chapter Thirteen

Oakley Glover hadn't been feeling well for days. Her due date had come and gone last week, but the doctor didn't want to induce labor yet. She said the baby was alive and well, and Oakley could feel her son moving around inside her.

She sure was miserable though, and she'd read about the onset of labor and how much it could affect a person. As she finally made her way down the stairs from the second-floor suite where she and Ranger lived, she prayed that the baby would come that day.

"I hope it's not too much to ask," she said to herself, navigating each step carefully so she wouldn't fall. Her balance wasn't what it normally was, what with this beach ball weighing an extra thirty pounds stuck to the front of her body. "But Lord, if at all possible, I'd love to have this baby *today*."

She'd been waiting for years to have this baby, and as

she reached the kitchen and found Sammy there feeding Stetson, she told herself she could wait one more day. And then one more. And then another if she had to.

Her gratitude to even get this baby and keep him for this long outweighed any discomfort she'd endured. It would be nice to see her feet again though, and to be able to put her shoes on without causing her toes to protest violently. They'd swollen about two weeks ago, and Oakley had taken to either lying in bed with her tablet or making her way to the couch in the living room and putting something on the television.

"My goodness," Sammy said, jumping to her feet. "You look awful."

"I feel awful." Oakley tried to put a smile on her face, but a radiating pain arched through her back. It settled as fast as it had struck, and the resulting dull ache had been there for days.

"Come sit," Sammy demanded, and she took hold of Oakley's arm and guided her to the couch. "I'll get you whatever you need."

"Just toast," Oakley said. "One piece. I can't eat very much before I'm stuffed."

"I remember that," Sammy said with a laugh. "I'm not looking forward to that again." She bustled off while Oakley lowered herself on the couch.

"Again?" she asked.

A clatter sounded in the kitchen, and Oakley twisted to see Sammy had dropped the spoon she'd been feeding Stetson with on the metal toaster. Her face turned bright red, and she spun away from Oakley.

"Oh, I know what's going on here," Oakley said. "You're pregnant again!"

Sammy didn't deny it, and Oakley squealed, trying to get back to her feet. She managed it and by the time she reached Sammy in the kitchen, she'd put down her single piece of toast and cleaned up the crumbs that had exploded from the toaster when it had been hit by the spoon.

She faced Oakley with tears in her eyes. "I'm pregnant again." The water slipped down her face.

Oakley grabbed onto her and held her tight. "Why are you crying about this?"

"I can't even keep up with one baby," Sammy said. "I'm terrified of having two. And it's really three, because Lincoln is my son too. He's just barely adjusting to Stetson now, and what's going to happen when I bring home another one?" She hiccuped and wiped angrily at her face.

She turned away from Oakley, her anguish so raw. "I am a horrible person. I'm so sorry. Please forgive me."

"For what?" Oakley tried to step around her to see her friend's face, but Sammy dodged her again. "Sammy. You're my very best friend. We live together. I love you like a sister."

Sammy finally lifted her eyes to Oakley. "I literally just complained about being pregnant again when you and Ranger had to work so hard to get your baby. I'm a huge, selfish jerk, and I'm sorry."

"You're not a selfish jerk." Oakley took Sammy into another embrace. "Everyone has their own path to trod," she whispered. "Their own cross to bear. It's okay to be frightened of dealing with two children under the age of two. And to be legitimately concerned for Link's welfare."

Sammy cried into her shoulder until the toast popped up. She snatched it and buttered it as if Oakley couldn't do it now that she stood in the kitchen too. She handed her the toast gently. "I really am so sorry."

"I know that." Oakley bit into her toast, another wave of pain flowing from the center of her body outward. She groaned, and Sammy smiled and shook her head.

"It's just toast, Oak."

But Oakley dropped the toast as a tearing, searing pain ripped through her. She flung her hand out to grab onto the counter, her first thought to drop into a crouch to alleviate this torture.

Something must've shown in her face, because Sammy's expression changed in an instant. "I'm calling Ranger." She darted over to the table where she'd left her device and her baby, and she called Ranger while Oakley tried to blink her way out of the white vision that had come over her eyes.

She groaned as every muscle in her body tightened to the point they couldn't get any tighter. Then they did, and she cried out as tears pressed into her eyes.

"I'm right here," Sammy said, putting her hand in Oakley's. "You can squeeze my hand. Ranger is two minutes away."

"Did it hurt this bad?" Oakley asked, some color coming into her vision again. "I feel like someone is sawing me in half."

"She's in labor," Sammy said. "I already called Ranger, but you need to let everyone know."

"No," Oakley said. "I don't want everyone at the hospital."

Sammy said something else to Bear, and then hung up. She looked right into Oakley's eyes. "Trying to stop the Glovers from coming to the hospital is like trying to stop the tide from coming in," she said gently. "They're going to come, just like this baby is." She grinned at her. "Your son is going to be born today."

Oakley's eyes filled with tears, and she nodded, her happiness almost as intense as the pain still echoing through her body.

Just as another contraction started, Ranger called her name. His footsteps ran toward her, and the next thing Oakley knew, everything in the world was exactly right. Because Ranger was there, and Ranger could handle anything.

Ranger knew what to do in every situation, and Ranger provided her with all the strength she lacked. "Can you stand, baby?" He put both hands under her arms and helped her. "Sammy, her bag is in the coat closet."

"I'll get it and the door." Sammy ran out of the kitchen while Oakley followed at a much slower pace. Ranger stayed right at her side, his comforting scent of flannel and horses reminding Oakley of where she was and how far she had to go to get to the hospital.

Ranger took the bag from Sammy, and he guided Oakley down the steps to his truck. With him behind the wheel, he said, "All right, love. Here we go."

The drive there took less time than Oakley anticipated, though she had at least ten contractions along the way.

Ranger had called ahead, and three nurses and a wheelchair met them at the entrance to the hospital.

From there, everything happened far too fast. The doctor took too long to come, or Oakley had progressed really rapidly. No matter what, by the time she was checked, she was dilated so far that she couldn't have an epidural.

She sobbed as Dr. Monroe told her she'd have to have the baby without any drugs, and she called for more nurses and all the equipment they needed. "She's at a nine," she heard the doctor say. "She's been in labor for days."

"Is that okay?" Ranger asked. "Is the baby okay?"

"We'll see," Dr. Monroe said, turning to another doctor.

Panic gripped Oakley's whole chest. "Range," she said. "Ranger!"

He turned back to her, his own brand of anxiety on his face. "Make her explain more. Why wouldn't the baby be okay?"

"Doctor Monroe," Ranger said, stepping to the end of the bed again. "Would the baby be damaged from being in labor for so long?"

"It's not good for the baby to go through contractions for very long," Dr. Monroe said, all business-like when she'd been so personable in her office. Oakley attributed the success of this pregnancy to her and her alone, for her kind care, and all the progesterone treatments, blood work, and monitoring she'd done.

"Every time she contracts, the baby loses some oxygen." She whipped her attention to the monitor as it started to wail. Oakley's muscles tightened and gripped her with the power of the sun. She groaned, everything turning to fire inside her. The doctor kept talking, but Oakley couldn't focus on the woman's voice.

Ranger returned to her side and took one of her hands in both of his. "Baby," he said, and she opened her eyes and looked at him. "Listen to me. You're going to push when I say, okay? Squeeze my hand as hard as you can. Doctor Monroe says you're ready."

"It's only been ten minutes," Oakley said.

"I know, sweetheart, but you progressed really fast." He wore a watery smile. "I'm going to listen to her, and you're going to listen to me. Okay?"

She nodded, feeling her body tense up again. The monitors started wailing again, and Ranger said, "Oakley, right now. Push now."

She did, bearing down the way she'd been taught in their labor classes. Exquisite pain tore through her, and she let her tears stream down her face.

"Here he is," Dr. Monroe said, and that cut through the noise in Oakley's soul. The doctor, seemingly masked from head to toe, held up a wailing, messy baby.

Oakley's pain disappeared, and she reached for her son.

"It's a boy, just like we thought." Dr. Monroe wrapped the baby and handed him to Oakley, who cradled him against her chest, still crying uncontrollably.

"Ranger," she whispered. "Look at him. He's perfect."

"They won't let you keep him long," Dr. Monroe said. "Kiss him quick."

Oakley did, and so did Ranger, and two nurses whisked the baby away from them.

"Okay," Dr. Monroe said. "You're not done, momma. A little further, and then we'll get you comfortable and feeling better."

"Ranger, go help him," Oakley said, anxious as the baby's cries intensified.

Ranger didn't hesitate as he walked away from Oakley, and she focused on Dr. Monroe. She could do this, because delivering the placenta couldn't be as hard as what she'd just done.

An hour later, Ranger entered the room where they'd put Oakley under a heated, weighted blanket. He carried a blue bundle with him, and love haloed his face in such a way that only new parents could achieve.

He came toward Oakley as she tried to shake off the dregs of sleep and push herself up a little further. "Here you go, my love." He passed their son to her and pressed a kiss to her forehead, and in that moment, Oakley held the world and everything good worth having in her hands.

An amazing man stood at her side, the father to her son. "Hello, my baby," she whispered to the child. "We're still naming him Wilder, right?"

"Wilder Hatch Glover," Ranger said.

Oakley looked up at him, surprise darting through her, further waking her. "I thought you wanted to name him after your granddaddy."

"I think he should have your name," Ranger said, gazing at her now with that adoration streaming from his eyes. "There's no one else to carry it, and he's strong enough to bear your name and mine."

Oakley wept again and kissed her husband sweetly,

their precious son they had waited for and agonized over for so long between them.

Ranger's phone buzzed a few times, and Oakley suspected what was happening. "How long can you hold them off?" she whispered.

"A few more minutes," he said. "I can take him out to them if you don't want them in here."

"They'll only let a few people in at a time anyway," Oakley said. "So I don't care. Your mother can come back right now."

"I'll go get her and the twins," Ranger said, stepping toward the door. He turned back to Oakley and stared at her. "I love you, Oakley. With everything I have." He returned to her and kissed her again. "You were so strong and so brave in there. I can't even imagine what you've gone through, and I love you all the more for it."

Oakley accepted his praise and said, "I love you too, Ranger." He left, and she let her eyes drift closed as baby Wilder seemed to snuggle closer to her heart and chest. "You were worth every ounce of pain," she whispered to him. "You are a wonderful, wonderful spirit, and I am so grateful to be your mother."

She wept then, her gratitude for Wilder overflowing and combining with her love and gratitude for God, who had allowed her to have the greatest desire of her heart...at long last.

# Chapter Fourteen

Etta Glover stood at the counter in the district office, waiting for Susan Thayer to print the paperwork she needed. Now that spring had arrived, the ranch was preparing to have elementary students up to the property three days a week for gardening, agriculture, and animal care workshops. As she oversaw all of that for Shiloh Ridge, right down to which class received which lesson, she needed to make sure all of the permissions were in place.

Etta worked with individual teachers in third through sixth grades, the bus garage to schedule transportation, and the nonprofit organization with her and Ida's name on it to pay for everything. Buses weren't free, nor were the lunches Shiloh Ridge provided for the students.

Her schedule for the next ten weeks was packed to the brim, with some classes coming more than once for different workshops. Ida had added beekeeping to the schedule last year, but it was really more of an autumn workshop, and they'd decided to offer it to the general public instead of students.

With the older students, Etta recruited Mister to do rodeo demonstrations, and since Wyatt Walker had moved to Three Rivers, those demos filled a year in advance.

"Here you go," Susan said, handing her a stack of papers. "You know the drill."

A tug of exhaustion moved through Etta, but she put a smile on her face. "I do." Without their partnership with the Three Rivers School District, she and Ida wouldn't have anything to do with the ranch. Etta believed in the work she did to show students that ranching was a viable career, and something vital to the health and well-being of the country they all lived in.

She thought of the words she'd said to Susan as she took her paperwork and a clipboard over to a chair. It would take about twenty minutes to fill everything out and get it all signed, and then Etta would drive through Bob's to get her favorite burger.

She didn't care that she'd put on fifteen pounds in a year. She'd been dating Noah Johnson, and he didn't seem to care if she gained or lost weight.

Her wedding sat on the calendar in just twenty-four days, and Etta bit her lip, the black letters on the white paper in front of her blurring. She was done crying though, and the words had fuzzed because of her nerves over saying I-do to Noah as they stood at an altar in front of everyone they knew and loved.

In her heart of hearts, she didn't know if she could go through with the wedding. She'd been on her knees morning, noon, and night, trying to find an answer. Begging and pleading with God to just tell her what to do.

She didn't want to be the only Glover without someone to bring to parties, meals, and holiday celebrations. She loved Noah Johnson with a love she hadn't felt for anyone else.

The man was Texas royalty, with a refined air about him that Etta really enjoyed. He was intelligent and kind, and he could tame any horse into his best friend in a matter of minutes. She'd watched him do it for a neighbor down the street who'd thought she'd have to put the horse down.

Then along came Noah, and he had that horse saddled and ridden in under ten minutes. He continued to work with Glory, as well as her owner, and everyone was so much happier.

Noah made Etta happy too, but there was one thing he would never make her. Something she'd wanted since she was a four-year-old toddling alongside Mother as she swept out the kitchen and put fresh dough in the window to rise.

A mother.

Noah had been married before, and he had three teenage children. They all lived with their mother in California, and Noah hardly saw them except for video calls and the occasional holiday if he flew there. They never came here, and while he'd explained things to her, Etta didn't understand the vitriol his ex-wife still held for him.

Of course, Etta had never been married and divorced, and she didn't understand a lot of the pain and anguish others had gone through. She praised the Lord for His gentleness in her life, and that she hadn't had to endure anything too heartbreaking yet.

That word *yet* caught in her throat, and she pushed against the lump of emotion there. That was where her tears had gone—into a hard ball right against her vocal cords. She couldn't clear it away. Swallowing didn't help.

Until she made a decision, Etta suspected the knot in her chest would stay, as would the bees in her stomach, and the sudden clenching in her muscles.

*Twenty-four days*, she told herself, trying to focus on the paperwork. This wasn't the only task she had to accomplish today, and she needed to get out of here so she could finish designing the flyers for their summer horse care classes.

She also had a meeting with Bishop to go over how he'd push out the advertisement for the classes on Two Cents. They were just starting to experiment with advertising, and he wanted to monitor everything from the time of day it went out to select groups they could target it to. She didn't understand a lot of it, but Bishop did and that was all that mattered.

She'd just finished the last signature when another woman asked a question. Etta got up to join her at the counter, recognizing the voice from somewhere. She glanced at the blonde, and she looked familiar.

"Be right back," Susan said, and the other woman looked at Etta too.

She did a double-take, surprise and recognition on her face too. "Etta, right?"

"Yes," she said. "I know you...Charlie?"

"Yes." Charlie looked like she'd just won the lottery, and she grabbed onto Etta.

"Oh." She grunted at the strength in the other woman's arms.

"Sorry." Charlie stepped back. "I just haven't met many of you Glovers."

"You did the ice cream at Ida's wedding."

"That's right." Charlie wore a pretty smile on her beautiful face. "You're getting married soon, I think. Right?" She wasn't really asking, at least Etta didn't think she was. The woman knew exactly what was going on.

"Yes," she said. "Are you coming with Preacher?"

"Yes." Charlie's expression melted into one Etta had seen on her sister's face when she looked at her husband. One Ranger wore when he held his new baby. One everyone who'd fallen head over heels in love with someone or something often wore.

Etta wondered why Preacher hadn't brought this lovely woman up to the ranch yet. She wasn't going to ask Charlie, and she had more tact than to bring it up to anyone at all.

Susan returned, and she handed Charlie the form she needed and looked at Etta. "Got it, hon?"

"Yes," Etta said, handing over the packet. "Thank you, Susan." She turned to leave, pausing next to Charlie. "It was lovely to see you, Charlie."

"You too," she said, beaming up at her.

Etta left the district office, and when she got to her car, she contemplated texting Preacher to ask him why he'd kept such a fabulous woman hidden. In the end, she didn't, because she knew better than most what it was like to bring someone up to the ranch. She'd seen her siblings and cousins do it, and every new addition looked like they'd been hit with an eighteen-wheeler the first time they walked into the homestead at Shiloh Ridge.

She'd prepped Noah for two weeks before he'd gone for the first time, and he'd still been astounded by the wealth and size of the ranch, as well as the many, many cowboys that ran it—most of them with the same last name as her.

Having to go through that again...Etta didn't want to do it. She didn't want to start over at zero. Square one. Whatever.

At the same time, was it fair to marry Noah when she might end up resenting him? When he couldn't give her what she wanted? Could she really love him the way she should if she considered the wedge between them?

Even now, it festered.

"Please," she begged as she closed her eyes. "Please help me know what to do."

---

A WEEK LATER, ETTA STOOD IN HER KITCHEN, ALL OF HER favorite people with her. Ida had just arrived with Mother, and Oakley, Sammy, Montana, and Holly Ann had been flitting around the house for about thirty minutes already.

Stetson had learned to walk, and Sammy spent the majority of her time trying to keep the rambunctious fourteen-month-old out of trouble. Wilder was about three weeks old now, and he'd pinked right up and gotten the chubbiest cheeks in the world since Etta had first met him in the hospital.

Oakley was generous with her baby, despite the trials she'd gone through to get him, and currently, Holly Ann held the infant while Oakley went to greet Mother and help her to the couch. Holly Ann then got up and handed Wilder to Mother, who sighed in pure contentment.

Ranger had delivered the first grandbaby for her, just like Ranger did everything first for their branch of the family. Etta loved her brother deeply, and while Ida had asked Ward to walk her down the aisle, Etta had asked Ranger.

"What's Ranger doing today?" she asked Oakley as she joined her and Montana in the kitchen. "You can peel those carrots. They just need to be shredded and added to this."

"You got it."

Etta stirred the cabbage—red and green—together, adding a bit of celery salt to her cole slaw.

"Ranger is out on the range," Oakley said. "He and Ward got out your daddy's guns to clean them, and they got all nostalgic."

"Ace went with them." Holly Ann joined them in the kitchen, and Etta hated cooking in front of her. She never said anything, because she was literally the nicest person on the planet, but she was such a good chef that Etta felt like she existed under a microscope with Holly Ann at her side.

"I think they all went," Sammy said, chasing after Stetson as he giggled down the hall. "Bear said he'd be heading out this afternoon too." She came back into the kitchen with her son in her arms. "I need a leash for this one."

Etta grinned at the boy and reached for him. "Holly Ann, would you finish that cole slaw for me?"

"Of course." She picked up the spoon Etta had left behind while Etta took Stetson from Sammy.

"Come read with Auntie Etta," she said, taking the boy to the rocking recliner in her living room. She bent to pick up a board book from the basket she'd put between the chair and the window and settled down with the child. "Once upon a time, a black and white puppy lived...."

Etta loved the warmth of the child, and the way he called out and pointed to the different animals as the puppy went to visit them. She patiently listened to him babble, and she asked him what sound each animal made. He knew some of them, like the dogs and cats and even the frog. Any he didn't, Etta made the sound for him and had him repeat it.

The moment the book ended, Stetson leaned over the side of the chair, looking for another one. Etta could hold the boy and read to him for a long time, and she glanced into the kitchen to find all five women standing there staring at her.

"Is lunch ready?" she asked. "Sorry." She shifted Stetson to one knee so she could get up, adding, "We'll have to read after we eat, my sweet boy." She gave him a kiss and stood. He clung to her, all smiles again, and Aunt Lois's nickname for him—Smiles—sure did fit.

"I've got a highchair for him," she said, moving over to

the pantry and opening the door. She pulled it out with one hand and buckled Stetson into the seat. He slapped both of his hands on the tray, and Etta simply smiled at him.

"Mother," she said. "I think we're eating."

No one had said anything, and Etta found she couldn't meet any of their eyes. Their thoughts were so loud, they screamed through the silent house. Baby Wilder gurgled as Mother stood, and Ida hurried around the couch to steady her.

"I'll take him," Oakley said. "He can chill in his car seat while we eat."

Mother passed the baby over, and everyone positioned themselves around the island in Etta's kitchen. She realized a moment too late that they were in her house, and everyone was looking to her to lead them.

"Uh, Mother would you pray?" Etta folded her arms and cast a look at Ida, the older twin. She was weeping, and Etta frowned at her, sending questions across the few feet between them.

Ida just shook her head, one hand pressing over her heart and one resting on her stomach.

Etta knew in that moment that Ida was pregnant. A punch of vertigo hit her, making her head swim and the room sway with it. Her stomach dropped to her feet and then went lower. Jealousy roared through her, and Etta had to work hard to tame it back inside the box where she kept it.

She'd told herself for many months last year that just because Ida got married first didn't mean Etta wasn't going to find someone to fulfill all of her dreams. Just because Ida had a baby didn't mean Etta never would.

Thankfully, before the end of the prayer, she'd caged all of her negative emotions. When she stepped over to Ida and drew her into a hug, all she could identify inside her was pure joy. "Congratulations," she whispered.

"Thank you." Ida clung to her, and Oakley said, "What is going on here?"

Etta stepped back from her twin and looked at her. They could have entire conversations without a single word, and Etta needed to know if Ida was ready to tell people yet or not.

She blinked, and Etta stepped to her side, slipping her hand into her slightly older sister's.

"Brady and I are expecting a baby," Ida said, her voice breaking on the last word. "I can't stop crying, and every time I see Wilder or Stetson, I'm a blubbering mess." She lifted both hands to cover her face, and Holly Ann and Montana—the two closest women to her—engulfed Ida in a hug.

Mother wasn't far behind, and Sammy and Oakley brought up the rear. With all of the hugging and congratulating done, Etta went over their food, and they sat down to eat. While everyone here was married—or in Mother's case, had been—Etta didn't feel out of place. She sat right next to Stetson, and she put bits of bread on his plate, and small bites of meatball. She gave him cole slaw and macaroni, and the child ate it all.

The women who lived up at Shiloh Ridge started getting packed up to go home. Ida's phone rang and she stepped out onto the porch to take it, leaving Etta with Mother in the kitchen. She spooned the leftover macaroni salad into a plastic container and glanced at Etta.

"Thank you for lunch, honey." She dripped sweetness on the last word.

"Of course, Mother," she said. "I love having everyone here for a meal."

Mother nodded and opened a drawer to find a lid. "Still going to marry Noah?"

Etta froze, wondering if this was the push she needed to say no. "I don't know, Mother."

That got her mother to stop. She looked at Etta, her eyes still as bright as ever despite her hair having lost all of its color. They flashed, and she said, "Etta, you do not owe him anything."

"We've been dating for over a year, Mother. I do love him."

"But?"

Tears came to Etta's eyes, after weeks of control. She hadn't told anyone that Noah didn't want more children. She shrugged, but she wasn't sure how much longer she could push away her feelings.

"He doesn't want more children, Mother," Etta whispered. "He's forty-seven years old, and he's got three kids." She didn't have to explain further. Mother knew how badly Etta wanted children of her own, and she didn't need to spell it out.

"Etta," Mother said. "You must follow your heart. I can't tell you what to do, but I know your heart, and I saw you with that baby today. You have a mother's heart, and you are not in a race with your sister."

Etta turned away from her mother and put the leftover cole slaw in the fridge. "If I was, Mother, I'd have already lost, wouldn't I?"

"I'm worried about you," Mother said as Ida came back inside.

"Not a word, Mother," Etta murmured.

"Call me later," she said as Ida said, "Ready, Mother?" She looked back and forth between Etta and their mother, her eyes widening. "What's going on?"

"Nothing," Etta said, putting a smile on her face. "Thanks for bringing Mother."

"Sure." Ida wasn't as proper as Etta, and she linked her arm through Mother's to help her out to the car. "I'm still coming over tomorrow to help with the dress, right?"

Etta nodded, avoiding Mother's eye. "As long as you come after two," she said. "I'm making all of the phone calls in the morning."

"Okay, see you then." Ida and Mother left, and Etta stood in the doorway and waved to them until Ida backed out of the driveway and drove away. She went back inside and pressed her back to the door.

She still had no idea what to do, and her wedding was only nineteen days away.

## Chapter Fifteen

Ward Glover knotted the tie around his neck, his fingers moving deftly through a task he'd done countless times before. Etta, the most formal of all of the Glovers, had opted for some of the least formal wedding attire.

No bow ties or tuxedos. She'd simply wanted dark brown suits with matching cowboy hats and boots. No flashy belt buckles. All of the ties had been sewn by Etta herself, and they were a beautiful pale pink, teal, and purple plaid that Ward would actually wear to church again.

He set his cowboy hat on his head, and cocked it, studying himself. He couldn't make himself look any better. He kept his beard trimmed and neat. He brushed his teeth religiously. He worked constantly, and he didn't carry much extra body fat and plenty of muscle.

Something seethed in his stomach as he left his bathroom and bedroom. Mister sat at the kitchen table, dressed in a similar suit and cowboy hat, his tie equally as pristine as Ward's. "I'm going to get Brenda," Ward said.

Mister looked up in surprise. "Really?" He looked at his phone again. "The wedding starts in an hour."

"She lives on Quail Creek Road," Ward said. "It's only twenty minutes from here, and I don't need to be there early."

"Oh, got it."

Ward went to get in his truck, wondering if he was wasting his time with Brenda. He found her beautiful, and they got along well. There had been sparks in the beginning, but he'd been out with her a couple of times now, including Aunt Lois's wedding over three months ago now, and he just wasn't sure about her.

He sighed as he drove under the arch and down the hill to the highway. He wanted fireworks. He wanted snap. He wanted crackle. And not just once. Every time he saw the woman. Every time he walked in the room or she did. Every day, every night.

He wanted someone who excited him. Someone who inspired him to be a better man. Someone who wanted to be better for him.

And he just wasn't sure that she was Brenda Fielding. Still, he'd asked her to accompany him today, and he wasn't going to call ten minutes before he was set to arrive and cancel. He parked in her driveway and walked up to the door.

The doorbell rang in the country silence, and a few moments later, the brown-haired woman opened the door. A smile sat on her thin lips, and she wore a pale pink dress that had tiny straps that went over her shoulders. The fabric shimmered in the sunlight, and Ward was physically attracted to her. Several sparks flowed through him. Enough to put a smile on his face.

"Hey, gorgeous," he said.

"We match," she said, indicating his tie.

"I did tell you the colors," he said, reaching for her hand. She slipped her fingers between his easily, a giggle coming from her mouth.

"Will we have to dance tonight?" she asked.

"I sincerely hope not," Ward said. "I nearly killed you last time." He added a chuckle that was more nerves than anything else, and he hated that. He shouldn't be nervous with a woman he'd been out with several times in the past. Nor should he be nervous with her after three months.

She definitely wasn't the one for him, but he couldn't tell her that now. He kept the conversation moving as he drove back up to the ranch and down the newly graveled road to True Blue.

He frowned at the gravel dust hanging in the air, and as he got out, he bent to examine the rock at his feet. "This isn't right," he muttered, a certain level of fury flowing through him now. He hadn't been able to get his preferred landscaping company to deliver the gravel he wanted, and he'd had to go with another supplier.

He'd paid a lot for this rock, and he shouldn't have dust hanging in the air and the gravel breaking into tons of tiny pieces after only a few months.

"Are you okay?" Brenda asked, and Ward straightened.

"Yes." It was his sister's wedding day, and he didn't need

to be thinking about work right now. Especially not gravel, which had become the bane of his existence for the past year. He wasn't going there again.

He offered his arm to Brenda, and they went inside the magnificent barn Bishop had redone. Today, the women had draped roses on every available surface, and straw had been brought into the foyer of the barn.

Noah Johnson had quite a few friends in Three Rivers, and the barn teemed with people. Ward didn't mind the people, because he generally thrived on the energy of other human beings. He smiled around at his family members and took a seat on the front row next to Oakley, who had an empty chair next to her for Ranger, who was in the back so he could escort Etta down the aisle.

Ward wondered if Daddy had thought about the weddings and grandchildren he'd miss after his death. He wondered if he knew how much he was missed at events like this. Ward closed his eyes and said a little prayer for Etta and Mother and his father too.

Mother held Wilder in the seat next to him, and Ward smiled as the baby made a grunting sound and squished into her further. The chatter went on and on, and Noah stood at the altar with Pastor Summers, talking as if they were at a picnic.

Ward checked his phone to see the wedding should've started ten minutes ago, and the energy in the barn shifted. More nerves ran through him, and Ward glanced down the aisle to Oakley, who tapped furiously on her phone.

"What's going on?" he asked her, and behind her, one of his cousins asked if the wedding was still on.

Ward glanced toward the back of the barn, sure Ranger and Etta would arrive at any moment. He looked at Noah standing at the altar. The man had obviously sensed that something had changed, because he'd stopped chatting with the preacher and he too watched the doorway at the back of the hall.

"Mother," he whispered. She had tears in her eyes, but she just kept bouncing Wilder. "Should I go check on them?"

She nodded, and Ward stood up. He buttoned his suit coat as he walked toward the back of the hall. He knocked lightly on the door to the bride's room, and he leaned closer to try to hear something. No one came to the door, but Ward wasn't going anywhere.

"Etta?" he said into the seam of the door. "Ranger? It's Ward."

The door opened a few seconds later, and Ranger stood there, his eyes wide and afraid. Ward stepped into the room, scanning for his sister. He found her standing in front of the wall of windows, her back to him.

She wasn't wearing her wedding dress.

He swallowed and exchanged a glance with Ranger before making his way over to Etta. He might not have the same type of friendship with her as he did Ida, but Ward had always been close to both twins. "Etta," he said, his voice soft and hopefully non-judgmental. "You're not marrying Noah today."

He didn't phrase it as a question.

A sob came from Etta's throat, and she turned into Ward.

"Okay," he said, taking her into his arms and holding her right against his chest. "It's okay, love. You don't have to marry him if you don't want to."

Etta cried for a good, long minute, and Ranger came to stand next to them too. Ward searched his face, trying to get answers without having to ask his sister.

"I do want to," Etta said, finally calming enough to speak. She stepped away from him. "I love him. He'd take such good care of me." A wild look resided in her eyes, even after she wiped the tears away.

"What's the problem?" Ward asked as gently as possible. He put his arm around Etta so she'd know he didn't much care what she did as long as she was happy.

"I just can't do it," she said. "There's—I want things he's unwilling to give me, and I—" She hiccuped and shook her head. "I should've done this months ago, and I feel so stupid." She dissolved into tears again, and Ward had no idea what to do. He'd never attended a wedding that didn't actually happen.

He stood with Etta until she quieted again. "Sissy, should I go get Noah? Do you want to talk to him?"

"I have to," Etta said, drawing in a deep breath. "I can't be the woman that stands up her fiancé at the altar and then runs away. That's not who I am." She shook her head, drawing all of her strength and sophistication right back into her shoulders.

"I'll go get him," Ward said, suddenly feeling like he might throw up if he had anyone looking at him, and it wasn't even him that had just been dumped. "Do you want Ranger to stay with you?"

Etta turned to Ranger and grabbed him in a hug. "Thank you, Ranger. I'm so sorry."

"Etta," he said. "I don't know what's going on or why you can't marry him. I just want you to be happy. If it's not him, you'll find someone else."

"Too soon," Ward muttered, and Ranger stepped away from Etta. Ward had no idea what he needed to do next. Ranger handled things like this, but his oldest brother hadn't followed him.

Ward slowed his pace as he approached the doorway, but he couldn't stop completely. He could do this for Etta. He could. He walked through it and every eye in the room zeroed in on him. He walked down the aisle alone and stepped right over to Noah.

"Etta would like to talk to you," he whispered. "In the bride's room."

Noah nodded once, a look of resignation on his face. "Thank you, Ward." He patted Ward's shoulder and held his head high as he went down the aisle.

Ward stood at the altar and faced the people who'd come. Etta hadn't asked him to make any announcements, but it was pretty dang obvious there was not going to be any I-do's said today.

"Uh, everyone," he said. "Etta and Noah aren't going to get married today."

Everyone started talking at once, and Ida stood up instantly and headed toward the back of the hall. Oakley jumped to her feet too, then paused and looked at Mother. She waved at her as if to say, *I've got the baby*, and Oakley met Montana in the aisle and off they went.

Sammy handed her baby to Bear, who'd stood and was watching the doorway. He came over to Ward, Smiles babbling as if nothing bad was happening. "What's goin' on?" Bear asked.

"She didn't say," Ward said. "Only that she couldn't marry him."

"Do we think he hurt her?"

"I don't know."

Holly Ann was the last woman to go down the hall, and Ace came to stand with Bear and Ward. "What in the world?"

"She's going to need a lot of support," Ward said. "Not questions."

Ace nodded, a look of pure compassion on his face. "Poor Noah."

"Yeah," Bear said. "Poor Etta too. She must be in so much turmoil."

Ward saw the panic in her eyes, heard the anguish in her voice. "She is," he said. "But we'll be there for her. Right? Because that's what we do. We're there for each other in this family." By the end of his sentence, his voice was the loudest one in the barn, and he looked around at everyone.

"Let's be as supportive as possible," he called just as loud. "She's not going to need questions or everyone staring at her. In fact, let's get this place cleaned up so she can exit with some dignity. Noah too." He nodded to Noah's friends who'd come.

To his surprise, everyone did as he said, and Ward got to work too, putting up chairs and thanking the pastor for coming. He dreaded getting everything done, because then he'd have to take Brenda home, and he was going to break up with her then.

He didn't want to drag things out that didn't need to be prolonged. She didn't deserve that, the way Noah didn't deserve to be standing at that altar, waiting for his bride-to-be to come down the aisle.

Ward didn't blame Etta, but he didn't want to do that to Brenda. Ranger had said she'd find someone else, and Ward clung to that idea with every fiber of his strength.

There was someone out there for him. There was. He just needed to keep looking.

# Chapter Sixteen

Cactus Glover hurried down the front steps, though the ache in his back told him to slow down. "I'm comin'," he called to Bishop and Bear, who both struggled with one end of a bureau. Bishop, who walked backward, stopped, and that made Bear pause too.

"You two will never get this up the steps." Cactus took one corner so Bishop could shift down to the other. "Ward's right behind me."

"Coming," Ward said, and he joined Bear's end of the dresser a few moments later. "This is her biggest piece. We get this in, and it's just boxes and lamps."

The solid wood bureau was a Glover family antique, and Cactus admired the lightly stained cherry wood as he took painstaking steps up to the porch. Inside the homestead, he and Bishop went straight back while Bear and Ward swung around, and then they had to walk backward through the arch.

"Whoa," Sammy said as she tried to come through the arch. "Everyone out of the way. They're bringing the dresser."

The activity and excitement about the homestead and the ranch had a lot to do with spring, sure. The winter hadn't been terribly long, but the wind had been murder. It wreaked havoc with a man's soul, and a lot of the re-fencing they'd done last autumn had to be redone now.

But the garden Ace and Mister labored over for six weeks was finally growing, and that brought a smile to everyone's face.

And today, Etta was moving into the homestead. When Mother had married Donald Parker in January, she'd vacated the small suite on the main floor. Ranger and Bear and their families lived upstairs in spacious suites, and the one that took up the back part of the main level had been empty for months.

Cactus actually looked around for Etta as he cleared the archway and entered the kitchen. He didn't see her, which wasn't surprising. After she'd left Noah Johnson standing at the altar, she'd disappeared from the family meals and activities. Cactus knew keenly how that felt, and he gave thanks to God that Etta was coming back.

It had taken him a decade to work out what she'd learned in only five weeks. He told himself the situations were radically different. They were. He'd lost a son and a wife, which had been everything to him.

He knew Etta was in a great deal of pain, and he never let more than three days go by before he called her, texted her, or simply drove down the hill to her house in town.

She'd listed it for sale before the wedding, as she'd been planning to move into Noah's house.

It had sold last week, and Etta needed somewhere to live. With Ida married and pregnant now, and Aunt Dawna living in the assisted living facility, the homestead was the perfect choice.

Cactus had suggested it to her, actually. They'd had some real bonding talks over the past few weeks, and Cactus wondered if the Lord had given him his particular trials so he could help Etta with something similar.

As he reflected on such a thing, his fingers protested his tight grip, but he wasn't about to let go. Bear and Ward led the way through the double-wide doors and into the suite, and Ida said, "Etta, the dresser."

"In the bedroom, please," Etta said. "Thank you guys so much." Every time Cactus saw her, she thanked him. True, he usually brought something tasty from the bakery or a loaf of homemade bread after he and Mitch pulled them from the oven. After the first few visits, Etta had asked Cactus if he'd bring Mitch and Link with him, and since Cactus loved the boys with his whole heart—which was actually whole now—he had. Etta had been learning sign language, and she had a real gift with children.

No one had known the reason Etta had called off the wedding at the twelfth hour. After a week, Aunt Dawna had stood up during their Sabbath meal and told everyone. Noah Johnson had three teenage children, and at his age, he didn't want more kids. Unwilling to negotiate, he'd thought Etta was okay with it.

She'd said she was.

In the end, though, she wasn't. She wanted her own children, and Cactus couldn't fault her for that.

"She feels terribly for what she did," Aunt Dawna had said. "She's working through a lot of grief and a lot of guilt for not calling off the wedding sooner, and she'd appreciate anyone who feels like they should to reach out. She's open to talking about things, though she has bad days like anyone would."

Cactus had already been to see her twice, because he didn't want her to retreat as far from the family as he had. He'd wept with her. He'd sat with her while she slept. He'd given her the name of the office where he still saw Dr. Thompson every so often.

"Right here," Bear said, his voice strained. "Down in three, two, one." They all groaned as the heavy bureau got placed on the ground, and Cactus backed up, shaking out his fingers.

"Granddaddy made this," Bishop said, running his fingers along the top of the chest of drawers. "It was a wedding gift for Uncle Bull and Aunt Dawna."

"I didn't know that," Cactus said, appreciating the dresser even more. He'd known someone in the Glover family had made it, because there always seemed to be someone with the gene for carving and building. In their generation, that person was Bishop himself.

"No time to be standin' around," Preacher said, depositing two boxes on the unmade bed. "The second truck just pulled up."

"Standing around?" Bear repeated, and Ward scoffed.

"Did you see us just haul that in?" He stretched his back. "I'm too old for this."

"Yeah," Cactus agreed. "You carried in two boxes. That was two tons. We can catch our breath."

Preacher grinned at them. "Old men," he quipped, and Cactus simply smiled and shook his head. He wanted to ask him about Charlie, but Preacher didn't like to talk about personal things in large groups. The two of them had been meeting for months about the veterinary care Cactus completed around the ranch, and he'd ask about her at their next get-together.

Every time he had, Preacher had simply said, "Yep, still seeing her." That was all, and it was slowly driving Cactus mad. At the same time, he knew what it was like to want to keep some things private. He knew exactly how it felt to not want to answer questions.

He'd just stepped over to his brother to ask when they could get together to go over market day preparations when Etta came out of the bathroom. Bear and Bishop had already started to leave the bedroom, but Cactus hung back.

She met his eye, and a smile curved her lips. "Thank you, Cactus," she said.

He changed directions and went to embrace her. "How's today? Hard? Hurting? Okay?"

She clung to him, a slight vibration in her chest that steadied quickly. He marveled at her strength. His embarrassment and humiliation had kept him from rejoining the family for such a long time, and he had no idea how she could face everyone with such a sunny disposition.

"It's a little of everything today," she whispered.

"I'm so sorry." Cactus stepped back and cleared his throat. "It's okay to let it hurt."

"I know." Her chin wobbled, and she moved to hug Ward. His eyes closed and he said something in a voice as equally as quiet as Cactus's had been. Ward had always been close with the twins, and Cactus turned to leave the suite, Preacher at his side.

"How's Charlie?" Cactus asked.

"Good," Preacher said. "Real good."

"You've worked out a way to see her more than once a month?" Cactus watched his brother as they passed through the living area of the suite. Beyond the doors was the massive family room where they gathered for meetings and meals, and he estimated Preacher could say maybe three sentences before they'd be surrounded by people.

"Yeah," Preacher said. "I gave up sleeping." He gave Cactus a smile, and he did notice the tiredness in Preacher's eyes. He also didn't say anything else, and why Cactus thought the man would ever string three sentences together was a mystery to him.

He followed Preacher back into the main part of the house, and someone said, "There he is. Cactus, Willa's looking for you."

He turned to Holly Ann, who held concern in her eyes. "Where is she?" He switched his gaze to Sammy, who nodded out the side door.

Everyone had gone quiet, and Cactus's heart flung itself against his ribcage, protesting this new tension in the house. "What's going on? Is she okay?" He strode toward the door that led out onto the deck.

"Those windows are open," Bear said. "Word to the wise—take a walk before you start talking."

Cactus had no idea what to expect as he left the homestead. Why hadn't anyone come to get him? Bishop and Bear knew where he was. And if Willa was hurt or upset, why? How?

"Willa?" he called once he arrived on the deck. He rounded the corner, where the deck ran along the entire front of the house too. It wrapped around the other side, and she appeared way down on that corner. Even from this distance, with the sun shining partially in his eyes, he could see she'd been crying.

He hurried toward her, already signing. *What's wrong? Are you hurt?* He took the last several steps at a jog, trying to find the source of her injury, her pain.

She shook her head, tears falling down her face. "I'm okay," she whispered.

He took her face in his hands, examining her and trying to quiet his fears and his pulse at the same time. "Talk to me." He thought of the open windows, but he didn't care. Down on this end of the house, there was only the lobby, and if someone wanted to loiter there and eavesdrop, that was all on them.

He pushed his hands through her auburn hair, every cell lighting up at the softness of her skin. He loved her so much, and if something caused her grief or pain, he'd go to any length to fix it. "Baby," he whispered. "You're scaring me."

"I'm sorry," she said, laughing now. "I'm just processing and enjoying the feeling so much."

"What feeling?"

She looked up at him, her eyes wide and vulnerable. "Last time I got pregnant, I was actually devastated. I cried for an entirely different reason."

Cactus searched her face, her words entering his ears at the speed of light but his brain processing them much slower. "Last time...." Joy filled his soul, and he grinned. His chest expanded as his heart grew. "Willa, are you pregnant?"

"Yes." Tears streamed down her face again.

Cactus whooped and engulfed her in a hug, his excitement slowly twining with gratitude that the Lord had found a way to replace everything Cactus had lost.

He stepped back quickly, reality taking over. "Okay, well, we have to go to the doctor."

"We do?"

"Willa, you have a son who was born deaf. My son died in four days from congenital heart failure. Yes, we have to go to the doctor, so we can make sure the baby is okay."

Willa looked up at him. "And what if it isn't, Charles?"

That brought him to a full stop. "I—"

"We still want the baby, don't we? Even if it's deaf?"

"Of course," he said, swallowing. "I just meant...." He wasn't sure what he meant. New fear bloomed inside him, and he turned away from Willa and looked toward the cemetery where generations of Glovers rested. "I think I might be able to handle anything with you at my side," he said. "But I'd like to know if I need to prepare myself for another infant funeral."

She laced her arm through the crook of his elbow and leaned into his bicep. "So you're worried about the heart."

"Yes," he said. "Mine. Yours. The baby's." How had he gone from complete elation to utter despair in only ten seconds? He pushed against the negative feelings. He cleared his throat. "This is a happy occasion," he said. "I'm not going to worry about it." He turned into her and took her into his arms again. "Will you help me not to worry about it?"

"I'll do my best."

He leaned down and kissed her, a slow, sensual kiss that he hoped conveyed to her how very much he loved her and how very much he wanted this baby. "I love you," he whispered.

"I love you too." She smiled softly at him. "Do you want a boy or a girl?"

"You know what? There are not enough girls in this family, so I'm going to start praying for a baby girl."

Willa giggled, the sound of it exactly what Cactus needed in that moment. "You know that's already been decided, right?"

Cactus slid his hand down to her stomach and rested his palm there. He felt nothing but the connection between him and Willa strengthen and grow. "I know," he whispered. "Maybe I'll just pray that he or she will be healthy."

"Mm." Willa covered his hand with hers. "Do you want to find out what the baby is? You know, when we can."

"Yes." He lifted his eyes to hers. "You?"

"Oh, I'm going to decorate the nursery from top to bottom," she said with a large grin. "So yes. We need to find out if it's a girl or a boy."

Cactus chuckled with her, but then Willa said, "Last time, Charles, I didn't enjoy the pregnancy. I hid it for months, and I didn't have a nursery at all. I wasn't married, and I lived every day in shame until the baby came. Many after that too."

"It's different this time," he said, finally getting what she meant about enjoying the feeling of being pregnant. She hadn't done that before. "It's a blessing, Willa. A true miracle."

"When should we tell Mitch?" she asked.

Cactus shook his head. "I don't know. I think when the moment is right, we'll know, and we'll tell him then."

Willa nodded, and Cactus slung his arm around her and looked at the cemetery again. "Let's go tell Daddy."

"Okay," she said. "But if we get in trouble because we skipped out on helping Etta move, I'm blaming you."

They laughed together, but Cactus knew Etta would understand. He wouldn't be telling the family about Willa's pregnancy for a while, and he'd actually tell Etta first. That way, she'd be prepared to hear the news that would hurt her. She'd be happy for them, of course, but it would still hurt.

Cactus knew the dichotomy of things, and how he could be thrilled for someone that they'd found a wife and were having a family and also be suffering through the pain of wanting those same things and not having them.

*Yet*, he thought.

Etta would heal, and she'd find someone else, and Cactus believed with the energy of his entire being that the Lord would provide a way for her to have what she wanted and find happiness. After all, he'd just experienced that very thing in his own life.

---

CACTUS HAD JUST LEFT THE CANDY SHOP WHEN HE caught sight of a bundle of giant balloons tied to the top of one of the kiosks in the mall. A line had formed while he'd been inside ordering caramel apples for Mitch's birthday party, and he edged around another kiosk selling sunglasses to get a better look.

The sign boasted the words: *Below Zero, an ice cream experience*, and Cactus instantly wanted to get in line. As he watched, a huge plume of white smoke lifted from the kiosk, and a murmur ran through the crowd.

Then a woman Cactus recognized instantly emerged from the mist, really digging into the bowl and producing perfectly round spheres of ice cream at a fast clip. Charlie Perkins put the ice cream in little tasting cups and another woman—identical to Charlie—picked up the tray and started passing out the samples.

She had to be Charlie's twin—or maybe she was Charlie herself. Cactus took a sample and said, "Are you Charlie?"

"Davie," she said with a smile. "I'm just helping my sister for her grand opening."

Another puff of mist filled the air around the mixer,

which had tubes running out of the top of it and into the kiosk. Cactus had seen this same thing at Ida's wedding, and all of the pieces started fitting together.

"The ice cream is made at three hundred and twenty-one degrees below zero," Charlie said, her voice loud but not shouty. "Here at Below Zero, your treat freezes in only fifteen seconds, and it produces ice crystals smaller than any other ice cream, which is why it's smoother, richer, creamier, and won't melt as fast."

She whipped together something in another big bowl. "The grand opening is tomorrow, right here at the mall, and my assistants are handing out coupons for anyone who comes this weekend. I'm going to mix up a few of our signature flavors, and you're welcome to try them all or just come back tomorrow with your friends and family."

Cactus took a coupon from Davie and looked at it. Buy one single cone, get one half-price. He scooped a bite of ice cream into his mouth, half his sample gone with that one taste. One bite was all it took, because Charlie was positively right. This ice cream was smoother, richer, creamier, and still incredibly cold.

He waited for the chocolate samples, which literally only took thirty seconds to arrive, and he stood and listened to the spiel again to get the bananas foster. As the crowd started to thin and new people moved in, Cactus figured three samples was enough. He'd drive down to the mall just to get this, and he knew Link, Aurora, and Mitch would come with him. Heck, he could probably steal Stetson away from Sammy for an afternoon too.

As he edged out of the way, he caught sight of Preacher

holding one of the trays on the other side of the kiosk, handing out samples and coupons just the way Davie had.

Cactus grinned from ear to ear. He never had asked his brother more about Charlie, but it was obvious the man liked her. He wouldn't be standing in the mall, talking to strangers and handing out ice cream for the woman if he didn't.

Before Preacher could see him, Cactus ducked his head and walked away. Preacher hadn't brought Charlie up to the ranch to meet the family yet, and there had to be a reason why. Cactus wanted to respect that, because Preacher had always given him the space he'd asked for. He'd given him respect and distance, and maybe, if Cactus did the same, Preacher would come to him if and when he needed help.

## Chapter Seventeen

"Grab that extension cord, would you?" Charlie lifted the heavy mixer while Preacher reached back into the pickup to get the cord.

"I can get that, baby," he said, taking the mixer from her. She grinned at him and danced a few steps in front of him. Summer had arrived in Three Rivers, though it was Memorial Day and technically still May.

"What are you smilin' about?" he asked, kicking a grin in her direction too. She sure did like the way his biceps bulged as he carried her equipment. They'd been working in the downtown park for an hour, getting her ice cream booth set up. She'd be here from noon to five today, and then Preacher had promised her a romantic birthday dinner.

He'd already left the ranch, which meant he wouldn't be canceling. In fact, he hadn't canceled in months, and he came down the hill from his ranch and up into the hills to her house on the opposite side of town at least three times a week. If he didn't come play games with her in person, they met for dinner somewhere. Once or twice, he'd even snuck away from Shiloh Ridge to take her to lunch.

"Just happy to see you," she said.

"I was at your place until midnight last night," he said, shaking his head. "I'm really going to pay for it today."

Preacher did look tired, but his smile was just as handsome and just as playful as it always was.

"You can go take a nap while I'm here," she said. "I won't need you to help once I'm set up and going."

"You don't know that," he said. "It could be insanely busy."

"I have three machines now," she said. "And I'm only offering three flavors." One for each machine. Charlie had been open in the mall for exactly two days, and she'd wrapped her kiosk in a huge purple bow and put signs to come find her at the opening summer craft fair here in the park today.

The past few months had been a whirlwind of firsts for her. Lots of new experiments. Lots of first times teaching students. First time the mint chocolate chip ice cream turned out right. First grand opening.

First time she'd hit half a million live views during a stream—and Preacher had been there for a lot of it.

Charlie felt like she was definitely falling in love, and while it wasn't the first time, it felt like it. It was only the second, but her first love had been warped. Looking back, she could see how dysfunctional her relationship with Forrest had been. She hadn't set a date to marry him despite their engagement lasting for just over a year, and she thought of Etta and the look on her fiancé's face as he waited for her to come down the aisle.

Charlie actually admired Etta, though she hardly knew Preacher's cousin. She'd been at the wedding-that-wasn't, and it took serious strength to refuse to walk down the aisle once everyone had already arrived. Charlie hadn't even been able to get a venue booked.

She glanced at Preacher as he hefted the mixer onto the remaining spot on the table they'd already set up. "So, uh, we've never really talked about Mindi," she said. "Or anyone else you've dated."

Preacher stilled and only cut his eyes toward her from under the brim of that cowboy hat. "Do we need to?"

"I don't know," she said lightly. "But yeah, I kind of want to." She opened the lid on her big, gray bin and took out the portable fan. She clipped it to the newly reinforced post on the end of the booth. Preacher had brought a hand-held welder down from the ranch and put better supports on the front of her stand, which was an old cattle trough she'd cut the bottom off of. She'd distressed the front of it, and her old logo had been painted on the front.

But she'd had her new one made into a huge magnet, and it stuck right over the old one—Preacher's idea. He'd also added a counter to the back of the trough that went along the side too, where she lifted her coolers next. She had prepared fifty servings of each flavor of ice cream she'd be making that day, and she'd brought ingredients for a hundred more. If she sold four hundred and fifty servings of ice cream in five hours, it would be a miracle, but she hadn't wanted to run out.

Chocolate, vanilla, and mint ice cream. Those were her best-selling flavors, and she had brought a dozen mix-ins. Truth was, Nutella was her best-seller, but she wanted to bring mint today to see if people would buy it in this Texas heat as a cooling treat.

"I was engaged once," she said, and Preacher stopped fiddling with the tube that connected to the canisters of liquid nitrogen.

"You were?"

"Five or six years ago," she said, pulling out the first container of Oreos from the bin. "His name was Forrest Millhouse. He was a gamer." She worked methodically, the same way she did when working on her chemistry problems or experiments. "He pretended like he was happy for me when I started to get really popular on Nexus. The real truth was he was jealous, and he only stayed with me because of my success."

Preacher moved down to the next mixer to hook up the tubes. "Did you break it off, or did he?"

"I did," she said. "We were engaged for over a year, and I still hadn't set a date. I finally told him I wasn't going to, and I didn't think we should get married."

Charlie wished that ended the story, but unfortunately, there was more. There always was. In real life, the stories behind the stories also had tales to them.

"At least he wasn't standing at the altar when you decided you couldn't marry him," he said.

"How is Etta?"

"She's doing really well, actually," Preacher said. "She moved into the homestead a week or two ago. Everyone came to help, and there was food for miles."

"Sounds amazing," Charlie said, her voice pitching up. She hadn't said anything to Preacher about meeting his family. Once he'd settled into his new role as foreman on the ranch, they'd managed to start seeing each other more often.

She knew the man who was currently giving up his holiday to help her with her ice cream booth liked her. She'd started to fall in love with him, and that was why she wanted to know his dating history.

"It was fun," Preacher admitted. "No one was looking at me this time."

She'd heard about the celebration his brother and cousin had thrown for him when he'd started as foreman a few months ago.

"Anyway," she said when he didn't continue. "Things with Forrest didn't just end. He sued me for half of my income, citing that he'd supported me and made it possible for me to build my subscribers and my channel. That without him 'sacrificing,' I wouldn't have found the same success."

"You're kidding."

"I am not." Charlie lined up her mix-ins along the top shelf and turned back to him. With the base ready, the mix-ins organized, and the mixers set up, she just needed cones and spoons. She bent to get out the paper goods. "He didn't win in court. I didn't pay him a single dime."

"I'm glad," Preacher said. He took the two boxes of

sugar cones she handed to him. "I've never been married or engaged."

Charlie said nothing, because she'd learned that Preacher had things to say. He just needed space to say them. He needed silence to say them into.

"I met Mindi a couple of years ago," he said. "She was pretty, and boy, could she flirt. She seemed to like me, and I didn't have anyone else on my radar. We went out a few times, and then her ex-boyfriend came back into the picture."

Charlie dumped a box of plastic spoons into a large, silver bucket, and Preacher paused while the noise filled the air between them.

"She preferred him over me," Preacher said. "But the man didn't respect her or like her. Every time he'd fade into the background, she'd bring me off the shelf where she'd put me." Preacher opened the container of peanut butter cups and shook a few into his palm. "And I let her, because she was beautiful, and I didn't have anyone paying any attention to me, in any aspect of my life. I guess she made me feel wanted, demented as the relationship was."

"And before her?" Charlie asked.

"Before her." Preacher drew in a deep breath and blew it all out. "Before and after her, I just dated anyone I found that I was remotely attracted to."

"No one else got hundred-dollar bills with your name and number on them?" She finally stopped stacking bowls and looked at him.

He grinned and shook his head. "I'm going to live that down one day."

Charlie returned his smile. "I thought you were really arrogant."

His eyebrows went up. "You did?"

"You were on a date when you gave me your number."

"I knew I wasn't going to go out with Cami again." He trained those pretty, dark blueberry eyes on her. "Once I met you, sugar, I haven't even thought about anyone else."

Warmth filled Charlie. "Is that so?" she asked, repeating something he said often.

"That's so." He slid his hand along her hip and brought her closer to him. He bent down and kissed her, and Charlie sure did like the taste of him, the heat pouring from him, and the way he made her feel like a strong, sexy woman.

"Okay, you two," Davie said, and Charlie broke the kiss quickly. Embarrassment filled her, and she pressed her cheek to Preacher's chest, her face turned away from her twin.

Davie entered the small space and bent to put her purse in the corner. "You guys are all set up already."

Charlie slipped away from Preacher and hugged her sister. "Thanks for coming to help."

"Of course. This is so exciting. I wouldn't be anywhere else." She stepped back and surveyed the area. "Okay. Teach me."

"You're going to take the orders," Charlie said, and she continued to show Davie where to put them. Charlie would man the mixers and scoop the ice cream. She'd mix in the toppings, and Davie would deliver the finished product.

Preacher stayed out of the way, and when Charlie finished, she checked the time on her phone. Fifteen minutes. "I'm going to walk Preacher to his truck," she said. "I'll be back in ten minutes."

She took Preacher's hand, and they walked away from the booth. "You really can go to my house and take a nap."

"I'm afraid of your cats," he said dryly.

Charlie laughed, because such a statement warranted it. "They're sweet."

"When you're around," he said. "They turn into demons when you turn your back."

"Let me tell you how you charm felines," she said. "They're a lot like men."

"Oh, boy."

"You feed them, Preach. I've got liver snacks in the pantry. Give them a few, then go in the guest bedroom, and close the door. You'll sleep like a baby, and when you come out, they'll be your besties."

He chuckled, quickly stepping in front of her. "You know I don't want to be friends, right?"

Charlie blinked at him. "We are friends, Preacher."

He shook his head, his eyes flashing. "I don't want to be *just* friends. Your bestie—that's not me."

"I do want my boyfriend to be my best friend."

"You're just being difficult on purpose now."

"Maybe." Charlie tiptoed her fingers up the front of his shirt. "Kiss me again, and then go take your nap. We'll be done here at five, and we have to break down the whole booth."

"I'll be back at five," he said, leaning down to kiss her

again. The coolness of the shade and the heat from his hands in her hair created opposites she really liked. "Did I pass with my dating history explanations?"

"Yes," she whispered against his lips. "And Preach, I don't want to be just friends either."

He smiled and kissed her again, but he pulled away quickly when someone said, "Preacher," in a somewhat shocked tone.

He turned toward the man who clearly belonged in his family. Those Glovers had a dark, rugged look to them that identified them easily. This man stood just as tall as Preacher, but he clearly wasn't as old. He held hands with a blonde woman, and a teenager stared at Preacher too.

"Hey, Bishop," Preacher said, stepping halfway in front of Charlie.

"What are you doing here?" he asked.

Annoyance threaded through Charlie. Was he going to introduce her or try to hide her? He'd brought her to two weddings up at the ranch, and that was it. She hadn't tried to sit with him at church again, and because she got to see him more often, she'd told herself it was okay. Preacher would introduce her to his family when the time was right.

Before Preacher could answer, a little boy ran over to them. He spoke with his hands, and Charlie had seen him at both weddings.

"Is Cactus here too?" Preacher asked, looking around.

"Yeah, we came together," Bishop said. "Aurora is meeting her new boyfriend."

"You've got a new boyfriend?" Preacher asked.

"Yeah," the teen girl said, shooting her parents a glare.

"And I'm old enough to wander around a craft fair with him."

"Not when I haven't met him," the blonde on Bishop's arm said, not giving her daughter one single inch. She reminded Charlie of Mama, who'd insisted on meeting every boy who even looked Charlie or Davie's way.

She found herself smiling at the woman, who clearly worked out and carried strength in her shoulders. She didn't want to hover in Preacher's shadow, and she stepped around him and extended her hand toward the couple. "I'm Charlie Perkins."

She looked at Preacher, her meaning obvious. *Introduce me. Introduce them. Something.*

"Sorry," he muttered. "Charlie, this is my brother, Bishop, and his wife, Montana. Aurora is her daughter." He indicated the boy and made a few signs. "This is Mitch. Everyone, this is Charlie." He didn't take her hand to claim her, and for some reason, that bothered her.

"Nice to meet you," Montana said, smiling at Charlie warmly. "I've seen you at the weddings, but I didn't realize Preacher was dating anyone." She trained her eyes on Preacher, and Charlie did the same.

He shifted his feet and glanced up as another couple approached them.

"Pastor Knowlton," Charlie said in surprise, looking from the Glover she held hands with to Preacher.

"It's Pastor Glover now," she said, stepping away from her husband and hugging Charlie. "How are you, Charlie?"

"Just fine, ma'am," Charlie said, smiling at her as they

parted. She glanced at the other man, and he didn't break the mask on his face.

"Have you met Cactus?" Willa asked. "He's Preacher's brother. Cactus, Charlie Perkins."

"Older brother, I'm assuming?" Charlie shook his hand, a smile on her face despite his near-frown.

"What gave it away?" he asked, and his voice was pleasant enough.

"It's the sexy gray in your beard, dear," Willa said, gazing up at him with extreme love in her eyes.

"Gross," Aurora said, and she giggled as all of the adults looked at her. "Sorry, Cactus. I just don't think of you as sexy."

"Thank the Lord," he said, glaring at her.

"You think of this Val-Jay as sexy though," Bishop said. "Which is why you need a babysitter today."

Aurora rolled her eyes, but she didn't argue.

"Okay, Charlie has to get back to her booth," Preacher said. "I have to go. I'll see y'all later." He nodded at Charlie as if they were merely business partners, but he didn't walk away. No one moved, in fact.

Finally, a bull horn sounded, and someone came over a megaphone. "Welcome to the opening summer craft fair! Vendors, get yourselves ready. We're going to cut the ribbon and let everyone in."

"I guess that's my cue to get to my booth," she said, glaring at Preacher for a hot moment before turning to his family. "Lovely to meet you all. Please excuse me." She walked away from Preacher, her chest vibrating in a strange way.

# Chapter Eighteen

Preacher watched Charlie march away from him, and he sighed, knowing he'd made a mistake. Probably more than one.

"You know," Cactus said. "I thought I was the worst one with women, what with the way I basically told Sierra I'd been stalking her."

Preacher finally looked at his brother as Charlie rounded a corner and disappeared from his sight.

"But I think he beats me." Cactus kept his gaze fixed on Bishop.

"Oh, he wins," Bishop said. "I want a proper introduction to this Val-Jay character." He looked at Aurora, who just rolled her eyes. "I'm just saying, it can't be that hard to tell your family who your significant other is."

"Okay," Preacher said, glaring at the lot of them. "That's great. Enough."

"What's with you?" Cactus asked. "It's obvious you're

dating that woman, yet you literally just told her to get back to work instead of introducing her to us."

"She had to do it herself for us," Montana said, cocking her eyebrows at Preacher.

"I saw you at the mall on Friday," Cactus said. "You're down there helping her with her ice cream shop, and now you're here, doing the same thing. What's going on?"

"Nothing's going on." Preacher folded his arms. He had neither time nor patience for this. He just wanted to sleep, and a very loud clock ticked in his head.

Bishop's eyes widened, and he shook his head. "Did you hear that, baby? He said nothing's going on, but I'm pretty sure we walked up on the two of them kissing." He leaned around Montana and looked at Aurora. "If you kiss someone, is something going on?"

Aurora met Preacher's eye, and he wished he could laser her lips closed. "Sorry, Preacher," she said. "But something's going on."

"You brought her to the weddings," Cactus said. "What are you trying to hide?" He peered at Preacher as if he could get the answers just by staring hard enough.

*Us*, he thought. *You guys. All the crazy up at the ranch.* Preacher said nothing.

"She seems lovely," Montana said gently. "Are you not sure about her?"

"This isn't about her," Willa said slowly. "It's about…."

Preacher simply looked at her, because Willa was smart. She saw and understood things others took longer to arrive at.

"It's about us," Cactus filled in for her. "He doesn't

want to introduce her to *us*."

"Etta did the same thing," Preacher said defensively. "I'm just trying to make sure she likes me enough before I try to incorporate her into this massive hoard at the ranch. I don't want to scare her off."

"Etta couldn't get herself down the aisle," Bishop said, as if Preacher needed a reminder. "How long have you been seeing Charlie?"

"A little while," Preacher hedged, cutting a glance at Cactus.

"There are a lot of you," Willa said.

"Thank you," Preacher said. "Now, I really do have to go. This is the only naptime I get, and I'm exhausted."

"You're going to go take a nap?" Cactus asked.

"It's not a crime." Preacher glared at his brother and started to turn. Just then, two boys approached the group, and he recognized one of them. Oliver Walker.

The other boy had blonde hair and blue eyes, and he swaggered right over to Aurora with a horribly sweet grin on his face. "Hey," he said.

"Val-Jay," she said as if surprised to see him there. She glanced at Oliver, and while Preacher might not know or understand everything about teenagers, he could tell there was still something there between them. "Hey, Ollie."

He simply nodded, his mouth set in a tight line. Aurora looked like she wished the ground would swallow her. "Mom, you remember Oliver. This is a friend of ours, Val-Jay Rigby." Aurora swallowed and looked back at Val-Jay.

"Val-Jay, this is my mom, Montana. And my step-dad, Bishop." She nodded to Preacher. "His brother, Preacher, and another brother, Cactus. His wife, Willa." She nearly choked on the last name. "And Mitch."

"Nice to meet you," went around, and Val-Jay shook Montana's and Bishop's hands.

"Wait," Cactus said, looking at the teens. "You and Ollie are friends?"

"Yeah," Val-Jay said.

"And you're both friends with Aurora."

"Cactus," Aurora said, plenty of warning in her voice.

"I'm just trying to understand," he said, and since he spent a lot of time with the kids around the ranch, he knew Aurora really well. "You dated Ollie for what? A year? Then you break-up, and you're dating his best friend now? Is that how this works?"

"We're not dating," Aurora said quickly, shooting a look at her mom.

"I'm gonna go," Ollie said, hooking his thumb over his shoulder.

"You picked me up," Val-Jay said.

Preacher felt bad for both of them. What a sticky situation.

"We're just hanging out," Aurora said.

"See if you can get a ride home," Ollie said, and Preacher couldn't keep up with all the conversations. Oliver left, and Aurora glared holes into Cactus's skull.

"I was just starting to talk to him again," she said. "You shouldn't have said anything."

"I just don't get it," Cactus said. "You just move around to all the boys? Is that how it works?"

"Basically, yes," Aurora snapped. She grabbed Val-jay's

hand. "Come on, VJ. Let's go."

"You're staying with us," Bishop called after her, but she just walked away anyway.

"I am so glad I'm not seventeen," Preacher said.

"Yeah," Bishop said with plenty of sarcasm. "Because hiding your girlfriend of five months is *so* much more mature." He turned to follow Aurora. "I'm feeling like ice cream, baby. Are you in?"

"I am," Cactus said, giving Preacher one last meaningful look before he followed Bishop and Montana.

Preacher stood there as they walked away from him, his ribs burning and his lungs flopping around in his chest.

---

PREACHER SAT ON CHARLIE'S FRONT STEPS, WATCHING AS she pulled into her driveway in her truck, the trailer with the booth in it coming along behind it. He kept his head low enough to barely see her, the brim of his hat draping his eyes in shadows.

She'd texted him several times over the course of the last five hours since he'd left the craft fair that she didn't need him to come back and help her with her booth.

When he'd woken at four-fifteen, he'd seen them all, and he'd tried to call. She hadn't answered, and he'd apologized profusely via text. Over and over.

She'd only responded with, *It's fine, Preacher.*

He knew when a woman used the word *fine*, nothing was fine.

He'd asked if they were still on for dinner, and Charlie

had said, *I'll see you soon.*

Her truck grumbled with its large engine, and Preacher stood as it cut off. He went down the steps to the sidewalk and on over to the truck. Charlie got out, her eyes flitting toward him and then away.

She turned away from him and headed toward the back of her truck. Preacher walked parallel to her on the other side of the pickup, meeting at the tailgate. "What do you need to take in right now?" he asked quietly.

"Just the mixers," she said. "The canisters. My coolers."

"I'll get it," he said. She'd already said she wanted to shower after the fair, and he'd said he'd unload everything while she did.

But she reached up to release the tailgate and then picked up a cooler.

"Charlie," Preacher said, a note of pleading in his voice.

To her credit, she paused and looked at him.

"I'm so sorry," he said.

"Are you hiding me from them?" she asked.

"Yes," he said.

"Why?"

"Because," Preacher said. "You don't get it, Charlie. They're so...loud. My family is huge. Like, legit huge. There are twelve of us Glovers. Twelve. A whole dozen. And that doesn't include my mother or my aunt. And now we've got several marriages. Babies everywhere."

He sighed and reached up to remove his cowboy hat from his head. "It's just so much, and I get so little time with you as it is, and I didn't want—I *don't* want—to share you with them."

"They seem to want you to."

"Of course they do," he said. "Because they're nosy and intrusive." He looked away, a sigh pulling through his body. "Sorry. They're great. I do love my family. I do. Sometimes I just wonder...if maybe I was born into the wrong one."

He sighed and reached for one of the liquid nitrogen canisters. It lifted much easier than he anticipated, because it was empty. "Did you do well?"

"Three hundred and twelve servings," she said.

"Holy cow, Charlie." He looked at her in surprise. "That's amazing."

A smile sprang to her face. "It really was amazing."

He put the canister back and took her into his arms. "I really am very sorry."

Her arms wound around his back, and he did enjoy his presence in her arms. "I know you are, Preacher," she said. "And you weren't born into the wrong family. You're a Glover, and you belong to them. They belong to you."

A thought jumped into his head. Could she belong to them too? Would they welcome her as easily as they had Sammy? Oakley? Montana? Holly Ann? Willa?

Preacher knew the answer to that, and it was *of course they would.*

Charlie pulled back and looked up at him. "Are a lot of your brothers and cousins having children, then?"

"Yeah," he said, gazing past her and into the horizon. A slight breeze blew up here, bringing with it the scent of dirt and wild things, and he sure did like it. It reminded him of the ranch with its stillness and fresh air.

"Do you want children, Preacher?"

He focused on her, blinking a couple of times. "I suppose so." He'd thought about being a father once or twice. He adored Stetson and Wilder, Lincoln and Mitch. He didn't get to spend much time with the kids at Shiloh Ridge, and in that moment, he hoped that would change.

"Not seven," he said. "Maybe not even five."

"Three?" Charlie teased.

"I suppose however many my wife and I decide we want."

"Mm." Charlie's blue eyes flickered as with flames.

"Do you want children, Charlie?" he asked, bending down and touching the tip of his nose to hers. Their breath mingled as he waited for her to answer.

"I'm not very nurturing," she said. "Or very maternal. Or very girly even."

"Yes, I've seen the sweat pants you wear when you game." He grinned, glad when she did too. She pushed one palm against his chest, but he wasn't going anywhere.

"You said you liked them," she said, giggling. "I believe the word you used was *sexy*, even."

"Oh, I doubt that," he said, sliding one hand along her waist and moving the other up into her hair. "And you didn't answer my question. Do you want children, sugar?"

"I honestly have never thought of myself as a mother." She stepped away from him, and Preacher let her go. "Or even a wife, to be truthful."

Preacher wasn't sure how to respond to that. He picked up the canister again and reached for a mixer. He could take them both into her garage in a single trip. His mind worked overtime as he did, and when he returned to get another load, Charlie stood there with her purse over her shoulder and a worried look on her face.

"I never thought I'd find the right man," she said. "To be a wife to and a parent with."

"You don't owe me any explanations," he said, reaching past her. She put her hand on his forearm, and he froze.

"With the right man," she said with power and strength in her nearly whispering voice. "Yes, I'd want to be a mother. I like the idea of a small family. Me and him and a couple of kids. No minivan needed. I am *not* driving a minivan."

Preacher burst out laughing, because he could never see her at the helm of a minivan. "Sounds like a great life," he said. "Because I'm with you. No minivans."

She smiled too, and he said, "You better go shower, baby. We have reservations in a little bit."

"Right." She stepped away from him and then came back, tipping up on her toes to kiss him. He forgot about the canisters and his blunder from earlier that day. He kissed Charlie, because that was all he wanted to do. Every day. All day. For a long, long time.

He knew he was falling in love with her, though he'd never fallen in love with anyone before. This had to be love, because it felt so good and so right.

He pulled away and pressed his forehead to hers. "Charlie," he whispered. Specific words sat on the tip of his tongue, but he didn't dare say them. He couldn't get them out. So he simply said, "Happy birthday, sugar," and kissed her again.

# Chapter Nineteen

Charlie had never been so full in her life. "I'm going to pop," she said even as she forked off another bite of chocolate tuxedo cake. "But I can't stop eating this."

Preacher scooped up a bite too. "It's the best thing I've ever eaten. Next time we come here, we should order dessert first."

"Yes," Charlie said, grinning. "Why didn't we think of that?" She put the rich chocolate cake in her mouth, with a layer of vanilla cream cheese, with the chocolate drizzle over the chocolate frosting completing the beautiful flavor in her mouth.

"Next time," Preacher promised, his smile absolute perfection. They stayed for several more minutes, and Charlie liked that he didn't tell their waiter that it was her birthday. He fussed over her, but he didn't call attention to her. In her mind, that was the perfect combination in a boyfriend.

"Let's get back to your place," he said. "I fed those beasts of yours and made them promise not to touch your birthday present."

Charlie laughed, tipping her head back and letting the joy fly from her throat. Every day had ups and downs, highs and lows, and today had been no different. She simply hoped to end this day on a high, with a kiss from the man she'd been steadily falling for.

He drove back to her house, where Davie had left on all the outside lights. Her sister had texted to say she'd stay out of the way tonight, but Charlie knew she'd poke her head out of her bedroom the moment Preacher left the house.

They met at the hood of his truck, where he took her hand and gave her another stunning smile. "I hope you like what I got you."

"I'm sure I will."

"I'm not great at giving gifts. That's Mister."

"He's younger than you, right?"

"Yes," he said. "He used to live with me and Judge. But he and Judge didn't get along very well." Preacher cleared his throat. "You seem to get along real nice with Davie."

"Yeah, sure," Charlie said. "Most of the time I know what she's thinking. We have this weird twin thing."

"What about your brothers?" he asked. "Do you get along with them?"

"Sure," she said. "I haven't seen them in a while, but we text. We get along."

Preacher nodded as they went up the steps. Charlie opened the front door and caught a black streak as Archie ran across the foyer from the direction of her office. "Archie," she said in a warning voice. "Paulie?" she called.

The gray and white cat didn't appear, which wasn't surprising. He only came out from his hiding spots when food got involved. She rustled the paper bag carrying her leftovers. "Come on, kitties."

Archie peeked out from behind the wall leading into the living room, and she grinned at him. "What were you doing in my office?" She let Preacher close the door behind them as she went to nab the cat.

She managed it, and she said, "You need to go on a diet, Mister Archuleta. You're fat."

He yowled in response, and she laughed as she set him back on his feet.

"He was in your office?" Preacher asked from behind her.

Charlie turned in time to see him go through the doorway that led to her office. She changed direction and did the same, coming to a stop when she saw the enormous painting leaning against her extra-wide monitor.

Her breath caught in her chest as she took in the beauty of it. One hand pressed over her heart as she gaped at the exquisite artwork, a gasp sticking halfway in her throat. "Preacher," she said. "It's Three Rivers. The skyline of Three Rivers." She looked from the gorgeous painting to the man beside it.

He seemed nervous as he watched her reaction. "Do you like it?"

"I love it," she said instantly, returning her eyes to the painting, trying to find every detail. The two tall buildings stood proudly in the skyline, but they hadn't been overdone. It was the grocery store on the east side she liked, and the black snake of road that led into town from the south and out of it in the north and northeast. One highway ran west, and she picked out the apple orchards and the cider mill, the police station and the courthouse on Main Street. The fountain with the statue of the pioneer woman, and the gardens, red barns, and quaint homes the small town boasted.

"Did you paint this?" She couldn't look away from it, because Preacher had been right. Three Rivers possessed a small-town charm that would be ruined with high-rises and skyscrapers, thousands more people, and all the traffic.

She suddenly didn't want that any more than Preacher did.

"Heavens no," he said with a chuckle. "Mister did. He's quite gifted with a paintbrush."

"I love this." She stepped over to it and traced her finger along the top of the painting, still trying to absorb the wonder of it. "Thank you." She turned toward him, seeing Preacher Glover with brand-new eyes. Eyes that could see past the handsomeness. Eyes that saw beyond his exterior. Past his faults and shortcomings.

Eyes that saw all the way to his heart, and she stepped up to him and took his face in her hands. "You are a wonderful man," she whispered, taking a piece of his heart and burying it inside hers. "Thank you."

"Happy birthday," he whispered back, kissing her again—a slow, sweet, sensual birthday kiss.

Truth be told, it was Charlie's happiest birthday ever,

out of thirty-seven full years on the planet, and she couldn't imagine ever having to go through another one without Preacher at her side.

---

"I DON'T UNDERSTAND," CHARLIE SAID AS PREACHER clicked on one of her computers. He'd come down from the ranch to play games with her that night, and their livestream started in forty minutes. "You have to buy Christmas light now? Why?"

"It's such a long story," Preacher said with a touch of darkness in his voice.

"I'll make ice cream," she said. "You can talk until it melts."

"Deal."

Charlie grinned at his back, watched him click around to find the Christmas lights he wanted at an online retailer, and left him in the office to get the task done.

In her garage, she quickly attached the liquid nitrogen tube to her mixer and twisted the handle to release the gas. Back inside, she found both cats on the counter as if they knew what she would do next—get out the food.

"It's not for you two," she said. "Now go on. Get down." She shooed them away, but only Paulie actually jumped down from the counter. The stubborn black cat stayed right on the edge of the countertop, his tail swishing back and forth as he watched her.

Charlie switched on her Internet radio and started putting together the ice cream base. Preacher loved chocolate and fruit, and as she sang along to her rock song favorites, she got out the orange liqueur and added half a capful to the base.

Back in the garage, she set the bowl in place, turned on the mixer, and relished the cold puff of cloudy air that came from the release of the liquid nitrogen. Thirty seconds later, she scooped the ice cream into bowls, grabbed two spoons, and went back toward the office.

She'd barely made it out of the kitchen when a horrible, metal clanging sound meant Archie had knocked the mixing bowl onto the floor. Charlie cringed, her adrenaline spiking. Then she shook her head, not even bothering to go back and chastise the cat. It wouldn't do any good anyway, and she had left the bowl sitting there on the counter, the cat only a few feet away.

"Everything okay?" Preacher called, coming out of the office.

"Yes," she said. "It's just Archie." She gave him a bowl of the chocolate orange ice cream and watched him. "Time's ticking."

He took a bite of the ice cream first, surprise moving through his expression. "Wow, this is *amazing*."

"I knew you'd like it." She smiled, because she enjoyed providing treats for people that they liked. "Chocolate orange. You were telling me you and your siblings got them in your stockings every year. You'd end up with four, because Bear, Cactus, and Judge don't like them."

"That's right." He grinned at her. "Come look at these lights."

Charlie followed him back into the office.

"We need more lights, because Judge enters the Ranch House in the lawn light competition every year. It's all done by public vote, and I don't have the heart to tell him he's never going to win. He starts pulling—"

"Why won't he win?" she asked.

"Because Shiloh Ridge is too far for very many people to drive. So they just go around town and then vote for their favorite they've seen. It's not a requirement to see them all before voting. Or even one."

"Interesting," she said, scooping up a mouthful of ice cream.

Preacher sat down in the chair he'd been in earlier. "Judge starts to pull out the bins and bins of lights and decorations we've got in late June or early July. That way, he can assess them, order new things, design the scene, and start to stage the music."

"Insane," Charlie said.

"He needs new lights for the house," Preacher said. "The ones we've been using are all white, which he doesn't like, and they're about five years old."

"Does the age matter?" she asked.

"Just in the technology to get them to time with the music." Preacher pointed to the screen. "So these are multi-colored, and you can program them to do all red, red and white, red and green, all blue, blue and white, all green, green and white, or all white." He sat back in his chair and took a bite of ice cream.

"They look great," she said. "That's a lot of choices."

"He'll like that," Preacher said. "I'll have to hear about it for the next six months, but he'll like it."

"How long does it take him to set up the scene?"

"About two months," Preacher said. "He works on it in his spare time. Evenings and stuff."

"Then what does he do from September to Thanksgiving?"

"Makes us all go watch it, give feedback, and suggestions. Then he tinkers. He tinkers with it for three months before the public finally starts showing up to vote." He spun in his chair so he faced her. "Three *months*, Charlie. I'm dealing with this for months."

Rarely did Preacher talk about something he wasn't passionate about. Especially with so many words at once. "I think you like it," Charlie said, teasing him, though she actually thought that. "You like this lawn light thing."

"It's a pain," Preacher said, without much oomph behind the words.

"Yeah, and you like it," Charlie insisted. "It's okay to say you like it."

"I mean, he builds a really great scene," Preacher admitted. "I'll take you to see it when it's done."

"You will?" Her eyebrows shot up. "Up to the ranch?"

He shook his head, a dark glint in his eye even as a smile curved those lips. "Yes, up to the ranch."

"I'm beginning to think Shiloh Ridge is just a myth. That you just disappear into the void or something after you leave here."

"It's a real place," he said in a deadpan. "You've been there twice."

"Three times, actually," she said, grinning back at him.

"See? Three times."

A couple more weeks had passed since he'd been unable to introduce her to his brothers. Charlie had accepted his apology and his explanation, but in the back of her mind, she really wanted to meet his family. She wanted to experience that roar of sound a lot of people could make together. She wanted to feed off the energy she'd felt once when she'd basically forced Preacher to sit beside her at church.

She told herself to be patient. Preacher just needed time to process the idea of her meeting his family as his official girlfriend, and Charlie could admit she liked the fact that he didn't want to share her.

He did come down from the ranch more often, especially now that it was summer, though he'd said he'd need to work a lot in the next couple of weeks to get everything set for market day in September.

Charlie hadn't realized how many moving parts there were on a ranch, but she knew a little bit more now. Every time she spoke with or spent time with Preacher, she learned more about him. She knew what to make for dinner for him on his birthday, and she enjoyed the quiet, steady way he approached life. No problem was too big for Preacher Glover, because he'd study things out, then dig right in to get them done.

An alarm sounded on her phone, knocking her out of her thoughts and back to the present moment.

"I'm buying these," he said. "I'll be ready in two minutes."

Charlie silenced the reminder that she was streaming that night, and she took another bite of her ice cream before waking up her large computer and getting the camera working.

She called up the game with slightly trembling fingers, and Preacher finally rolled his chair over next to hers.

She turned on the stream and said, "Hey, hey, everyone out there in the Nexus. It's y'girl The Chemist here tonight. We're going to start the one-minute countdown, where I'm going to finish my ice cream, and Preacher is going to guess what game we'll be playing tonight."

She started the clock, took a bite of her ice cream, and looked at Preacher.

"Solitary Ops," he said.

Charlie cocked one eyebrow and turned to face the camera. "Not Solitary Ops." The comments flew by again, several about how happy they were to see Preacher back. He hadn't come around the Nexus on The Chemist's feed for a few weeks now.

Someone asked about her ice cream, and because they had an orange slug next to their name, she wanted to comment. "That's right, Nuts-About-Berries, I made the ice cream. It's done with liquid nitrogen, and when I'm not here gaming with all of you, I'm making the smoothest, richest, creamiest ice cream in Texas."

Charlie paused to scan the comments. "Oh, Mint Brownie wants Preach to guess again."

"It better not be a flight simulator."

"It's not," Charlie said, grinning at him. The clock was almost out, so she took a small bite of ice cream and set her treat aside. She looked right into the camera and said,

"It's something brand new. Something no one can even get. And something he's going to love."

"Better just tell us what it is then, Chemist," he said. She loved that he fell into his role during their broadcasts, and she couldn't help taking a moment to smile at him in a way that would have her subs going wild.

Sure enough, when she faced the screen again, the comments were going crazy, most of them saying some version of, *Aww, Chemist, you like him so much!*

She did, and anyone with half a good eye could see it. In fact, she was pretty sure Lambchop only had one eye....

"It's Hoops Next Level," she said, watching Preacher in the screen that showed the two of them in the corner. "I got a demo copy in the mail the other day, and I've been dying to get Preach down here to play it. I happen to know he adores sports games, and I bet he's ultra-excited to try out a game no one else has even seen yet."

He blinked, his shock palpable. "You got Hoops Next Level?" he asked, his voice cracking in his excitement.

"Pick up your controller, cowboy. Let's see what you've got."

# Chapter Twenty

Preacher lifted his right fist into the air as the ball went in. On the screen, the crowd went wild. His grin couldn't be contained, and he switched his gaze from the basketball game to the side of the screen with all the comments from Nexus.

That crowd was going wild too. How Charlie kept up with the commenters while she played, he had no idea. He didn't have to do that, and he was sure that was why he'd just beaten her at their Hoops game.

"Well, he finally did it, you guys." She turned and grinned at him too, and if there was anyone more beautiful in the whole world, he wouldn't believe it. Focusing back on the screen, she added, "He beat me. Some of you have been waiting months for this to happen, and I hope you're happy."

She trilled out a giggle, and Preacher put his controller on the desk in front of her extra-wide monitor. He slid forward a little more, so they were more side-by-side, and he put his hand on her knee.

He simply liked being close to her. He liked touching her and listening to the sound of her voice. He liked learning about her, and he sure did like watching her work toward what she wanted. He liked her analytical mind, and he liked her out-of-the-box ideas. He liked holding her hand, and he liked kissing her.

He liked her faith, and if he had to admit everything, he even liked her cats.

She continued to chat with her subscribers, going back through the feed to answer their questions and talk more about Hoops Next Level. He knew she got paid to do that, but she worked the information and endorsements for the video game into the conversation naturally.

"Oh, we've got a question here about us." Charlie put her hand over his on her leg. "Do you want to answer it, Preach?" She turned and looked at him, her eyes shining like sapphires. "It's from Killer Whale."

Preacher followed her finger to the screen, where she pointed to a user comment with the orange slug next to it. He'd spoken on her Nexus feed before, and while he had an account and had done a few livestreams in the past, he didn't have the following Charlie did. Still, since he'd been dating her, he'd picked up about five hundred new likers on his stream. No new subscribers, because he didn't provide content the way Charlie did.

She'd told him he should record it when they all gamed together, but Preacher didn't think anyone would care. She live-streamed it, but that made sense. She made a lot of money from her station.

"Brands and saddles," he said after reading the comment. He exchanged a glance with Charlie, who simply glittered at him, a sly smile on her face. "Killer Whale wants to know if we're dating, and I'm pretty sure The Chemist has answered that. But yes," he said, looking right into the camera. "We're dating. Have been for about six months now, I guess."

More comments flew in, most with the special, exclusive emojis Charlie's subscribers got to use. Hearts and smiles and things like *I knew it!* came up the chat channel.

"Haven't you told them that before?" he asked her, and she lifted one shoulder in a shrug. He didn't watch every one of her videos, but he felt certain she'd mentioned the words "her boyfriend" on her stream.

"Anyway," he said, clearing his throat. "The second half of Killer Whale's question was if we were going to get married." He glanced down, showing everyone the top of his cowboy hat. "It's hard to say, you know?" He turned his hand over and laced his fingers through Charlie's. He squeezed and looked up into the camera again. "I sure do like her, but I've never been in love before. I'm not super sure what that looks like or sounds like or feels like. Right now, we're taking things one step at a time." He nodded, done with that question. He wasn't going to answer any more either.

Charlie seemed to know it, because she nodded too, did her wrap-up message, reminded everyone to get on in the morning for he special broadcast, and ended the livestream.

The high in the air started to come down, and Charlie turned her whole chair toward him. "You're a saint."

He just shook his head, a chuckle coming from his mouth. "No, I'm late getting back up to the ranch, because while you say you never play sports games, you sure are good at them."

"Luck," she said. "Plus, I'd played this before." She stood, and Preacher got to his feet too. "Do you have to go?" She wrapped her arms around his back, and Preacher sure did like the way she wanted him to stay.

He gazed down at her. "The fireworks are this weekend," he said. "Me and you? Spend the day at Centennial Park, starting about one? We can get lunch there or go somewhere first."

"I have to get the stand set up by eleven," she said. "But I can have Parvati and Ben run the booth starting when you get there."

"You sure? I can come later if you'll be busy with Below Zero."

"Nah, I can get everything going, and then they can run it."

"I'm glad you found good people to help."

"I pay them a lot," she said with a smile, her face tipped up toward his.

He grinned back at her, leaned down, and kissed her. He'd spoken the truth when he'd said he wasn't sure what the future would hold with him and Charlie. But right now, he knew he liked her a lot.

A whole lot.

---

PREACHER TURNED TO A FRESH SHEET OF PAPER AND started a list. He'd been talking to Ranger and Bear about market day, though it sat two months away. July and August could disappear into smoke faster than Preacher could breathe, and market day had a couple dozen moving parts, many of which needed to be set up well in advance.

He put a number one and put *Schedule semis* next to it.

Below that went *Hire seasonal cowboys.*

Number three became *Talk to Holly Ann about providing lunch on market day*.

He needed to make sure they had enough horses for everyone. He needed to check their tack. He needed to figure out where to feed everyone. Bear usually just set up some tables near the chutes, but they had True Blue now. Maybe Preacher should schedule that on the family calendar and entertain in style.

Then, though, someone would have to clean the barn, and Bishop acted like he personally owned it.

He clicked on his computer to get to the schedule for the barn, but as far as he knew, no one was getting married in September. They used True Blue for family luncheons and other big get-togethers too.

The date in September was open, and he scheduled it for market day. Then he picked up the phone and flipped the pages in his notebook back to the one where Bear had written down the phone number for the trucking company.

"Dale Mendelson, please," he said, hating the sound of his voice. It came out too much like a professional and not at all like who he really was. He waited on hold while the line got transferred to the scheduler, and Preacher then identified himself.

"So I need to schedule trucks and tractor trailers for market day at Shiloh Ridge."

"Let's see," Dale said. "You got twelve trucks from us last year. Is that what y'all need again?"

"Yes, sir," Preacher said.

"Okay, let's see...." The sound of typing and clicking came through the line. "What's your date with the weigh station, and I'll see what I can do."

"Date at the weigh station?" Preacher asked.

"Son, you've got to have the date on the calendar at the weigh station first. Otherwise, you're gonna load up your cows and have nowhere to take 'em."

"Okay, sure," Preacher said, wondering how he'd missed this crucial step. Humiliation started to creep into his mind, and he listened as Dale rattled off the number for someone named April at the weight station.

Preacher scribbled the number and name down and got off the call as quickly as possible. He made the necessary call to April and got September sixth as the official market day for Shiloh Ridge Ranch.

He went back to the family calendar and changed the schedule, then made the call to Dale again. "September sixth," he told Dale, and the man at Wolf Trucking told him he could have a dozen semis and tractor-trailers at Shiloh Ridge at eight a.m.

Since the weigh station sat two hours away, that was a great time. They could get their cowboys there in the morning. Get the cattle loaded up and off to market. Get some branding done. Eat lunch.

Done by two.

Preacher knew things never went according to his plans, and he wouldn't schedule anything on market day except dealing with market day.

His phone bleeped, and he picked it up, hoping it wasn't Dale telling him something else he'd forgotten to do. Thankfully, Ace's name sat on the screen. He tapped to call him, and he asked, "Where are you, Preach?"

"In the office at the Ranch House," he said. "Why?" He shuffled some papers around, trying to find his paper calendar.

"We're meeting at the homestead this morning."

Preacher frowned as he peered at his calendar. He just wanted to get as much done this morning before he went down to town to spend time with Charlie. "Who's we?"

"Me and Ward, Ranger and Bear. You're the other foreman, and we're waiting for you."

"I never got confirmation on today," he said, picking up his cowboy hat and heading for the door. Annoyance sang through him, but if he had a meeting this morning, he had a meeting. "I'll be there in five minutes."

"Okay," Ace said.

Preacher got himself down the road and under the arch to the homestead. When he walked into the house, the sound of chatter, a dog barking, and a baby crying—maybe two—greeted him.

He paused for a moment and took a deep breath. He'd grown up in a household full of boys, and one sister he'd never really gotten along with. He'd never found a quiet patch to really be himself, and he'd stayed in the background a lot of the time.

He thought of his father's words as he considered his role in the family. He saw Charlie stomping away from him after he'd done a poor job of introducing her to his family —and just two brothers. Not six. Plus Zona.

"He's here," Lincoln yelled, and Preacher opened his eyes to find his nephew running toward him. Benny, the black and white dog that lived at the homestead, followed him. He wore a smile on his face as big as the boy's, and Preacher crouched down to accept a hug from Lincoln, and then scratched Benny's head.

"Hey, boys," he said, smiling at them both. "What's goin' on today?"

"Daddy is taking us to the park in a little bit," Lincoln said. "But Momma says I have to shower first."

"Better go get it done then," Preacher said.

"Yep." Lincoln headed for the steps, taking them two at a time for the first few. He slowed quickly, and Benny didn't go with him. Preacher went with the dog into the kitchen, where he found more people than Ace, Ward, Ranger, and Bear.

Oakley sat on one of the couches, her baby in her lap as Wilder slept. The General, her snooty cat, hovered near her feet, and she spoke quietly with Willa. Cactus wasn't there, but Mitch came in the side door with his hearing dog, Frost, and surely the prickly man wouldn't be far behind.

He didn't see Sammy, but it had to be Stetson's crying that he'd heard. She'd be around, and he made his way over to the long dining room table, where Frost nosed his hand before going with Mitch further into the kitchen while the boy found something to drink.

"There you are," Ace said, and he didn't look very happy that Preacher was late.

"Sorry," Preacher said, taking a seat at the table beside Bear. "I must've missed a text."

"It's fine," Bear said with a smile. "Ace might lose his mind, but I'm fine."

"I'm not going to lose my mind," Ace said, and it could've been classified as a snap.

"Okay, what's going on?" Ranger asked. "You're in a terrible mood."

"Seriously," Ward said. "I asked you if you wanted sugar for your coffee and you bit my head off."

"I did not," Ace growled.

"He's definitely more grizzly than I've ever been." Bear leaned back and folded his arms.

Preacher kept his head down and let Ace stew for a few moments. Finally, he said, "I'm just in a hurry to get down to the grocery store."

"You're going to the grocery store on a Saturday?" Ranger asked.

"Not just a Saturday," Ward said. "A holiday Saturday."

"Seems odd," Bear said.

"Can we just start the meeting?" Ace asked.

"No," Bear said, leaning his elbows on the table. "Tell us what's going on."

Ace looked at Preacher, who just looked steadily back at him. He hadn't said anything, and Preacher wasn't going to. He got along with Ace really well, and he saw no reason to jab at that. He raised his eyebrows as the war continued to march across his cousin's face.

"Fine," Ace said, his shoulders slumping. At the same time, though, his eyes lit up and a smile crept onto his face. "Holly Ann is pregnant, and she's been really sick in the mornings. She needs a few things at the store. That's all."

"That's great," Ranger said, smiling too. "Congrats, Ace."

Preacher added his voice to the others telling him congratulations, and a flush crept into Ace's face. "Thanks," he said. "Sorry, but thanks."

"You should just go," Bear said. "We can talk about the stuff you wrote down without you."

"Yeah?" Ace asked.

"Yeah." Bear turned as Sammy came into the kitchen from the deck, carrying Stetson in her arms. His brother turned and took the still-sniffling boy from his wife and settled the one-year-old on his lap. Bear leaned down and touched his lips to Stetson's head, and the toddler snuggled into his father's chest and put his thumb in his mouth.

Preacher's heart grew and grew and warmed and warmed. Bear was such a good father, and he looked up at Sammy, who still stood at his side. "Did you say Holly Ann was pregnant?" she asked.

"How did you hear that?" Ranger asked. "You were outside."

"Holly Ann is pregnant?" Oakley asked from the couch, and Willa stood up. She was pregnant too, and she wore a look of hope and happiness in her eyes.

Preacher thought of what Charlie had said about how she wasn't very nurturing. Would she fit in with all the women up here? They seemed to all want big families and were fixated on having babies.

*At least we'd be black sheep together*, he thought, smiling.

"What are you smiling about?" Sammy asked, one hand on her stomach too.

"Good question," Bear said, half under his breath.

"When are you going to bring your girlfriend up here?" Sammy actually sat down on the bench, and Ace got up.

"I'm going to go," he said.

"Bye," Preacher said, wondering if he could follow Ace out the door.

He met Sammy's eyes, and he couldn't ignore her. "I don't know," he said honestly.

"Are you embarrassed of us?" Sammy asked.

Oakley and Willa joined the conversation, taking seats at the table. Preacher didn't want to be grilled by his sisters-in-law, and he glanced at Ranger for help. But Ranger was busy taking his sleeping son from his wife, so Preacher looked at Ward.

He wore a frown between his eyes, and he wasn't going to be any help for Preacher.

"No," he said. "We're just loud, and I don't get to see her—"

"Yeah, yeah," Sammy said. "Cactus told us that you don't get to see her very often, and you don't want to share her with us."

"It's true," he said, annoyed that Cactus and the others were talking about him behind his back.

"How often do you see her?" Bear asked.

"A few times a week." Preacher shifted on the bench and cleared his throat. "We're going to Centennial today. Her ice cream booth will be there, and we're going to watch the fireworks from the front porch at the Ranch House."

"Oh, so she'll be up here," Sammy said, her voice pitching up. "What time are the fireworks?" She casually tucked her blonde hair behind her ear.

"You're not invited," Preacher said darkly. "Plus, won't it be too late for you?"

"Too late?" Sammy asked. "What does that mean?"

Preacher didn't answer. Bear said, "Because you go to bed at nine, sweetheart." He chuckled, but Sammy didn't look amused.

Cactus walked in the door at that moment, a long sigh leaking from his mouth. "We've got pinkeye in the cattle in grassy pasture six," he announced. He sank onto the bench at the table with Willa at his side. He gave her a smile, but exhaustion lined it. Preacher knew that level of tiredness, as it currently streamed through him.

Alarm joined the flow, because pinkeye in their herd meant a ton of work for Preacher, who was over animals on the ranch.

"Holly Ann is pregnant," Willa said to Cactus. "That's three of us."

"Three?" Preacher asked, his eyes flying to Sammy, though Montana could've been pregnant. Zona too. "Who's keeping secrets now?"

Sammy's head bobbled like a toy. "We just haven't made an official announcement," she said. "It's not a secret."

"Okay." Preacher stood up. "I'm assuming we're not meeting?"

"Let's cancel," Bear said. "You and Cactus need to go check the herd." Normally, Bear would've jumped to his feet to do that the moment pinkeye was uttered. Now, he got to hold his dozing son and stay in the air conditioning.

"All right," Preacher said. "Come on, Cactus. I have to leave here by twelve-thirty."

"To go see your not-so-secret girlfriend?" Cactus stood up, his dark blue eyes shining with teasing.

"That's right," Preacher said. "So let's get this done. Talk to me about treatment for pinkeye...."

## Chapter Twenty-One

Charlie smiled as she handed over a chocolate cone with banana and peanut butter mixed in. She'd brought four flavors to Centennial Park today, and she was almost out of chocolate already.

"Parvati," she said. "I'm going to make more chocolate base. Can you handle the orders?"

"Yep." The twenty-year-old could do anything, and she reminded Charlie of herself from seventeen years ago. She moved around the booth in quick spurts, taking an order and then delivering one. Behind her, Ben only worked on making the ice cream. Charlie had been helping him and doing all the mix-ins, so they'd definitely be short-handed while she made more base. But it had to be done. The clock had barely touched one-thirty, and the crowd surrounding the booth hadn't let up for longer than five minutes since opening at eleven.

At this rate, they'd be out of ice cream completely

before dinnertime. Charlie didn't mind. She wanted to spend a lazy, casual, fun afternoon with Preacher, and she'd actually considered closing the booth completely.

"I'm going to call Sal too," she said, having dismissed the idea of closing down. "We need more help." She wanted everyone in Three Rivers to know about Below Zero. Then her kiosk in the mall would thrive, and she'd get asked to do more festivals and fairs and events.

Since opening over Memorial Day, Charlie had booked three weddings in the past six weeks. Below Zero operated in the black already, and she'd been able to hire three people to help run the kiosk so far.

The ultimate goal would be to have the kiosk open at the same time as the booth, but she couldn't do that unless she hired even more people. Right now, she didn't have the funds to do that unless she dipped into using personal money to fund payroll, and she didn't want to do that.

She got out her oversized burner and plugged it into the power brick that supplied her mixers with electricity. Into a huge pot over the burner, she put in a little water and set a bowl over it. Broken pieces of semi-sweet and dark chocolate went into that bowl to melt. Meanwhile, she measured cream, milk, sugar, and salt into individual mixing bowls and cups.

Around her people started to gather, and Charlie looked up. This felt so much like Nexus, and she smiled at them, wondering if she should do a demo. She had a speech prepared from her samples and demos they'd orchestrated at the mall when Davie had been in town.

"What are you making?" someone asked, and Charlie turned her attention to the deep, familiar voice.

Preacher stood there, a sparkle in his eye and a smile on his face. Charlie giggled and ducked her head. Yes, he was late. Apparently pinkeye in cattle was a serious condition that took longer to discuss than either of them knew. But he was here now. Perhaps he could help her get caught up before they started their afternoon together.

"We're almost out of chocolate ice cream base," she said. "So I'm making more. Would you like a demo?"

"Yes," several people in the crowd said, and more started to gather.

"Okay," Charlie said. "Cooking is simple chemistry, and I'm a chemist, which is how I got into ice cream making. First, I'm going to melt the chocolate over low heat. You don't want to microwave chocolate. It heats it up too fast. A double-boiler—where you put a bowl over a pot of simmering water—is a slower method and helps prevent the chocolate from breaking, splitting, or heating too fast. It's called tempering."

She bent and got out the large carton of eggs. "We do the same thing with egg yolks. No one wants scrambled eggs in their ice cream, right?"

Several people made faces, and Charlie laughed. She did love performing, and she realized that was why she loved live-streaming so much. It was why she'd loved doing assemblies at schools as well.

"So we'll crack our eggs and separate them. Who wants to come help?" A few hands shot up, and Charlie nodded to

Preacher. "What about you? You're the one who started all this."

"Yes, ma'am," he drawled, and he entered the booth and used hand sanitizer to clean up. After wiping his hands on a towel, he said, "Tell me what to do."

"We need thirty egg yolks," she said. "That will make thirty more servings of chocolate ice cream base."

"Wow, thirty," he said, picking up an egg and cracking it expertly against the table.

"The egg yolks have a protein in them that makes your ice cream smooth. And the way we freeze your treat here at Below Zero adds another element of creaminess as well." Charlie continued the demo, thriving on the energy from the crowd as she heated the milk, cream, and cocoa powder.

"You whisk the sugar into the egg yolks to dissolve it," she said as Preacher got the job done. "Who thinks they know why?"

Lots of hands went up this time, and Charlie didn't have a plant in the audience. She pointed to a woman decked out in red, white, and blue from head to toe. Well, if Charlie could see the woman's feet over the counter in front of her.

"It dissolves the sugar," she said. "Then it's not grainy."

"That's right." Charlie beamed at her. "Once it's glossy and forms little ribbons. Show 'em, sir."

He lifted the whisk, where ribbons of sugared egg yolk hung.

"Then you temper these too. Basically, you add the hot liquid a little at a time to make the two items the same temperature *before* you mix them together." She ladled the hot milk mixture into the bowl with the egg yolks, and Preacher kept whisking. Several ladles later, steam rose from both the bowl and the pot.

"And that's it." Charlie nodded to Preacher. "He'll pour the eggs into the pot, and whisk. Once a single bubble pops on the surface, it's good. We'll add the melted chocolate and a dash of vanilla, and that's the ice cream base. It's actually a chocolate custard, which is smooth and rich."

She turned to the mixers and picked up the next order. "We've got an order here for vanilla ice cream with Oreos." She grinned. "Very popular." Several people twittered, and someone asked her what her favorite flavor was.

"I love vanilla and caramel," she said. "So I usually do a vanilla base, add a caramel swirl, bananas, and some almonds for crunch." She giggled as she took out a bag of vanilla base. "My mouth is watering already. It's like a banana split."

She poured the vanilla base into a mixing bowl and started to go through the properties of liquid nitrogen, and the process for how the ice cream went from liquid to solid in only fifteen seconds, the higher melting point and slower process, and said, "Viola. Your ice cream delivered to you in under a minute."

She turned to the counter, where Parvati had three more orders she hadn't even laid out for Ben yet. "Stein?" she called, and a man came forward to get his Oreo ice cream.

Charlie returned to the counter where the newly-made ice cream base cooled in a bowl of ice. "Any questions?" As she answered them, she portioned the ice cream base into thirty more servings and put them in a single layer in the cooler. Ice on top of that, and then another layer. By then the crowd had gone, and Charlie noted that Preacher had been working the mixers to help get caught up on orders.

"Hey, baby," she said, touching his arm. "Thanks for that."

"You loved it," he said with a grin. He leaned down and kissed her quickly. "I don't mind staying to help you for a bit. You're slammed."

"It's been crazy-busy," Ben said, wiping his forehead with the back of his wrist. "You're saving us." He looked at Charlie meaningfully, and she sighed.

"Yeah, we better stay for a while and get caught up."

With four of them in the booth, Charlie was able to make more vanilla base and more birthday cake while the other three worked on orders. With the coolers full and the line dwindling, she switched over to mixing in flavors and handing out orders while Ben ran the mixers exclusively and Parvati only took orders.

Half an hour later, everyone had been served, and Charlie had sweat running down the side of her face and between her shoulder blades.

"Holy fireballs, it's hot," she said. "You're all getting a bonus for being here today."

Parvati smiled at her and Ben said, "Thanks, Char," as he wiped down the table that held the mixers.

"What's my bonus?" Preacher asked, his voice really flirty. "I don't even work here."

Charlie laughed and said, "I'll think of something." She

checked on a few more things, asked if Ben and Parvati would be okay, and once assured they would be, she left with Preacher.

"I'm sticky," she said. "I need to clean up in the bathroom."

"No problem, sugar." He waited for her while she washed her hands. She also splashed cool water over her face to get rid of the sweat and the redness in her cheeks. She slicked back her hair and redid her ponytail so it was nice and tight on top of her head.

Looking at herself in the mirror, she said, "Well, that's all you can do."

She found Preacher talking to someone several feet away when she exited the restroom, and she stalled. This wasn't a family member, because they weren't nearly tall enough. He shifted as he fell back a step, and she saw a dark-haired woman with way too much make-up on. She'd really gotten into the Fourth of July spirit too, and Charlie realized she was woefully underdressed for the holiday.

She wore a pair of cutoff denim shorts that could be classified as blue, but this woman had on a pair of navy blue cotton shorts, a white tank top with a huge red star splashed across the chest, and dangling earrings with three sizes of stars, the largest very nearly touching her shoulder.

Charlie swallowed and looked at her own red tank top. No stars in sight. No stripes. Just a red tank top and jean shorts, with a pair of white sandals. She did have the red, white, and blue, but Charlie never wore jewelry, and even if she had put on make-up this morning, it would've just been washed off as she cooled down under cold water.

She stepped toward Preacher and this other woman, the tension swimming toward her and telling her Preacher didn't like the conversation. "...okay?" he asked. "So you need to stop texting me."

He turned and looked at Charlie as she arrived at his side. "Hey, baby," she said, looking only up at him. She wanted to ask if he was okay, but she didn't. She took his hand and squeezed, the communication between them silent and meaningful—and crystal clear.

She'd just told him, *I'm right here if you need me.*

The frown between his eyes disappeared, and he said, "Hey, sugar." He looked at the other woman. "This is Mindi Freeman. Mindi, my girlfriend, Charlie Perkins."

Mindi's mouth dropped open, and she didn't even try to hide her surprise.

"Nice to meet you," Charlie said, extending her free hand to shake Mindi's. This woman was her polar opposite, and she remembered the giggling girl he'd had at his side at his cousin's wedding, where he'd first dropped that hundred-dollar bill into her tip jar.

"I love your Nutella ice cream," Mindi said. "You work at Below Zero, right?"

"She owns it," Preacher said, and Charlie liked how proud he sounded.

"I'm glad," Charlie said, smiling. "That recipe took a long time to perfect." It sold well out of the mall, but not at fairs. The mint did much better in the heat, and Charlie didn't bring the Nutella to parks or events anymore.

"We need to go," Preacher said. "Good to see you, Mindi."

"Yes," she said. "You too."

Preacher guided Charlie away from her, and finally the tension in his shoulders broke. "She seriously just asked me to go to a family barbecue with her, because one of her exes is going to be there. She didn't want to go alone."

"I'm so sorry," Charlie said in a low voice. "Sounds like you told her exactly what you've wanted to say to her."

"I hope so." He glanced over his shoulder. "She's a little relentless."

"Has she been texting you?"

"Yes," he said.

"You didn't tell me that."

"It wasn't a big deal."

Charlie wondered if it was, though. If things started to crumble between them, he'd have a beautiful woman waiting in the wings. She shook the thoughts from her head. Nothing was crumbling between her and Preacher. They were rock-solid, and their relationship grew stronger each day.

At least in Charlie's mind, it did. Shaking off the late start to their date, as well as the heat, and all of her doubts, she said, "Okay, cowboy. I'm starving, and you promised me something good to eat. What's on the agenda as far as food goes?"

---

SEVERAL HOURS LATER, CHARLIE SAID, "I'M SO EXCITED to be coming up here." She reached out and ran her hand along the armrest. "I can't believe you have two Mustangs."

"Don't be too excited," Preacher said, bumping along the dirt road he'd turned onto a few minutes ago. "We're not even officially going onto the ranch."

"You don't live on the ranch?"

"I mean, I do, yes," he said. "But there's this big arch that hangs over this road, and that's the official entrance to Shiloh Ridge. We turn off to the right before that and go around the side of the hill here. The Ranch House is over there. That's why it overlooks Three Rivers."

His headlights came on as darkness gathered fast now. He'd proposed the idea of coming up to his house to watch the fireworks, and Charlie had said yes before he'd even finished asking. He'd chuckled, but she hoped he'd gotten the hint that she wanted to go to his house. She wanted to see his ranch. She wanted to meet his family.

All of them.

She'd been shocked to learn he'd left his beloved pickup truck at a storage unit, swapping it out for Wanda, this gorgeous, vintage Mustang the color of dark plum skin. He clearly cared about the car, and he'd told her his father had loved fixing up old cars and driving them.

He'd told her about the Corvette he'd had in his garage until very recently, when he'd given it to his sister, who'd also shared their daddy's affinity for sports cars and tinkering with old vehicles.

"Will Judge be home?" she asked.

"I don't know Judge's plans," Preacher said.

Charlie looked out the window, the town of Three Rivers becoming more visible as they went steadily up into the hills. He did turn right, and then she could see the town out the front windshield. A short few minutes later, he pulled into the driveway of a fairly big house, with a wide front porch that charmed Charlie the moment she laid eyes on it.

Outside, the heat still hung in the air, but up here, a breeze cooled her skin. "This is gorgeous," she said, pausing near Wanda's taillights to look out over the valley. "It looks just like my painting."

Preacher joined her and slid his arm around her waist. "The sunrise is stunning."

"I want to see that," she said, leaning into his body. This moment felt perfect, and a sigh slipped between her lips. "It's so peaceful here."

"That it is," he whispered.

"You like the ranch, right, Preach?"

"I love the ranch," he admitted.

"So you'll live and work here forever."

"Yes."

"In this house?"

"No," he said. "Judge is slated to have this house for his family. He's not seeing anyone right now, but since several of my brothers and cousins started getting married in the past five or six years, we've been adding houses and making plans for remodels or new builds, so everyone has a place here if they want one."

"Where will you live?"

He sighed, his chest deflating all the way before he breathed in again. "We own all the land right down to the highway. There's an old ranch there that my dad bought years ago. The Kinder Ranch. It's on the schedule to be rebuilt and remodeled. We'll probably put some cowboy cabins down there, so it'll be a whole community. I'm most likely going to live there."

"Most likely?"

"There's another plot of land we own," he said. "We call it the Cornish Plantation, because we bought it from the Cornish family. It's really far out, along this road, and it needs a ton of work too. I could live out there, but it doesn't make much sense for me to do that. Not as foreman. I need to be more accessible."

"Mm." Charlie soaked in the sound of his voice, the heat from his body, and the comfortable feeling between them.

"Let's go sit, sugar," he said. "I'm tired of standing."

She went with him to the front porch, where he pulled two rocking chairs forward so they could see past the eaves. The breeze didn't quite reach her face now, but Preacher went inside the house for a few minutes and returned with popcorn and ice-cold bottles of sweet tea lemonade.

He also had a plastic bag filled with red licorice and M&Ms, and he handed it to her. "Mother never took us to the fireworks without Red Vines," he said, a smile riding in his voice. He'd turned off all the lights in the house so the countryside was dark in every direction. "I love them, and every time I have one, I think of a summer night just like this. She and Daddy would take sandwiches to the fireworks, and I always wanted a hot dog or a piece of pizza. Instead, I had to eat ham and cheese." He chuckled. "It's funny what you want as a kid. I don't even like hot dogs all that much now."

Charlie smiled at his childhood memories, because they felt pure and good. "What else?" she asked when he didn't continue.

"Oh, there were so many of us," he said. "I didn't get along with Arizona, so I sat by Ace and Bishop. Sometimes Mister and Judge. Whoever would let me draw in their notebook while we waited for the show to begin. Every year, they have a concert before dark, and as I got older, I started thinking I'd be in a band. Ward plays the guitar real well, and so I started hanging out with him more."

"So you're good friends with a lot of your family members."

"I even made up with Zona finally," he said quietly. "By giving her that Corvette. She's wanted it since Daddy died."

Charlie glanced at him, but his focus sat beyond the porch. Out in the wilderness somewhere where only he could see the thoughts and memories. "My parents took us to the stadium at UT Dallas," she said. "That's where I grew up, for the most part. There was always a lot of noise and a lot of cops. It took forever to park and walk in, and my daddy used to make us wait in the stands for a half an hour before we even started walking to the car. That way, he claimed the lines to get out of the parking lot wouldn't be so long."

She smiled at the memories. "The last Fourth of July my parents were together, my youngest brother spilled pop all down the front of himself, and Mama said we had to leave." She sobered, this last Fourth of July not quite so charming. "They argued, but Daddy finally got up and started packing up the blankets and stadium seats. We left before any of the fireworks, and after that, Mama didn't take us."

Preacher reached over and threaded his fingers through hers. "I'm sorry, sugar. How old were you?"

"Fourteen," she said. "I lived with Mama, because she got the house, and I wanted to finish high school with all of my friends. We all stayed with Mama most of the time. Daddy got to see us every other weekend and for months in the summer."

"You said once that it was a fairly bad divorce."

"It was," Charlie said.

"And that you weren't sure about marriage."

Charlie's pulse started to pounce around in her chest. "I said I needed to be really sure about that."

"Mm." He didn't say anything for a few minutes, and the only sound between them was the crunching of popcorn and the rocking of chairs against the porch. "We can turn on the music," he said. "Do you want to?"

"Sure," she said.

He got up and went inside the house again, returning a few minutes later with a speaker. He connected his phone to it and said, "I think the link for the radio station is on the town website."

Sure enough, a few moments later, patriotic music blared out of the speaker. He yelped and turned it down quickly, all while Charlie giggled at him.

As soon as he settled again, she reached for his hand. "I'm more and more sure of us every day, Preacher."

"Is that so?" he asked, flirting in that throaty voice she adored.

"That's so."

"Get on over here then," he said as a new song began to play. He tugged on her hand, and Charlie got up out of her rocking chair to join him in his. He slid his hand up her bare arm, sending ripples of pleasure through her. He curled his fingers around the back of her neck and brought her face closer to his.

"I'm definitely falling in love with you," he whispered. "All the way. Completely."

"How do you know?" she whispered back. "You said you've never been in love before."

"I think it's something you just know." He kissed her, and Charlie knew he was right. She just knew how she felt about Preacher, and that it had become a deep, rooted feeling inside her. Deeper than anything she'd experienced before.

As he kissed her slowly and deeply, Charlie experienced true love for the first time, despite her past engagement.

"Oh, Preacher's got the music going," someone said, and Charlie pulled away from her boyfriend.

"Someone's here," she whispered.

"Yeah." Preacher sighed, and Charlie stood up so he could too. "Etta?"

"Oh, he's right there." Etta came up the steps, emerging from the darkness as the first fireworks started to fill the sky. She glanced at Charlie, who offered her a smile. "I didn't mean to interrupt. This is just the best place to watch the fireworks. Can we join you?"

"Of course," Preacher and Charlie said at the same time. She did sound happier about it than he did. "Etta, this is my girlfriend Charlie Perkins. Sugar, Etta's one of my cousins. Ace's sister."

"Of course. I remember," Charlie said, because she'd come to Etta's wedding. The woman looked tired, but she wore a smile as she shook Charlie's hand.

"Ida and Brady are putting blankets down," Etta said. "Ace said he and Holly Ann might come."

"Okay," Preacher said. "We'll just stay up here."

"We won't bother you," Etta promised, and she turned to go back down the steps.

Charlie stepped into Preacher again and wrapped her arms around him. "Let's sit down, baby," she whispered. "It's dark, and it's okay."

"Yeah," he said, sighing as he sat down.

She settled onto his lap again, and he toed them back and forth as the glorious fireworks filled the sky at about eye level, right in time to the music.

They lasted about thirty minutes, and that half-hour became one of Charlie's favorite time spans of her whole life. She had Preacher's arms around her, and his breath slipping across her shoulder, and the scent of his skin in her nose.

He took her heart in those thirty minutes, and Charlie had given it to him freely. She hoped she hadn't just made the biggest mistake of her life—the way Mama had once said she had by falling in love with Daddy.

# Chapter Twenty-Two

Ward Glover kept his head bowed even after the prayer, adding his own pleas to the Lord for himself. He'd been making a conscious effort to find someone he could share his life with. Since he'd ended things with Brenda, the woman he'd brought to Etta's wedding a few months ago, he'd been out with three more women.

He honestly wasn't sure if Three Rivers would have any women left to date by the time he finished embarrassing himself. He'd considered joining an app and expanding past his own zip code, but he hadn't quite taken that step yet.

"Thanks for joining me on this glorious summer morning," Pastor Corning said, and Ward looked up at the preacher. He was Willa's brother, and he'd come up to Shiloh Ridge several times over the past couple of years as Cactus and Willa had been dating and now that they were married.

He had two little girls, and Ward wondered if he was looking for a new wife for himself and a new mother for those kids. Ward said an extra prayer for him too, whether he was or not, because it had to be hard to be a single dad.

Ward had gone out with a single mom for a few dates before she actually told him there was "no sizzle," and she was real sorry. Ward was too, but at least she'd been honest with him, and he'd moved on.

*You're not going to another summer dance though*, he told himself in his sternest mental voice. He'd tried that last week, and he'd felt practically geriatric. Ward was thirty-seven years old, and he swore some of the men at the summer dance that had taken place in the downtown park had been boys. Barely out of high school. Big flirts, who liked to dance with every girl there.

*Girl* being the operative word.

Ward was not interested in finding a girl. He wanted a woman, and one that was as strong as him. One who could put up with his insane work schedule, and actually get out there on the ranch and join him. He preferred women with lighter hair, though he wasn't limiting himself in any way besides age.

Thirty was as low as he was willing to go, and it had taken him all of ten minutes to figure out the summer dances drew the twenty-something crowd. He'd heard that from some other cowboys around at other ranches, but he'd wanted to see for himself.

"Today I want to talk about quitting," Pastor Corning said. "Sometimes, it can feel like our efforts are getting us nowhere. That no matter what course of action we try, the result is not one we desire. Sometimes, we start to wonder if the Lord hears our prayers at all."

Ward nodded, thinking, *Amen*, because that was exactly how he felt. And yet, he couldn't stop himself from praying.

"Don't withdraw from the Lord. He's not testing you. He's not trying to push you away. Sometimes life is complicated, and there are things to learn. We're here to learn how to think for ourselves, choose for ourselves, and I hope we'll always choose to incorporate the Lord into our decision-making process."

He continued with encouragement and ways the Lord gently led and guided His children to their ultimate happy ending. "And you know, I've come to realize over the past few years, that sometimes that happy ending might not happen in the days of our mortal lives. That's the hardest part of this." He looked out over the crowd, his face earnest and his fingers gripping both sides of the podium where he stood.

"We want the happily-ever-after, and we want it now. Some people struggle through their whole lives with illnesses they can't overcome. Some of you are lonely, desperate for a partner or spouse to spend your lives with." He paused, his neck moving as he swallowed. "I count myself in that boat, my friends, and the seas can be stormy. But remember when the apostles were fishing, and the storm arose? They were scared, and they were being tossed to and fro in the sea. Who was there to calm the troubled waters? Who held out his hand and sent away the winds and the waves?"

"The Lord," Ward whispered as Pastor Corning said it.

"The Lord," the pastor said again. "He's there. He doth not sleep. He is with you, even when you don't realize it."

"Amen," Ward said along with several others. He loved coming to church, because his soul got fed and he found the energy he needed to keep trying. Live another day, refusing to give up.

The sermon ended a few minutes later, and Ward stood with Mister and Aunt Lois. Donald led the way out into the aisle, putting his hand on Lois's lower back and letting her go in front of him. Ward liked watching the two of them, because they genuinely seemed to love one another, and he wanted that in his life too.

At the back of the chapel, the pastor's girls stood, one at each exit. "Don't forget," the younger one said as Ward approached. "We're having our potluck today. Everyone is welcome to stay after and eat."

Like a flash of lightning, the thought struck Ward that he should stay for the potluck. He'd never attended one before, and he immediately resisted now. He could handle the crowd at Shiloh Ridge, because they were all family. He didn't particularly like crowds otherwise, especially if he didn't know anyone.

*You know the people here*, he told himself. He'd been attending this church for years, and he dismissed that excuse, searching for another one. When he couldn't find one, he reached up and took off his cowboy hat. Reseating it, he turned back to Mister, who followed him. "Do you think you could get a ride back to the ranch?"

"Why?" Mister turned toward Ward and away from someone he'd been looking at. Ward followed his gaze and found a couple of women standing over by the bulletin board.

"I'm going to stay for the potluck," Ward said.

"Maybe I'll stay too," Mister said, not immediately jumping to a question. Ace would've done that—demanded to know why Ward wanted to stay for a potluck he'd never attended before. Just another reason Ward sure did like living with Mister.

"Yeah?" Ward asked. "Isn't that Libby Bellamore?"

"Yeah," Mister said. "And she's with someone I don't know." He gestured for Ward to follow him. "Let's go see if she'll introduce us."

Ward decided to take another leap of faith and follow his cousin.

"Heya, Libby," Mister said, and the sandy blonde turned toward him with a bright smile on her face.

"Mister," she said, her eyes shining like stars. Ohhh, she liked Mister. Ward looked at his cousin, and he didn't even see it. He didn't even see the pretty woman in front of him. "Hello, Ward."

"Hullo, Libby," he said, noting how the brightness in her eyes dimmed when she looked at him. How could Mister not see this? He looked at the woman next to Libby, and after she'd glanced at Mister again, she startled.

"Oh, this is Sandy Keller," she said. "She just started at our ranch."

"Nice to meet you," Mister said, and he spoke in that ultra-Texas swagger voice that almost made Ward roll his eyes.

"These boys work at Shiloh Ridge," Libby said. "Pretty close to us on the south side of town. Mister Glover and Ward Glover."

"Your first name is Mister?" Sandy said, her bright blue eyes fixed on Mister.

"That's right," he said with a smile, and Ward did roll his eyes this time. "Are you ladies staying for the potluck?"

"Yes," Libby said while Sandy tucked her hair. She looked between her friend and Mister, her expression falling in an instant. Ward felt bad for her, and he wished he could kick Mister and get him to open his eyes.

"So are we," Mister said, cocking one elbow. "Let's head out, should we?"

Libby smiled and took his arm, and he offered the other one to Sandy. She took it, and Ward marveled at how he'd gotten two women in a single conversation. He watched them walk down the hall and out the door that led into a garden, thinking maybe he'd just stay here and enjoy the air conditioning.

In the end, though, he'd driven with Mister, and if he was going to wait, he might as well go eat. Besides, he'd had the thought to stay for a reason, and he didn't want to ignore the promptings from the Lord.

He'd only taken two steps down the hall when the scent of something salty and cheesy met his nose. The kitchen sat at the back of the church, with a door that led into the same garden where Mister and the women had gone.

Ward continued that way, picking up the pace when he heard someone say, "All right, let's say a prayer."

So focused on the door, Ward didn't look left or right. A woman dashed out of a doorway just as he passed it, and the next thing he knew, he'd been knocked into the wall. He grunted, a pain flying through his shoulder.

Something cold smashed into his other shoulder and part of his chest, and Ward looked down at the sticky, pink dessert before he met the eyes of the woman who'd been carrying it.

"Dot," he said, heavy annoyance in his voice. She'd just smashed something the consistency of pudding into his white shirt. Bright pink, wobbly, creamy gelatin.

"Ward," she said just as icily. "I didn't see you."

"Obviously," he said, stepping out of the way and trying to push the Jell-O salad off his clothing. How could he go to the potluck and expect to meet the woman of his dreams now? Irritation fired through him, and not just because of this untimely meeting with Dorothy Crockett.

The woman wouldn't return his calls about coming up to Shiloh Ridge to look at his gravel either. An idea formed in his mind, and he seized onto it. "Looks like you're going to owe me one," he said, giving her a Cheshire Cat-like grin.

"What does that mean?" she said, looking from the plate of ruined dessert to his face.

He took a tiny step closer to her, getting near enough to be in her personal space. She didn't back up an inch, and a fizzling firecracker moved through Ward's bloodstream. Dot had her hair down today, all curled in pretty silver-blonde waves that fell to her shoulders. She had dark hazel eyes and a bright smile—most of the time.

Right now, she frowned at him.

"It means you just ruined my shirt, sweetheart, and I'm going to need you to pay for it."

## Chapter Twenty-Three

Dorothy Crockett did not like the arrogance she saw in Ward Glover. The man was incredibly good-looking, but boy did he know it.

"Fine," she said, nearly snapping the word at him. "Send me a bill."

"Ho, no," he said, chortling a little as he blocked her from going past him. "You're coming up to Shiloh Ridge to look at my gravel. That's the payment."

"You don't get to decide how I'll pay you for the shirt."

"Don't I?" he asked, those blue eyes shooting sparks at her. She felt them all the way down in her stomach, and she sure did like the way he made her cells tremble.

*No, you don't*, she told herself even as a vein of excitement moved through her that she hadn't felt in a while. The man had been calling her office for months, so he obviously couldn't take a hint.

"I don't have the gravel you want," she said. "That's why I didn't have my secretary call you back."

"Come on, Dot," he said, rolling his eyes. "You have every type of gravel, and you should *see* this junk I got from Twin Cities."

Her curiosity piqued, but she still didn't want to go up to Shiloh Ridge. She'd done work up there before, and she always got paid. That was more than she could say about some other ranches and businesses and even private citizens she'd dealt with.

But the foreman was extremely demanding, and he barked orders at her as if she worked for him.

She didn't work for Ward Glover, thank you very much.

In fact, Dot had worked very hard to establish her landscape company in Three Rivers so she could work for herself. She loved driving the big dump trucks and shoveling bark, gravel, or lava rock out of the back. She loved picking through rock samples for her inventory or wandering through the rows of trees with a customer.

Dot loved everything about making a piece of land look like a million bucks, and it had been a steep climb to learn everything she needed to know to run the biggest and best landscape company in the Texas Panhandle.

"Didn't you just re-gravel your whole ranch?" she asked.

"Last year, yes," he said. "Not even a year ago. The stuff I have is already crumbling and breaking. It's going to have to be redone already." Ward dropped those baby blues to the stain on his shirt. "What is this? Some sort of Jell-O dish?"

"Raspberry cream whip," she said. "It's my mother's

recipe." And her offering for the potluck that had already started. She hadn't wanted to put the cold dessert out in the heat until the last minute. "It's about the only thing I can make without burning the house down."

Ward chuckled, and Dot's mouth actually dropped open. Who knew the man could even smile? He transformed in front of her, and her pulse sent erratic beats through her whole body.

Ward Glover....

*No*, she told herself. *Absolutely not.*

The man had been demanding and barely grateful in the past, and she wasn't interested in him simply because he was good-looking and older than twenty-five.

Wow, her criteria for a potential boyfriend had really dwindled.

"Can you *please* just come look at my gravel?" he asked, a pleading note in his voice and the same look in his eye.

"You should call Twin Cities," she said. "They should replace it."

"I did," he said. "They won't."

Annoyance sang through Dot. "I can't believe they're still in business." She hated companies that didn't take care of their customers. Dot worked tirelessly to make sure her patrons left happy, without a single complaint. Her reviews showed that, and From the Ground Up had been number one on the Two Cents app for months. Maybe a year now. It was no wonder she couldn't keep up with the business that came her way.

A wave of exhaustion threatened to overcome her, and Dot sighed as she sagged into the wall.

“Whoa, are you okay?” Ward jumped forward and put his hand under her elbow, as if that alone could hold her should she faint. The hallway spun, creating four more Ward Glover’s in front of her, all of them with those intense blue eyes inside a handsome face. His beard all trimmed nicely, and his hair shaved on the sides but long on top.

“Dot,” he said, but his voice echoed in her ears. Something clattered on the floor, and Dot felt too hot with his skin touching hers. At the same time, a cold sweat had formed along her hairline, and Dot closed her eyes.

“Dot?” Ward asked, his arms around her fully now. The scent of raspberries filled her nose, along with the woodsy, clean scent of Ward’s cologne and shirt. “Hey, Dot, talk to me.”

“I’m right here,” she slurred, but she wasn’t all the way there.

“Come on,” he said, and he got her to walk. She didn’t want to leave raspberry cream whip all over the hallway, but Ward didn’t give her a choice. Stupid man. He didn’t always have to get what he wanted.

“Sit on down here, Dot,” he said, his voice tender. Not at all like what Dot had expected. The world stilled, and the room came into focus. He’d brought her into the pastor’s office, and the chair beneath her was soft and padded.

He crouched in front of her, his eyes earnest and concerned. Also something new for Ward Glover. She honestly hadn’t believed the man could be anything but a beast.

"Are you okay?" he asked, his voice low and slow.

"Yes," she said, everything coming back into clarity. "I dropped the plate the cream whip was on."

"I'll clean it all up," he said. "I think you should stay here. You're white as a ghost."

"I'm okay," she said, but she wasn't in any hurry to get up.

"I'll go get you some food," he said, straightening. "Okay? Anything you don't like? Allergies?"

Dot's brain wasn't quite working all the way, and she shook her head. "Anything's fine."

"Please stay here," he said, and that reminded her of the demanding foreman she'd known and worked with in the past.

Ward left the office, and Dot stared at the painting hanging above the pastor's desk. It was of the Savior, and he looked steadily back at her with kind, knowing eyes. In that moment, she realized that she'd been projecting some of her ex-fiancé's qualities onto Ward, simply because they had the same name.

The cowboy returned quickly—at least in Dot's mind. She wasn't sure how much time had passed while she sat there inside her own thoughts. He'd piled a plate with pulled pork and macaroni salad, and she thought he must've called her sister to ask what Dot liked best.

"Thank you," she said quietly, taking the plate and then the fork.

"I'll be right back," he said, and he quickly left the office again.

Dot started to eat slowly, the food bringing back some

of her strength. She sometimes forgot to eat while working too, and it really wasn't very healthy for her to do that. She needed to monitor her blood sugar levels better, and she should've dug into her pocket and pulled out one of the hard candies she kept there the moment the vertigo had hit her.

Ward returned to the office several minutes later, another plate piled with food in his hands. "Can I eat in here with you?" he asked.

Again, he was so much nicer than she'd ever given him credit for. "Okay," she said, and he rounded the desk and sat where Pastor Corning usually did. Dot speared a piece of macaroni and put it in her mouth, racking her brain for something to say to Ward.

She couldn't come up with anything, and they ate in strained silence. *Well, that's about how all of your relationships with cowboys have been*, she thought. Why should she expect things to be different with Ward?

Just because he'd been kind once didn't mean they were going to start dating. Even if he asked her out, she'd say no. The man carried power and arrogance in his very stride, and Dot had had enough of cocky cowboys. The end.

So she'd eat her pork and her pasta, collect her plate, and get on home—where she'd make another batch of raspberry cream whip and eat it all herself.

## Chapter Twenty-Four

Arizona Rhinehart paced in the kitchen, wearing the old linoleum beneath her booted feet. A sob filled her chest, where she tried to swallow against it. "Where is he?" she asked, stepping over to the back door and opening it.

The early August heat hit her squarely in the face, and her first reaction was to slam the door and keep the hot air out. The air conditioner in the old house where she lived with her husband, Duke, could barely keep up as it was. They lived only a hop, skip, and jump from the southern border of Shiloh Ridge, and Zona could see the fence separating the two properties from the back door.

She didn't see her husband.

She'd called him twenty minutes ago, and he'd said he'd come right in. She'd been crying on the phone too, but she wanted to tell him in person.

She put one hand on her flat stomach, trying to feel the

life there. She couldn't, of course, though she did feel drastically different today than she had yesterday. Knowing she was pregnant had changed everything.

Feeling calmer, Zona closed the door, a new wave of fears and doubts threatening to crush her. She was a loud, obnoxious Glover. Every time she got together with her family, she had to coach herself mentally to stay quiet. She didn't have to have an opinion on everything. Other people could talk. They could be right, even if she knew they were wrong. She didn't have to call everyone out on everything, the way she'd done in the past.

Duke had taught her that, and a powerful swell of love for the man filled her. "Please hurry," she whispered, leaning against the counter in front of the kitchen sink so she could look out the window.

Just then, her husband's truck came into view, and she spun away from the kitchen sink. She hurried to the door and yanked it open just as he jogged around the front of the pickup. "Zona," he said when he saw her. "What's going on?"

She sobbed as she flew into his arms, and finally, finally, everything was okay in the world.

"Baby," he said, stroking her hair. "What's wrong? Are you hurt? I came as quick as I could, but we've got flooding out in the second acre, and I had to wait for the stupid cows to wade through it to get by."

She nodded against his shoulder, just so glad he was there. She drew in a long breath, and then another one. Finally able to think, she pulled away and looked up at him.

He wore concern in his dark eyes, and he searched her face for an answer.

"I'm pregnant," she said, a smile bursting onto her face. "I got the call from Dr. Sudweeks right before I called you."

"You're pregnant," he repeated, and then his own smile took up his whole face. He laughed as he lifted her right off her feet. "That's great news, baby." He spun her around before setting her down, both of them laughing now.

He wiped her face and gazed at her with such love and adoration in his eyes. Most of the time, Zona didn't know what he saw in her. She wasn't especially pretty, and she had strong opinions and plenty of vocal cords to express them. Not only that, but she didn't want a man telling her what to do. She considered herself extremely feminist, and she could do anything Duke could do.

She'd never particularly wanted to be a mother, though she'd once told Duke if they could have all boys, she'd give him as many as he wanted.

She had no idea what to do with a girl. She barely did her own hair, and she only wore makeup when she went to church. If then. She didn't paint nails or bake or even like to shop all that much. She had a few pairs of boots for working around the ranch, a pair of sneakers, and a couple of pairs of sandals she wore with her skirts on the Sabbath Day.

No closets full of shoes. No jewelry. No desire to learn how to braid hair or dress a child in the latest fashions.

"I hope it's a boy," she whispered as they both quieted. "Can you please pray that it'll be a boy?" She leaned her forehead against Duke's, taking the comfort she needed from his touch. He was so good to her. He cared about her, and he took care of her from morning until night. Every day. All week.

They'd been married for over eighteen months now, and they'd been talking about starting a family for the past six.

Duke took her face in his hands and said, "We'll love it no matter what it is."

"I can't do hair," she said. "I don't know how to paint nails. I—"

"Honey," he interrupted. "It'll be born a *baby* girl, not a teenager." He grinned at her, the smile sliding off his face. "Are you not happy about being pregnant?"

"I am," she said.

"Honestly?" he asked. "I don't want you to be unhappy about this. I thought we'd agreed to try for a baby."

"We did."

"I pushed you into it." He stepped back, his eyebrows drawing down.

Zona saw him slipping away from her, and she reached for hm. "No, Duke. No, you didn't." She took both of his hands in hers, and the sun blazed down on them. "Let's go inside. It's too dang hot out here."

They went into the house together, and Zona busied herself with getting out glasses and sweet tea. "You didn't push me into having a baby," she said. "I'm just nervous about a lot of things. Life changes when you have kids."

"I know," Duke said.

She set a glass of tea in front of him and joined him at

the table. "I'm happy about this," she said. "So happy I cried, and when do I ever cry?" She gave him a smile, and thankfully, her husband returned it.

The grin slipped away quickly though. "I'm going to fix up the house for you," he said. "I am."

"The house is fine," Zona said.

"It's not fine." He shook his head. "Arizona, I want to give you the world. I just don't have the money."

She took a drink of her tea. "If it's that important to you, baby, we have the money.

"No," he said firmly, shaking his head before she'd even finished speaking. "Absolutely not. I'm not using your money to build us a house."

"It's *our* money now, Duke," she said, imploring him to understand. "Bear's not telling Sammy she can't use his money. Ace and Holly Ann don't have separate assets. I know for a fact Bishop paid off all of Montana's debts. It's what people do when they get married. They merge their lives, money and all."

A storm blew across his handsome face, and indecision raged in his eyes. "I don't want to feel weak," he admitted. "I already took so much from your family, and I can't fix that."

"Baby." She took his hand in hers again. "You *have* fixed that. No one even thinks about it anymore but you." Arizona wondered if she could pull out just one particle of her Glover DNA and get through to Duke. "I want a beautiful nursery for our new baby. I'm going to call Bishop and Montana and ask them to come meet with me. She'll design us a gorgeous house, and then they'll build it for us.

If there's no land here on the Rhinehart Ranch, I know we can find a spot at Shiloh Ridge."

She spoke with confidence, but she hoped not too much. "Tell me what you're thinking."

"I'm thinking that we could raze this house and rebuild right here," he said. "Kind of like how Bear did with the homestead."

Zona's hopes lifted. "And we can live in the Top Cottage until the house is done."

"Okay," Duke said with a sigh. "This is hard for me, Zona. *I* want to provide everything for you."

"Don't you know you already do?" she asked, getting up and moving to sit on his lap. "You do, Duke. You're my whole world." She gently removed his cowboy hat and set it on the table in front of him. "Just you, baby. You and me. Isn't that what we said?"

"Yes," he murmured.

"The money doesn't matter," she said, lowering her mouth toward his. "It's just you and me. That's all that matters."

"And the baby now," he whispered, touching his lips to hers. He kissed her slowly, with plenty of passion, and Arizona fell in love with him all over again.

"Yes," she said after she'd pulled away. She snuggled into his chest. "And the baby now."

---

"HOLY BRANDS AND SADDLES, ZONA." PREACHER GAPED at her and then the Corvette. "It looks brand-new."

"It nearly is brand-new," she said, running her hand along the hood. "I've been working on it for months."

"Does she run?"

Zona scoffed, irritated with Preacher's question. "Of course she runs," she said. "Do you think I'd have invited you to come up here if she didn't?" She wasn't going to tell Preacher about the completion of the restoration, but something had been nagging at her for a week. Her conscience. The Lord. Something.

Preacher didn't have to give her the Corvette. Daddy had left it to him in his will, legal and fair and square and all that. He'd done nothing with it, though, because Preacher had always worked like a dog around Shiloh Ridge.

"You went with the red," he said, stepping over to the trunk to admire the paint job.

"I decided the black would be too hot." She'd texted him a few things over the months, little questions about what type of upholstery to put on the seats or what color to paint the Corvette. "I named her Stony. You know, for Daddy."

Preacher grinned, his examination of the sports car just beginning. "This is so great, Zona. Have you driven it?"

"A few times," she said. "You can take her for a spin if you want. That's why I called."

"I'd love that."

Zona dug the keys out of her pocket. "Sammy's been helping, so she runs pretty great."

"Sammy is pretty great," Preacher said. "Don't you think?"

"Bear definitely lucked out when he got her to marry him," Zona said with a smile. "I'm still not sure how he did it."

"Yeah, no kidding." Preacher's expression took on a slight edge, but Zona didn't know why. She and Preacher weren't exactly close, though their friendship had been growing and changing over the past seven months since he'd given her the Corvette.

Preacher reached the front of the car where Zona stood. He hesitated for a moment, a mere breath of time, and then he took her into an embrace. "Thank you for calling me to come see it," he said, his voice low and filled with emotion. "I apologize again for keeping it from you for so long."

Zona's emotions had been on a roller coaster since she'd learned she was pregnant. She and Duke hadn't told anyone yet, not even his parents or Mother. She pressed her eyes closed as they filled with tears, sincerely hoping and praying she wouldn't be weepy for the next nine months.

She didn't have time for that.

"You're welcome," she managed to say, and when she stepped back and looked into her brother's eyes, all of the trouble between them simply washed away. It went right under the bridge and downstream, where neither of them had to deal with it anymore.

They smiled simultaneously, and Preacher, never one to mince words said, "Forgive, and you will be forgiven."

"I do forgive you, Preach."

"And I forgive you," he said, ducking his head. He drew

in a deep breath and looked down the length of the car again. "Now, should we drive this thing? How fast can she go?" His eyes lit up like a child's on Christmas morning, and Zona tipped her head back and laughed.

As they buckled into the Corvette, she said, "Get 'er on the highway, Preach, and let's see how fast she can go."

"Daddy would've loved this," he said, twisting the key. The engine roared to life, chugging along for a few moments while they looked at one another, both of them smiling like fools.

"Yes," Zona said as he shifted into first gear and got the sports car moving forward. "Daddy would've loved this." She missed her father deeply in that moment and all the way down the road from the Rhinehart Ranch.

She thought of his first line of her letter, and a smile touched her soul. *My dearest, most precious daughter, how I love you.*

And right then, Zona knew that she'd love her baby even if it was a girl, and that the Lord wouldn't give her anything she couldn't handle.

# Chapter Twenty-Five

Judge pulled on an old pair of jeans—one of his favorite articles of clothing, because they were well-worn and soft. They were also two sizes too big because he'd once weighed more. But he couldn't stand the thought of getting rid of the jeans.

Judge Glover didn't get rid of much of anything. The basement in the Ranch House had four bedrooms, but his Christmas lights had started to creep into a third. He told himself it didn't matter, because no one lived down there anyway. Mister had moved out a long time ago, and a pang of regret cut through him as he cinched a belt around his waist.

He pulled it, his hand flying to the right as the buckle broke through the leather. "Shootin' stars," he grumbled, removing the belt from the loops and dropping it on his unmade bed. He opened his top drawer to look for another belt, but he didn't have one.

"Great." He looked at himself in the mirror on the back of his door, deciding he could work on the Christmas light display without a belt. When he went out onto the ranch to get the horses fed and the cattle rotated, he'd put on a pair of pants that fit and pull a rope from one of the barns to use as a belt.

In any spare time he could find, he'd been steadily putting up the display for this year's lights. He'd been sketching designs for a couple of months, and as August had dawned a few days ago, he was actually quite late physically getting the lights out to the yard.

Downstairs, he lifted two boxes full of soldiers and mice and carried them upstairs. Out on the porch, he set them down and returned to the basement for more. He had to keep pulling up his pants, but he didn't care. Comfort trumped everything, in Judge's opinion.

He got busy setting the soldiers in a straight row along the edge of the lawn on the west side of the Ranch House. He ran the cords and tested to make sure every light lit up the proper way.

With one earbud in and his favorite eighties music podcast playing, Judge could easily spend hours on the light display. He could hear Mister's mocking voice when he threw Judge's hobby in his face, and he frowned.

He needed to do something about Mister. "What you need to do is apologize." He hitched up his pants and returned to the porch for a string of red lights to put along the fence behind the soldiers. He could animate that to flash when the soldiers were off, right on the beat they'd marched to earlier in the show.

No one would even realize how perfect it was, but it would complete the show in a way that would leave them feeling like they'd just seen something great. All of those feelings lay in the details no one paid any attention to except for Judge.

The sun started to bake the Earth, and Judge wiped the sweat from his face. He removed his cowboy hat and pushed his hair back before putting it back on. Preacher had left early that morning to work out on the ranch, because he had a date with Charlie that night.

Judge assumed he did, anyway. Preacher always seemed to be going to Three Rivers, and he didn't check with Judge before or after. He was his own person, that was for sure, and Preacher valued his privacy above a lot of other things. Judge didn't mind giving it to him. He didn't need to know every detail of his brothers' lives, though he often felt a little removed from them because he didn't ask more questions.

Parched, he went into the Ranch House, searching the kitchen at the back of the space when he heard someone talking. All of the Glover men had a similar twang, but none as pronounced as Mister.

The man had ridden the rodeo circuit for a few years, and that had added swagger and salt to his personality that Judge didn't care for. His accent had deepened, and his opinions gotten louder. Judge couldn't seem to hold his own tongue when it came to Mister, and he paused, thinking maybe his footsteps hadn't been heard.

Mister said something else, and irritation burst through Judge. What was Mister doing here anyway? He hadn't lived here for over two years now. True, no one really knocked at the houses out here on the ranch, and Judge himself walked into the homestead any old time he wanted.

Mister turned toward him though, which meant he'd heard the footsteps. Judge lifted his hand in a wave, the lines from his father's letter running through his mind.

*When Grandmother gave you the nickname Judge, I wasn't happy. I told her that was too much for a boy of nine years old to carry. It's not up to you to judge anything. I still believe that, Judge, because there is only one Master and one God who can truly judge us.*

*But your brothers will need you in the years ahead. You have a strong personality and a good head on your shoulders. When they come to you, don't turn them away. Seek counsel from the Lord and help them as lovingly and as gently as you can.*

*As you grew, you grew into your name, my son. It fits you now, and Grandmother once again proved how very smart she was.*

*Stay close to your family, Judge. They'll need you, but you'll need them just as badly.*

"Hey," Mister said, and Judge blinked. They'd had such a great dance going, where they seemed to know instinctively where the other was, and they simply avoided each other. Shiloh Ridge was plenty big, with plenty to do. "Sorry, I was dying to use the bathroom and I needed a drink. I didn't think anyone was here."

"It's okay," Judge said automatically. He even took a step closer to the kitchen. Mister had lowered his phone, which he'd been talking into, and tucked it into his back pocket. He now held a bottle of water, which he drained half of while Judge took a few more careful steps toward his brother.

"I want to talk to you," Judge said. "I just never know how."

Mister wore a leery look in his eye, which Judge didn't blame him for. Suddenly, the right thing to say popped into his mind.

And it was so simple.

Yet it hurt as it came out of his mouth. "I'm sorry, Mister." He swallowed as his younger brother's eyes rounded in surprise. "I'm sorry for what I said. Of course you weren't wrong for feeling the way you did when Bear got married. All of us struggled. And of course Daddy's letter was right about you."

Mister's eyes hardened at the mention of the letter, and Judge hated that his brother regretted showing it to him. "I was wrong to say you were acting like a baby, and I was wrong to say you've had everything handed to you. It's just not true. You work as hard as any of us. More, because you actually went out there and made your own career."

His chest heaved, and Judge couldn't remember the last time he'd spoken so much at once. "I'm sorry for the pranks. Everyone hates them, and I've been doing them less and less. I just felt...." He didn't know how to finish. It didn't matter how he felt anyway. All that mattered was how *others* felt when he moved their vehicles or took stupid pictures on their phones when they left them lying around.

"Insignificant," Mister said, and Judge's eyes flew back to his.

"Yes," he said. "Somehow, me getting after you for how I interpreted you to be failing made me feel less like a loser. Less like a failure. Less insignificant." He could barely see, but he'd started and come this far. "I'm sorry. I'm so, so sorry."

Because he wasn't less of a failure when he judged Mister. He'd become a bigger one.

Mister held his gaze for several long moments, and Judge knew he might not grant his forgiveness. That was a consequence Judge couldn't control.

"I know I didn't make things easy for you," Mister said, ducking his head. "I'm sorry too, Judge."

Relief cascaded through Judge. He continued into the kitchen, pulling up his pants and smiling at his brother. "Okay."

"Okay." Mister barely returned the smile. "I was on the phone with Wyatt, and he wants to meet about doing another rodeo camp." He held up his phone. "I better go." Just like that, Judge nodded, and Mister walked out, and the door clicked closed behind him.

Judge took a moment to realize how different he felt, and then he pressed his eyes closed and said, "Thank you, Lord." He felt better. He felt cleansed. He felt like he'd done something wrong and made it right.

Finally.

---

AN HOUR LATER, JUDGE SANG ALONG TO THE SONG playing through his earbuds. He'd gotten properly hydrated and cooled down before returning to the yard to get the next section of the train set up.

He hadn't used the train in a while, and he had his doubts it would work this year. He didn't have a sophisticated enough system to run the train and a whole bunch of other lights. He needed a dedicated hotspot just for the lights display, but all of his calls to Juniper Nichols had gone unanswered and unreturned.

She probably thought his pleas for help were a ploy just to get her out to the ranch. She wouldn't be wrong. Judge did want to see her, but he needed an upgrade to his network too. June was a whiz with modems, the Internet, WiFi connections, and all of that.

She'd founded and run Nichols Networking twenty years ago, and they had branches in Oklahoma, out in Lubbock, and as far south as Abilene.

They'd been the main service provider in Three Rivers and Amarillo for years, and she traveled a lot between the two cities. She also had a sixteen-year-old daughter named Lucy Mae that she was fiercely protective of.

Judge had met the teen a couple of times, and he'd liked her just fine. She'd seemed to like him.

But June had ended their barely-there relationship pretty quickly, citing that she wasn't interested in dating until Lucy Mae was grown and out of the house. Judge had some daytime personality on the radio to thank for that, as June listened to Stacy Says religiously and agreed with a lot of what the parenting and relationship expert said.

Heck, Judge agreed with a lot of what Dr. Stacy Brown

said too. He wasn't a single father, so he wasn't sure how he'd feel about bringing someone new into his child's life. What he did know was that no one had intrigued him and excited him as much as June Nichols had and did in at least a decade.

He'd called her several times to come look at the network she'd installed a few years ago—which was how Judge had met her in the first place. The attraction between them felt like a north pole coming close to a south, and he couldn't fight against it.

June certainly could though, and she was so much stronger than him. He knew, because she hadn't called him back. Not only that, but she hadn't even allowed one of her secretaries to return his calls.

His thoughts caught in a loop that went around June, he bent over, sticking pins in the ground to keep the cords down so they wouldn't be seen. One of his favorite songs came on, and he started to sing along with it.

Out at the Ranch House, it didn't matter if he yelled. No one would hear him, so he really poured the energy of his soul into the song. Down the row he went, pinning the cord in place and adjusting a few of the bigger lawn lights to make sure they sat just-so.

The song ended, and in that tiny fraction of silence, he heard something.

Applause.

Horror filled him as he spun around, expecting to see Preacher or maybe even Mister again. They'd heard him singing, and they'd be mocking him with their false applause. After all, Judge wasn't the singer of the Glover family. In fact, he could barely carry a tune at all.

When he saw the gorgeous blonde standing at the end of his sidewalk, he dang near ripped his earbuds out. Trying to process her stunning, crooked smile, all Judge could say was, "June. What are you doing here?"

"Keep your pants on, cowboy," she said in her perfect Texas drawl. She wore a pair of khaki shorts and a polo with the double-N logo of her company on the front of it. "I came to help with your network."

"You're kidding," he said.

Her eyes slid down to his boots at back. "Not kidding—about either of the things I said." She nodded to his lower half. "You're losing your pants."

Double horror struck him in the form of hot embarrassment as he looked down and saw his jeans were nearly off his hips. And he'd had his back toward the sidewalk... bent over....

*Dear Lord*, he thought. *Please don't—Please let her not have seen anything too humiliating.*

He hitched up his beloved jeans and looked at June again, heat filling his face faster than the sun rose in the morning. June grinned like she'd definitely seen something he hadn't wanted her to, and she lifted her briefcase. "Show me where the network is, cowboy. I'll see what magic I can work."

She'd already worked some sort of mysterious magic on his heart, and Judge couldn't believe she stood in front of him. His heart wailed at him to ask her out before she left today, but his brain told him he absolutely would not be doing that.

He liked seeing her, and if that meant only professionally, he'd take it...for now.

## Chapter Twenty-Six

Charlie swayed in the safety and warmth of Preacher's arms, everything about this night filled with wonder and love. He'd taken her dancing at a new hall that had gone in on the west side of town.

Clippers had amazing fried pickles and delicious hush-puppies. Preacher had eaten the tavern pretzels nearly by himself, and after they'd had the biggest, juiciest hamburgers Charlie had ever seen and tasted, he'd brought her onto the dance floor.

He really was a very good dancer, and he'd spun her around during the more lively tunes, then pulled her close and allowed their two heartbeats to mesh into one during the slower numbers.

Neither of them had spoken during this song, and Charlie's adrenaline had faded a few minutes ago.

"Ready to go?" Preacher asked as the song ended.

Charlie nodded as she applauded for the live band providing the music that night, and she followed Preacher back to their table to get her purse and their leftovers. He held her hand on the way out to his Mustang, and she smiled at the convertible. Darkness had stolen the light from the day about an hour ago, but plenty of heat remained in the air. Driving back to her house with the wind in her hair, the stars plainly visible overhead, and her hot cowboy boyfriend behind the wheel sounded like a fantasy.

But she was living it.

Once they'd pulled away from the dance hall, Preacher cleared his throat. That alerted Charlie, because she knew his tells by now. He was nervous about whatever he was about to say.

"I've been thinking," he said.

"Mm?" Charlie kept her eyes closed and her face turned into the wind, everything warm and wonderful about this night.

"Are you awake?"

"Yes," she said, turning toward him and opening her eyes. "I'm listening."

He focused on the road again, though they were the only vehicle on the road. "Maybe you'd like to go look at engagement rings with me."

Charlie choked on her own tongue. Or maybe her breath as it went down into her stomach instead of her lungs. Either way, she ended up coughing a couple of times and then squeaking, "What?"

"I don't know," Preacher said. "We've been dating for seven months, and—"

"Eight," Charlie said, her voice back to normal, thankfully. "We've been dating for eight months."

"Eight months," Preacher said, glancing at her. "I feel good about us. I'm thinking it might be time to take the next step." He looked at her for a few moments, the silver moonlight casting his into glowing shadows. "What do you think?"

Charlie looked out the windshield, the breeze trying to steal her hair and whip it into the sky behind them. "I think...I think if that's something you're really serious about...." She looked at him, waiting for him to say he wasn't really all that serious about marrying her.

"I am," he said. "I know you said you needed time to come to the idea of marriage, and that's fine. I just was thinking we could *start* looking at rings. Just start."

Charlie nodded, because she wanted to go right now. "I think it's time I met the family then."

Preacher jerked his attention to her, shock undulating from him in great waves. When he didn't say anything, she added, "I want to come up to the ranch, Preach. I've never been up there. Not really. I've never seen what you do for a job. Don't you think that's kind of weird?"

"No," he said.

"You're ingrained into my life and culture," she said. "You've been on my stream several times, and you've met my sister. I think my neighbors think you've moved in for how often you're at my house. I've never been inside your house. I've never met your mother. Or all of your brothers. I know precious little about your ranch. I just—"

"It's not my ranch," he said.

"Okay," she said, instantly frustrated. "You know what I meant."

He didn't argue, because he did know what she meant. "Are you embarrassed of me?" she asked.

"Of course not. If anything, you're a step up from me."

"That's not true," she said quietly, the magic in the breeze completely gone now. "You're embarrassed of them, then."

"Not entirely."

"They're just too loud."

"They *are* loud," he said.

"I can handle loud," she said. "I'm *asking* you for the loud."

"I hear you."

"Do you?" she asked. "This isn't the first time we've talked about it, and nothing changes."

"We haven't had any big family things," he said.

"So there has to be a big family thing to introduce me to them?" She shook her head, her anger starting to bloom. "I don't buy that, Preacher. You could take me to sit by them at church. You don't. You could invite me to the ranch to eat lunch with you. According to you, everyone gathers in the homestead, no matter what day of the week. You don't. I sit at home, eating some take-out while strangers watch me."

She shook her head, because he was being ridiculous. "I don't know what you're waiting for. If you're really serious about looking at engagement rings and getting married, I need to meet your family. All of them."

"I realize that." He left the town of Three Rivers behind and started up into the hills where her gated community sat concealed behind and beneath trees.

She didn't think he did. "Because you're not going to move into the northeast hills and my house. You're going to live right there on that ranch. Which means I am too. Am I just supposed to automatically be friends with everyone? Have you ever thought that I might need time to fit into your family too?"

"*I* don't fit into my family."

"So you're worried I'll fit better, and you'll be an even bigger black sheep. Is that it?"

"No," he bit out. "You're making stuff up now."

"You're the one making things up," she said as the car started to move faster. "You're the one who's been feeding yourself stories about why your family won't like me. Or why you need to keep me away from them. Or whatever it is you've been doing."

"I never said they wouldn't like you."

"You think they'll like me more than you?"

"No."

"Then what?" she demanded. "Why have you kept me from them?"

Preacher gripped the steering wheel like he wanted to rip it from the column and throw it away while they were still in the car. "I don't know. I just like having you to myself."

"Sounds like an excuse." She folded her arms and

pressed her lips into a tight line. The rest of the drive to her house happened in tense silence, and Preacher got out of the car with her and walked her to the door.

Normally, she'd kiss him goodnight right there on the stoop. More often than not, she invited him inside and doctored him up with coffee. *Then* she kissed him goodnight until she couldn't breathe, and he was whispering about how early he had to get up in the morning. Then he'd kiss her some more, and he'd finally leave a half an hour from now.

Tonight, she simply fitted her key into the lock, and said, "Thanks for taking me dancing. I think I'm getting better."

"You are," he said from behind her, and Charlie hated it. Like, hated it with the power of a dozen suns.

She stepped into the house and faced him, one step higher than she normally was when looking at him. She stared at him, waiting for him to say something. But he wasn't a character in one of her video games, and she couldn't prompt him to tell her what she wanted to hear.

She rolled her eyes and fell back a step, her finger curling around the door. "What's next for you at the ranch? Your next big event?"

"Market day," he said. "Remember, it's next week?"

"Right," she said. "I could come for that?"

"It's noisy," he said. "We're rounding up cattle for days, and then all these semis come. I'm in charge this year, and I won't be around at all. Everyone is busy. We don't have a shared meal or anything."

Another excuse. Charlie nodded, her insides burning

and ready to burst. "Goodnight. Drive safe." She started to close the door.

"Charlie."

She didn't stop the door from swinging closed, and for good measure, she locked it too. He knocked, the sound loud and booming through her double-story foyer. "Come on, Charlie," he called from the other side of the door.

"Come on what?" she muttered to herself as she dropped her purse and phone on the front table. Paulie came around the corner to see what all the banging was about. Charlie bent and scooped him up, saying, "He doesn't have a good reason for keeping me from them. At least one I can make sense of. What's inside his head?"

Her cat simply snuggled into her, no answers in sight. Preacher didn't knock again, and after Charlie had changed into her pajamas and brushed her teeth, she tiptoed into the office without turning on the light.

The Mustang was gone. Preacher had left.

Sadness draped over her, because she didn't want to lose him. But he came with a family, and she wasn't going to spend her life as a kept woman, away from and out of all the family activities simply because he didn't want to share her with the men and women at Shiloh Ridge Ranch.

Acting quickly, she strode back to the foyer and picked up her phone. *Call me when you get home so I know you made it safely*, she typed out and sent to Preacher, hoping he'd be able to read between the lines and know that while she was mad at him, she didn't want to break up with him. She wanted to talk to him again tonight.

He didn't respond, and Charlie told herself he had an

hour-long drive back to the ranch. She returned to her bedroom, plugged in her phone, and got underneath her puffy comforter. With Archie on her left and Paulie on her right, Charlie fell asleep without a response from Preacher.

## Chapter Twenty-Seven

Preacher slammed his open hand against the steering wheel as he drove away from Charlie's. He wouldn't be so angry if she wasn't so right.

"Go back and apologize," he told himself. He wouldn't though, because he knew Charlie, and she wouldn't open the door tonight. She needed a few minutes to calm down and then she would.

Preacher slowed to pull over. Maybe he could just hold here for a few minutes and then go back. A tidal wave of exhaustion overcame him, and he kept going. He still had an hour drive in front of him.

His phone rang, and his heart leapt into the back of his throat. Mister's name came up on the screen, and that sent a dash of surprise and a lash of disappointment through Preacher. He still tapped to answer and said, "You're up late."

"Yeah, I was wondering if you had a minute."

"Yeah, I just dropped off Charlie. What's up?" Preacher prayed it had nothing to do with the ranch. He didn't have the mental capacity to deal with pinkeye or pasture rotation, mechanical issues or market day. Not right now.

"Remember how you and Ward said Libby Bellamore liked me?"

Oh, this was a woman problem. Preacher relaxed, the tension in his muscles simply evaporating. He hadn't even realized how tight he'd been. "Yeah."

"I asked if I could come out to Heritage and bring lunch, and she acted weird."

"Weird, how?"

"She's normally all bubbly and nice. We're friends, you know?" He continued to say that she hadn't really answered him, and Mister felt lost as to what to do next. He and Liberty Bellamore had grown up together and were the same age. They had been friends for a lot of years and while Preacher himself had never tried to expand that box, he supposed it could be a challenge to do so.

"Maybe you weren't real clear," Preacher suggested. "You didn't really ask her out. You made it sound like you were coming to hang out and bring food."

"I guess." Mister sounded miserable, and Preacher wished he could help. But it all honesty, he should be the last person to offer relationship advice. Heck, his own girlfriend—a very serious girlfriend—had just closed the door in his face.

He sighed too, and said, "She probably doesn't want you to try to get her to set you up with anyone else."

Mister stayed quiet for a minute and said, "That was really stupid, wasn't it?"

"She probably got her feelings hurt," Preacher said, grasping onto that. "Maybe apologize for that and then ask her to dinner. Not lunch on her ranch. That's what *friends* do, and you want to be *more* than friends." When Mister remained silent, Preacher asked, "Right?"

"I don't know what I want."

Preacher looked out the side window at the darkness streaking by. He'd left Charlie's gated neighborhood behind a few minutes ago, and the road wound down out of some shallow hills to Three Rivers. He'd skirt the town and take the east highway out toward the Bellamore's actually, and then go past Seven Sons to the main highway that connected to Shiloh Ridge.

"Anyway, thanks," Mister said, and Preacher felt like he'd missed something.

"Yeah," Preacher said, and the call ended. Thankfully, the relaxation and comfort he'd gotten from talking through a problem with his brother stayed, and Preacher sank back into his seat even more. The big bucket seats in his Mustang cradled him, and he let out a long sigh.

His mind wandered, and there were no other cars on the road, so he drove right down the middle of the highway. He made the turn to head south around Three Rivers, the country Texas silence soothing him further.

"Charlie is right," he said. "I should've brought her to meet the family before talking about buying engagement rings." He shook his head at his idiocy, once again wondering why he didn't just ask Ace or Bishop for help. Heck, Bear and Cactus knew more about how to deal with women than Preacher did. Ward always had a new date, and Ranger had seemingly done everything right with Oakley, if their fast courtship, engagement, and marriage indicated anything.

The long line of monotonous road stretched before him, and Preacher yawned, his tiredness a physical, palpable being in the car with him. It kept tugging at his conscious, trying to drag him under when he needed to stay awake and get home.

He reached over to switch on the radio, just to have something to jolt him back awake. The music worked for a few minutes, and he even sang along to one of his favorite country songs. He was going to make it back to Shiloh Ridge Ranch just fine, despite the way his mind turned soft and his attention wandered.

His eyelids lowered, and Preacher jerked himself awake again. He rolled down the window, but the air outside was hotter than the air conditioner blowing inside the sports car.

He pressed on the gas to get himself closer to the road at Seven Sons. Closer to home. He just had to make it home.

After a few seconds—he didn't know how long—his head drooped again. He'd taken his eyes from the lonely ribbon of road for maybe a second. Maybe two or three.

No matter what, when he looked out the windshield again, two deer were right there in front of him.

A yelp flew from his throat.

He hit the brakes, but it was too late.

He jerked the wheel to the right to avoid them.

The Mustang didn't handle the same way as his pickup truck, and the next thing Preacher knew, he was upside down.

Rolling.

Off the road.

The horrible crunching sound of metal and glass filled his world.

Pain sliced through his legs.

His vision went dark.

The last thing he heard was the sound of his own voice groaning.

---

SOMETIME LATER, PREACHER BECAME AWARE OF HIMSELF again. Something throbbed from his hip down, and his eyes snapped open.

The radio played.

Gasoline scented the air.

He lay with his head against the doorframe, because the car sat on the side.

Panic filled him, and Preacher could blink, but he couldn't move. After what felt like a very long time, he managed to say, "Help."

He definitely needed help. And fast.

*Get your phone*, he thought, and he lifted his head from the side of the door where he normally rested his forearm if he'd rolled down the window in the Mustang.

His phone...had been plugged in. He'd spoken to Mister several minutes before the car accident.

He fumbled around in the dark, the music he'd turned on to keep himself awake only increasing his headache now.

He found the cord and pulled on it gently, as if teasing a fish to bite.

His phone came up, but the bright light from the screen caused a round of vertigo that sent nausea through him. He clenched his eyes closed and then squinted at the screen, trying to find Mister's name.

His vision swam.

His hips were on fire. His leg throbbed.

He stabbed at the phone, saying, "Don't let me pass out. Please, Lord, don't let me pass out."

As the line rang, Preacher passed out.

---

AGAIN, PREACHER SWAM TOWARD THE SURFACE OF consciousness. Someone was yelling his name. He needed to tell them where he was. He needed to tell them he needed help.

Another groan dribbled from his mouth, and he recognized the voice.

*Mister.*

He must've gotten through.

"Help," Preacher whispered. "Off the road...."

"Where?" Mister demanded. "Preacher, *where?*"

*East highway*, Preacher thought as the darkness tugged at him again. As the pain overcame his ability to speak once more. All he could do was pray he'd actually said the words out loud and that someone would find him before it was too late as he drifted into unconsciousness yet again.

## Chapter Twenty-Eight

Mister Glover needed another phone. He didn't want to hang up with Preacher, though his brother had obviously passed out. The radio still came through the line, and Mister had never felt so frantic.

He burst out of his bedroom, already calling, "Ward!"

His cousin would be asleep. Mister should be too, as the clock had ticked to eleven just as he'd called Preacher the first time. Something had kept him awake that night, and he'd originally thought it was Libby Bellamore.

He knew now that it was the Lord, and that it was up to Mister to save Preacher's life.

"Ward," he yelled again as he rounded the corner from one hallway to another. He kept his phone in front of him, the blasted radio playing through the speaker, and he banged on the door as he entered.

"Ward, I need your phone."

"What in the world?"

"Preacher called, and he's in trouble." Mister thrust his phone at Ward, who sat up in bed. "I need to call Wyatt with your phone." He snatched the device from the nightstand and tapped in Wyatt Walker's number. "Let him pick up. He needs to pick up."

"Mister," Ward barked. "What's going on?"

"That's the radio in Preacher's car," Mister said as the line connected and started to ring. "He called me, but he wasn't there. I yelled his name a few times, and he woke up. He said help, and then he said he was off the road."

"Hello?" Wyatt answered, his voice froggy and filled with sleep.

"Praise the Lord," Mister said. "Wyatt, it's Mister Glover. My brother was up in your neighborhood maybe twenty minutes ago. His girlfriend lives up there. Charlie Perkins?"

"Sure, I know Charlie," Wyatt said easily, as if Mister hadn't woken him near midnight.

"I think Preacher got in a car accident, and I hate to ask it, but he passed out before he could tell me where."

"I'm pullin' on my boots now," he said without further explanation. "What was he driving?"

"He owns a couple of Mustangs," Mister said. "He drives 'em all summer, and this one has the radio playing. I still have him on the line, but he's not responding."

Ward had gotten out of bed, and he had his boots and jeans on too. "I'm going to hang up on my cousin's phone and call Bear. We'll leave the ranch as soon as we can and work our way toward you." His mind spun, but he had to keep everything together. Bear wasn't the only one who could come up with solutions, and Mister's emotions choked in his throat.

"I'll call this number if I find him," Wyatt said.

"Thank you, Wyatt," Mister said, his voice thin and barely able to come out his narrow throat.

"You got it." The call ended, and Mister immediately swiped and flipped to Bear's name.

"Let's get next door," Mister said, tapping to get the line open. "We need all the phones we can get. We need Mother to pray, and we need Brady to call his police friends." He left Ward's bedroom, his cousin right on his tail. "They won't see a text, I don't think."

"Did he say he was hurt?" Ward asked.

"He literally said *help*, and then *off the road*," Mister said, practically running now. The moment he left Bull House, he did break into a jog. He just had to get down the driveway and past the shed. Over to the homestead.

Bear answered with, "Ward, what in the world?"

"It's Mister," Mister said. "Preacher's been in a car accident. I've got him on my line, and I went to get Ward's phone." His breath came so fast, and his pulse sprinted. "I called Wyatt Walker, because Preach was up in that area at Charlie's house. He's already gone to look for him."

"I'm getting dressed," Bear said.

"Bring your phone. Bring Sammy's phone. We need everyone to know."

"Will do."

Mister entered the house, and Ward went to wake Etta. Bear came thundering downstairs with Ranger only a few minutes later, and Ward joined them in the kitchen. "Etta's calling Ida right now. She said she'd keep Ranger updated once she talks to her and Brady."

"I called Mother," Ranger said. "She's praying, and she's calling Aunt Lois."

"Let's go," Mister said. "How long since he called Ward?"

Ward looked at Mister's phone. "Seventeen minutes."

"Mostly passed out," Mister said, his throat clogged. Bear grabbed him and they held one another tightly.

"I'm not going to say it's going to be okay," Bear said, his voice breaking. "But let's go, and Ranger pray on the way down."

The four of them hurried out of the house, and Etta said, "I'm praying too," behind them.

"Thank you," Ward said, and he closed the door as the others went down the steps. Bear got behind the wheel, and Mister got in the back seat behind him. Once Ward was in the back with him, Bear took off down the hill.

"Lord," Ranger said right out loud. "We beseech Thee for protection for our brother and cousin Preacher Glover. We don't know where he is, and we don't know how he is." He paused, and Mister sniffled as he let himself cry.

He never cried. The last time was when he'd injured himself on the back of a bronco and the doctor had told him he couldn't ride in the rodeo anymore. His world had cracked then, and when it had crashed down, Mister had cried and cried.

Mother had told him he could cry as much as he wanted, because what he'd thought his life would be had suddenly changed. His dreams and everything he'd worked for over the course of a decade gone in less than five seconds.

"Protect him," Ranger finally said again, his own tears right there in the words. "Guide us. Sharpen our eyes, and those of Wyatt Walker, and help us find him quickly. Bless any who work on him or try to help him tonight with clear minds and steady hands."

Ranger stopped again, and it was Bear who said, "Amen, Lord."

"Amen," Ward said, but Mister couldn't get his voice to work. He exchanged phones with Ward and put his up to his mouth.

*Preacher*, he wailed silently. *Wake up*.

He took a deep breath. "Preach?" No answer. Only that stupid radio playing country music, Preacher's favorite.

The truck bounced down the dirt lane, and Bear paused at the highway. "Which way does he come back from Charlie's?" he asked.

"He didn't say," Mister said.

"Judge says he takes the east highway," Ward said, lifting his phone. "They're all coming in to the homestead. Etta's going to get Mother and Aunt Lois."

"East highway," Bear said, turning left. "We can go out past Seven Sons for that."

"That's the quickest way," Ranger said, his voice tight.

"Preacher?" Mister asked again. "We're on our way, okay? We're coming to the East Highway, but we're at least thirty minutes out. I called Wyatt, and he's looking too." He looked at Ward. "Maybe we should call nine-one-one right now too. Get them headed in that direction."

"Where?" Ward said. "We can't just send them out along a stretch of highway."

"I'll call," Bear said, tapping on the screen of his truck. Just before the turnoff to Seven Sons, he turned down another road, this one paved and a long, straight shot to the highway that ran north and past Three Rivers on the east side.

"Nine-one-one, state your emergency."

"This is Bear Glover," he said with utmost confidence. "My brother's been in an accident on the east highway, and he's not responding."

"Where on the east highway?" the woman asked.

"Just south of the turnoff that goes up to the gated community in the hills," Bear said. "He's been on the line for twenty minutes."

"Is he conscious?"

"No, ma'am."

"You don't know the exact location?"

"No, ma'am. His car is running, because we can hear the radio. We assume his lights will be on, and he won't be hard to find. We're just quite far away, and we're not doctors."

"I'm sending two police units and a paramedic unit."

"Thank you, ma'am."

Mister marveled at the calmness in Bear's voice. In his very mind, as Mister should've been able to zero in a little closer on where Preacher was. He hadn't left Charlie's that long ago, and Bear had picked up on that.

"Duke is on his way down from the Rhinehart's,"

Ranger said from the front seat. "He called Brit, who left Heritage a minute ago. He'll be closer than us."

"He will," Bear said.

The headlights cut through the darkness, and they fell into silence. The only noise was the tinny warbling of the country music playing in Preacher's car.

## Chapter Twenty-Nine

Wyatt Walker kissed his wife and said, "I'll call you as soon as I know anything."

"Wyatt, you have three children," she said. "Don't you dare put yourself in danger."

"I'm just going to be driving."

"In the middle of the night," his wife said, folding her arms.

"What can I do to make you more comfortable? They're friends. They need help."

"Call Jeremiah," Marcy said. "Rhett. Liam. I don't care. Someone who knows you're out there who I can call if you don't come home."

"I'll call Micah," Wyatt said, smiling at her. "Okay?"

"If I don't hear from you in thirty minutes, I'm calling Micah."

"Okay."

Marcy stepped into him and held him tightly. "I love you, Wyatt Walker. Please be safe."

"I love you too, Marce. I'll be home soon." With that, he went into the garage quickly and fired up his truck. He put the beams on high as he went down the road. He looked left when he passed Charlie Perkins's house and found only the porch light on. If she knew there'd been a problem with her boyfriend, the house didn't show it.

"She probably doesn't know," he said to himself. He wondered if he should stop and tell her, but the urgency to find Preacher nagged at him. Wyatt knew all the Glovers, as a couple of them rode out at Three Rivers Ranch, at the equine therapy unit there.

He'd seen them at Momma's parties, at church, and around town. He knew Preacher had recently started a new job up at the ranch as one of their foremen, and he knew Jeremiah regarded Bear Glover and everything up the hill at Shiloh Ridge in high regard.

"Wyatt?" Micah asked. "What's wrong?"

"Preacher Glover has been in some sort of car accident. Long story, but I'm headed down to see if I can find him, and Marcy's worried about my safety. I told her I'd call you, and if I don't check in before thirty minutes pass, she's calling you."

"I'll call everyone else," Micah said. "Update me, and I'll keep everyone appraised."

"Thanks." Wyatt let his brother hang up, and he slowed around every corner, scanning left and right, right and left.

His pulse bobbed in the back of his throat. He honestly had no idea what he'd do if he came upon the scene of the accident. He had some first aid training, only because he'd had to patch himself up a bit while riding bulls, and Marcy had wanted him to be able to help the kids if she was flying and he was home with the boys.

Boys tended to get into a lot of trouble, and Warren had definitely already had more than one skinned knee though he was only seven years old.

He made it all the way to the intersection without spotting any headlights or hearing any music. He had all the windows down, and he listened and looked straight ahead. Would Preacher have gone that way? He certainly wouldn't be going right, as that led north to Oklahoma.

"South," he said, but he didn't let off the brake. "Lord, did he go left?" If it were Wyatt, he'd take the east highway to get to Shiloh Ridge. He'd driven that road plenty of times to go to Seven Sons, unless he had to go into town for some reason.

Preacher wouldn't have a reason to go to town this late at night. His nerves settled, and Wyatt felt like taking a left and going down the highway toward Heritage Ranch and the road that led due west toward Seven Sons—and thus, Shiloh Ridge.

Wyatt eased his truck around the corner and got going again. "Lord, bless me to find him." He went twenty under the speed limit, constantly looking forward to both sides of the road simultaneously, and then scanning both sides as he got closer.

No headlights.

No music.

What if he'd chosen wrong?

He noted each mile marker he passed, knowing that would help emergency services should he need them.

Then, all at once, he saw a light on the horizon. Right side of the road. He pressed on the gas pedal and sped up, not even bothering to look anymore. He'd found Preacher Glover.

He pulled to a stop, nearly giving himself whiplash as he did, and grabbed his phone before jumping from the truck. Adrenaline drove him around the truck and out into the wild grasses and sage brush lining both sides of the highway.

Preacher's car sat on its side, all four wheels facing the highway. Country music filled the air, and Wyatt called, "Preacher," as he ran toward him. He fumbled his phone, but he managed to dial nine-one-one just as he arrived at the car.

"I need help," he said before the emergency operator even finished talking. "Mile marker twenty-three on the highway running north and south east of Three Rivers." He went around the front of the car, which had smoke leaking from it at a slow clip. "The car is smoking. He's strapped into the driver's seat with his seat belt. Should I get him out?"

Wyatt had no idea what to do, but he noticed the front windows were down.

"Is the car on fire?" the operator asked.

"No." Wyatt moved around to the top of the car, as he could get closer to the open window and Preacher that way. "Preacher? Can you hear me? It's Wyatt Walker."

"Is he bleeding, sir?"

"I can't tell," Wyatt said. "Wait, yes.... I think I can see some blood on the side of his face. His eyes are closed. He's leaning against the door on his side, down on the ground. The car is on its side." Wyatt remembered Mister was on the line with Preacher, and he spoke up. "I can see his chest moving up and down."

"Leave him, sir," the operator said. "We got a call about this accident about ten minutes ago. Mile marker twenty-three."

"Yes," Wyatt said as Preacher's hand moved. "He's waking up. Preacher," he called louder. He reached into the car and tapped the volume button on the radio to turn it off. The silence felt all-encompassing, and Wyatt said, "Preacher, it's Wyatt Walker. Mister called me. Look at me now, cowboy."

Preacher groaned, and Wyatt actually smiled. He scanned his body, the grin disappearing. "His legs are pinned beneath the dashboard. The blood on his face looks superficial. He's coming around."

With every word Wyatt said, Preacher became a little more aware. He turned his head toward Wyatt, his eyes fairly blank. "It's Wyatt, Preacher," he said. "The paramedics are coming, and your brothers are on their way too."

"I can't feel...." Preacher trailed off, his eyelids fluttering.

"Don't talk," Wyatt said. "Just stay with me. Look at me, Preach. Right here."

Preacher did what he said, his eyes filling with pain as he became even more aware. "Wyatt?"

"That's right," Wyatt said as he heard the first sounds of a siren. "Help is on the way, Preacher. Just look at me. I rode this horse named Nine Inches once in the rodeo...." He continued the story, asking Preacher to repeat parts of it along the way, until the paramedics arrived.

From there, they took over, and Wyatt retreated to his truck, where he leaned as he watched the six people who'd shown up get Preacher out of his car. He called Marcy and told her he was all right, and that he'd found Preacher.

He called Ward Glover's phone, and the man said, "We're five minutes out. Thank you, Wyatt."

Another truck pulled up to the scene, but only one man got out. "Brit," Wyatt said, stepping toward the other man. "Did the Glovers call you?"

"Yes." He stepped to the edge of the asphalt and stared out toward the car. "You called them?"

Wyatt stepped next to him. "Yes."

"How is he?"

"He woke up," Wyatt said. "But...he's going to have some problems with his legs."

"Oh, boy." Brit took off his hat and smoothed his hair back. "As if that family hasn't been through enough."

"They have?"

"Their daddy died when he was only forty-five. Then their uncle a few years later. Those boys have been running that ranch for decades by themselves. Doing a dang good job at it, sure. But I didn't have to take over my father's ranch until I was almost fifty."

"Mm." Wyatt watched as they finally got Preacher out of the car. Relief filled him, and he thought about Daddy and the car accident he'd been in several years ago. He'd been in a coma for months, and he couldn't stand the thought of anyone else having to go through that.

Moments later, another truck arrived, this one huge and growly. It had barely stopped before all four doors burst open. Bear, Ranger, Ward, and Mister Glover arrived, and they went right past Wyatt. Mister alone paused and clapped him on the shoulder with the words, "Thank you, Wyatt."

They crowded around the stretcher, one of them asking a lot of questions. They followed the paramedics to the ambulance, and Bear got in the back of it. The rest of them returned to the truck, and this time they all thanked Wyatt.

"Ranger," Brit said. "What do you need?"

"Let all of the ranch owners know, would you?"

"Yep. Food?"

"My sisters will keep us fed," Ranger said. "Willa will have called her brother, and the pastor will let everyone know to pray."

"Of course," Wyatt said. "Anything else?"

"I'll let you know." Ranger got into the truck and they left.

Brit sighed and turned back to Wyatt. "All your family okay?"

"Yeah," Wyatt said, still staring at the car. "Yours?"

"Yep. I best be gettin' home. Then Gabi won't be worrying for no reason."

"Me too," Wyatt said, but he waited until Brit had left. Then he walked back out to the Mustang and took the keys out of the ignition and reached way down to get Preacher's phone. The Glovers would want it, and Wyatt called Marcy as he went back to the truck.

"Baby," he said. "I'm good. They've got Preacher on the way to the hospital. He was awake. I've got his car keys and his phone, and I'm going to head over there and make sure they don't need anything."

"Wyatt," Marcy said, a hint of warning in her voice. Then she sighed and added, "Be careful, Wyatt. I love you."

"Love you too." He couldn't wait to get home to kiss his wife, but he just had to take a phone to a family first.

## Chapter Thirty

Bear Glover had to hold everything together, though the threads of his composure were unraveling one by one. Quickly too. He went with Preacher into the emergency room, his voice stuck somewhere down behind his ribcage.

"You're at the hospital," he said to Preacher. "You're going to be fine."

"Mister?" Preacher asked.

"He got us all in the loop within minutes," Bear said. "Smart calling him."

"It was...accident." Preacher's eyes closed, and the doctor that approached said, "Sir, you can't be here."

"He's my brother."

A monitor wailed, and the paramedic pushing him on the left side put one hand on Bear's chest. "Sir, he's just passed out. Please. Let us work on him."

The other paramedic started reciting stats and numbers

to the doctor, who pressed his stethoscope to Preacher's chest. "He's wet. Status on the legs?"

"He said he can't feel them," Bear said as they continued down the hall and he didn't. Numbness spread through him and he felt like an island in the middle of the hallway. Nurses flowed around him as he watched the stretcher and all the people hovering around Preacher disappear through a set of double doors.

"I can't help him," Bear said to himself. "Daddy, I can't help him. I can't protect him. I can't fix this." He pressed his eyes closed against the burning tears gathering there.

His phone rang, and that snapped him out of the bubble where he'd fallen. "Cactus," he said.

"Willa called her brother," Cactus said. "I've got Judge, Bishop, and Ace with me. We're just getting on the highway."

"They just took him from me," Bear said, still staring at the doors.

"How is he?"

Bear dropped his head, the first sob wrenching from his throat. "Not good, Cactus. Get here fast."

---

Bear hated hospitals, at least right now. His mood worsened by the minute, and as he'd spent the night in an uncomfortable chair, waiting for word about his brother, he was particularly cranky.

Sammy had texted to say she'd taken care of the ranch by asking the full-time cowboys to do the essentials that day. She was bringing the kids down to see the family, and she wanted Bear to go up to the homestead and take a nap.

Like that was going to happen.

Two doctors came out, both wearing surgical gear. Bear recognized one of them, as he'd come out to talk to them earlier. He jumped to his feet, as did several others.

"He's out of surgery," the doctor said. "He'll be waking up soon, and once he does, we'll be moving him into a room."

"Which one?" Bear barked.

"We don't know yet," the surgeon said. "We'll have the nurses let you know once he's been assigned. He'll be waking up when we take him up there." He glanced at the crowd, and there weren't even any wives there. "He can't have this many visitors. Two or three."

"All right," Mother said. "I'll make sure we don't overwhelm him. How is he?" She linked her arm through Bear's, and he tucked her against his side.

"He has a broken hip," the doctor said. "We set it, and both of us think it'll heal just fine. The dash pinned his legs, but thankfully, they're just bruised. No breaks on the x-rays that we can see. We'll monitor that, though to make sure. We've got him pinned back together, and he has two rods holding his pelvis together."

"My word," Ranger said. "What else?"

"Nothing abnormal on the CT scan," the other doctor said. "No concussion has manifested itself, though he definitely hit his head. He's got some minor facial lacerations from the broken glass. Some on his arms. Mostly, he's exhausted and dehydrated, which we're treating with an IV."

"How long will he be here?" Mister asked.

"Depends," the first doctor said. "Four days. Maybe five, depending on how he does. We'll know more as soon as he wakes up. The nurses will have him up and walking before long." He smiled and glanced at the other doctor.

"He did great in surgery. No problems. He's strong and healthy. He's going to recover from this."

Bear nodded, and the two doctors left. Mother clung to him, and Bear held her hand just as tightly. He needed an anchor right now, because Preacher was the middle child of seven. *He* held the family together, and without him... without any of them, Bear's heart would break and he wouldn't be the same man he'd once been.

"There's enough of us to stay with him all the time," Bishop said, causing Bear to turn back to the family.

"He won't want that," Judge said, and Bear agreed with him.

"Someone should call Charlie now that it's morning," Cactus said. "She should know."

"Should she?" someone else asked.

"They're serious," Mister said. "I can call her."

"Wyatt brought Preacher's phone."

Things shuffled around, and Mister ended up with Preacher's phone. He looked at Bear, and Bear saw a man of great integrity, filled with worry and guilt.

"Will you call?" Mister asked, extending the phone toward Bear.

"Of course." He had to be strong. For himself. For the

whole family. He took Preacher's phone, finding Charlie's last text that had come in.

*Call me when you get home so I know you made it safely.*

His heart fell to his boots. How did he call her now and tell her that Preacher hadn't driven safe? Preacher hadn't called. Would she be worried?

He walked away from the group, trying to find courage and strength. He prayed for it, but he didn't feel any different as he tapped the button. As the line rang, he felt all of the wobbly things inside him button up. His shoulders straightened, and he swallowed back his nerves.

"Preacher," Charlie said. "Finally."

"Charlie," Bear said gruffly. "It's Preacher's brother, Bear. There's been an accident."

# Chapter Thirty-One

"I don't know, Mama," Charlie said, her voice tinny and breaking on every other syllable. "His brother said he's in the hospital, but I don't know if I should go or not."

"Why wouldn't you go, honey?"

Charlie paced away from the huge windows at the back of her house. "I don't know. We argued last night." Tears fell down her face, and she hated them. She didn't like not knowing what to do. She didn't want to be on-air in ten minutes, but she had a schedule to keep.

"Char," Mama said. "He's your boyfriend. You really like him. He's in the hospital, and you should go."

"I'm in love with him," Charlie whispered. "But Mama, he hasn't told his family about us. Not really." She sobbed now, not caring how she looked. She'd get on with a black screen and tell all of her subs that she had an emergency, and she'd be back online when she could. The end.

Heck, it might even make her more popular.

"What do you mean?"

"I've never been up to his ranch to meet his family. Not all of them. The ones I have met were by accident. He's hidden me from them, and I was angry about it."

"If you go, sweetie, you won't be hidden anymore. Plus, his brother knew about you."

"I don't want to meet them like this." She collapsed into a chair at the dining room table and put her head in her hand. "Without him."

"Did his brother say what was wrong with him?"

"Only that he'd been in a car accident, and he's out of surgery, and he's sure Preacher would like me to be there."

"I'm sure he would too, baby. If you really love him, Charlie, how are you still at home?"

Everything in her life slowed and stopped. She looked up, the movement in the room from Paulie as he stalked into the kitchen, clearly looking for something to eat. Her own stomach growled, but she didn't get up and get her SlimDown out of the fridge, the way she normally did at this time in the morning.

"You're right, Mama," she said. "I have to go." She left her phone on the dining room table and strode toward her office. She'd be early for her livestream, but that didn't matter. She had to deliver a fast message, and then she had to get to the hospital.

---

CHARLIE HELD HER BREATH ON THE ELEVATOR. THAT worked, because it only took ten seconds to go from the first floor to the third. The doors opened, and a man stood there.

"Judge," she breathed, and he opened his arms. Charlie flew into them, wishing she was strong enough not to cry. She pressed her eyes closed, taking a leaf from her feline's book and hoping that meant no one would see her weeping.

"He's okay, Charlie," Judge whispered. "I'm going to introduce you to everyone. There's a lot of names. Don't worry about remembering them. We're just glad you're here."

She nodded and stepped back. She wiped her eyes and met Judge's. "Is he awake?"

"Yes." Judge gave her a warm smile. "When Bear told him we'd called you, his heart monitor did a little melody." He chuckled. "I don't know you real well, but I hope that changes. All I know is my brother likes you a whole lot."

Charlie nodded, because she knew that too. She wondered with every step she took if that was enough. If he couldn't include her in his life, did it matter if he liked her? Did it matter if she was in love with him?

She didn't know the answers to her questions, and she stuffed them away to examine later. Judge put his hand on her back, and they walked down the hall and through a lobby. Around a corner. Down another hall, and then another waiting area opened up before them.

Cowboys and women waited on the couches, on their feet, and in little groups. Every single one of them seemed to detect her arrival, and all conversations ceased as they turned toward her.

"Everyone," Judge said, and Charlie couldn't count them all fast enough. "This is Charlie Perkins. She and Preacher have been datin' for several months." He held up one hand as one of the men stepped forward. "I'm going to come around and introduce her. She doesn't need to be mobbed. Then she's going to go talk to Preach alone."

He nodded, and Charlie's gratitude for him multiplied. Judge indicated the couple closest to him. "This is Bear. You spoke to him a bit ago."

The man standing there stood well over six feet, with shoulders as wide as a grizzly bear. He flashed her a pained smile and took her right into his arms.

"Oh." Charlie grabbed onto him so she wouldn't fall.

"His wife, Sammy," Judge said when Bear stepped back. "They've got a couple of kids around here somewhere."

Sammy took her into a hug too, her eyes wet. Charlie fed off the emotion, and while she'd never been nurturing, she could experience real emotion. She'd never been broken up over not having a boyfriend, but the level of love and acceptance she felt pouring from just these first two people was more than she could take.

"He's okay," Sammy whispered. "And it's so lovely to properly meet you." She stepped back and smiled at Charlie in such a friendly way. "This is Preacher's mother."

"Yes, I've met his mother," Charlie said. "I attended your wedding, ma'am."

Lois Glover embraced Charlie, and she was so glad she'd decided to come to the hospital. "You come with me, dear," she said. "I'm going to take you back to Preacher. You can meet everyone else later."

"Are you sure?" Charlie asked.

"Preach only stays awake for an hour or so," Lois said. "I just went to see him, and he's doing well right now. Just eaten and the nurse just took him for a walk, and he's back in bed with painkillers." She smiled at Charlie warmly, but Charlie couldn't return it.

She had no idea what to expect when she walked in that room. She didn't spend time in hospitals. She and Preacher hadn't left things on the best of terms.

Still, she took the first step with Lois, and then several more until she stood outside his room. "You go on now," Lois said, and Charlie could hear Preacher in her manner of speech.

She nodded, took a breath, and knocked before opening the door.

"Yeah," Preacher said, his voice slightly hoarse. He came into view, and he looked so different than Charlie had ever seen him before. Her throat closed and tears came to her eyes.

"Charlie," he said, relief in his tone. He reached his hand toward her, and she hurried to his bedside, taking his face in both of her hands.

"You were supposed to call when you got home," she whispered.

"I haven't been home, sugar."

She kissed him, tears streaming down her face. "Why are you so stubborn?" She kissed him again, and then again, before she stepped back.

"I'm sorry," he said. "I'm so sorry, Charlie."

She fell back a step and shook her head. Turning away

from him, she wiped her face and collected her emotions into one single box so they weren't flying all over the place. "You shouldn't have stretched yourself so thin."

Preacher didn't say anything, and that only fueled Charlie's anger.

"You should've let me come up to the ranch. I don't get up early. I don't work fifteen hours a day."

"You do too," he said quietly.

Charlie turned back to him, a storm buzzing in her chest. "I can schedule my morning broadcast whenever I want. You put in five hours on the ranch before I even go online."

She didn't want to fight with him. She wasn't even sure how she'd gone from relief and gratitude to see him alive, to kissing him, to arguing about her work schedule with him.

"This doesn't matter."

"No, it doesn't." Preacher continued to glare at her for a few moments before his expression softened. "I didn't... I've been fine for months."

"Yes, but even you're not immortal," she said. "Even you need to sleep more than four hours each night." Charlie shook her head, her anger with him familiar on her tongue.

"I don't want to argue." He closed his eyes in a long blink, and Charlie saw how slowly they opened. He looked different in a gown, without a cowboy hat, and with a hint of grayness still in his skin.

"I don't want to argue either," she said. "Judge is introducing me to everyone out there, and I wish it was you."

"I wish it was me too," he whispered, studying his hands in his lap. "I've told you before I'm not as good as you."

Charlie didn't want to have this discussion. "Only at Solitary Ops."

He lifted his eyes to hers. "Charlie, I'm not kidding. I can't...I can't even walk. They say it can take anywhere from six to twelve months to heal from a broken hip, and they found a hairline fracture in my lower femur too." He shook his head, his jaw tight and his eyes growing brighter as they filled with tears.

"I can't—" His voice broke, and he looked away from her, focusing on a spot above her shoulder. "I can't ask you to doom yourself to a life of taking care of me."

"That's not your choice."

"It kind of is."

"Preacher."

"Are you saying you still want me?" he demanded, lifting his chin and looking directly at her. "Look at me, Charlie. I can't walk. I can't do anything. It'll be a year before I can. A year before I can walk down the aisle. A year before we can get married." He shook his head. "I don't believe it. And the problems don't end there. My hip is broken—badly. Because I fell asleep at the wheel. Because I made bad decisions with you. I have to live with that my whole life, but you shouldn't have to."

His chest heaved, and his heart monitor showed it. Her pulse rioted too, and she was sincerely glad she didn't have a machine to broadcast it. "What are you saying?"

"I'm saying I think you should think really hard about

what you want, and honestly, if it's not me and taking care of someone with a chronic health issue for the rest of their life, then...that's that."

"That's that?" she repeated. "Preacher, I'm in love with you."

He opened his mouth to say something but stalled. Nothing came out, and Charlie wiped angrily at her face again. "I don't understand why you want to push me away. I don't understand why you don't see yourself the way I do. I don't understand why you kept me from the love that abounds in your family." She gestured toward the door. "Do you know how many of them are out there?"

He looked away, that jaw muscle jumping. "I'm guessing all of them."

"All of them," she said. "*All* of them—and I don't understand why that upsets you."

"I don't need the spotlight on me," he said quietly. "I never have."

"They're your *family*," she said. "You're extremely lucky to have them, and you know what? I would've liked to have known them too, as I'm really far from my family up here in the Panhandle." Her chest vibrated and collapsed, and she had no idea what the next step should be.

She sank onto the recliner in the room. "I don't want to fight with you." In that moment, she realized what she'd said to him.

*Preacher, I'm in love with you.*

And he hadn't said it back.

Thunder rolled through her, and she hadn't been this confused in a long time. Charlie loved puzzles, and she loved solving problems. Those things made her very good at being a chemist and coming up with new medicines to help animals.

In matters of the heart, though, she was useless.

"I think you're right," she finally said.

"About what?"

"I need to think long and hard about what I really want." She stood up and tried to give him a smile. Her mouth only turned down, though, and she couldn't steady the wobble in her chin. "I'll talk to you later, okay?" She shouldered her purse and started to turn toward the door.

"Charlie," he said, and she turned back to him. "I...I'm not good with words; you know that. I want to dance with you, though." A flash of a smile touched his face, and it looked painful.

"I want you," he said. "If you decide you want me, but I completely understand if you don't."

"Preacher," she said. "Can you just answer one question for me?"

"Of course."

"When you say, *I want you*, is that the same as *I love you?*"

"Yes," he whispered, a hint of redness touching his cheeks.

Charlie wanted to rejoice, but her frustration level only climbed to a new level. "You shouldn't have kept me a secret," she said. "I feel so foolish out there. You wouldn't have fallen asleep at the wheel if you'd let me shoulder some of the burden by coming to see you at Shiloh Ridge instead of you being so proud you always came down to town to see me."

"I can't change what I've done," he said.

"I'm going to go," she said. "I just need some time to think." She stepped back over to him, her eyes searching his face. "Will you give me some time?"

"Take what you need." He gestured to his legs, which a blanket covered. "I'm not going anywhere."

Charlie wanted to tell him she wasn't either. That she'd be at his side every step of the way—even if he couldn't physically take a step. She just needed some time to come to terms with her anger and her fear and everything else swirling within her.

"Thank you," she whispered, just before pressing her lips to his forehead. Then, she turned and left the room. Part of her wanted to go out a different way than she'd come in, but in the end, she didn't want to hide from the Glovers.

So she rejoined them in the waiting area, and she went around with Judge and met them all. Each and every one, and they were all warm, and welcoming, and wonderful.

Which only made her angrier that Preacher had kept them from her.

## Chapter Thirty-Two

Preacher stared at the television mounted to the wall above his door. Mister sat on one side of the bed, with Judge on the other. That alone would've freaked Preacher out, as they hadn't gotten along for years now.

But they'd come in together, and they'd brought bags of food from Preacher's favorite burger joint. He'd eaten entirely too much, and his stomach hurt.

His head hurt. His hip hurt.

Worst of all, his heart hurt.

Something pressed on his chest, and he struggled to breathe against it. Mister glanced over at him, but Preacher just let his eyes drift closed in what he hoped looked peaceful and serene. He was just tired and needed to rest. Nothing to see here.

His guilt would not allow him much rest. Surely, he'd worried Mister. He'd gotten everyone up in the middle of the night, and most of them had been at the hospital for hours before they'd been able to come see him.

His body seemed to know it now had metal in it, and the bones and ligaments nearby were not happy about that. He groaned and tried to shift to bring some relief to his hip.

"You need more meds, Preach?" Mister asked.

"Yes," Preacher said, though he didn't think the nurses would let him have them. They'd brought him pills only an hour ago.

"I'll call the nurses," Judge said, and he lifted the remote attached to the bed and pressed the big red button.

"What can I do for you?" a saccharine-sweet voice asked.

"He's in pain," Judge said. "What can you bring him?"

"Let me get Patty."

"Patty doesn't like me," Preacher muttered.

"Impossible," Mister said. "What with you being so personable at all."

Preacher opened his eyes and looked at Mister. "Charlie broke up with me."

"She did?" Mister asked.

"She did not," Judge said. "She stayed for a good hour out there, talking to everyone. She said she'd be back later."

*Then she's a liar*, Preacher thought. But he didn't want to say anything bad about her in front of his brothers.

"You must really like her," Mister said.

"He does," Judge said, and that earned him a glare from Mister. "Sorry," he muttered.

"I do though," Preacher said. "We were talking about going ring shopping and all of that."

"Hmm." Mister didn't add anything as two nurses came into the room. Preacher actually tried to sit up straighter and couldn't.

"You're in pain, sir?"

"Yes," Preacher said. "It never stops. I just want it to stop."

"He had four hundred mills of ibuprofen ninety minutes ago," one of the nurses said, tapping on the computer mounted to the wall beside Preacher. Judge had stood and retreated further into the room.

"He can have another four hundred," the second nurse said. "And I can put in an acetaminophen drip. It'll be slow, sir," she said. "But constant."

"I want to go to sleep," he said. "Can you give me something for that?" Preacher was done talking. He'd entertained everyone all dang day, and he just wanted them all to leave him alone. They could go back to Shiloh Ridge, as surely the work had been piling up all day.

"Let me check with Doctor Snellson," the nurse said. "I'll be right back with that drip."

The first woman stayed at the computer, typing something in. The moment she left, Preacher said, "You guys can go. I don't need anyone sleeping overnight in the hospital with me."

"You sure?" Judge asked.

"Yes," Preacher said. "I'm fine here. They're going to give me something to sleep, and then they'll make me walk around, and I'm just cranky. You should go."

"I'll stay until you fall asleep," Mister said. "You can go now if you want, Judge."

"No, I sent the girls in my truck. I need a ride back up to the ranch."

"Oh, okay."

It seemed to take forever for the nurses to return. One shot something into Preacher's IV, and the other hung a new bag of clear liquid behind him. He didn't care what they were doing, as long as he got some relief.

"Doctor Snellson said you can have a low dose of a sleeping pill. I'll bring you that. When did you eat last?" She looked at the hamburger wrappers on the rolling table that went under his bed.

"An hour ago?" he guessed. "My brothers brought dinner."

"You should be fine to take it then." She flashed him a smile and walked out. She returned a moment later with a pill in a paper cup, and Preacher swallowed it. He sighed as he lay back, a shooting pain going from his shoulder to his ankle. It hurt enough to make him groan, and everyone alerted on him.

"Preach?" Mister asked.

"I just get these shooting pains," he said, his lungs still seized up. He panted for a moment. "They don't last long."

"How bad is the pain?" The redheaded nurse stepped over to him and put her stethoscope against his chest.

"It's a ten for sure," Preacher said. "For a moment. Then it fades to maybe a four or a five." He tried to push himself up and didn't get very far. "I just need to sit up more."

"I can move the bed," the nurse said. She did, lifting the back of it so he sat up easier.

"Yes," Preacher said. "Like that."

"Oh, Mother brought over a blanket," Mister said. "I'll go grab it." He hurried out of the room, and Preacher's embarrassment knew no end. That he even had to be in this hospital room was bad enough. His family had brought pictures, flowers, food, and balloons, and it looked like he'd be hosting a party later for all the people staying on the third floor that night.

Now Mother had sent over a blankie?

He dang near shook his head, his frustration rising with every breath he took. The nurses left, and Judge walked to the foot of the bed. "Preacher, I can stay. I brought pajamas and my own pillow. I was planning on it."

"I'm fine." Preacher closed his eyes, feeling anything but fine.

"You're a bad liar," Judge said.

Preacher didn't care. He just shook his head. He wanted to cry, but the last time he'd broken down like that was when Daddy had died. Then again at the funeral. Was a break-up with Charlie Perkins worth feeling like someone had hollowed out his eyes with steel wool? That was how Preacher felt whenever he cried.

*She's worth it*, he thought, the first hot tears gathering in his eyes.

"I'm going to stay unless you specifically tell me I have to leave," Judge said.

Preacher couldn't say that. In truth, he didn't want to be alone. Only his ego did. His embarrassment and humiliation would really like to be left alone. But deep inside his heart, Preacher did not want to spend the night in the hospital by himself.

Mister returned with his blanket, and he laid it over Preacher's body. "There you go," he said. "Mother said she'd made it for you for when you got married, but she figured now was as good as then."

Preacher basked in the new warmth from the quilt, and he let Mister pull it all the way to his chin. The soft, clean scent of his mother came with the blanket, and Preacher couldn't help the sob that came from his throat.

"I'm going to stay with him," Judge said in a very quiet voice. "You go on ahead without me."

"I'm staying until he falls asleep," Mister said, and he took up his guard position on Preacher's right-hand side. He put his hand on Preacher's forearm under the blanket, and he added, "You cry as much as you want."

"I'm fine," Preacher said, but his voice broke and he heard the lie inside the words. Loud and clear. His heart broke too, and he didn't think the doctors could pin it back together with metal rods.

---

PREACHER WOKE TO THE SOUND OF VOICES. ONE CLOSE, and one farther away. One male. One female.

"He's asleep," Judge said, and Preacher knew that voice.

"I'll just sit with him if you don't mind."

*Charlie.*

Preacher couldn't believe it, but that voice absolutely

belonged to Charlie. He'd heard her speak in that soft, reverent tone many times. He wondered how much time had gone by. Was he still in the hospital? Had she thought through everything and decided she still loved him and wanted to be with him?

Her cool fingers slid down his arm and into his, and he tried to curl his around hers. "Are you awake, baby?" she asked.

He wanted to say he was. Of course he was. He could hear her. But his voice didn't work, and he couldn't get his eyes open either. Thankfully, there was no pain in his hip or leg or heart, and that was the best part of the sleeping pills and the constantly dripping drugs going into his system.

"I'm still plenty mad at you, cowboy," she said, a tear in her voice that made his heart rip in half. "I feel so guilty. Like, if you'd just told me how tired you were. Or that you'd given up sleeping to see me in the evenings. Or that you couldn't see me because you really couldn't drive an hour home. I would've understood. At least I'd like to think I would have."

*You don't need to feel guilty*, he thought, wishing he could say it out loud.

"It's not fair, you not telling me," she said. "I can't read your mind, Preacher. You're so good at hiding things, and you know what? That's *not* a good thing."

*I know. I'm sorry.*

She sniffled, and her hand tightened in his. "Everyone's asking about you on Nexus," she said, her voice steadier now. "I had a livestream scheduled for tonight, but I canceled it. The one I did this morning mentioned that you'd been in an accident and I wasn't going to be available for a little bit. I left that one up. You know, so people could watch my latest, even though it wasn't live."

*I know what a my-latest video is, sugar*. He'd smile at her if he could get his mouth to work.

"I don't know what to tell them, Preach."

*You don't owe them anything.*

"I don't owe them anything," she said as if reading his mind. "But they love you. They're concerned. What do you want me to tell them?"

He tried to move, but none of his muscles would cooperate.

"I'm just going to tell them the truth," she whispered. "That's what I wish you would've done, and then I wouldn't have gone dancing with you last night. I'm so, so sorry, Preacher."

*Hey, it's not your fault.*

Charlie wept for a minute. Maybe two. It was impossible for Preacher to tell time. He drifted, her cool hand in his, and when he woke again, it was gone.

She'd left, and all Preacher could do for that moment of consciousness was pray that she'd come back.

---

"NO," HE SAID WITH PLENTY OF BITE IN HIS TONE. "I don't want to go for a walk. It hurts. Everything hurts." He glared at Cactus and Bear, the pair who'd come today. "I want to go home. I'm fine. If I can hobble around this blasted hospital on crutches, I can do it at the Ranch House."

"They're working on it," Cactus said.

"Not fast enough." Preacher glared at the nurse who came in, the idiotic walker in front of her. "I'm not going."

"Oh, I'm sorry to hear that," Jenny said, her smile not even moving one centimeter. "Well, not really, because if you don't show us you can get around, you'll stay another night. Then I'll get to bring you dinner and try to beat you at cards again."

The blood drained from Preacher's face. "I have to walk to go home?'

"That's right, Mister Glover." She stepped between the two burly cowboys beside his bed, not nearly as tall as them. "You show me you can do this, and I put in your discharge paperwork."

"Fine." Preacher could walk around the stupid halls if that was what it took. The fracture in his lower leg turned out to be nothing, but he had three screws and pins in his hip. That hadn't been a complete break, or he'd have gotten a hip replacement.

In all honesty, that wasn't off the table yet, but his doctors and physical therapists wanted to see how he would heal. If his range of mobility didn't allow him to live the rest of his life independent of others or a wheelchair, he could get a hip replacement and probably regain that ability.

He got himself to his feet and gripped the walker. He hated feeling weak, and in front of Bear and Cactus, everything he did—even at his best—made him feel weak. "You guys comin'?"

He moved toward the open door as quickly as he could, which was about the same speed as a snail. Mother had brought him loose-fitting basketball shorts and he wore those under his hospital gown. He had no idea where his clothes from the night of the accident had gone, and Judge had brought down a couple of T-shirts, a new pair of running shoes, and fresh socks for Preacher to wear when it was time to go home.

Preacher took a right out in the hall and started toward the station. He wanted them all to see how well he was doing. Maybe then they'd let him leave faster. He walked around the unit five times with Cactus and Bear trailing in his wake, talking in low voices.

When they got back to the room, Jenny grinned at him widely. "Let me go get your paperwork started. You're going to have a lot of follow-up appointments." She looked at Bear and Cactus. "He can't drive with that hip. He can't ride a horse for at least a month. The doctor will go over all of that. He has someone who can get him to his appointments?"

"He is right here," Preacher said. "And yes, I have someone I can ask to drive me to whatever you're going to make me do."

"Preacher," Bear said, staring at him in shock.

"Sorry," Preacher said. Charlie hadn't come back to the hospital, and he'd learned from Judge that she'd snuck in just after ten p.m., which was hours after the normal allowed visiting timeframe. "I'm sorry, Jenny. Honestly."

"Oh, Mister Glover, I can handle you. Believe it or not, you are not my surliest patient." She gave him a giggle and a grin, and Preacher knew that some people were just born to be nurses. Jenny was one of them.

She left, and Preacher looked at his brothers. "Will you help me get this gown off?"

"Yep." Cactus stepped over to him and untied the back of it.

"Judge brought down T-shirts," Preacher said. His house mate had stayed with him the first night. Mister had come the second. Ward the third. Bear last night. Cactus had drawn the short stick for tonight, but it looked like he wouldn't have to sleep away from his pregnant wife and step-son after all.

"Listen," he said as he dug a T-shirt out of the backpack Judge had brought. "We've been talking about you, and we're wondering if you'd like a dog."

"Who's been talking about me?" he asked, taking the shirt from Cactus.

"Everyone," Bear said, his voice booming like it did when he went into grizzly mode. "So get over it, Preach. You rolled your car. We're allowed to be concerned."

"I know that," Preacher snapped. He pulled his shirt over his head and glared at Bear. If he didn't hold onto the anger, he had nothing left but despair. And he would not cry in front of Bear and Cactus the way he had Mister and Judge.

He would *not*.

Without warning, Bear stepped forward and grabbed Preacher in a hug. He grunted as he lost his balance. Frantic, he had to grab onto Bear too, and then he was safe. His eldest brother held him up, the way he'd done for the whole family for years and years now.

"I love you," Bear said. "We all love you, and we're all concerned about you."

"I know that," Preacher said again, much softer this time. "I'm grateful for that. I am. I just don't like having the spotlight on me. I don't like thinking about people talking about me. I like being in the background."

"Is that why you didn't bring Charlie up to the ranch?"

"Part of it," Preacher said, knowing Bear had been trying to find a reason Preacher had kept Charlie a secret for days now. "I don't need the spectacle."

Bear released him and held onto his shoulders as he looked at him. They stood almost the same height, but Bear possessed the same powerful personality Daddy had. He was bigger and better than them all, simply because he was Bear. He never made anyone feel small on purpose, but Preacher absolutely felt leagues behind Bear in most things. His brother could see things no one else could. He led effortlessly, and Preacher had always admired him.

They'd had a really good talk last night about it, actually, and Preacher smiled at his brother now. "Forgive me," he said, his voice pitching up. "I'm not myself, and I just want to go home." He glanced at Cactus. "I'm sorry, guys. Really."

"Of course, Preach," they said together.

Bear stepped back. "I'm sorry we're a spectacle, Preacher."

"It's not your fault," Preacher said, easing himself onto

the bed and motioning for Cactus to hand him the shoes. "It's Mother's and Daddy's. They're the ones who had a million kids."

Cactus burst out laughing, and Bear joined in only a beat later. Preacher took his sneakers—blasted *sneakers*, because the doctors had told him he couldn't wear cowboy boots for a while—and tried to stifle his own laughter.

He couldn't, and it felt really good to laugh with his brothers.

## Chapter Thirty-Three

Bishop caught motion out the window above the sink as he washed his hands. "They're back," he bellowed. "Ace."

His cousin turned and whistled through his teeth, one long, loud shrill note that filled the homestead and got all the people to quiet down. Benny barked, and Frost looked at Ace like he'd just done something terrible.

"They're here," Bishop said, holding up both hands. "Cactus says he's in a bad mood. We know how to make someone feel welcome, right?"

"Someone like Preacher," Mister clarified as he stood from across the room. "He doesn't want questions. He doesn't want fawning. He literally wants to sit somewhere and be left alone."

"We got it," a couple of people said, but Bishop wasn't sure everyone could really act that way. He knew Zona couldn't, as every time he'd seen her in the past few days since Preacher's accident she'd been weeping.

Legit weeping, something Bishop hadn't seen her do for decades. Arizona was a tough woman, who worked with sneaky cows and even tougher men. She didn't cry about anything, and he glanced at Montana.

She'd been crying a lot lately too, but she actually had a reason for that. He grinned at her and extended his hand toward her. "How are you feeling?" he asked under his breath as he moved to press his lips to her temple. "Not too many smells, are there?"

"I nearly lost it when Ida brought in that green bean casserole," Montana whispered. "Did you see me go out onto the deck?"

"I sure did." He kept her close to his body, because he wanted to share in the joy and wonder of the life she carried inside her. Life that belonged partially to him. He loved their child already, though the baby wouldn't be born for seven more months.

The front door opened, and a couple of people went through the arched doorway to the lobby. One of them was Arizona, and she did exactly what Bishop had asked her not to do. He sighed in frustration, but he reminded himself he couldn't make his sister do anything. She got to choose for herself, and if she wanted the wrath of a hangry, hurt Preacher coming down on her...well, that was up to her.

"Brands and saddles, Zona," he said from the foyer. "I'm fine. You're gettin' my shirt all wet." Preacher appeared in the doorway a few moments later, Bear on his right and Cactus on his left.

"All right," Bishop said, tossing a smile in their general direction. "Everyone's here. We're having Mother's famous meatloaf and mashed potatoes and gravy tonight. Ida brought green bean casserole, and Etta's been in the kitchen making rolls and caramels for hours." His throat turned sticky, though Bishop had been announcing things to the family for a long time now. He spoke in almost all the family meetings, as his role as construction manager at Shiloh Ridge had him intimately involved in everyone's lives.

He cleared his throat and looked at Montana. She nodded, her blue eyes bright with joy and hope. She'd been wanting to tell her friends she was pregnant for a week, but things had taken a turn when Preacher had rolled his Mustang.

"We'd like to make an announcement before we pray," he said, glancing over to where Mother stood with Donald. "Montana and I are expecting a baby next March."

A pin could've been heard for a breath. Half a second.

Then an uproar happened, and a couple of women rushed at Montana. She laughed as she embraced Oakley and Holly Ann, and Mother came toward Bishop. "Congratulations, my baby," he said, beaming at him. "How exciting."

"Thanks, Mother."

With Montana pregnant, that made four women at Shiloh Ridge expecting babies in the next several months.

"If we're doing pregnancy announcements," Arizona

said into the lull that happened. "Duke and I will have a new baby in April. Beginning of April."

More noise. More congratulations. Bishop just grinned at her, suddenly all the weeping making so much more sense.

"I've got an announcement," Preacher said, and that pin-dropping silence returned. He cleared his throat. "Charlie Perkins broke up with me, and I don't want to talk about her." He surveyed the crowd. "Okay?"

"Deal," Bishop said, though his heart ached for his brother. The pain on his face wasn't all from the hip or the way he limped toward the long island holding all the food. Others gave similar votes of assent, and Preacher looked at Bishop.

"Can Aunt Dawna pray?"

"Of course I'll pray for you, Preacher," she said, only a couple of seats away from him at the island. "Bishop?"

"Please," he said.

Aunt Dawna took a moment to stand, and Ward held onto her elbow while she found her footing. Bishop watched her and then switched his gaze to Preacher. He also watched, a frown filling his entire countenance.

"Dear Lord," Aunt Dawna said. "We come before Thee as a family tonight to offer Thee thanks for Preacher's life. He is such an amazing example of strength and hard work, and we ask Thee to please pour out Thy blessing of healing upon him. Heal his body. Heal his mind. Heal his heart. Shoulder the burden for him, so he doesn't have to suffer alone."

Bishop's eyes burned as his tears filled them, and he

didn't have a pregnancy excuse to be sniffling the way Montana, Holly Ann, Zona, and Ida did.

"Bless all those carrying babies that they will be mindful of their bodies. Bless them and their babies with health and strength. Bless the cowboys in this family to be good to their wives and children. Bless Etta with the spirit of discernment as she tries to find someone who will bring her untold joy. We are grateful for Thy bounteous blessings in our lives, and we acknowledge Thy hand in all aspects of our lives."

She paused for a moment, the moment powerful and sober. "Lord, I feel there are several in our company who are missing our loved ones right now." Her voice choked, but that only added to the reverence in the room. Aunt Dawna had such a special relationship with the spirit, and she could feel things others couldn't.

"I miss my beloved Bull with the energy of my heart. I know there are others who miss him as well, and his brother Stone, who would surely be here to hold all the babies he could. He would tell Preacher to work hard at healing and not worry about the ranch. He would tell Bear to rely on his mother for strength when he feels like he has none."

Bishop reached up and wiped his eyes, because he missed his father terribly. He did most days, and he loved walking past the cemetery every day to get from his house to the homestead. He always threw a salute to Daddy and Uncle Bull, because they'd built this ranch into what it was.

"We're grateful for our knowledge of Thee, and we ask

a special blessing on any here that might need it that we are not aware of. Amen."

"Amen," Bishop said, wiping his eyes again.

"Oh, and bless the food," Aunt Dawna said into the silence. She turned into Ward, who gathered her into a hug and held her tightly, his eyes closed. Bishop suspected he was hurting in some way.

His gaze moved to Etta, who wept openly. She'd definitely been in healing mode for the past few months, and Bishop had sat with her in the living room a couple of times when he'd come to the homestead and found her here.

Ward released his mother, and Preacher got to his feet painfully and took a turn hugging her. She whispered to him, and he nodded. When she released him, Mother embraced him, then linked her arm through his and led him over to the table.

People had started moving to form a line to get food, and Bishop got out of the way.

"Bishy," Lincoln said, and he turned toward the boy.

"Yep." He grinned at him. "You want the orange juice, right?"

"Can you help me get it out?" he asked. "It's full, and Momma says I can't do it myself."

"I'll get it."

"Thanks."

Bishop delivered the juice to the table where Lincoln and Mitch had claimed a couple of seats. Aurora sat there too, looking at her phone, and Bishop sat down next to her at the same time Mother did.

"I got you something," Mother said, sliding a fairly hefty package across the table to the teenager. Her eyes looked lit from within, and Aurora abandoned her phone.

"Lois," she said, grabbing the package. "You didn't." She giggled and started ripping into the wrapping paper.

Bishop watched as his step-daughter opened the present and lifted the lid on a department store box. She squealed and lifted out a dark green gown.

A very strapless gown.

"Mother," Bishop said, frowning at the garment.

"It's going to be perfect for Homecoming," Aurora said, standing to hold the dress against her body.

"You're not wearing that out of the house," Bishop said, frowning even more. So far, he could barely see out of his eyes.

"Bishop," Mother said. "It's an original, and Aurora is going to jazz it up."

"Jazz it up?" He shook his head, ready to put his cowboy boot down on this issue. "It has no straps." And Aurora was a beautiful girl. She was smart and funny, and she had a new boyfriend every few days. Scratch that. They weren't boyfriends, as she'd told him over and over.

She was dating a lot of boys. She went out on dates with them. Some were friends—but Bishop knew they wanted more. He'd been a seventeen-year-old boy, thank you very much. He knew they were ruled by hormones and a tight pair of jeans—or a strapless gown on a girl like Aurora.

"She's going to add straps, Bishop," Mother said, standing. "Tell your step-dad what's going on." She took

Donald's hand and together, they walked toward the food.

Bishop looked at Aurora. She looked nervously back. "You know how I like to sew?" she asked. "Well, I don't really like to sew. I like to take pieces and well, make them a bit different. Remember how I added those panels into my skirt to make it fuller?"

"Yes," he said, folding his arms.

"This will be like that." She looked down at the gown again. "I actually want to try something with a cap sleeve on this, but sort of like a shoulder pad too. You know, from the eighties."

"I am not old enough to be from the eighties," he said with plenty of disdain, though he'd actually been born in 1985.

Aurora giggled, her anxiety gone. "It's going to be modest, Bishop, I promise."

"Oh, my goodness," Holly Ann exclaimed as she set a plate of food on the table. "Is that the Ashton-Winston?" She reached out and touched the fabric. "Girl, you have to let me do your hair."

"Do you even have a date to this dance?" Bishop asked.

"Okay," Aurora said. "Can you help me with the makeup too? Your eyeliner always looks so good. I can't make the wings like that."

"You're not wearing eyeliner like Holly Ann," Bishop said.

Both females looked at him. Holly Ann, pregnant and just barely starting to show it, settled onto the bench at the long picnic-style table in the homestead. "You don't like my makeup, Bishop?"

"Of course I like it," he said. "On you. You're thirty-five years old. *She's* seventeen." He nodded at Aurora.

"I'm not sure if I should be flattered you think I'm only thirty-five or horrified you don't know how old your favorite sister-in-law is." Holly Ann smiled at him. "I won't put too much makeup on her."

"Ooh, is Holly Ann going to do your makeup for the dance?" Oakley asked. She passed Bishop her five-month-old, as if he was her built-in babysitter. Fine, maybe he'd told Ranger and Oakley he'd take Wilder any time they needed him to. "What are you going to do with your hair?" She sat down on Aurora's other side.

The teen folded the dress and laid it carefully back in the box. "I'm not sure. I want to look amazing for my first dance back with Ollie."

Her eyes met Bishop's, all the anxiety back.

"You're going to Homecoming with Oliver Walker?" he roared.

"Oh, dear," Holly Ann said.

"I told you he wouldn't take it well," Aurora said.

"I thought you said your mom was going to tell him." Oakley pushed Aurora's hair off her shoulder. "I think you should just go with something curled. And down."

"But I'm going to do something amazing with the shoulders and sleeves on my dress," she said.

Bishop didn't know what to do or say. Montana arrived and she took Wilder from him. "Why are you yelling over here?"

"She's going to Homecoming with Ollie."

"I know, dear," Montana said. "He's coming for movie night tomorrow too." She smiled down at baby Wilder, and the baby smiled on back.

"Why am I always the last to know everything?" he grumbled, getting up.

"I told you last week," Montana said. "You were just in a hurry to get out to the stable and didn't listen."

"That is not true," Bishop said. "I listen to you when you talk." He knew exactly the situation she was talking about, and he'd made sure he'd stayed to listen before going horseback riding with Bear, Ward, and Ranger. "You probably said it after I closed the door."

The way Montana grinned at him told him he was right, and he shook his head as he walked away. He didn't really care who Aurora went out with. She and Ollie had broken up a while ago, and she hadn't really been happy since.

He'd just need to make sure he had a talk with the boy about boundaries and being respectful. And that he and Aurora couldn't do this on-again, off-again thing again.

"So, you're going to have a baby in March," Bear said, grinning at Bishop and handing him a paper plate. "That's great news, brother."

"Thanks, Bear," Bishop said, immediately forgetting about Aurora's boyfriend issues. He loved being in her life, and he couldn't wait to be a biological father too.

## Chapter Thirty-Four

Ward stood next to the couch while Preacher got to his feet. "There you go. We're going to the stables and back. It's farther than you've ever been."

"I can do it," Preacher said, giving Ward a smile. He'd take it, because anything was better than the growling and glaring Preacher had done the first week home.

He still didn't move very fast or very fluidly, but the physical therapist had said he was recovering at a normal speed for someone his age with his injuries.

Ward didn't touch Preacher, and he never had. He was there in case his cousin needed him. Nothing more. Preacher didn't want to be babied, and he didn't want to be coddled.

Mister did too much of it, and Ward sat on the other end of the spectrum.

Today, Preacher wore sweat pants, as he hadn't been

able to get into his jeans yet. They put too much pressure on his thigh and hip, and he'd slept for a whole afternoon after simply trying them on.

He wore sneakers all the time now, even when napping on the couch, and he reached for things to balance himself when he'd never done that before.

The first few days Preacher had been home, he'd taken more painkillers than Ward thought any animal of any size ever should, and he'd still complained about the pain. Even now, Preacher took pills in the mornings, at lunchtime, and at night to manage the pain in his legs and pelvis.

They'd not spoken about Charlie, but Mister had entertained them with stories of his failed attempts to ask Libby Bellamore to dinner, and Judge had told a story about how he'd basically been walking around in his underwear in front of the woman he'd been trying to go out with for over a year.

Ward had heard of June, but Judge had clammed right up when questions started getting asked. Ward himself had no room to talk when it came to women. He was currently seeing three at the same time, and while he'd not agreed to date any of them exclusively, he still felt a bit guilty.

And none of them excited him all that much.

Whenever he thought about who did excite him, he saw the streaked blonde-haired woman who drove a big dump truck and kept insisting she couldn't get him the gravel he wanted for the ranch.

Dorothy Crockett.

Dot didn't seem to like him all that much, and that only made her more intriguing to Ward. They'd eaten a meal together in the pastor's office a while ago, and she'd gone back to ignoring his phone calls at From the Ground Up.

He wasn't going back to Twin Cities for gravel, he knew that. No one had said a word about the shoddy gravel on literally every surface of the ranch, but Ward knew. Ward could see it. Ward hated it.

Preacher opened the back door, and Ward followed him outside. The day had barely begun, and Ward felt the oppressive heat. It never really left in September, and he had the fleeting thought that he'd like to trade places with Preacher. At least his cousin got to sit inside in the air conditioning.

At the same time, Ward wouldn't want to be dealing with pain and injuries—and he knew there were more than just the physical, obvious ones people could see. Especially for a man like Preacher, who held everything so close to the vest.

He hated people looking at him, talking about him, or even thinking about him. The past couple of weeks had likely been excruciating for him, which was why Ward and Mister had moved over to the Ranch House temporarily. That way, Preacher only had to deal with three people instead of the whole family.

Of course, only God himself would be able to stop Etta from bringing food to someone who was ill, and she'd come by several times. Ward certainly wasn't complaining, because while Preacher had a lot more time on his hands, he hadn't taken up the idea of perfecting his cooking skills while he healed.

Preacher started to pant about halfway to the stables,

but Ward said nothing. He'd told Preacher he better dang well ask for help if he needed it. Otherwise, Ward was going to assume he was okay. He had asked for help a couple of times, but it had been hard for him, Ward could tell.

"Physical therapy at eleven," Ward said just to have something to say.

"With Bryan or Hart?"

"Hart, I think," Ward said.

"Thank goodness."

"You don't like Bryan?"

"Jackson's...I think he thinks I'm faking."

"He doesn't, I'm sure," Ward said easily. He'd never gone into the appointment with Preacher. He dropped him off and slept in his truck while Preacher went and did whatever the physical therapy entailed. When he came back out, Ward woke up. They drove through the cinnamon roll hut that had come to town a couple of months ago, and they ate their sweet treats on the way back to the ranch in silence.

"Tyler's gentler too," Preacher said. "I just like him better."

"Fair enough."

Preacher began to slow, and Ward did as well. He had nothing else to do for now, and he didn't need to be in a hurry. On days where Preacher had appointments, one of the men in the Ranch House took the whole day with him. Ward would work on some paperwork tonight before his date, and he'd fiddle with Two Cents before bed.

"Market day tomorrow," Preacher said.

"You gonna at least come over?"

"And risk Bear yelling at me again?" Preacher shook his head. "No thanks."

"Oh, don't listen to Bear," Ward said.

"Easy for you to say," Preacher muttered. "He's not your perfect older brother."

"I have one of those too," Ward said. "And besides, if he's yelling at you in front of the other boys, he's clearly not perfect." He tossed Preacher a smile, but the other man didn't even look at him.

Preacher went all the way to the stable wall and reached out and touched it. "I did it." He paused, his chest lifting and lowering, lifting and lowering. "I feel so weak."

"Need to sit for a minute?"

"Yes." Preacher put both hands on the seat of the bench and lowered himself carefully. Ward sat next to him, his eyes tracing the road he'd created for Willa and Cactus to get out to the Edge. It hadn't existed until February, and now they didn't have to go over rutted dirt or ride a horse to get to their house.

"You thinkin' about that dog?" Ward asked as Preacher bent carefully to get out his whittling kit. He'd been doing a lot more of that since the accident, and Ward thought it helped him mentally.

"I actually was," Preacher said, taking out his knife and the latest item he'd caused to emerge from the wood. "How'd you know?"

"You relaxed." Ward looked casually left, away from Preacher.

"I don't think Bear or Cactus will let me back on the

ranch without one," Preacher said with a sigh. "I have to admit, it's not a bad idea."

"It's just to keep everyone safe," Ward said. "Plus, you want a dog." He looked at Preacher now. "Right?"

"Right."

"What kind?"

"Do I get a choice?"

"Why wouldn't you?"

"I don't know. Cactus seems to have my life worked out for me now."

Ward chuckled, the sound growing into full-blown laughter after only a few seconds. "Yes, for someone who hates being told what to do, he sure likes dictating things for others."

Preacher laughed too, but he cut the sound off after a few seconds. "Don't make me laugh, Ward. It hurts." He continued a low-level chuckle, and Ward did too.

His fingers flew across the wood, sending shavings to the ground. After a minute, Preacher asked, "Who are you going out with tonight?"

Ward sighed and took off his cowboy hat. "I don't know." He set his hat on his knee and ran his hands through his hair.

"You don't know."

"At the moment? No, I don't know. I'll shower tonight after work, and when I look at my phone when the alarm goes off to remind me it's time to leave, the address will be there." He shrugged. "If I cared...."

"Why are you going out with her if you don't care?"

"I'm just trying to find the right person," Ward said. "Everyone seems to have this magical meeting, and then a month later they're in love, and I've been out with oh, I don't know." Ward ran his hand down his face. "Ten women in the past few years? At least ten. And there's nothing. There's no spark. There's no magic."

Preacher remained silent for a couple of minutes as the sun started to send golden rays across the ranch. Ward loved mornings like this, but his favorite time came in October, when the air cooled at night a little bit more than early September, and the sun took longer to spread light over their land.

"I love Texas," Ward said.

"No magic?" Preacher asked as if Ward hadn't even spoken. "With anyone?"

"There's someone," Ward said casually. "But it feels like a lot of work, and I don't know. She didn't seem to like me much."

"You went out with her?"

"No," Ward said. "We...ran into each other at church."

"So you know her."

"Yes," Ward said. "I know her."

They sat in silence for a few more minutes, and then Preacher said, "I think I want a Labrador retriever."

"Black or yellow?"

"Yellow," he said. "And Ward, if there's no spark or excitement, don't go out with whoever it is tonight. Call the woman who you're thinking about and see if you can fan those sparks into flames."

"What if she's like Libby, and she won't say yes?"

"Oh, Mister just needs to go over to Libby's," Preacher said. "He needs to show up there with her favorite flowers and his hat in his hand. He needs to tell her he's sorry for asking her to set him up with her friends, and that he really wants to get to know her as more than a friend. That's all."

"Wow, Preach," Ward said, chuckling. "You've got all the answers."

"Yeah," someone else said, and Ward looked up to find Mister standing at the corner of the stables. "And it's just *so easy* when he says it too, right?" He gazed off into the distance, and Ward couldn't argue with him.

"I *do* have the answers," Preacher said. "And you, Ward, just need to call whoever that woman is that you ran into at church."

"Dot?" Mister asked.

"No," Ward said, but he clipped out her name way too fast, and that definitely meant yes, Dot.

"Dot Crockett?" Preacher asked. "The landscaping lady?"

"That makes her sound eighty years old," Ward said with disgust. "And no, it's not Dot." But it so was Dot.

"Is she the one who won't call you back about the gravel?" Mister asked.

"Yes," Ward said darkly. "And neither will Twin Cities. The gravel is literally a huge mess."

"It's fine," Preacher said. "I don't even notice it."

"That makes me feel so much better, Preach. Thanks." Ward got to his feet, noticing the shape of the wood in his cousin's hand. It looked suspiciously like a video game controller. "Come on, know-it-all. Time to walk home."

Preacher smiled and stood. The three of them started the slow waltz back to the Ranch House, where Preacher got right back on the couch and promptly fell asleep.

Ward set an alarm so he'd be back in time to wake Preacher and get him to his physical therapy appointment. Then he went back outside to go through his morning meeting with the men and women who worked full-time at Shiloh Ridge.

With Preacher out of commission, Ward was back to running the ranch as the only foreman, and he didn't hate it. He didn't love it either, but he could do it for Preacher.

"All right," he said once he'd arrived at the cowboy cabins that sat directly west of the homestead. "We've got plenty to do today. The harvesting is in full swing, and I need my B-crew on that today."

"You got it, boss," someone said.

"I want A-crew on rounding up cattle and bringing them to pastures one through seven."

"Yes, sir," a cowboy said.

"I need two people doing sprinklers today." He surveyed the group. "Lindsay and Floyd?"

"Yep," the cowgirl said. "And Bear asked me to check in the maintenance shed to make sure the harvesters are humming along."

"That's fine," Ward said. "That's important." He glanced down at his clipboard and adjusted his cowboy hat. "I need one extra man in the stables with Judge this morning."

"I can," Ed said, raising his hand. "I'm good with the horses."

"Thank you," Ward said. "Wait. You're on cattle round-up." He frowned. "You can't do both."

"I can," Ed said. "I'll go to the stables now, and then I'll catch up with the herd."

"If you think you can."

"I can."

"Okay," Ward said, because he didn't need to cause a problem if there wasn't one. "Last thing. Tomorrow is market day. I need everyone ready an hour early. We're going to do our holiday essentials for the animals, and everyone will be on that. Then, we'll all be rounding up the calves to our corral, and the trucks will be here at eight."

He looked around at everyone. "We really appreciate you all working here with us. We can't do what we do without you." He grinned at a couple of the career cowboys that had been at Shiloh Ridge for years. "Lunch will be provided tomorrow, and it'll be served in True Blue. Everyone will have a little bonus there too, so be sure to look for your name on an envelope."

"Yeehaw!" Russ said, throwing his hat up into the air. Several others copied him, and laughter and chatter broke out. Ward knew how important verbal praise was, but he liked following it up with cash. They got better help that way, and they had very little turnover at Shiloh Ridge—which made life easier for Ward.

The meeting broke up, and he joined the crew going over to the sprinklers. He'd told Preacher he'd make sure that was done today, and he'd check in with Cactus too, as they were gearing up for birthing season once they got the cattle back in from the range.

He worked through the morning, stopping only for a few minutes for lunch at the homestead. He got to hold his nephew Wilder while Oakley ran to take a shower. Both he and the baby fell asleep, and he didn't wake until Oakley put a plate with a sandwich and potato salad on the table next to him.

"Thank you," he said sleepily. "Holdin' this baby put me right out." He looked down at the six-month-old, who seemed so perfect and so peaceful. Ward smiled at Wilder and shifted him so he could reach for the food.

"I can take him."

"I'm okay." Ward ate his sandwich with the sleeping infant in his arms, but he had to yield Wilder to eat his potato salad.

As he left the homestead, Ward's desperation and loneliness quadrupled. He wanted the wife and family. He wanted to bring his wife something for lunch while he held their infant to give her a break. He wanted a son to teach the world of ranching, the way his daddy had taught him.

"What do I do?" he asked the heated sky. "Lord, tell me what to do." He'd prayed for this exact thing in the past and gotten nowhere.

But today, his only thought was, *Call Dot*.

He wasn't going to ignore that anymore. He wasn't going to go on dates with women who didn't excite him.

He wanted to go out with Dot.

He pulled up her number and hit call. The line rang and rang, and Ward prayed and prayed.

"Ward Glover," she said, and even her voice got his blood vibrating in a new way. "I don't have the thirty-five."

"Dot," he said. "I'm not calling about the gravel." He cleared his throat, his mind going with it. "You intrigue me, Miss Crockett, and I want to get to know you better. Would you consider going to dinner with me sometime?"

## Chapter Thirty-Five

*The second baby is a girl!*

Charlie looked up from the text, the parking lot where she waited starting to fill up. Messages continued to pour in, and Charlie read them as the other women on the group text congratulated Ida Burton.

Once a Glover.

Charlie tapped out a message of her own, but her thumb hovered over the *send* button. She wasn't really one of them, though she'd been added to this group the day of Preacher's accident. She'd labeled it *The Women of Shiloh Ridge Ranch*, and she surely didn't belong in that group.

Her brain misfired as she tried to remember who'd added her a few weeks ago. "I think it was Pastor Knowlton."

She scrolled up in the text to the very top, where it said, *Willa Glover has added you.*

"Of course," she murmured. Willa had told her once that it was Pastor Glover now.

Charlie wasn't married to a Glover. Heck, she wasn't even seeing Preacher anymore.

Ida was pregnant with twins—apparently one boy and one girl—and due just after Christmas. Sammy was due with a baby just before Christmas. She and Bear didn't find out the gender of their baby until it was born, and Charlie felt a bit of stress on their behalf just thinking about that.

Willa was having a boy before the end of January, and the other three women currently pregnant didn't know if their babies were boys or girls. Holly Ann was due first, in mid-February, and then Montana in March, and finally Arizona in April.

Why Charlie had kept up with their family drama, she didn't know. All she knew was that she couldn't bear to ask to be taken off the group text. She looked down at her message again, suddenly panicked about sending it.

If she did, they'd realize she was still in their group. Then someone might remove her, because she really didn't belong there. It was for the Glover women, and she wasn't one of them.

If she didn't send her text, she'd feel guilty and left out.

A sigh escaped as she contemplated what to do. Why couldn't life be simple? Why had she gone and fallen in love with the cowboy? Because he could dance? Because he played video games? Because he was handsome and smart and hard-working? Because he treated her like royalty?

Tears entered her eyes, and she fought against them. She didn't have time to cry this morning. She'd done her morning broadcast two hours early for her Nexus fans, because school had started again and Charlie had a demonstration at the high school this morning.

She erased the message congratulating Ida, stuck her phone in the pocket of her lab coat, and got out of her truck. She'd been carrying in her own bins and setting everything up herself. It was hard work to get all of the supplies in and unpacked, but then she enjoyed the experiments and demos.

Usually. Today, she could already tell her patience wavered on the edge of a thin line, and she really just wanted someone to put a hot breakfast in front of her and then stay with her while she went back to bed. When she woke, Preacher would be there to take care of her. Both of her cats would be on his lap or very nearby, as they really seemed to sense those who didn't like them, thus prompting the felines to stay by them even more.

Charlie half-smiled, half-sobbed at the thought. Archie and Paulie had been stalking around the house since Preacher's departure, throwing her nasty looks as if she were the one who'd driven him away.

Maybe she had driven him away. She wasn't sure. She'd asked for time to figure out what she wanted, but she knew already.

She wanted him, and yes, that was code for she loved him. She didn't know when she'd fallen in love with him—she couldn't go back and pinpoint the exact moment—and she didn't know how to stop loving him.

With Forrest, Charlie had learned over time that she'd never really loved him at all. It had been somewhat easy to move on once she'd realized that. But this? This daily living without Preacher's calm, steady influence in her life felt like someone screwing a key into her back, slowly, painfully. Every twist dug a little deeper, hurt a little more. They wound her up, and she went about her day like a toy doll, with memorized lines and plastic smiles.

"There you are," someone said as she juggled opening the door to the gymnasium with two bins she'd stacked on top of one another. The man took one of the bins. "I'm Doctor Samuels. I was just beginning to wonder if you were coming."

"I'm here," Charlie said, slipping into her role as chemist. She was very good at moving from one persona to another. Doting cat mom. The Chemist the gamer. Miss Perkins, the extraordinary woman who did experiments for children.

She wasn't sure what label she'd put on herself when she laid in bed and wept that Preacher was injured and she wasn't there to help him. She'd gone to the hospital late at night that first day. His brother had barely let her through the door, but she'd convinced him she just wanted to sit with Preacher for a little bit.

She had, and she'd talked to him and wept over him. Leaving him there and not going back had been the hardest thing she'd ever had to do. Not only that, but the regret that she'd done such a thing gnawed at her a little bit harder every single day.

At this point, though, Charlie didn't know how to open a line of communication with Preacher. He seemed so far away. Untouchable, and it had only been three weeks.

Every day put an additional layer between them, and Charlie felt smothered beneath the distance she'd have to cross to even speak to him again.

"Oh, good," she said, making her voice as chipper as possible for this time of the morning. "You found the tables I need."

"I had to borrow them from the faculty room," Dr. Samuels said with a smile. "You've got more in your truck, right?"

"All the bins in the back have to come in," she said. She left him to do that, as he was only about ten years older than her and her point of contact here at the high school for experiments. Today, she was demonstrating the different types of chemical reactions, and she'd need her protective glasses and plenty of ventilation. Groups were coming to the gym in pairs—two classes at a time—throughout the entire day, and then Charlie needed to stop by the kiosk in the mall to go over the schedule.

She had seven employees helping her run Below Zero now, and while she was thrilled with the growth of her ice cream company in such a short time, it could sometimes feel like a burden too. She had payroll to deal with now, and scheduling teens and young adults who had constantly changing lives. She'd been developing a new ice cream base—banana—and she still didn't have the ratio of real fruit flavor to synthetic right. The last batch had come out tasting too much like chemicals, but the one before that had barely tasted of banana at all.

The truth was, Charlie's heart wasn't in any of this. She didn't carry the same passion for her demos as she had last winter and spring. She'd go by the kiosk and smile at the sign for Below Zero, but it didn't hold the same satisfaction and joy.

Without Preacher, everything existed in shades of gray.

*What are you going to do about it?* she asked herself as she got out the row of fuel tanks. All she had to do was coat the fibers with the fuels, and she could produce a rainbow effect when the fires got lit. She did love this experiment, and she started to cheer as she set it up.

Meanwhile, Dr. Samuels brought in her supplies to show an exothermic reaction she really liked doing. The "elephant toothpaste" was one she could have students come up and do, then she'd ask them questions to help them figure out what chemical reactions were happening, and how they could recognize one.

When two things interacted and produced heat, that was almost always a chemical reaction. A change in color showed something similar, and that was why she'd brought her rainbow flames today.

She'd also be filling a balloon through a chemical reaction, because the production of a gas usually showed chemical changes happening, and the only way to do that was to collect the gas somehow.

She busied herself with getting each station set up with the supplies she needed, and then she went over her notes while the first bell of the day rang. The students would be arriving shortly, and Charlie looked at her phone again.

*The second baby is a girl!*

The text that had started today's flurry of messages burned into the back of Charlie's eyes. She'd never considered herself very maternal, nor did she want a big family. She did want to belong somewhere, and she would like to be a mother at least once.

She scrolled to the bottom of the text string, where Montana had asked what Ida would name the babies. *Do you have any particular names in mind?*

*Not quite yet,* Ida said as Charlie watched. *Besides, they'll just change anyway, right? LOL.*

Charlie smiled at the text, at the memory that Preacher's name was really Paul. She'd never really gotten the whole story as to why the men at Shiloh Ridge had different names. Etta, Ida, and Arizona didn't, and she wondered if it was something reserved only for males.

Did she dare ask? If she did, would she have to answer a bunch of questions about her and Preacher? Surely his family knew the status of their relationship, which made her continued presence on the group text even more baffling.

*Congratulations, Ida,* she typed out, gathering her courage as the first of the students started to enter the gym. *Two babies at once. You're a saint. I'm intrigued by the names up there. Is it something only for the boys? How did they get chosen?*

Before she could chicken out—if they removed her, they removed her—she sent the text and pocketed her phone. Dr. Samuels said, "All right, settle down," and Charlie wouldn't have a chance to get back to her texts for a few hours. That was probably fine, because then she wouldn't have to face reality until then either.

# Chapter Thirty-Six

Preacher strained against the weight in his hand, lifting the barbell up into a curl as he exhaled and lowering it as he inhaled.

Jackson Bryan, his physical therapist, watched, making notes. Preacher had decided a couple of weeks ago that he didn't care what the man thought of him. He did the work, and his hip and leg and back were getting stronger.

Sometimes he wanted to throw a string of swear words to Jackson, and not the brands and saddles kind. The kind that told the trainer just what Preacher thought of the leg lift he wanted him to do.

Preacher wasn't too proud to admit he'd cried more than once after physical therapy. Usually only with Judge in the truck with him, because his more emotional brother wouldn't well, judge him.

"Okay," Jackson said. "You're great in your upper body strength."

All of Preacher's superficial wounds had healed too. The cuts and bruises on his face had lingered for a while, but Mother had a tincture she claimed would clear up anything, and boy had it worked on his scrapes, scars, and scuffs.

Now, he just needed to get his hip in shape. The doctors seemed pleased with the way it had been healing, but they still wouldn't authorize him to drive, nor would they let him get back on a horse. He had to rely on his brothers and cousins to get him where he needed or wanted to go, and he had to do all of his work from behind a desk or with nothing heavier than a shovel in his hand.

Jackson wouldn't even let him clean horse stalls, saying that one put far too much pressure and torque on their hip when forking out old straw and replacing it. Chores Preacher had taken for granted were completely off-limits. He'd taken over feeding the chickens and roosters, because that was tossing feed and refilling water containers.

He fed the pigs too, lifting about as much weight in fifty-gallon buckets as he did right here in the gym with the barbells.

He did have to be more mindful of how he twisted and turned while out on the ranch, and if he'd done something he shouldn't have, he paid the price. First, he usually had to suffer through some serious pain for a day or two. Then, when he came to his now-weekly physical therapy appointments, Jackson or Tyler always seemed to know which rule he'd broken.

"Let's see you walk and pivot," Jackson said, studying

his board. "I want you in the pool today too. Do you think you can do that?"

"I can try," Preacher said. Those three words had almost become a mantra for him over the past six weeks since his car accident. *I can try to get out to the stables. I can try to climb the stairs. I can try to pick up all the hoses from the yard.*

The Ranch House had never been so clean and organized, and that was because Preacher was slowly going insane inside its walls. Ward and Mister lived in the basement now, and one of them made him walk down there every night. Then to the main level, then out to the stable and back. Three times. Up, down, out.

He spent a lot of time with his knife and a piece of wood. He'd carved horses and dogs, joysticks and video game controllers. He'd started to paint some of them, and he thought he might give them to Lincoln or Mitch for their birthdays. Cactus would take the ones of his dogs, and Preacher was currently working on a Corvette—a replica of the one Zona owned and had fixed up. He planned to paint it blue and keep it for himself, and Lord knew he had time to do all of that.

His mind got to go where it wanted while his hands were busy, and he liked that he could lose hours of time, have something he'd created, and feel like he had a better handle on the world after a good whittling session.

*I can try to stop thinking about Charlie Perkins.*

He never did accomplish that, and something was going to have to be done about her. He pictured her pretty blue eyes as he walked the length of the room and turned around until Jackson was satisfied his hip could take the twisting pressure. Then he said, "Get your trunks on, cowboy."

Getting dressed had presented its own unique set of challenges. Simply stepping into a pair of jeans didn't happen anymore. Preacher had to think so hard about what every movement would do to his hip, his lower back, and his knee. Could he lift his leg that high? If he tried to balance on his left leg, would he fall down?

The answer to that was still yes. He couldn't balance on his left leg alone, and he walked with a slightly stumbling gait that he hadn't been able to even out yet. Jackson said he may never be able to, and that his body would adjust.

The chiropractor Preacher had started to see really wanted his stride to be even, because yes, the body adjusted. But it did so in ways that caused other problems and pains. A shooting arc of pain through his lower back, for example. A tension in the left side of his neck and through his shoulders. A twist in his knee that would wear him down over time.

The fact was, Preacher was doing better, feeling better, and performing better, but he was not whole. He may never be whole again.

He changed out of his sweatpants and T-shirt and into his swimming trunks. He was still under strict orders not to walk anywhere without shoes on his feet, and he only broke that rule in the middle of the night when he had to go to the bathroom. No one had called him on such treachery yet.

He slipped his feet back into his sneakers and went into the physical therapy pool room. At least five swim spas took up this room, and three of them had people in them. Jackson waited for Preacher in the one against the far wall, his clipboard now inside a waterproof plastic sleeve.

Preacher hated the pool therapy. Number one, he'd never enjoyed swimming all that much. Number two, he always ended up wrong-side-up underwater. The way the water moved and pressed against him, sloshing him this way and that, made him disoriented and unbalanced.

He "fell" in the pool, and that left him breaking the surface, sputtering for air, and wondering why he hadn't been able to maintain his balance.

Of course, regaining the strength in the left side of his body so he could balance was the whole point.

"All right," Jackson said once Preacher had joined him in the water. "I just want to see an easy front stroke for a minute or two. I want to see how that left leg does in a kick."

"All right." Preacher adjusted his goggles over his eyes and waited for Jackson to get up on the side of the swim spa.

"Sixty seconds," Jackson said. "You're on a three, Preacher. It shouldn't be hard."

"All right.," he said again, this time letting his body float up a little bit as the water rushed at him from the front of the spa. His feet lifted off the ground, and he stroked into the water coming toward him.

"Kick," Jackson barked, and Preacher growled into the

waves. But he kicked. He didn't want to argue with anyone. If they thought this was going to get him well, he'd do it. He didn't want to be a burden to his family forever, and he didn't want to saddle Charlie with an invalid for the rest of her life.

Just the fact that he thought he might still have a shot with Charlie was fairly laughable. She hadn't texted or called him in forty-three days now, and Preacher felt each one keenly. Each hour stabbed at him. Each minute reminded him of how hard it was to breathe without her.

*You'll get her back*, he thought as he stroked, stroked, stroked through the water. He had no plan to get her back, only that once he was well enough to drive himself to her house, that was where he'd be.

Her favorite flavor of ice cream in his hand, and the newest joystick under his arm. He'd beg her to forgive him, plead with her to give them one more chance. She simply lit something inside him that had to burn, and right now, it was lifeless and limp.

*Soon*, he promised himself as Jackson blew the whistle and said he could stop. Chest heaving, Preacher tried to find his footing so he could stand. He couldn't quite get his left foot under him, despite Jackson's encouragement.

He treaded water while the trainer said, "Try again, Preach. Get the left foot under you first. You've got all the support of the water here to hold up your body weight."

"The water trips me," Preacher complained, skating the toes of his left foot along the bottom of the spa. "I can feel it. I just can't get it...." He pressed his hip forward, because that should bring his leg forward too.

The sole of his foot touched the bottom, and Preacher put his weight onto it as much as he could. The undulating water immediately tried to push him back, but Preacher put his right foot solidly on the ground too.

His back straightened, and the next thing he knew, Preacher was standing after his swim.

"You got it," Jackson said, a smile in his voice. "Nice job, Preach."

That was the best praise Preacher would get from the relentless trainer, and he turned to face him. They smiled at one another, and Preacher felt like he'd conquered the world. If he could really do that and then show up on Charlie's doorstep with the world in his hands, maybe—just maybe—he'd have a shot at getting her back into his life.

---

A WEEK LATER, PREACHER OPENED THE DOOR OF WARD'S truck and turned his whole body so his legs dangled out of the doorway. "Thanks, Ward. Zona will bring me home."

"Okay, but you two be safe in that blasted sports car."

"We'll be fine," Preacher said, annoyed at Ward's opinion of sports cars. It wasn't the Mustang's fault Preacher had rolled it. It was his. His and his stubbornness. His pride.

Well, God had knocked that right out of him, and Preacher had been apologizing to the Lord for a while now. He'd been begging for a speedy recovery too, and as his sister came out of the house where she lived with her husband, Preacher did feel more like himself than he had in a while.

"Afternoon," she drawled, and Preacher grinned at her. She still had six months to go before she'd deliver her baby, and he didn't detect the slightest rounding in her belly at all. She'd always been tall and thin, just like her brothers, and she drew him right into a hug that reminded him of Mother. "I've got the ham sandwiches about ready to come out of the oven."

"Sounds great," he said. "How is she?"

"She's missin' you," Zona said with a smile as he pulled back. "I told her I'd have to drive, but that you'd be behind the wheel soon enough."

"I don't know," Preacher said, glancing at the Corvette parked at the side of the house. "I think I'm gonna sell my other Mustang."

"You don't have to do that, Preacher."

"I know, but I just don't know if I can drive it."

"You do what you think is right." Zona led the way into the house and the blessed air conditioning. Though October had arrived in the Panhandle, Three Rivers was experiencing a heat wave that had most people blowing the air conditioning during the day and then their heaters at night.

Soon enough, Mother Nature would decide to get her act together, and she'd throw wind, rain, and even snow at them. Preacher wanted to tell her to bring it on, because nothing had been worse than him watching everyone around the ranch on market day, riding horses and herding cattle. He couldn't help with the branding, and he couldn't be out on the range with other cowboys and cowgirls as they brought in their bounty for the year.

He'd spent a great deal of time going over their final numbers and projections for breeding season. He'd balanced every budget and bank account the ranch had, and he still had hours in his day to fill.

"I made you something," he said, reaching into the backpack he'd brought to take out the carving. "I have a lot of free time these days, so...."

He handed her the present he'd wrapped in newspaper, sudden nerves attacking his stomach.

Zona's face lit up. "Preach. You're whittling again?"

"I have the time," he said again. "Might as well take advantage of it, right?" He held up his hand, where two fingers had been bandaged. "I've nicked myself a couple of times."

She tore the newspaper off the object to reveal a baby cradle. She pulled in a breath and said, "Oh."

"I didn't paint it blue or pink," he said. "I figured once y'all knew what you were having, I could do that for you."

"Thank you." Zona threw her arms around him, but not before he saw the unshed tears in her eyes. He felt like he barely knew her, because his sister had always been as tough as nails. Hard as steel.

He held her tight, so glad they'd managed to rebuild this bridge between them. *Thank you for the inspiration*, he prayed, because it hadn't been his idea to give Zona the keys to Dad's Corvette for Christmas last year. That inspiration had come from God.

He and Zona sat down to eat lunch, and he listened to

her chatter about a class Terelyn Michaels was doing for hair-cutting. "I'm thinking of taking it," Zona said. "Duke has a ton of hair, and I'm sure I'll need to cut our son's too."

She didn't know if she was having a girl or a boy yet, but having a girl terrified Zona to the very core. She'd decided to only talk about the baby with male pronouns in an attempt to convince the universe to send her a boy.

"Take it," Preacher said as Zona's phone lit up with texts. "That must be the family string. I mute mine."

"Oh, mine's muted too," she said, practically knocking down her lemonade to get to her phone and flip it over. She glanced at Preacher, something nervous in her expression.

Part of him wanted to let it go. If she didn't want him to know who was texting her, fine by him. He'd never been that involved in her life anyway. She was a grown woman, and she could message and talk to whomever she pleased.

The phone continued to vibrate, though, and Zona's face turned a rather unhealthy shade of pink.

"What's goin' on?" Preacher finally asked.

Her phone began to vibrate steadily against the table, and she finally reached for it. "Oh...someone's calling."

Preacher's eyes had been unaffected from the accident, and he clearly saw Charlie's name on Zona's screen. She swiped the call away and stuck her phone in her back pocket.

Preacher's pulse pounded through his whole body. His throat narrowed to the point where he couldn't take another bite of his hot ham and cheese sandwich. He had to know, and he prayed his voice would work as he opened his mouth.

"Why is Charlie calling you?" he asked.

Zona stuffed the rest of her sandwich in her mouth, and she had at least a third of it left. Impressive. But Preacher had the wait-time of an elephant, and she should've known it. Sitting around the Ranch House for the past seven weeks sure had helped his patience, and he simply took a more appropriately-sized bite of his food and waited.

"Zona," he said once she'd swallowed.

"Fine," she said. "Willa put her on the girls' text a while back, and she texts us."

Preacher opened his mouth, his mind racing. Nothing came out. No words could be formed.

"Oh, close your mouth," Zona teased. "It's harmless."

"What does she say?" Preacher asked, his voice pitching up.

"Stuff," Zona said nonchalantly. She even tried to shrug it off. "It's just the girls up here in the southern hills. You know, the wives at Shiloh Ridge."

"She's not my wife."

"I...yeah, I know."

"What does she say?"

"Stuff," Zona said again, her voice turning a touch harder. "She participates in our conversations."

"Are you friends with her now?"

"Yes, that's right," Zona said. "Just because you two

aren't dating anymore doesn't mean she can't be friends with us."

"With *us*?" Preacher asked. "She's friends with everyone?"

"I think so," Zona said, getting up and taking her plate to the kitchen sink. "She's nice, Preacher. We like her."

"Why didn't you take her off the group text?"

"Did you hear what I just said?"

Preacher had heard it. He just didn't know what to do with the information. His family—all the wives at Shiloh Ridge—had been texting and talking to Charlie for weeks. Seven weeks.

He wasn't sure if he should be happy or horrified. And that only made him angry. *Of course* he should be happy Charlie had friends, and there was no one better to be friends with than his sister and his sisters-in-law.

He just hadn't known this was going on, and he needed a few minutes to think about it.

"Does she ever say anything about me?" he asked, trying to play it off as nothing. In reality, if Zona said no, she'd be driving a pick right into Preacher's heart.

"I'm not answering that," she said, returning to the table for his empty plate. "Are we driving this Corvette today or what?"

"Yes," Preacher said, but he didn't get up. "You wanted to talk to me about the angel tree, though." He could circle back to Charlie later.

"Oh, that's right." Zona turned toward the living room. "Be right back." She bustled off past the sofa and recliner, the only two furniture items that would fit in the small space. They'd mounted a TV to the wall, and a fireplace took up the front corner of the house. This was nothing like the houses Bishop could build—and had built—for family members, and Preacher wondered if Zona was happy at this ranch.

She sure seemed happy with Duke Rhinehart, and that was all that really mattered.

Preacher thought about where he'd live, and he couldn't picture it. Over the past few weeks, he'd realized not having a place to call his own home had put a wedge between Charlie and the rest of the ranch. He hadn't known it, but he did now.

How could he offer her the world if he didn't even have a home for her to live in?

"Okay," Zona said, bustling back into the kitchen. "The tree broke when we were taking it down this year. I ordered a new one—or rather, I'm going to order a new one." She put three printouts on the table in front of him. "Which one do you think will be the best? Remember, Grandmother loved a flocked tree."

"The one we have now is all white," he said. He loved the pure white pine needles, and all the white lights. Angels wore white, and that had made the tree into what it was.

"All white trees are very hard to find now," Zona said. "That tree was at least two decades old."

"Sad it broke."

"Yes," she said, but she sure didn't sound sad. She tapped the pictures one by one. "One, two, or three?"

"If I'm picking right now, two," he said. "It's the closest

to what we've been using." The tree had a wide base with dark green needles that had been flocked to look drenched in powdery, white snow. He could just see Grandmother's crocheted ornaments hanging from the limbs, and hear the Christmas carols as they played from a speaker someone had put on the bottom step of the grand staircase that led up to the apartment-suites on the second floor.

"Okay," she said. "Second choice?"

"One." Preacher did like a robust tree, and while this one didn't have a stitch of white anywhere, it would hold a lot of ornaments.

He looked up to find Zona frowning. "Okay, thanks." She swept away the photos almost as quickly as they'd arrived, and she stood. "Come on, Preach. Time to get your lazy bones off that chair."

"Hey, I've done my walking for this morning already," he said. "Ward pushes me to go farther every single time."

"Good," Zona said without a trace of compassion. "You need it."

"I do what I'm supposed to do," he said.

She gave him an arched brow, stepped over to the back door, and took her keys off the hook there. "Do you?"

"What does that mean?"

She left the house, and Preacher hurried after her as quickly as he could. "Zona, what does that mean?"

"What are you going to do about Charlie?" she asked, not meeting his eye as she rounded the sculpted, nearly pointed hood of the Corvette.

"I—" Preacher stared at her over the top of the low-riding car. "What should I do?" She'd been talking to Charlie. She was a woman. Maybe Zona could tell him what to do to get Charlie back into his life.

"The angel tree celebration is in twelve days," Zona said. "Everyone brings their significant other. Bishop brought Montana before they were engaged. Sammy brings her parents. Holly Ann brings her whole family."

Preacher stared at her, trying to find the solution to his problem with Charlie inside what she'd said. "You think I should bring her to the angel tree celebration. With the whole family."

"I think it's the perfect thing to do if you want her to know how welcome she is in your life, and our lives," she said, grinning. "What a great idea, Preach." She got behind the wheel of the Corvette, and Preacher looked down at the top of the car.

This was a huge mistake. There was no way he could get into or out of this car without help. He wasn't even sure his hip could bend like that.

The window rolled down, and Zona said, "Get in, Preacher. I'll help you get out." The locks clicked, and Preacher opened the door.

He put his left foot in first, making sure he moved slowly so the sideways motion didn't cripple him with pain. When it only gave him a sharp warning, he quickly sank into the seat and brought his other leg inside. He stretched his legs out and leaned back with a sigh.

"Zona?" he asked. "Where were you planning to go?"

She twisted the key in the ignition, and the engine roared to life. Looking at him, she said, "You tell me. This is your ride."

Preacher's mind spun. He wasn't sure he was ready to face Charlie yet. He had nothing to offer her. No home. No health. Definitely not the world.

"Will you take me to Charlie's?" he asked. "I need to talk to her."

## Chapter Thirty-Seven

Charlie spooned banana chocolate chip ice cream into her mouth, the consistency of it absolute perfection. "The flavor's pretty good too," she said to Paulie, but he simply stalked on by as if he had somewhere feline and fabulous to be.

The wind whipped against the windows, and Charlie got up to close the blinds. Now that it was getting darker earlier, she didn't like letting the world see inside her house. Not that anyone could see back here, and not that the clock was anywhere close to evening.

In fact, Charlie was eating ice cream for lunch, and she should probably get some real, solid food in her stomach before too much longer. She also had to prep for her livestream that night, as she was demoing a new product she hadn't even opened yet, and she needed to find time to buy more extension cords for that weekend's Fall Festival.

"Oh, and you better get online and get another order of

cones in." The kiosk at the mall had been going through ice cream cones like crazy, what with the heat wave that had hit the Panhandle. It would last a few more days, and then rain was supposed to come to Three Rivers.

Charlie honestly wanted to hunker down this winter, and she hadn't booked any schools in November or December. She wouldn't either, and she'd told the curriculum coordinator at the district office exactly that.

A weight had been lifted from her when she'd made that decision, and her mind went to Preacher as she walked into the kitchen. She'd wanted to tell him about how overwhelmed she'd felt, and that she'd actually done something about it. He'd have held her close, swayed with her, and whispered that he was glad she'd have more time to do what she loved.

Charlie did love doing the chemistry experiments. She loved chemistry and figuring out how to put compounds together to create something beneficial. She loved watching the students' faces when the rainbow fire burst to life, or when one of their classmates touched her electrified ball and all of their hair stood straight out from their head.

But she loved developing ice cream recipes too. She loved entertaining a group of people at the stand at a fair, teaching them about liquid nitrogen and freezing points and chemical reactions right there in their food.

She loved sitting in front of her extra-wide screen and playing video games. She liked interacting with her friends online. In so many ways, she had everything she could ever possibly want.

But without Preacher, none of it mattered. "Maybe just

drive up there and see him," she said to herself. She opened the fridge and pulled out the box of leftover pizza. With two slices of it rotating in the microwave, Charlie pulled out her phone and checked the group thread with all the Glover women.

Holly Ann had posted the menu for that month's luncheon, and Charlie had already committed to going. It would be her first one, and a wave of nerves twittered through her. What if these women were just like her other girlfriends in real-life? What if all they talked about were their kids and pregnancies? Did she have any chance of fitting in at all?

She knew better than most that online relationships weren't entirely real. Two people could get along swimmingly well via chat or even video calls, but once they met and existed in the same physical space, the sparks fizzled.

Others started commenting on the menu, and Charlie sent a quick message about how much she loved fried macaroni and cheese, and that she was thrilled to see that as an appetizer. Just the fact that Holly Ann had appetizers for a monthly luncheon with all the ranch wives made Charlie smile and shake her head.

She'd called Arizona a little over an hour ago, mostly just to chat. Charlie did want to prime her for more information about the luncheon, and she needed to ask what everyone wore. Was it casual? Should she plan time to curl her hair and put on makeup? Where was the luncheon? In the homestead? At Holly Ann's?

When Charlie didn't know something, she asked Arizona off the main group text. That way, she didn't have to feel foolish in front of all of them, and she'd actually become real friends with Arizona.

The doorbell rang, and Charlie looked up, startled. "Who could that be?" No one ever came by the house in the middle of the day. Or at night. Only Preacher, but he'd stopped coming around obviously. Charlie hadn't even realized how lonely and isolated she was until he'd vacated her life.

She left the kitchen and crossed through the living room. Both cats waited for her on the rug in the foyer, and she told them to, "Stay," as she passed. She hated it when one of them ran out the front door, as they had a cat door in the back that led into a fenced yard.

Of course, she couldn't herd cats any better than she could figure out how to call Preacher, and both Paulie and Archie followed her to the door. "It's not for you," she told them as she opened the door.

She looked up from the felines and into the most beautiful pair of eyes she'd ever seen.

"Preacher," she said, her voice more of a gasp than anything else.

He stood on her front porch, the picture of cowboy perfection though he didn't have the boots on his feet today. He wore a regular pair of sneakers, a pair of sweatpants, and a T-shirt that stretched across his shoulders and biceps.

"Do you maybe have a minute to talk?" He reached up and swiped his cowboy hat from his head, about the only thing that still made him a cowboy.

She had no idea what to say. The sound of her pulse

beating through her veins made a white roar fill her ears, and even if she had said something, it would've echoed through her head.

"Just for a minute," he said, the sound of his voice clearing her mind.

"Yes," she said, stepping back and opening the door further. Both Paulie and Archie streaked past her ankles, and each of them rubbed against Preacher's legs as they went by. Charlie couldn't look away from him, but she definitely heard the grumble and rumble of a very big engine as a sporty red car backed out of her driveway.

"Arizona brought me down," he said. "She has a couple of things to get in town, and then she'll come get me." He kneaded the brim of his hat. "I can't drive yet." He cleared his throat. "I can't do a lot of things yet, but I'm working on them, Charlie. I'm going to give you the world one day. That is...if you'll let me."

"I don't need the world," she whispered.

"But you deserve it," he said. "I know I said you should take the time you need to decide if you really wanted to be with someone like me." He gestured down his body, but he looked fine to her. More than fine. Perfect.

"You still can. I'm just...." He glanced left and then right, but Charlie had plenty of land surrounding this big house, and no one would overhear them.

He focused on her again, those eyes filled with bright hope. "I'm just in love with you," he said, a smile touching his lips. "Every time I think of you, I smile. When I think about my future, you're in it. When I imagine who I want at the side of my bed when I'm hurt or old and gray, it's you."

Charlie pressed one hand to her chest as she studied his face.

"I know I should've introduced you around to my family. I told myself I was right because I didn't want to share you. I still don't, by the way, but I know it's important that I do. I've spent so much of my life thinking I was on the outside of the family, when really, I've done that to myself. I'm the one standing on the other side of the door and refusing to walk through."

"Preacher," she said, her voice wavering.

"I'm sorry," he said. "I'm *so* sorry, and I'm here begging you to please give us a second chance. I'll do better. I'll be better. Well, the best I can be."

"You don't need to do better," Charlie said, tears filling her eyes. "You're good enough exactly the way you are."

"Sometimes I can't get off the couch," he said. "Trust me, I need to get better."

"I don't care," she said. "I don't care if you can't walk or you make mistakes. We all make mistakes." She searched his face, wondering if what she'd said made sense to him. It didn't to her.

"I'm miserable without you," he whispered. "There's this chemistry between us I can't live without." He reached one hand toward her. "Please."

Charlie had fallen back to allow him room to enter her house, but he hadn't. She stepped out onto the porch with him, her hand touching his. Their fingers intertwined, and a sigh moved through Charlie's whole soul. "I love you too," she said. "So much. I've been miserable without you too. I didn't call or come by, because honestly...." She looked past him, the sunny day so hot and yet so far removed from her.

"I'm not good at talking about stuff," she said. "I'm not romantic or eloquent or any of the things you are."

"That's why we're so good together." He lifted his other hand to her hip and drew her against his body. "I want to dance with you every day," he whispered. "Every morning when we get up and every night before we go to bed."

"I'd love that," she said.

As they swayed on the front porch, he asked, "Will you come to the angel tree celebration at the ranch?"

"What is it?"

"It's this family tradition in the Glover family. We set up a tree in the foyer at the homestead. It's usually white, but it broke last year, and Arizona is ordering another one. My grandmother used to knit ornaments, and we have boxes and boxes of them. We gather for a big meal and sometimes a family meeting."

Charlie closed her eyes and let herself experience the warmth of him in front of her. She let herself float with him, the scent of his shirt in her nose and the strength of his arms around her.

"I'm not sure what they're doing this year, because I've been so out of things lately."

"Understandable," she murmured.

"Anyway, once we eat and meet, we set up the tree and we decorate it with her ornaments. It's a physical reminder of our ancestors. Of the people who've come before us and are no longer with us. Anyone can hang ornaments on the tree, and some people give whispered tributes to the people they've lost. They don't even have to be dead to be lost."

"No, they don't."

"It's the last Sunday of October, so in about a week and a half. I can have Judge or Ward or someone drive me down to get you."

"Nope," Charlie said. "I have five vehicles here, Mister Glover, and I know the way to Shiloh Ridge."

Preacher hesitated, which told Charlie how he felt about that. "If it gets late, you can stay at the homestead. I'll talk to Etta."

"I can talk to Etta about it," Charlie said, her chest vibrating in a strange way. "I've been texting your family." She pulled out of his embrace. "They're lovely women, and I really like them. Holly Ann is doing a luncheon next week, and they've invited me to come." The words just spilled out of her mouth, like water falling over a cliff. "I want to go, and I'm...how do you feel about that?"

Preacher took her face in both of his hands. "I feel great about that, sugar. You should go, and you should text them, and I apologize I kept them from you."

"You don't need to keep apologizing."

"I will until you kiss me." Light danced in his eyes, and Charlie giggled as she shook her head.

"Is that a no? You won't kiss me?" Preacher slid one hand down the side of her neck. "I'm sorry, sugar." He trailed his lips along her jaw. "I'm really sorry."

Charlie held onto his shoulders, zips and pops running

through her. Heat filled her from head to toe, and she definitely felt so much with this man.

"Please forgive me," Preacher said. "Don't you know it's required of all men to forgive?"

"Okay," she said dryly. "That's good enough."

"Yeah?" Preacher straightened and looked down at her. "I really do love you, and I really am sorry, all kidding aside."

"I know that," she said. "So kiss me already."

He grinned and did what she said. As Charlie kissed him back, she finally felt all of the ragged edges that had been catching in her soul smooth out. She kissed him and kissed him and kissed him, hoping her love for him would ignite inside his soul the way his did in hers.

After a few minutes, he pulled back and said, "Can we go inside? My back hurts when I bend like this."

"Of course." Charlie stepped away from him quickly, and he stumbled forward. She hurried to reach out and steady him. "Sorry."

A flush entered his face as he gripped her forearms and used her to hold himself up. "I'm not whole yet, Charlie," he said. "But I promise you, I'm going to get all the way better, and I *am* going to give you the world."

"*You* are my world," she said. "Come in and sit down. I've just perfected my banana ice cream, and I need to tell you all about the stuff I'm doing on Nexus."

---

Charlie smoothed her hands down her thighs as she peered at the huge homestead standing tall and proud at Shiloh Ridge Ranch. At least half a dozen vehicles had been parked out front, and as she sat in her truck, two more pulled in.

The afternoon still held light, but the sun would yield to the moon within the hour. Mother Nature had blown her heat wave to the East Coast, and Charlie wore a skin-tight pair of jeans, a white camisole, and a sweater filled with autumn-colored stripes. She'd brought a jacket just in case.

Just in case of what, she wasn't sure.

Rain had soaked the Panhandle for a few days, and then the weak fall sun had started to dry it all out again. She watched as Arizona and Duke walked up the sidewalk and climbed the stairs. They didn't pause to ring the doorbell or knock, but simply went right into the house.

Charlies anxiety tripled. She wasn't like Zona. She wasn't like Holly Ann or Montana or Willa. She wasn't married to a Glover, and she'd never been inside this homestead before.

Ida and Brady followed, both of them moving much slower, as Ida only had eight more weeks until her twins would be born. Honestly, Charlie was surprised she'd come at all. They too went up the steps and inside, no knocking necessary.

"Go on," she told herself. "You can ring the doorbell. Preacher will be watching for you anyway." In fact, he probably knew she'd arrived and was giving her space until she got out of the truck.

With shaking hands, she opened the door, reminding herself that she'd met all of these people before. Under a stressful circumstance too, and they'd been kind and welcoming in the hospital. She had friends here—not only Preacher, but all of the women. They'd enjoyed lunch at the barn where Preacher's mother had been married. Holly Ann's house wasn't quite done yet, but she thought they'd be moving in before Christmas.

Charlie had loved the luncheon, and not only because of the delicious food. The company one kept could make any meal worthwhile, and she told herself that no matter what happened tonight, she'd be fine.

She slid from the truck and took a moment to reach back in to get her phone. Inhaling, she got the scent of fresh air, something cool and refreshing, with the underlying smell of horses.

"Right here, Hammy," a man said, and Charlie turned to find a man and his son arriving on a tall, proud, beautiful palomino horse. She remembered Cactus just fine, as she'd met him in the park and at the hospital. Mitch, his stepson, rode in the saddle in front of him, his face lighting up when he saw Charlie.

"Wow," Charlie said. "You guys arrive via horseback and everything."

"It's a nice night," Cactus said. "Willa's driving over."

Mitch started signing something, but Charlie didn't know the language. Blank, she looked up at Cactus as the boy slid down to the ground. His father followed him, saying, "He wants to know if you've played that new...small game?" He swung out of the saddle too and signed to Mitch. "Small game? Is that right?"

Mitch used both hands and started at his chest, his palms down. He made tiers going down, and Cactus still frowned when he looked at Charlie. "Short game? Little game? Something like that. I don't get video game talk."

"Mini-game," Charlie said, finally getting it. "Left Field just put out a *mini-game* for Genius Warfare." She grinned at Mitch. "Yeah, I've played it. They sent me a demo download. Do you play it?"

She glanced at Cactus, because Mitch couldn't be older than ten or eleven. The boy shook his head, indicating Cactus and then continuing to sign. He laughed in a loud voice that surprised Charlie, and Cactus beamed at him.

"He doesn't play," he said. "We don't let him, but he doesn't mind because Preacher's been lettin' him watch him sometimes." Cactus shook his head. "Good to know. I need to have a talk with my brother."

"Genius Warfare isn't bad," Charlie said. "It's more intellectual than just blowing things up."

"You do still blow things up, though, right?" Cactus indicated the sidewalk, and Charlie's lungs seized. Still, she took the first step, Mitch at her side and Cactus only a step or two behind her.

"I mean, yes," she said. "But only if you get the chemistry right." She glanced over her shoulder. "I consulted on that game. The chemistry and science is one-hundred percent accurate, and you have to be smart enough to get it right to progress through the game."

"Interesting," he said. "How long are mini-games?"

"They take ten hours or less to win," she said. "Since I know all the science, I can get through it in about five."

"Preacher has always liked smart women," Cactus said, his voice warm. They reached the steps, and they could walk up the width of them together. Charlie met Cactus's eye, and he must've been able to see something there. "Don't worry," he said. "There are a lot of people here, but it's a big house, and there are multiple exit points."

Charlie nodded, a lump in her throat making it impossible to speak.

"After my son died and my first marriage ended," Cactus said. "I stopped coming in from the Edge. When I started coming back—which was only a few years ago—everything above ten decibels annoyed me. All of my siblings irritated me. They wanted me to talk about things I didn't want to talk about, and they wanted me to do things I hadn't done in a decade." He paused with his hand on the doorknob. "Simple stuff, Charlie, like going to town. Cutting my hair."

She looked at him with wide eyes. "I'm so sorry about your son," she managed to say.

He nodded, somber and so much more real to her. "Thank you. Life is interesting," he said. "The Lord works in mysterious ways, but I believe He's always at work in our lives. He didn't bring you to the ranch for no reason, Charlie. You're here because you belong here."

Tears pricked her eyes, and she nodded, a new sense of warmth and peace flowing through her. It erased all of the doubt and all of the nerves, and she grabbed onto Cactus and hugged him. He chuckled as he lightly embraced her back, and then he said, "I can practically hear Bear growling about how late we are."

They parted, and he opened the door, waiting for her to go first. She looked from him to Mitch and then she ran her hand along the boy's face. "You can come play with me too, Mitch. Or watch me play. Have you heard of Nexus?" She cut a glance at Cactus, whose smile had slipped.

"She's the most popular female gamer on Nexus," Preacher said, and Charlie's eyes flew to his. Joy burst through her, and she found herself leaving Cactus and Mitch without a second thought and flying right into her boyfriend's arms. He chuckled as he held her against his chest, and Charlie grinned when she looked up at him.

"You found it," he said dryly. "For a minute there, I thought you'd gotten lost."

Noise and chatter came from her left. Cactus and Mitch went that way, and Charlie's nose told her to do the same. Something smelled sweet and browned, and her stomach grumbled for want of it. She took a deep breath, getting more of Preacher's scent now than dinner, and she tipped up onto her toes to kiss him.

"You smell great," she whispered.

"I've never been told that before," he said with a smile. "You look fantastic." The warmth of his hands along her waist sent shivers through her, and Charlie settled onto her feet and faced the arched doorway that clearly led into the heart of the house.

GLOVER sat above the arch, carved delicately into the wood there, and Charlie admired the work. "You said Bishop is a woodworker. Did he build this house?"

"No," Preacher said. "Micah Walker is behind the work here."

"It's beautiful."

"I agree." He took a step toward the archway.

They passed boxes and boxes that had been stacked in front of the windows, the last one being a flocked Christmas tree. "Oh, you set it up out here."

"Yes," he said. "That way, whenever you come in and out of the homestead, you can remember who you are. Where you came from. Why you're doing what you're doing. Our traditions and blood runs deep here at Shiloh Ridge."

"I can feel it," she said just before they entered the kitchen. To her left sat the refrigerator, but it wasn't just any old fridge one might get at an appliance store. This one spanned the width of two fridges, before yielding to a corner counter space. The kitchen sink sat beneath wide windows, and more counter space ran down the back wall, ending in double ovens and a range top with six full-sized burners.

A long island separated the back counter from the wide aisle Preacher now led her down. Two couches sat end to end on her right, and the biggest picnic-style table she'd ever laid eyes on took up the dining room space.

Men and woman sat at the table, at the bar, and on the couches and loveseats in the living room. A door led outside near the table, and another one led further into the house beside the fireplace.

"All right," Preacher said, and while some people had quieted down when he and Charlie had entered, they all did now. "I think most of you have met Charlie Perkins before, but in case you haven't, this is Charlie Perkins." He beamed at her, his hand in hers so wonderful but so tight. He was definitely nervous to have her here whether it showed on his face or not.

"My girlfriend," he said. "The smartest woman I know. Gorgeous and a genius." He gazed at her with love now. "The woman I hope to marry, so y'all better be nice to her."

Charlie pulled in a breath, because while she and Preacher had been back together for a little over a week now, they had not gone right back to talking about diamond rings and saying I-do.

She got tugged away from Preacher by Montana and Aurora, who wanted to show her something about Aurora's chemistry grade at school. Everyone seemed to want to speak with her and welcome her individually, and she met Montana's aunt and uncle, then Sammy's parents, and had just been introduced to Oliver Walker when Bear whistled through his teeth.

"Find a seat, everyone," he said. "We have a few things to discuss as a family, and then we'll eat."

She automatically looked for Preacher, who sat in an oversized chair that actually made him look small. He motioned for her to come sit with him, and she did, cramming herself into the chair beside him on his right side. He groaned a little but said, "I'm fine. Just have to find the right position." He shifted and moved until he did, and then he took her hand in his. Leaning down he whispered, "I love you so much for coming to this. Sorry if it's a bit overwhelming."

It *was* a bit overwhelming, but Charlie had the perfect response. "There's nowhere else I'd rather be." That was the gospel truth, because she did belong here at this ranch, and with this man, and she didn't need more time to think about any of it.

## Chapter Thirty-Eight

Preacher's nerves wouldn't settle. Bear started the meeting with prayer, and then he nodded to Ward. He got up and said, "Our market day was one of our best ever. We've got three choices for investments this year, and Mister is going to put those on the screen."

The huge television above the mantle brightened, but it stayed blue. Mister fiddled with the projector and his computer, to no avail. Preacher wouldn't jump to his rescue, because at least ten other people would. No one in the Glover family knew how to mind their own business, and they all possessed at least some level of intelligence. Enough to think they could solve most problems.

*You're the bridge, Preacher,* he thought, reciting the lines from Dad's letter. *You're the middle child, the bridge between the older brothers and the younger siblings. They'll come to you, because they need you. You need them, though I know you don't feel like it sometimes.*

He did need them, though. He'd never have survived the past two months on his own, and he thanked the Lord every day for his family's help. For them as people.

"I think it's the network," Judge said, and he got up to help Mister. Watching the two of them work together cleansed Preacher's soul, and he couldn't help grinning. Reverence filled the room, as everyone seemed to realize they were witnessing a miracle.

Right in front of him, Preacher saw the rift between Judge and Mister disappear. It had been going on since his accident, when Ward and Mister had moved into the Ranch House to help Judge with taking care of Preacher.

"God knows all things," Preacher murmured, and Charlie looked at him, questions in her eyes. "I'll tell you later, sugar." He pressed his lips to her temple, so many emotions streaming through him.

No, he didn't want to endure a broken hip and a terrible car accident. But he had, and because of it, he'd provided a bridge for Mister and Judge, where they could meet in the middle and make things right.

Daddy had been right. Preacher *could* unite his family members.

*Maybe in the future, can I do it without a massive accident?* he asked the Lord silently. *That would be nice.*

"Here we go," Judge said as the screen finally showed what Mister had put on the computer.

"We invest in local Texas companies," Mister said, turning to face the group. "Bear and Ranger think it's smart to continue to put money into Two Cents and the infrastructure hosting sites that Range uses to build and expand that app. So they're putting some of their gains into that."

He cleared his throat as he tapped on his computer. "Our new investment this year is fifty thousand, and we have a few choices. HealNow."

Preacher stiffened in his seat. He could admit that HealNow did good things in the pharmaceutical world. He simply didn't like their huge building and the traffic congestion they'd brought to Three Rivers.

"HealNow is a drug company," Mister said, continuing on to give a short speech about the stability of pharmaceuticals and how they wouldn't call their stock for at least four years.

"Essential Elements," Mister said next. "They're a utility company out of Austin, and they have a great mutual fund that has shown stable growth over the past decade."

He cleared his throat and clicked. "Below Zero."

Beside him, Charlie gasped. "No," she said.

"They're a start-up company," Mister said. "From right here in Three Rivers, and I'm sure most of you know Charlie owns Below Zero." He looked at her, and so did everyone else.

"You can't put fifty grand into my business," she said.

"Why not?" Ranger asked.

Preacher didn't know how to feel. No one had told him Below Zero was on the table for ranch investments.

"I don't even have stock," she said. "It's just me. I just run the company."

"What would you do with fifty thousand dollars?" Bear asked. "Expand to more cities? Have a storefront instead of a kiosk in the mall? Bring on a CEO who can take the company nation-wide?"

"I…." Charlie looked at Preacher for help, and he simply smiled at her.

"She'd expand to more cities," Preacher said quietly, though his voice was powerful enough to fill the room. "She'd set up storefronts and kiosks and stands at fairs. Ice cream trucks. She'd be the CEO, because she's that smart and that savvy, but she'd definitely bring on people to help her grow."

Mister and Bear nodded, and Mister said, "We vote on where we put our yearly investment. Get your phones out and put in this address, please." He changed the screen so it had a short web address on it, and Preacher got out his phone.

Charlie didn't, though Bear said, "Anyone can vote, even if you're not in the immediate family. Sometimes that helps us make decisions, honestly."

Charlie still didn't pull out her device, and she didn't look particularly happy either. Preacher finished typing in the website, and he tapped to vote for Below Zero. That done, he met Charlie's eye again. "I didn't know this would be on the agenda."

"I feel like…I haven't even *thought* about investors."

Preacher smiled at her gently. "Maybe this is why you didn't want to take on more school visits in the next couple of months," he said. "Let's just see what happens."

He knew what would happen though. The Glovers were family-oriented, and they loved small businesses. Ranger, Bear, and Ward especially, and they ran the finances on the ranch. They made sure Shiloh Ridge stayed profitable and healthy, and in fact, it was because of their excellent management of the resources on the ranch that Preacher had a bank account with ten figures in it.

Why all of them did.

"Results are in," Mister said, and he tapped on the link. The website loaded, and Below Zero came in with almost all of the votes. Only two people had voted for HealNow, and Mister nodded to Bear.

"Noted," Bear said, standing up again. "We'll discuss it in our next administrative meeting, and we'll send a memo out to everyone with the final answer. Bishop is going to go over our housing situation. Bish."

Preacher shifted again, but not because of the pressure in his hip. "This is the part I told you about," he whispered to Charlie.

Bishop put a new list on the television screen. "We've had a relatively quiet year," he said. "No termites. No major remodels. Montana and I completed the re-fencing, and we rebuilt two barns, a stable, and added another hay storage facility."

A map of the ranch came up, with all of the buildings highlighted. "This is Ranger's shed, and that's done. Ace and Holly Ann got their dream home." Bishop smiled at the two of them, and then he faced the crowd again.

"Y'all heard Preacher talkin' about marriage, and he's our next most pressing need." His eyes skated past Preacher and Charlie, and Preacher was glad for that. "I don't know when they'll get married, but Preacher's asked for the Kinder Ranch. The house there...." He sighed and flipped to a new picture.

The house looked like a stiff wind would knock it down. Old equipment littered the yard, and Preacher could see hours, days, weeks, and months' worth of work that needed to be done.

"Honestly," Bishop said. "Montana and I called in Micah and a couple of other builders, and we all came to the same conclusion. The house needs to be knocked down. Razed completely. The land cleared and a whole assessment made."

Another picture came up. "I asked Thelma Atgood to help me come up with a rendition of what the Kinder Ranch could be, and this is what she gave me."

Preacher pulled in a breath and leaned forward. The house in the middle of the picture stood two stories tall and had a charming white exterior like a farmhouse, not a homestead. It had a huge front porch that wrapped around the side, with trees and bushes out front.

The driveway extended from the front of it, with fruit trees along the lane, and to the left, back away from the highway sat a circle of cabins.

"We'd put six cabins there," Bishop said. "With Preacher being one of our foremen, it makes sense for him to be accessible to his people, as well as to have a place to offer seasonal workers should the need arise."

"That need always arises," Ward said. "I've been using the upper cabins this year, and I've been grateful for them."

Bishop nodded. "This project is huge. It includes an entire house, six cowboy cabins, brand new plumbing, as the Kinder Ranch is actually run on a well right now. We'd need the town to come in and approve new electrical poles, new roads, new addresses. We have to meet with the zoning commission, and we have about ten permits that need to be obtained. That all takes more time than I'd like to admit, because we're waiting on someone else."

"Once we get all of that, though," Montana said from her spot on the loveseat. "The building will go fast."

"Maybe," Bishop said. "We don't know what the land is like right now. We have to clear it and assess it. But then yes, once we know the stability of it and what we need to do, once the construction starts, it should go fast."

"Sounds like it's not going to be done in time for a wedding," Ward said.

"I doubt it," Bishop said. "We're looking at eighteen months of construction at the Kinder Ranch. That takes us from other projects around here." He surveyed the group. "Though both Judge and Ward have homes already, so when they get married, we won't need to deal with this issue."

He didn't mention Mister, but Preacher glanced over to his brother. Their eyes met, and Mister smiled, releasing the tension that had started to gather in Preacher's neck.

"Anyway," Bishop said. "This is a massive construction project, and it'll cost the ranch three-point-four million dollars."

"This is insane," Charlie whispered. "I don't need a three-point-four-million-dollar house."

"But you do," Preacher said, barely looking at her. This felt like the world to him. If he could provide this for her, as well as the investment in Below Zero, maybe she would get everything she wanted—and more.

"We have to vote on that amount," Bear said. "As well as agreeing to allow Bishop and Montana to work on this. Personally, I think it's worth it. Daddy bought that ranch decades ago and did nothing with it. It's time. Ranger?"

"I agree," he said. "There's no reason not to do it. We have the money, and Preacher will take good care of the land. He's good to his men, and it'll only expand the operation we have here."

"Ward?" Bear asked. "Cactus? Anyone want to add anything?"

"Say Preach gets married before the project is done," Cactus said. "I'm assuming he and Charlie will live in the Top Cottage?"

Bear tossed a look toward Zona. "Actually, Zona and Duke are going to be building a new place up at the Rhinehart Ranch, and they've asked to live there until it's finished."

"Well, when is Preacher getting married?" Zona asked. "Our house is already designed, and we'll be out before summer."

"Not before summer," Preacher said, glancing at Charlie, who shook her head.

"Okay," Bear said, casting Preacher a look. He nodded at his brother, because he and Charlie weren't in a huge hurry, and he didn't want to push Zona out of the Top Cottage.

Wilder started to fuss, and Etta got up to take him away from the meeting. He quieted right down under her care, and Preacher smiled in their direction as she took the boy into the kitchen to get a snack.

"I like the plan," Ward said, moving his eyes back to the screen. He'd watched Etta with baby Wilder too. "Like I said, it's always nice to offer men and women a good place to stay for a while, especially if they're working on the ranch for longer than a week."

"And with all the land we're not currently using," Ace said. "We can add in more grass pastures and more hay fields. That'll require more people on my agriculture crew. They can be full-time cowboys who'd live up here. We could transition some people to Preacher's crew over animals, and they could live down the hill."

"Let's vote," Ranger said as a timer went off in the kitchen. "Then we'll eat."

Another link came up, and this time, it was a yes or no question, with a spot for more questions to be asked. With a survey so easy, it didn't take long to get a unanimous yes from everyone who'd voted.

"Great," Bear said with a smile. "Let's eat. Etta you're over there already. Want to tell us what we've got tonight?"

She explained the burrito bar, complete with the Spanish rice and refried beans that she'd just taken out of the oven. "We have sweet pork and steak," she said. "Plenty of toppings. Come eat."

People got up, conversations breaking out and noise filling the homestead once again. He looked at Charlie, who hadn't moved. "What are you thinking?"

She shook her head, her eyes wide and somewhat glazed. "So many things."

"Is one of them about how we should go look at diamond rings sometime soon?" He ducked his head, in complete disbelief that he was having this conversation here, now.

"That's on my mind, yes," she said with a smile.

"What kind of wedding do you want, baby?" he asked.

"Preacher, you don't have to do everything I want."

"With this, I do," he said. "Because I don't care, Charlie. I want you to have what you want. That's it."

Mother appeared in front of them, and she sat on the ottoman he hadn't used. Sometimes he liked stretching his legs out in front of him, but he'd suspected that it would hurt his hip today. "I know your mother lives quite a ways away," she said, looking from Preacher to Charlie. "I'd love to help with the wedding planning, once you're engaged."

Preacher smiled at her. "Mother fancies herself a wedding planner," he said. "She's really quite good."

"I've heard," Charlie murmured. She gave Mother a small smile. "I'd like that, Lois. Thank you."

Mother wore glee in her expression as she stood. "This is going to be so fun."

Charlie watched her walk away, and when Preacher looked at her again, he chuckled. "If it's too fast, just say so."

"It's a little fast," she said. "I mean, we just got back together."

"So you don't want me to propose tomorrow."

"Are you going to propose tomorrow?"

Preacher laughed at the horrified tone in her voice. "No, baby. But...I would like to know what you're thinking.

Winter wedding? Spring? Summer? Am I looking at next autumn? Next winter? A vague idea would help a cowboy plan the perfect proposal...that's all I'm saying."

"Preacher," she said with a heavy dose of frustration in his name. "Remember how I'm not like other women? I've thought about my wedding, but I don't have it all planned out."

"Come eat," Mister said as he passed Preacher and Charlie. "The crowd is dying down, and you won't get jostled."

Preacher dang near rolled his eyes. He didn't need to be reminded that he couldn't handle getting bumped. "Okay," he said, but he didn't move.

"I have no grandiose ideas about what my wedding should be like," she said.

"We could get married in the barn here," he said. "Your back yard. Wherever."

"The barn here is nice," she mused.

"It can be big or small," he said. "You could livestream it or keep it quiet. You can wear these sexy jeans for all I care." He leaned toward her. "I just want you, Charlie, to be my wife. I love you. You tell me what you want—or tell Mother—and it'll happen."

"By the way," Bishop said, coming closer to them with a heavily laden plate holding three burritos. "You two can design the whole house. Where the bedrooms are, the arrangement of the kitchen, all of it. It's just a rendition. There's no blueprints yet."

"Great," Preacher said, feeling like maybe he'd gotten ahead of himself. "Thanks, Bishop." His brother turned back to the table, and Preacher started to scoot out toward the edge of the chair so he could get up. "Come on, sugar. Let's go eat. We can talk about all of this later."

She got to her feet first and offered him her hand. He took it, because he wasn't too proud to get the help he needed, especially from her. She tugged him closer, her bright blue eyes firing sparks at him.

"I want to marry you with the sun shining overhead," she said. "Outside, right here at the ranch. Then we can dance in that barn of yours, and you can take me on an amazing honeymoon to Europe, and then we can come back here and build our life together."

Preacher sure did like the sound of that. He searched her face, finding determination and happiness in her eyes. "So summertime?"

"May, June," she said.

"That's eight months," he said. "Only seven if you go with May."

"That's enough time, right?"

To harness the world and give it to her? No, he'd need a lifetime to do that, and he was absolutely willing to spend his life doing exactly that.

"Sure," he said. "I guess I can be ready to marry you in seven months."

She giggled and traced her fingertips down the side of his face. "I like this sexy beard you've grown, Mister Glover."

"Yeah?" he asked. "Finally, my laziness has paid off."

"You are one of the least lazy people I've ever met," she said.

"Oh, sugar, you have no idea," he said. "I've been taking a nap every day for two months, and I'm not going to give that up easily." He grinned at her, but she only laughed harder.

"A nap every day," she said between giggles. "How scandalous."

"What's scandalous is this blatant display of affection," Ward growled as he passed to take a seat at the table. "Stop flirting and get your food already."

In the past, Preacher would've been horribly embarrassed and irritated. Today, though, he simply laughed at his cousin and led Charlie over to the island so they could load up with burritos and salsas.

# Chapter Thirty-Nine

Charlie gazed at the beautiful tree as one of Preacher's brothers plugged it in.

"All right," Bear said, and he sure did lead the family well. "Welcome to our angel tree decoration. We're so glad to have all of you with us. The concept is pretty simple."

"All of Grandmother's ornaments are right here," Zona said, and Charlie smiled at the woman. "You take the ones you want, and you put them on the tree. Some people have specific ornaments that they like to hang for someone every year, so be kind and mindful of that, as we have a lot of new people in the family now."

"For example," Oakley said, moving toward the boxes. "My first year here, Cactus found this charming little car for me." She dug through the box and lifted the crocheted car from it. "See? It's for me. I don't know how their grandmother knew I'd need this car to make me feel like a part of the family, but she did." She smiled at the ornament and took it to the tree, which Mister, Judge, and Cactus were still fluffing and arranging the branches on.

"I think of her when I hang it," Oakley said. "I feel close to her, though I've never met her in real life."

"I hang the bear for Grandmother," Bear said, placing his ornament higher on the tree. "You can take a moment to remember them or not. We just want the tree to be a good reminder of who Glovers are." He stepped back and scanned everyone. "And you're all Glovers now, no matter your last name. So come get some ornaments and let's get this tree ready for the next couple of months."

Charlie stayed right where she was, though most everyone else surged forward and started spreading out the boxes. Even Preacher dove right into the fray, and he came toward her several moments later with a few ornaments in his hand.

He held up a delicately shaped set of two eighth notes. "I usually hang this one for Grandmother," he said. "She had a beautiful singing voice, and I loved listening to her sing the hymns on Sunday morning while we got ready for church."

Charlie marveled at the tenderness in his voice and on his face, and she teared up at the feeling of love and peace filling her.

"I thought you might want this one," he said, extending an ice cream cone toward her. It had two perfectly round scoops, and she imagined the flavors to be coconut and piña colada, because the ornament was snow-white and those would be white ice creams.

She took the ornament and smiled at it, feeling a

kinship with this grandmother the same way Oakley had described. "This is stunning." The cone fit in the palm of her hand, and she absolutely adored it.

"I always hang this one for my daddy," Preacher said, lifting a single cowboy boot. "He taught me the value of hard work. He taught me how to cure leather, and that a man could do anything if he'd just pull on his boots and get to work." He gazed at the boot and then smiled at Charlie. "I miss him the most at Christmas."

"I bet you do." Charlie linked her arm through him. "I want to know more about him, Preacher. You don't talk much of him."

"I know," Preacher said. "I don't talk about much of anything."

"That's gonna have to change a little," she said. "At least with me." She reached to hang the ice cream cone on a bough about halfway down the tree. "I want us to be open and honest and tell each other everything."

Preacher ducked his head, but his cowboy hat couldn't conceal his smile. "I want that too, sugar."

Charlie smiled at him, and she turned to the boxes along the wall. People came and went from them, and she watched Ranger hang a cage with a bird inside it, close his eyes, and smile. She loved this tradition, and the way all of these people let themselves think of their loved ones in such an open, raw way.

She moved over to the boxes when an opening became available, and she peered down into the ornaments. They didn't have a rhyme or reason to their organization, until she noticed the numbers on the boxes.

"These are older," she said, glancing into the box to her right. "Those are newer."

She stayed at the older box, though many others chose from the newer ornaments. Charlie reached in and pulled out a couple of ornaments to be able to see them better. She held a manger in one hand and a snowflake in the other.

"Zona," she said as the other woman turned toward her. "Look at this one." She held up the manger. "Do you want it?"

"I knew she'd made a manger," Zona said with a smile. She took the ornament, which bore a bit more yellow than some of the others. "Can I have it for my baby?"

"Of course," Charlie said.

Zona didn't immediately move back to the tree. "How are you, Charlie? Really?" She spoke in a very quiet voice, and that was saying something for Arizona. She'd been raised with six brothers and a bunch of cousins, and she's learned from birth to be loud or be ignored. She'd gone down the loud track while Preacher had chosen the one that kept him quietly on the sidelines.

Until the accident, at least. Now, everyone rotated around him, speaking to him and laughing with him. He *fit* with them, and if he couldn't see it Charlie would have to tell him every day of his life until he could.

"I'm good," she said, blinking to focus back on Arizona. "Really good, Zona." She leaned closer and moved her gaze to the snowflake. "Thank you for making Preacher invite me to this. And for driving him to my house last week."

"One thing real quick," she said almost under her

breath. "No one makes any of the Glovers do anything they don't want to do already." She smiled. "That man loves you, Charlie, and I could see it the moment I found out about you."

Charlie smiled and nodded. "Still, I think you inspired him to act."

"Maybe a little sooner than he would have otherwise," Zona said. "But that's all I'm taking credit for." She grinned too, turned and said in a much louder voice, "Duke, look what I found."

Charlie crouched in front of the box of ornaments and picked through them, trying to think of who she should hang them for. Her mama. One for Davie, of course. One for Daddy. One for each brother she hadn't seen in a while.

They got along—they weren't like Mister and Judge who hadn't spoken to each other in months until very recently—but weeks and months could go by where Charlie didn't talk to them all the same.

She needed five ornaments, and she picked out a sleigh for Davie, who loved the outdoors. A lamppost for Mama, who'd always shined a light on Charlie's path. A horse for Daddy, who was a born and bred Texan. She kept the snowflake for Mack, her oldest brother who'd never seen the stuff, and she found a Texas Sheriff's star for Ian, who was a police officer in San Antonio.

*Perfect*, she thought, standing to face the tree again. She felt Preacher's eyes on her, but she didn't look at him. She walked over to the tree and hung each ornament, saying a mental prayer for each of her family members as she did.

Now, she just needed one more ornament. She caught

Preacher's eye this time, and he raised his eyebrows. She crossed over to where he leaned against the wall, out of the way, and said, "I just need one for you."

"Me? I'm right here, baby."

"I know," she said. "But they said I could put one on for anyone I wanted."

"Who were all those others for?" He nodded toward the tree. Several members of his family had finished with the ornaments, and they'd moved back into the kitchen with talk of coffee and hot chocolate.

"My parents and siblings," she said. "One for each of them. One for your grandmother."

She turned to the nearest box, which held the most recent ornaments his grandmother had made. "What was your grandmother's name?"

"Priscilla," he said. "She married Ranza Glover when she was only nineteen years old."

"Wow," Charlie said. "I was trying to get through PE about then."

Preacher chuckled and said, "I'd just won the state championship in debate."

"You're kidding." Charlie looked at him with shock moving through her. "Preacher, you're a fascinating man."

He chuckled again and stood beside her as she sifted through the remaining ornaments in the box. She just needed something...something...she didn't know what. She'd know the very core of Preacher when she saw it though, and she moved over to the next box.

Her fingernails caught on the delicate threads his grandmother had crocheted into such beauty, and she gasped when she saw the horse with its mane flying behind it. He even looked like he was in a full gallop, only his front hoof connecting him to the curved bridge he was crossing.

"Preacher, look." She untangled the hook from the rest of the ornaments and stood. "It's a mustang."

Preacher's eyes widened, and he took the delicate ornament from her. It was larger than the ice cream cone by about double, and the horse wore a tiny red bow around his neck.

"It's a mustang crossing a bridge," Preacher said. He stared at the ornament, clear surprise in his eyes.

"It fits you perfectly," she said. "You're this wild, beautiful man, who's not afraid to do hard things."

"I wrecked my Mustang," he said, his voice barely above a whisper. "And Charlie, my daddy wrote all of us kids a letter before he died." He cleared his throat and lowered the ornament. "Mine said that I'm a bridge between my siblings. I can unite them, and that was why Grandmother gave me the name Preacher. Because I could bring them together through example, even if I wasn't a great speaker."

"But you were the debate state champion." She cocked her head, trying to see all the pieces that made Preacher Glover who he was.

"For a while there, I thought that was why Grandmother gave me that name," he said. "But it's not. It's because I don't *have* to preach to unite." He met her eye. "*This* is my ornament, Charlie. It's the one Grandmother made especially for me." He handed it back to her, and Charlie took it.

She grinned at the horse, then the man it represented, and she hung it on the tree right at her eye level. That way, every time she entered this house—which she hoped would be a lot over the next two months—she'd see it. She'd see him for who he truly was—and together, they'd belong at this ranch, in this family.

## Chapter Forty

"I better go," Charlie whispered. She didn't move though, and Preacher wasn't about to release his hold on her. She and Preacher lay on the couch in his living room, something playing on the TV neither one of them had paid any attention to.

Over the course of the past couple of months, Ward and Mister had moved back to Bull House, and Judge had been helping Preacher if he needed it. Now that it was almost Christmas, and nearly four months had passed since Preacher's accident, he was doing really well.

Well enough to cuddle with Charlie on the couch, and well enough to drive his truck. She still wouldn't let him come to her house, though, because it was far too long to sit in one position, and she had much more free time than he did.

"Mm," Preacher said, touching his mouth to hers again. "I have something for you before you go." His lips caught against hers, and Charlie pressed into his touch, making the kiss firmer and more real.

He sure did like that, and he prayed to the Lord that he could be strong enough to get down on one knee. He'd been practicing the movement for a solid week now. Morning, noon, night. First thing in the morning when he was rested and fresh, and as the last thing he did before he crawled into bed, exhausted and worn out physically.

He'd been able to do it no matter what time of day it was, and he really wanted to propose before Bear and Sammy had their baby. She was due tomorrow and set to go into the hospital to be induced bright and early in the morning, so he had to get the job done tonight.

Charlie pulled away first, and Preacher kept his eyes closed and breathed in the sweet, cinnamon coffee scent of her mouth.

"I'm going to go," she said, groaning as she sat up. The twinkling Christmas lights spurred Preacher to get up as she stood, and while she busied herself with finding her phone and putting on her shoes, Preacher went over to the tree and plucked the black ring box from the upper branches.

He'd taken her to three jewelers in the past few weeks, and he knew what she liked. Charlie didn't wear a lot of jewelry, and the stuff she did had to make an impact.

He took a deep breath and turned back to the house. She clicked off the TV and smiled at him. "What are you hiding, cowboy?"

"Just a little something I got for you," he said.

"I'm coming up for Christmas," she said, her smile slipping. "I didn't bring your gift since it's still a week away."

"This isn't your Christmas gift," he said. He brought the box out in front of him. "Charlie, I love you. I may have fallen for you the very first time I saw you emerge from the cloud of smoke when you made ice cream at my cousin's wedding."

She smiled, and it was so radiant in the holiday lighting. He grinned back at her, glad it was easy to say words like *I love you* to her.

"I want to dance with you every day. I want to be inspired by you every day. I want to share my life with you every day. I don't want to celebrate Christmas without you as my fiancée, so."

He took a big breath and got down on both knees, first using his good, healthy right side to lower himself to the ground and then letting his left knee sort of buckle and join the right on the floor.

He looked up at her, so dang proud of himself for not making a fool of himself. "Will you marry me?"

Charlie started nodding before he'd finished asking, and she covered her mouth with both hands as he opened the ring box and let her see the ring.

"Preacher," she gasped. "You got the Queen Anne."

"Almost," he said. "It's the same cut and setting, but the diamonds are colored. They're not all white." He tilted the box so she could see better.

"It's like a real bouquet," she said, her voice breaking. She dropped to her knees too, and he slid the ring on her finger. "I love it." She smiled fondly at her left hand. Lifting her gaze to meet his, she added, "I love *you*."

She took his face in both hands and kissed him, and Preacher poured all of his love and joy into this brand-new kiss with the woman he loved.

---

Read on for the first couple of chapters of the next book in the Shiloh Ridge Ranch in Three Rivers series, **THE DELIVERY OF DÉCOR**.

# Sneak Peek! The Delivery of Décor
# Chapter One:

Ward Glover paced in the hospital. How long did it take to have a baby? Honestly, he'd been here for three hours and his sister's babies should be tiny, seeing as how there were two of them being born at the same time.

He cast a look at his eldest brother, but Ranger didn't seem concerned about anything but the game on his phone. "You should sit down," he said when Ward went by again. "Pacing won't make Brady bring the twins out faster."

Ward simply grunted at him and kept walking. This time, he didn't turn around and go back by the chairs and couches the Glovers had claimed in the maternity waiting area.

He rounded a corner and pressed his back into it, breathing in deeply through his nose. He pushed it out the way the counselor at Courage Reins had taught him. He'd been going to the equine therapy facility for a few months now, and he'd doubled his sessions over the past three weeks.

Since Thanksgiving, when Dorothy Crockett told him she "liked him and all, but she didn't want to mix business and pleasure."

Ward didn't even know what that meant. She still didn't have the gravel he wanted, and they'd only been out a few times since he'd gotten brave enough to be straight with her. He'd held her hand and spent plenty of time talking and flirting with her, but he hadn't kissed her yet.

He'd been texting her in the twenty-four days since she'd told him that, and she responded. He suspected there was more at play than she'd said, but he hadn't been able to get anything more from her.

Thinking quickly, before he could change his mind, he took out his phone and tapped on her name right at the top of his app. He'd pinned her there, and he wasn't embarrassed about it.

*Ida's having the babies. I thought you might like to know.*

Dot lived only a couple of blocks from Ida and Brady, and one of their dates had been a double with Ward's sister and brother-in-law.

Since Dot was literally the nicest woman on town, she'd become fast friends with Ida, and Ward knew the two had spent some time together over the past few months.

*How exciting!* Dot said in response. *She must be thrilled. She was really hurting a couple of days ago.*

His sister had been experiencing some labor pains, as well as the reduced ability to breathe and swollen legs and ankles in the recent past. All pregnancy-related.

Ward stared at the conversation, wondering how he could get Dot to talk to him.

*You can't*, he told himself. She was a grown woman who was older than him, and she got to make her own choices.

And she hadn't chosen him.

The realization cut through him like an electric knife, and his breath caught somewhere between his throat and his lungs.

She *hadn't* chosen him.

*You'll never guess who I just spoke to*, Dot said, and Ward seized the opportunity to talk to her.

*Who?*

*Lionsgate Gravel. They have the thirty-five in bulk, and I got as much as I could.*

Ward's hopes lifted, and instead of texting her, he tapped the green phone icon to call her.

"I knew you'd call," she said, and she sure sounded downright flirty to him. "Nothing excites you as much as thirty-five gravel."

Ward cleared his throat. "Oh, I can think of a few things more exciting," he said.

She giggled, and Ward knew for certain she was flirting with him now. What he didn't know was *why*. Or why she'd turned cold a few weeks ago.

"You want the gravel, right?" she asked after she'd stopped laughing.

"How much do you have?"

"Enough to fill the order you put in a couple of years ago."

"Wow," he said. "Yeah, I want that. All of it." He stared

across the hall to the bland hospital wall looking back at him. "Maybe you'd let me take you to dinner to discuss delivery?" He almost coughed but managed to suck it back at the last second. "I mean, I'm already in town."

"At the hospital, Woods."

He grinned at her sarcastic tone and the use of his real name. "The cafeteria here has great food," he said.

"I'm not eating somewhere called a cafeteria. I'm not in grade school."

No, she wasn't. *Not even close*, Ward thought as he imagined the curvy blonde. And the first time he'd seen her rumble up in her dump truck and climb down like she owned the world....

Ward could barely breathe just remembering it. He didn't want to say, "Name the time and place, and I'll be there, darlin'."

He absolutely would not say that.

"I'm hungry almost all the time," he said. "If I can, I'll meet you somewhere."

Meeting her somewhere. That was low-key, right?

His brain misfired when he realized what else he'd said. *I'm hungry almost all the time.*

*My word, Ward*, he thought. *Get off the phone right now.*

"Hey, I have to go," he said, actually pulling his mouth away from the phone as if someone else needed his attention. "Let's talk later about the gravel delivery."

"Sure," she said. "Tell Ida hello."

"Yep." Ward hung up before he could tell Dot to come over and tell Ida hello herself. Then he'd get to see her, learn the color of her tank top, and what box of dye she'd chosen at the grocery store that week.

Dot never wore anything but jeans and a tank top, even in the winter. Not that Ward had much experience with her in the winter. "Or the spring, or the summer," he muttered to himself.

He thought about her flirty tone and teasing nature as he rounded the corner and went back toward the other Glovers. He sat next to Ranger, who didn't look up from his phone.

About twenty minutes later, right when Ward's patience was about to snap, Brady appeared at the mouth of the hall. The smile on his face couldn't be described in words, but the look of adoration and wonder could only be achieved by a new father.

"Here they are," he said, passing the baby boy wrapped in the blue blanket to Ward. "That's Jonathan Ryan Burton." He gazed down at the baby girl. "This is Judith Dawna Burton." The tiny baby gurgled, and Brady handed her to Ranger.

Ward couldn't look away from the sleeping child in his arms, and the little boy captured his whole heart in less time than it took for Ward to draw a breath. He knew Etta desperately wanted children of her own, and he'd have plenty of opportunities to see Ida plenty in the next few weeks.

So he turned to Etta and handed her baby Jonathan. The boy's face scrunched up, but Etta cradled him right against her chest and cooed at him. "You're okay, baby," she said. "It's Auntie Etta, and you and I are going to be great friends."

Ward smiled at her, and she grinned back at him. "How's Ida?" Ward asked, stepping over to Brady as Ace and Holly Ann crowded in around Ranger and Oakley, who now held Judith.

"She did great," Brady said, looking a bit overwhelmed now. "They put her in a recovery room with a bunch of heated blankets when she started shivering. They think she may be having a bad reaction to the epidural."

"But she'll be okay, right?"

"Yeah, they didn't seem worried." Brady watched as Oakley gave his daughter to Montana, who rested the infant on her own pregnant belly. Bear and Sammy hadn't come to the hospital today, because they'd just left it yesterday. They'd had their second baby boy four days ago, and they'd named him Russell, which was Sammy's mother's maiden name.

Montana went to sit by Mother and Aunt Lois, and Etta wandered that way too. The four of them sat on a single sofa, the twins more loved than they even knew.

"Stay there," Ward said, dropping to one knee right there in the hospital. "Look at me, and let me take your picture for Ida. She'll like that."

The women looked up at him, and he tapped his phone to get several pictures. "Perfect," he said, looking at the picture as one of the infants started to cry.

A flurry of activity happened around him as Brady got loaded up with both babies so he could take them back to their mother. Ward stayed down as he used his favorite editing app to make everyone look better by taking down the shadows and pushing up the contrast.

"Why are you down on the floor like that?" a woman asked, and Ward's attention got jerked from his device. "Are you praying or proposing?"

He looked up at Dorothy Crockett, his pulse shooting through every vein in his body simultaneously. "Dot," he managed to say. The problem was, he tried to get up at the same time, and shove his phone in his pocket, and combined with his sudden nerves, he stumbled forward.

He managed to catch himself before he fell flat on his face, but he had to grab onto Dot to do it. She grunted and braced herself, and because she owned and operated a landscaping company and shoveled bark and gravel for a living, she was strong enough to hold him for a moment. Long enough for him to get his footing, release her, and clear his throat.

"Sorry," he said.

Dot looked around at his family, most of whom were watching the two of them. Preacher looked mildly horrified, and Ward suddenly knew why Preacher had kept his relationship out of the Shiloh Ridge limelight. Then he didn't have to deal with awkward situations like this.

Of course, he now held hands with his fiancée, and Charlie fit right in with all the Glovers.

Ward turned his back on the group and stepped over to partially shield Dot too. "Did I miss a text?"

"You said we could talk about the delivery of your gravel." She looked from him to this family and back, a hint of nerves in her eyes. "I thought I might get to see the babies."

"You just missed them," he said. "Look." He turned his phone toward her, and she took it from him.

"Oh, they're perfect." She looked at him again, and as he'd crowded in beside her, their faces were only a few inches apart. He took a breath of her and got something green with dirt and something cottony fresh. Her tank top was a dark eggplant color, and it clung to all of her curves and revealed the muscles in her arms.

"What did they name them?"

"Jonathan and Judith," he said.

"Judith sounds just like Ida," Dot said with a smile. She focused back on the picture, studied it for a moment, and then handed it back to Ward. "Are you staying here for a while? I know you and Ida are close."

"I'd like to see her," he said, glancing over his shoulder. "But her husband said they had her in a recovery room. She'll be here overnight for sure. I can come back." He took a step closer to her, though they were already practically touching. "Might be better, since there's so many of us. We can be a lot to handle."

"You're kidding," she said without the trace of a smile. "I had no idea you Glovers could be hard to deal with."

"Hey, I'm not hard to deal with," he said. "Am I?"

"Oh, Ward," she said, patting his chest and sending excited tremors through every muscle in his body. "You're the worst one."

## Sneak Peek! The Delivery of Décor Chapter Two:

Dorothy Crockett could admit that a day hadn't gone by since she'd smashed her raspberry cream whip into Ward's white church shirt that she hadn't thought about him. She'd seen a different version of the cowboy that day at the church potluck, and when he'd called and said she intrigued him, Dot had changed her opinion of him completely.

At the same time, he still used his good looks against her, along with that Texas twang she found so sexy. Of course, Dot had always been a sucker for a strong, tall cowboy, and Ward had all the strength and all the height in the world. He could wear a cowboy hat like no man she'd ever met, and she'd never seen him without jeans and cowboy boots too. He changed up his shirts, and as the weather had cooled, he'd started wearing a leather jacket that made her heart pirouette every time she thought about it.

Today, he wore a T-shirt with the outline of Texas on it, and he must've bathed in pine needles and sugar, because he smelled masculine and delicious all at the same time.

He looked at her with those blue eyes that had probably broken dozens of women's hearts, and Dot saw the confusion he harbored there.

"I'm the worst one?"

Dot blinked, trying to remember what she'd said to him and what he'd said before that.

"What have I done that's been hard for you to deal with?" he demanded, and he fell back a step. Two, then three. He looked like she'd insulted his dog and his daddy, and Dot regretted teasing him.

"Do you know how many times you've called my office about gravel?"

"Do you know what it would've taken to get me to stop calling?" He folded his arms, and Dot didn't want to have a stand-off with him in the hospital. Especially not the maternity wing, with his whole family watching.

"One returned phone call, Dot," Ward said, rolling his eyes. He turned from her as if he'd really walk away.

"I'm returning your latest call," she said, and that got him to face her again. Something sparked in those eyes now, and Dot really wanted to get burned by it.

*No*, she told herself. *You don't.*

She'd told herself that a lot when it came to Ward Glover, and every time, she hadn't been able to convince herself.

"You want to go to dinner?" he asked.

Dot shook her curly hair over her shoulders as she drew them back, making herself taller. "Yes."

He took one step toward her, and it almost felt menacing. "Okay," he said. "But if we go to dinner, you have to tell me why you quasi-broke up with me three weeks ago."

*Twenty-seven days*, Dot thought. *That's four weeks.* But she didn't argue with him. She searched his face, wondering how he'd take the news.

"I thought we were going to discuss the delivery of your gravel."

"Oh, we are," he said, giving her a smile that made her stomach quake. "Are you okay to hang out for a minute? I need to talk to my brothers for sec."

"Yeah, okay," she said.

He nodded, his hand finding hers and squeezing before he walked away. That simple touch was what made Ward so extraordinary. It wasn't the things he said, but the small, minute details he did that told her what was really on his mind.

She didn't mean to stare after him, but she did. Her diverted attention meant she didn't notice immediately when two women sidled up to her and paused.

"I'm Etta," she said. "Ward's sister."

"Zona," the other woman said. "His cousin."

"Hello," Dot said, disappointed with herself that she'd let her guard down. She'd never gotten along all that well with other women, as she'd been a tomboy and an athlete her whole life. She was taller than the average woman, and she towered above Etta but not so much Zona. She'd dated a lot throughout high school and college, but she'd made bad decision after bad decision that had taken her a long time to come to terms with. Sometimes, she wasn't sure she'd made peace with her past, and she wasn't sure the Lord had forgiven her.

Then, every so often, she felt utterly loved and worthy of that love from On High. In those moments, she allowed herself to date again, but eventually, the things she'd once done sneaked back into her life and caused her grief.

"Do you have a name?" Zona asked, and Dot looked at her with a cocked eyebrow.

"Yes," she said. "Dorothy Crockett."

"Are you going out with Ward?" Etta asked.

"Just for dinner," Dot said. "We're not like...going out." She had no idea what that even meant, and as Etta cocked her head to the side and frowned, she obviously didn't either.

Zona snapped her fingers. "You own From the Ground Up."

Dot grinned at her. She could talk about her landscaping company forever. "Yes," she said. "Have you used us?"

"No," Zona said. "But my brother said you guys are great. I guess you put in a bunch of rose bushes and sod at one of our ranch houses."

"Oh, sure," Dot said. "I remember that. Something about re-landscaping after termites?"

"That would be us," Etta said with a smile.

"You look so much like Ida," Dot said.

"Oh, you know Ida?" Etta asked. "We're twins."

"Oh, *duh*," Dot said, trilling out a laugh. "I can't believe I forgot Ida had a twin. Ward's mentioned it too."

"How do you know her?" Etta asked. "Did she introduce you and Ward?"

"No," Dot said, cementing her smile in place, though she liked these two women. They weren't firing questions at her about Ward, at least. "Ward and I went on a double-date with Ida and her husband. Turns out, I live only a couple blocks away from them."

"Oh." Etta looked like Dot had thrown icy water in her face. "I see."

"Etta," Zona said.

"I have to get back to the ranch," she said, already walking away. "I promised Bear and Sammy I'd watch Lincoln and Stetson tonight."

Dot watched her retreat to the couch and pick up her purse. "What did I say?" she asked quietly. "I didn't mean to make her feel bad."

"It's not you," Zona said with a sigh. "She's going through a rough time right now, and she sometimes feels left out. That's all."

"I'm sure if I'd have kept dating Ward, we'd have gone out with Etta and her boyfriend. Husband. Whoever."

Zona watched Etta gather her things and hug a few people. "She doesn't have a boyfriend or a husband."

"Oh." And she was Ida's twin. Ida, who was married and now with two babies.

Zona put her hand on her own pregnant belly, and Dot nodded to it. "When are you due?"

"Not until April," she said, smiling down at her stomach. "Three and a half more months."

"Boy or girl?" Dot smiled at her, but Zona's smile slipped away completely.

"It's a girl," she said, and she looked like she might cry.

"Do you live up at Shiloh Ridge?" Dot asked, because she was really good at making small talk with strangers. She'd literally built her business doing such things, and she could ask someone questions forever.

"No," Zona said. "But I grew up there. I married Duke Rhinehart, and we live on his ranch. Or we will, once our house is done."

"I know the ranch," Dot said. "I did some tree removal up there a few years ago."

"Mm." Zona nodded, and she put another smile on her face. "Excuse me. I need to go talk to my mother. So nice meeting you."

"You too," Dot said, and thankfully, Ward returned a moment later. "Ready?" she asked.

"Yep." He hooked his thumb toward Zona. "You met my sister and my cousin?"

"Yes," Dot said. "You have a lot of family."

"Yes, I do." Ward indicated the sterile hall in front of them. "Do you have a restaurant in mind?"

"What about Small Plates?" she asked. "Or are you the type of man that doesn't share his food?"

"I can share food," he said. "Small Plates is getting great ratings on Two Cents."

"You use that app?"

"Ranger invented it," Ward said. "I work with him on

the back end of it, pushing out notifications and polls. I update the infrastructure of it. That kind of thing." He gave her a devastating grin that made Dot's pulse skip and hop through her ribs. "I get to see the results before anyone else."

"Wow, Ward, that's great." Sexy and smart. It so wasn't fair to bring so much to the battle, and Ward Glover seemed to have it all.

He led her to his truck, opened her door, and waited while she climbed in. He didn't touch her again, a fact Dot was keenly aware of as the man rounded the front of his truck and got behind the wheel.

"Um," she said. "I didn't mean to say you were difficult."

"What did you mean to say?" He buckled his seatbelt without looking at her, and Dot didn't like that. She also had no idea how to answer his question.

"I was just teasing," she finally said. "It wasn't very funny, obviously."

"You do think I'm difficult though," he said. "It's fine," he added quickly. "I know I can be a little intense about certain things. I guess I just didn't realize I'd done that with you." He shot her a look out of the corner of his eye as he left the hospital parking lot.

"I thought we'd been gettin' along real nice, Dot. Slow, but nice. And I'm fine with slow." He kneaded the steering wheel with those big hands, and Dot swallowed when she thought about holding one of them again.

*Tonight*, she thought. *Hold his hand tonight.*

"I am," he said. "I...like taking my time to get to know a woman, and I've been real busy at Shiloh Ridge." He finally relaxed as he finished talking, and Dot reached up to tuck her hair.

A smile formed on her face. "We do get along real nice," she said. "For a while there, before we really knew one another, yes, I thought you were demanding. I thought you were really arrogant. *So* good-looking, and you knew it. Boy, did you know it."

He turned and looked at her fully, blinking quickly. "What?"

"Come on," she said with a light laugh. "You know you're gorgeous."

"Am I?"

Dot coughed, because she suddenly felt like she'd say the wrong thing and Ward would pull over and demand she get out of his truck. Find her own way home. "Anyway," she said, clearing her throat. "It was nice getting to know you better. Intense is a better way of describing you, and I don't mind intense."

"You're not exactly the Queen of Relaxation," he said.

Dot burst out laughing, thrilled when Ward joined in. They quieted, and Ward drove steadily toward the restaurant. She'd been able to find something to eat every time they went out, and she'd already given herself a shot of insulin tonight.

"Ward, I...I thought maybe we...Okay." She took a deep breath. "I said we shouldn't mix business and pleasure, because I don't really know how to have a relationship with a man that lasts."

"Oh."

"And I'm diabetic, and I didn't want to tell you."

"Dot." He looked at her again, swiveling his head from the road to her and back. "Why is that a deal-breaker?"

"I don't like talking about it," she said to the passenger window. "I can manage it on my own, and I don't need someone fussing over me."

Ward didn't say anything for a few moments. He made a turn and came to a stop at a red light. "I think one of the nicest things about having a partner is that they can fuss over you. It's something I really miss."

Dot turned toward him, stunned at the vulnerability in his voice. "Who did you have fuss over you?"

"Mother," he said with a smile. "My sisters. It's why Ida and I are so close. I got the flu—like the demon flu. So bad I couldn't get out of bed for anything—once right after I'd graduated from high school and moved to town for a bit. Ida was still in school and living at the ranch."

He pressed on the gas when the light turned green. "I went to sleep on a Monday morning and woke up Wednesday night. Ida was right there, taking care of me. Fussing over me." He smiled to himself, and it only made him more attractive in Dot's eyes. "I've had a girlfriend or two along the way like that too." He cleared his throat. "Nothing's ever worked out though. Never been married or engaged."

"Me either," she said, and Ward nodded. This was definitely a deeper conversation than the ones they'd had on their previous dates, and it painted Ward in a whole new light.

"I don't mind fussing over the ones I care about," he

said. "And that would include you and anything you needed with your diabetes."

"Thank you," she murmured, because Dot had very few people she'd call on if she needed help. She had two really good friends she worked with, and a couple of people from church. And now...Ida and Ward.

Warmth moved through her, and she clasped her hands in her lap. "I'm sorry I said I didn't want to see you anymore. I think I was in complete denial when I sent that text."

"And now?"

"You ask a lot of hard questions," she said, grinning at him.

He returned the smile and ducked his head. "You don't have to answer that last one."

"I think I already did, Ward."

"I suppose you did, darlin'," he said. He slowed as Small Plates came up on his right. With his blinker on, he made the turn and found a place to park. "It's a miracle there's anywhere here." He peered through the windshield. "We might have a long wait. I forgot about the holidays, and it's smack dab in the middle of dinnertime."

"I don't mind waiting," she said. *With you*, she added mentally.

"All right," he said. "If you wait, I'll come open your door for you."

Dot nodded, and Ward killed the engine and slid from the truck. When he opened her door, he crowded right into the gap created between it and the truck. "Your fainting episode at the church makes so much more sense now. You had low blood sugar."

"Yes," she said. "I carry candy in my pocket everywhere I go. That's how serious it can be."

"Good to know," he said. "I've seen you eat dessert."

"I can eat whatever," she said. "I have to monitor the blood sugar and inject myself with insulin if I go crazy and have chocolate cake."

"But you love Black Forest cake," he said. "If I remember right." He gave her a smile that stole her breath again.

"You remember right." She smiled back at him. With her still seated in the truck, and Ward standing beside her, they were very nearly the same height. Dot reached out and ran her hand down the side of his face, the softness from his beard sending a thrill through her. "You really are extremely handsome," she said.

"Thank you," he said. "I think you're downright gorgeous yourself." He ducked his head, but he only kept it down for a moment before meeting her eyes again.

Without thinking or second-guessing too much, Dot curled her hand around the back of his neck, feeling the thick hair there too. She could only think about kissing him, and he clearly knew it.

Of course he did. Men like Ward Glover weren't strangers to women.

He reached up with one hand and swept his cowboy hat off his head. His other hand cradled her face, and he pressed his hat to her back at the same time he touched his lips to hers.

Explosions and waves of heat moved through Dot, and if she'd known kissing Ward Glover would be this magical and this blissfully intense, she'd have done it weeks and weeks ago.

She thoroughly enjoyed herself until an all-too-familiar *whoop! whoop!* of a police warning siren filled the air.

Ward broke the kiss at the same time the bright blue and red lights filled the parking lot.

"Sir," a man's voice said over the loudspeaker coming from the police vehicle. "Step away from the truck and keep your hands where I can see them."

"What in the world?" Ward asked, falling back a step.

Dot rolled her eyes and got out of the truck. "It's just my stupid brother," she said.

"Brother?" Ward asked, pausing near the hood of the truck and facing the cruiser.

"Yeah," Dot said, moving to stand next to him. She folded her arms and cocked her hip, glaring toward the windshield, behind which Tyson sat. "He's the third thing I didn't want to tell you about, because he gives every man I go out with a hard time."

"I didn't even know you had a brother," Ward said.

"You're about to find out why," Dot said dryly, hating that Tyson had interrupted the best kiss of her life and hoping that later that evening, she and Ward could pick up what they'd been doing before Tyson's rude intrusion.

**The Mechanics of Mistletoe (Book 1):** Bear Glover can be a grizzly or a teddy, and he's always thought he'd be just fine working his generational family ranch and going back to the ancient homestead alone. But his crush on Samantha Benton won't go away. She's a genius with a wrench on Bear's tractors...and his heart. Can he tame his wild side and get the girl, or will he be left broken-hearted this Christmas season?

**The Horsepower of the Holiday (Book 2):** Ranger Glover has worked at Shiloh Ridge Ranch his entire life. The cowboys do everything from horseback there, but when he goes to town to trade in some trucks, somehow Oakley Hatch persuades him to take some ATVs back to the ranch. (Bear is NOT happy.)

She's a former race car driver who's got Ranger all revved up... Can he remember who he is and get Oakley to slow down enough to fall in love, or will there simply be too much horsepower in the holiday this year for a real relationship?

**The Construction of Cheer (Book 3):** Bishop Glover is the youngest brother, and he usually keeps his head down and gets the job done. When Montana Martin shows up at Shiloh Ridge Ranch looking for work, he finds himself inventing construction projects that need doing just to keep her coming around. (Again, Bear is NOT happy.) She wants to build her own construction firm, but she ends up carving a place for herself inside Bishop's heart. Can he convince her *he's* all she needs this Christmas season, or will her cheer rest solely on the success of her business?

**The Secret of Santa (Book 4):** He's a fun-loving cowboy with a heart of gold. She's the woman who keeps putting him on hold. Can Ace and Holly Ann make a relationship work this Christmas?

**The Harmony of Holly (Book 5):** He's as prickly as his name, but the new woman in town has caught his eye. Can Cactus shelve his temper and shed his cowboy hermit skin fast enough to make a relationship with Willa work?

**The Chemistry of Christmas (Book 6):** He's the black sheep of the family, and she's a chemist who understands formulas, not emotions. Can Preacher and Charlie take their quirks and turn them into a strong relationship this Christmas?

**The Delivery of Decor (Book 7):** When he falls, he falls hard and deep. She literally drives away from every relationship she's ever had. Can Ward somehow get Dot to stay this Christmas?

**The Blessing of Babies (Book 8):** Don't miss out on a single moment of the Glover family saga in this bridge story linking Ward and Judge's love stories!

The Glovers love God, country, dogs, horses, and family. Not necessarily in that order. ;)

Many of them are married now, with babies on the way, and there are lessons to be learned, forgiveness to be had and given, and new names coming to the family tree in southern Three Rivers!

**The Networking of the Nativity (Book 9):** He's had a crush on her for years. She doesn't want to date until her daughter is out of the house. Will June take a change on Judge when the success of his Christmas light display depends on her networking abilities?

**The Wrangling of the Wreath (Book 10):** He's been so busy trying to find Miss Right. She's been right in front of him the whole time. This Christmas, can Mister and Libby take their relationship out of the best friend zone?

**The Hope of Her Heart (Book 11):** She's the only Glover without a significant other. He's been searching for someone who can love him *and* his daughter. Can Etta and August make a meaningful connection this Christmas?

**Rhett's Make-Believe Marriage (Book 1):** She needs a husband to be credible as a matchmaker. He wants to help a neighbor. Will their fake marriage take them out of the friend zone?

**Tripp's Trivial Tie (Book 2):** She needs a husband to keep her son. He's wanted to take their relationship to the next level, but she's always pushing him away. Will their trivial tie take them all the way to happily-ever-after?

**Liam's Invented I-Do (Book 3):** She's desperate to save her ranch. He wants to help her any way he can. Will their invented I-Do open doors that have previously been closed and lead to a happily-ever-after for both of them?

**Jeremiah's Bogus Bride (Book 4):** He wants to prove to his brothers that he's not broken. She just wants him. Will a fake marriage heal him or push her further away?

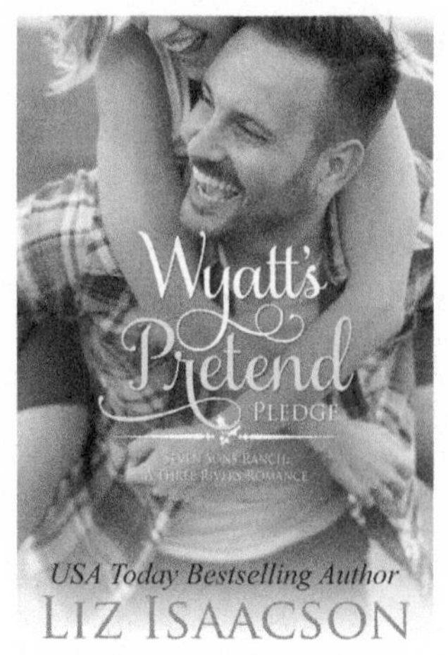


**Wyatt's Pretend Pledge (Book 5):** To get her inheritance, she needs a husband. He's wanted to fly with her for ages. Can their pretend pledge turn into something real?

**Skyler's Wanna-Be Wife (Book 6):** She needs a new last name to stay in school. He's willing to help a fellow student. Can this wanna-be wife show the playboy that some things should be taken seriously?

**Micah's Mock Matrimony (Book 7):** They were just actors auditioning for a play. The marriage was just for the audition – until a clerical error results in a legal marriage. Can these two ex-lovers negotiate this new ground between them and achieve new roles in each other's lives?

**Her Cowboy Billionaire Birthday Wish (Book 1):** All the maid at Whiskey Mountain Lodge wants for her birthday is a handsome cowboy billionaire. And Colton can make that wish come true—if only he hadn't escaped to Coral Canyon after being left at the altar...

**Her Cowboy Billionaire Butler (Book 2):** She broke up with him to date another man...who broke her heart. He's a former CEO with nothing to do who can't get her out of his head. Can Wes and Bree find a way toward happily-ever-after at Whiskey Mountain Lodge?

**Her Cowboy Billionaire Best Friend's Brother (Book 3):** She's best friends with the single dad cowboy's brother and has watched two friends find love with the sexy new cowboys in town. When Gray Hammond comes to Whiskey Mountain Lodge with his son, will Elise finally get her own happily-ever-after with one of the Hammond brothers?

**Her Cowboy Billionaire Beast (Book 4):** A cowboy billionaire beast, his new manager, and the Christmas traditions that soften his heart and bring them together.

**Her Cowboy Billionaire Bad Boy (Book 5):** A cowboy billionaire cop who's a stickler for rules, the woman he pulls over when he's not even on duty, and the personal mandates he has to break to keep her in his life...

Books in the Christmas in Coral Canyon Romance series

**Her Cowboy Billionaire Best Friend (Book 1):** Graham Whittaker returns to Coral Canyon a few days after Christmas—after the death of his father. He takes over the energy company his dad built from the ground up and buys a high-end lodge to live in—only a mile from the home of his once-best friend, Laney McAllister. They were best friends once, but Laney's always entertained feelings for him, and spending so much time with him while they make Christmas memories puts her heart in danger of getting broken again...

**Her Cowboy Billionaire Boss (Book 2):** Since the death of his wife a few years ago, Eli Whittaker has been running from one job to another, unable to find somewhere for him and his son to settle. Meg Palmer is Stockton's nanny, and she comes with her boss, Eli, to the lodge, her long-time crush on the man no different in Wyoming than it was on the beach. When she confesses her feelings for him and gets nothing in return, she's crushed, embarrassed, and unsure if she can stay in Coral Canyon for Christmas. Then Eli starts to show some feelings for her too...

**Her Cowboy Billionaire Boyfriend (Book 3):** Andrew Whittaker is the public face for the Whittaker Brothers' family energy company, and with his older brother's robot about to be announced, he needs a press secretary to help him get everything ready and tour the state to make the announcements. When he's hit by a protest sign being carried by the company's biggest opponent, Rebecca Collings, he learns with a few clicks that she has the background they need. He offers her the job of press secretary when she thought she was going to be arrested, and not only because the spark between them in so hot Andrew can't see straight.

**Can Becca and Andrew work together and keep their relationship a secret? Or will hearts break in this classic romance retelling reminiscent of *Two Weeks Notice*?**

**Her Cowboy Billionaire Bodyguard (Book 4):** Beau Whittaker has watched his brothers find love one by one, but every attempt he's made has ended in disaster. Lily Everett has been in the spotlight since childhood and has half a dozen platinum records with her two sisters. She's taking a break from the brutal music industry and hiding out in Wyoming while her ex-husband continues to cause trouble for her. When she hears of Beau Whittaker and what he offers his clients, she wants to meet him. Beau is instantly attracted to Lily, but he tried a relationship with his last client that left a scar that still hasn't healed...

**Can Lily use the spirit of Christmas to discover what matters most? Will Beau open his heart to the possibility of love with someone so different from him?**

**Her Cowboy Billionaire Bull Rider (Book 5):** Todd Christopherson has just retired from the professional rodeo circuit and returned to his hometown of Coral Canyon. Problem is, he's got no family there anymore, no land, and no job. Not that he needs a job--he's got plenty of money from his illustrious career riding bulls.

Then Todd gets thrown during a routine horseback ride up the canyon, and his only support as he recovers physically is the beautiful Violet Everett. She's no nurse, but she does the best she can for the handsome cowboy. **Will she lose her heart to the billionaire bull rider? Can Todd trust that God led him to Coral Canyon...and Vi?**

**Her Cowboy Billionaire Bachelor (Book 6):** Rose Everett isn't sure what to do with her life now that her country music career is on hold. After all, with both of her sisters in Coral Canyon, and one about to have a baby, they're not making albums anymore.

Liam Murphy has been working for Doctors Without Borders, but he's back in the US now, and looking to start a new clinic in Coral Canyon, where he spent his summers.

When Rose wins a date with Liam in a bachelor auction, their relationship blooms and grows quickly. **Can Liam and Rose find a solution to their problems that doesn't involve one of them leaving Coral Canyon with a broken heart?**

**Her Cowboy Billionaire Blind Date (Book 7):** Her sons want her to be happy, but she's too old to be set up on a blind date...isn't she?

Amanda Whittaker has been looking for a second chance at love since the death of her husband several years ago. Finley Barber is a cowboy in every sense of the word. Born and raised on a racehorse farm in Kentucky, he's since moved to Dog Valley and started his own breeding stable for champion horses. He hasn't dated in years, and everything about Amanda makes him nervous.

**Will Amanda take the leap of faith required to be with Finn? Or will he become just another boyfriend who doesn't make the cut?**

**Her Cowboy Billionaire Best Man (Book 8):** When Celia Abbott-Armstrong runs into a gorgeous cowboy at her best friend's wedding, she decides she's ready to start dating again.

But the cowboy is Zach Zuckerman, and the Zuckermans and Abbotts have been at war for generations.

Can Zach and Celia find a way to reconcile their family's differences so they can have a future together?

**Second Chance Ranch: A Three Rivers Ranch Romance (Book 1):** After his deployment, injured and discharged Major Squire Ackerman returns to Three Rivers Ranch, wanting to forgive Kelly for ignoring him a decade ago. He'd like to provide the stable life she needs, but with old wounds opening and a ranch on the brink of financial collapse, it will take patience and faith to make their second chance possible.

**Third Time's the Charm: A Three Rivers Ranch Romance (Book 2):** First Lieutenant Peter Marshall has a truckload of debt and no way to provide for a family, but Chelsea helps him see past all the obstacles, all the scars. With so many unknowns, can Pete and Chelsea develop the love, acceptance, and faith needed to find their happily ever after?

**Fourth and Long: A Three Rivers Ranch Romance (Book 3):** Commander Brett Murphy goes to Three Rivers Ranch to find some rest and relaxation with his Army buddies. Having his ex-wife show up with a seven-year-old she claims is his son is anything but the R&R he craves. Kate needs to make amends, and Brett needs to find forgiveness, but are they too late to find their happily ever after?

**Fifth Generation Cowboy: A Three Rivers Ranch Romance (Book 4):** Tom Lovell has watched his friends find their true happiness on Three Rivers Ranch, but everywhere he looks, he only sees friends. Rose Reyes has been bringing her daughter out to the ranch for equine therapy for months, but it doesn't seem to be working. Her challenges with Mari are just as frustrating as ever. Could Tom be exactly what Rose needs? Can he remove his friendship blinders and find love with someone who's been right in front of him all this time?

**Sixth Street Love Affair: A Three Rivers Ranch Romance (Book 5):** After losing his wife a few years back, Garth Ahlstrom thinks he's ready for a second chance at love. But Juliette Thompson has a secret that could destroy their budding relationship. Can they find the strength, patience, and faith to make things work?

**The Seventh Sergeant: A Three Rivers Ranch Romance (Book 6):** Life has finally started to settle down for Sergeant Reese Sanders after his devastating injury overseas. Discharged from the Army and now with a good job at Courage Reins, he's finally found happiness—until a horrific fall puts him right back where he was years ago: Injured and depressed. Carly Watters, Reese's new veteran care coordinator, dislikes small towns almost as much as she loathes cowboys. But she finds herself faced with both when she gets assigned to Reese's case. Do they have the humility and faith to make their relationship more than professional?

**Eight Second Ride: A Three Rivers Ranch Romance (Book 7):** Ethan Greene loves his work at Three Rivers Ranch, but he can't seem to find the right woman to settle down with. When sassy yet vulnerable Brynn Bowman shows up at the ranch to recruit him back to the rodeo circuit, he takes a different approach with the barrel racing champion. His patience and newfound faith pay off when a friendship--and more--starts with Brynn. But she wants out of the rodeo circuit right when Ethan wants to rejoin. Can they find the path God wants them to take and still stay together?

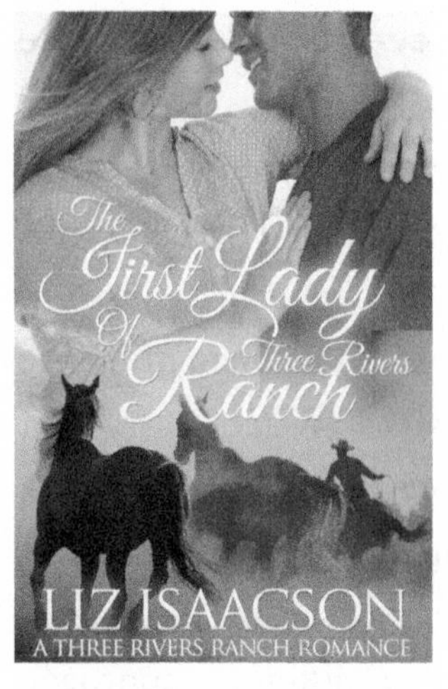


**The First Lady of Three Rivers Ranch: A Three Rivers Ranch Romance (Book 8):** Heidi Duffin has been dreaming about opening her own bakery since she was thirteen years old. She scrimped and saved for years to afford baking and pastry school in San Francisco. And now she only has one year left before she's a certified pastry chef. Frank Ackerman's father has recently retired, and he's taken over the largest cattle ranch in the Texas Panhandle. A horseman through and through, he's also nearing thirty-one and looking for someone to bring love and joy to a homestead that's been dominated by men for a decade. But when he convinces Heidi to come clean the cowboy cabins, she changes all that. But the siren's call of a bakery is still loud in Heidi's ears, even if she's also seeing a future with Frank. Can she rely on her faith in ways she's never had to before or will their relationship end when summer does?

**Christmas in Three Rivers: A Three Rivers Ranch Romance (Book 9):** Isn't Christmas the best time to fall in love? The cowboys of Three Rivers Ranch think so. Join four of them as they journey toward their path to happily ever after in four, all-new novellas in the Amazon #1 Bestselling Three Rivers Ranch Romance series.

THE NINTH INNING: The Christmas season has never felt like such a burden to boutique owner Andrea Larsen. But with Mama gone and the holidays upon her, Andy finds herself wishing she hadn't been so quick to judge her former boyfriend, cowboy Lawrence Collins. Well, Lawrence hasn't forgotten about Andy either, and he devises a plan to get her out to the ranch so they can reconnect. Do they have the faith and humility to patch things up and start a new relationship?

TEN DAYS IN TOWN: Sandy Keller is tired of the dating scene in Three Rivers. Though she owns the pancake house, she's looking for a fresh start, which means an escape from the town where she grew up. When her older brother's best friend, Tad Jorgensen, comes to town for the holidays, it is a balm to his weary soul. A helicopter tour guide who experienced a near-death experience, he's looking to start over too--but in Three Rivers. Can Sandy and Tad navigate their troubles to find the path God wants them to take--and discover true love--in only ten days?

ELEVEN YEAR REUNION: Pastry chef extraordinaire, Grace Lewis has moved to Three Rivers to help Heidi Ackerman open a bakery in Three Rivers. Grace relishes the idea of starting over in a town where no one knows about her failed cupcakery. She doesn't expect to run into her old high school boyfriend, Jonathan Carver. A carpenter working at Three Rivers Ranch, Jon's in town against his will. But with Grace now on the scene, Jon's thinking life in Three Rivers is suddenly looking up. But with her focus on baking and his disdain for small towns, can they make their eleven year reunion stick?

THE TWELFTH TOWN: Newscaster Taryn Tucker has had enough of life on-screen. She's bounced from town to town before arriving in Three Rivers, completely alone and completely anonymous--just the way she now likes it. She takes a job cleaning at Three Rivers Ranch, hoping for a chance to figure out who she is and where God wants her. When she meets happy-go-lucky cowhand Kenny Stockton, she doesn't expect sparks to fly. Kenny's always been "the best friend" for his female friends, but the pull between him and Taryn can't be denied. Will they have the courage and faith necessary to make their opposite worlds mesh?

**Lucky Number Thirteen: A Three Rivers Ranch Romance (Book 10):** Tanner Wolf, a rodeo champion ten times over, is excited to be riding in Three Rivers for the first time since he left his philandering ways and found religion. Seeing his old friends Ethan and Brynn is therapeutic--until a terrible accident lands him in the hospital. With his rodeo career over, Tanner thinks maybe he'll stay in town--and it's not just because his nurse, Summer Hamblin, is the prettiest woman he's ever met. But Summer's the queen of first dates, and as she looks for a way to make a relationship with the transient rodeo star work Summer's not sure she has the fortitude to go on a second date. Can they find love among the tragedy?

**The Curse of February Fourteenth: A Three Rivers Ranch Romance (Book 11):** Cal Hodgkins, cowboy veterinarian at Bowman's Breeds, isn't planning to meet anyone at the masked dance in small-town Three Rivers. He just wants to get his bachelor friends off his back and sit on the sidelines to drink his punch. But when he sees a woman dressed in gorgeous butterfly wings and cowgirl boots with blue stitching, he's smitten. Too bad she runs away from the dance before he can get her name, leaving only her boot behind...

**Fifteen Minutes of Fame: A Three Rivers Ranch Romance (Book 12):** Navy Richards is thirty-five years of tired—tired of dating the same men, working a demanding job, and getting her heart broken over and over again. Her aunt has always spoken highly of the matchmaker in Three Rivers, Texas, so she takes a six-month sabbatical from her high-stress job as a pediatric nurse, hops on a bus, and meets with the matchmaker. Then she meets Gavin Redd. He's handsome, he's hardworking, and he's a cowboy. But is he an Aquarius too? Navy's not making a move until she knows for sure...

**Sixteen Steps to Fall in Love: A Three Rivers Ranch Romance (Book 13):** A chance encounter at a dog park sheds new light on the tall, talented Boone that Nicole can't ignore. As they get to know each other better and start to dig into each other's past, Nicole is the one who wants to run. This time from her growing admiration and attachment to Boone. From her aging parents. From herself.

But Boone feels the attraction between them too, and he decides he's tired of running and ready to make Three Rivers his permanent home. **Can Boone and Nicole use their faith to overcome their differences and find a happily-ever-after together?**

**The Sleigh on Seventeenth Street: A Three Rivers Ranch Romance (Book 14):** A cowboy with skills as an electrician tries a relationship with a down-on-her luck plumber. Can Dylan and Camila make water and electricity play nicely together this Christmas season? Or will they get shocked as they try to make their relationship work?

Books in the Last Chance Ranch Romance series

**Last Chance Ranch (Book 1):** A cowgirl down on her luck hires a man who's good with horses and under the hood of a car. Can Hudson fine tune Scarlett's heart as they work together? Or will things backfire and make everything worse at Last Chance Ranch?

**Last Chance Cowboy (Book 2):** A billionaire cowboy without a home meets a woman who secretly makes food videos to pay her debts...Can Carson and Adele do more than fight in the kitchens at Last Chance Ranch?

**Last Chance Wedding (Book 3):** A female carpenter needs a husband just for a few days... Can Jeri and Sawyer navigate the minefield of a pretend marriage before their feelings become real?

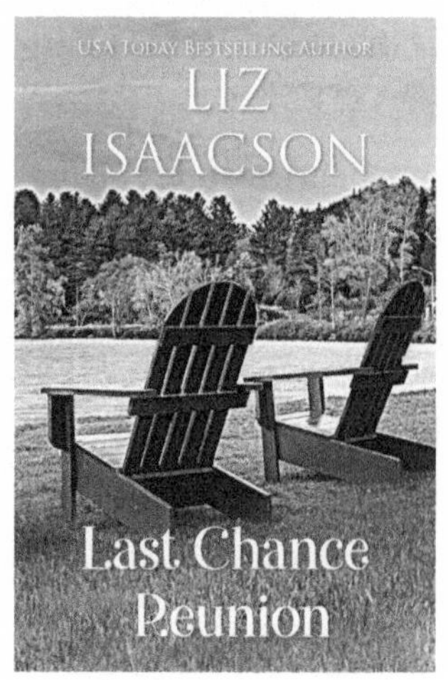


**Last Chance Reunion (Book 4):** An Army cowboy, the woman he dated years ago, and their last chance at Last Chance Ranch... Can Dave and Sissy put aside hurt feelings and make their second chance romance work?

**Last Chance Lake (Book 5):** A former dairy farmer and the marketing director on the ranch have to work together to make the cow cuddling program a success. But can Karla let Cache into her life? Or will she keep all her secrets from him - and keep *him* a secret too?

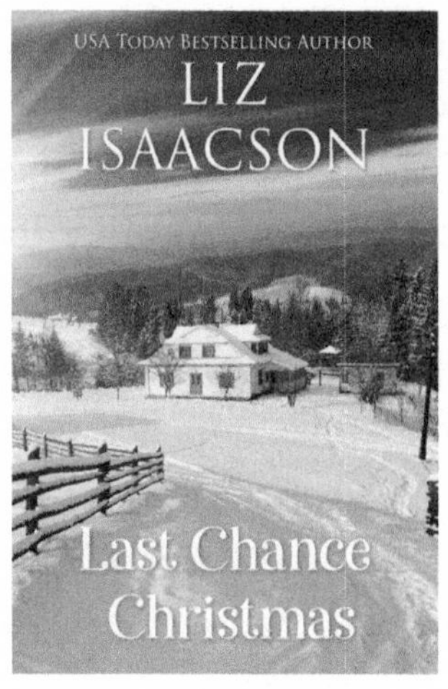


**Last Chance Christmas (Book 6):** She's tired of having her heart broken by cowboys. He waited too long to ask her out. Can Lance fix things quickly, or will Amber leave Last Chance Ranch before he can tell her how he feels?

Books in the Steeple Ridge Romance Series:

**Her Billionaire Cowboy (Book 1):** Tucker Jenkins has had enough of tall buildings, traffic, and has traded in his technology firm in New York City for Steeple Ridge Horse Farm in rural Vermont. Missy Marino has worked at the farm since she was a teen, and she's always dreamed of owning it. But her ex-husband left her with a truckload of debt, making her fantasies of owning the farm unfulfilled. Tucker didn't come to the country to find a new wife, but he supposes a woman could help him start over in Steeple Ridge. Will Tucker and Missy be able to navigate the shaky ground between them to find a new beginning?

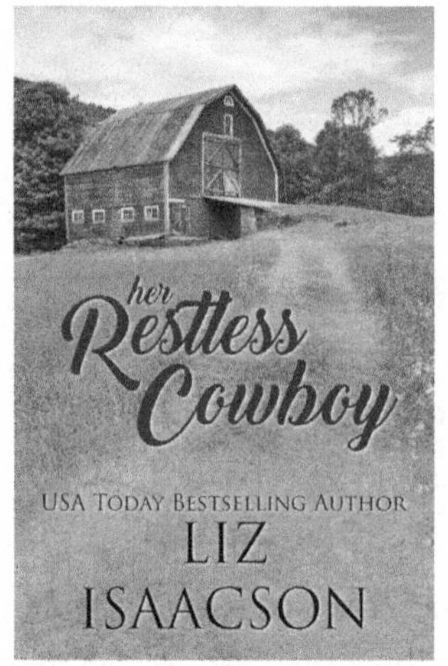


**Her Restless Cowboy: A Butters Brothers Novel, Steeple Ridge Romance (Book 2):** Ben Buttars is the youngest of the four Buttars brothers who come to Steeple Ridge Farm, and he finally feels like he's landed somewhere he can make a life for himself. Reagan Cantwell is a decade older than Ben and the recreational direction for the town of Island Park. Though Ben is young, he knows what he wants—and that's Rae. Can she figure out how to put what matters most in her life—family and faith—above her job before she loses Ben?

**Her Faithful Cowboy: A Butters Brothers Novel, Steeple Ridge Romance (Book 3):** Sam Buttars has spent the last decade making sure he and his brothers stay together. They've been at Steeple Ridge for a while now, but with the youngest married and happy, the siren's call to return to his parents' farm in Wyoming is loud in Sam's ears. He'd just go if it weren't for beautiful Bonnie Sherman, who roped his heart the first time he saw her. Do Sam and Bonnie have the faith to find comfort in each other instead of in the people who've already passed?

**Her Mistletoe Cowboy: A Butters Brothers Novel, Steeple Ridge Romance (Book 4):** Logan Buttars has always been good-natured and happy-go-lucky. After watching two of his brothers settle down, he recognizes a void in his life he didn't know about. Veterinarian Layla Guyman has appreciated Logan's friendship and easy way with animals when he comes into the clinic to get the service dogs. But with his future at Steeple Ridge in the balance, she's not sure a relationship with him is worth the risk. Can she rely on her faith and employ patience to tame Logan's wild heart?

**Her Patient Cowboy: A Butters Brothers Novel, Steeple Ridge Romance (Book 5):** Darren Buttars is cool, collected, and quiet—and utterly devastated when his girlfriend of nine months, Farrah Irvine, breaks up with him because he wanted her to ride her horse in a parade. But Farrah doesn't ride anymore, a fact she made very clear to Darren. She returned to her childhood home with so much baggage, she doesn't know where to start with the unpacking. Darren's the only Buttars brother who isn't married, and he wants to make Island Park his permanent home—with Farrah. Can they find their way through the heartache to achieve a happily-ever-after together?

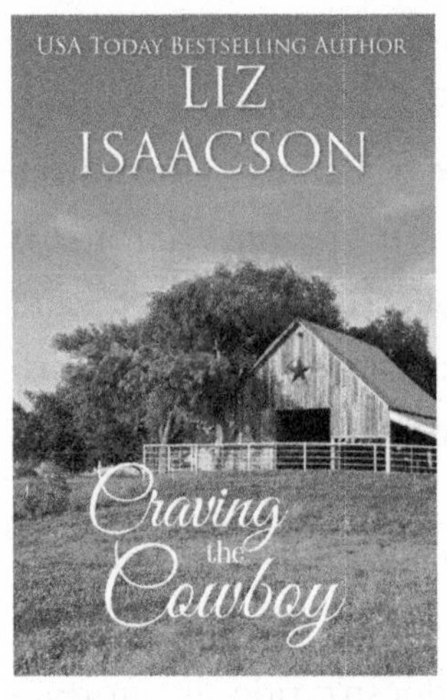


**Craving the Cowboy (Book 1):** Dwayne Carver is set to inherit his family's ranch in the heart of Texas Hill Country, and in order to keep up with his ranch duties and fulfill his dreams of owning a horse farm, he hires top trainer Felicity Lightburne. They get along great, and she can envision herself on this new farm—at least until her mother falls ill and she has to return to help her. Can Dwayne and Felicity work through their differences to find their happily-ever-after?

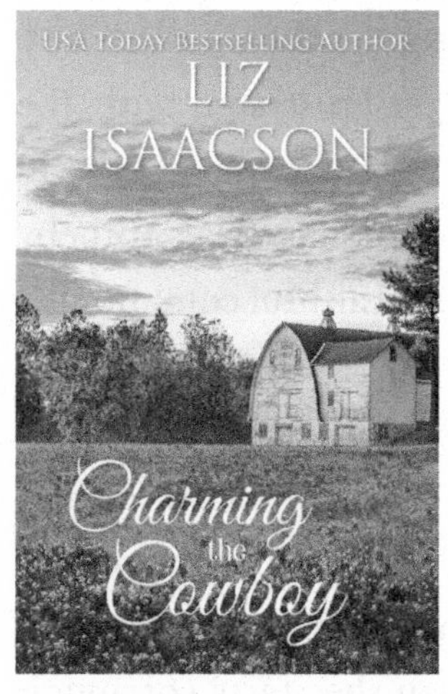


**Charming the Cowboy (Book 2):** Third grade teacher Heather Carver has had her eye on Levi Rhodes for a couple of years now, but he seems to be blind to her attempts to charm him. When she breaks her arm while on his horse ranch, Heather infiltrates Levi's life in ways he's never thought of, and his strict anti-female stance slips. Will Heather heal his emotional scars and he care for her physical ones so they can have a real relationship?

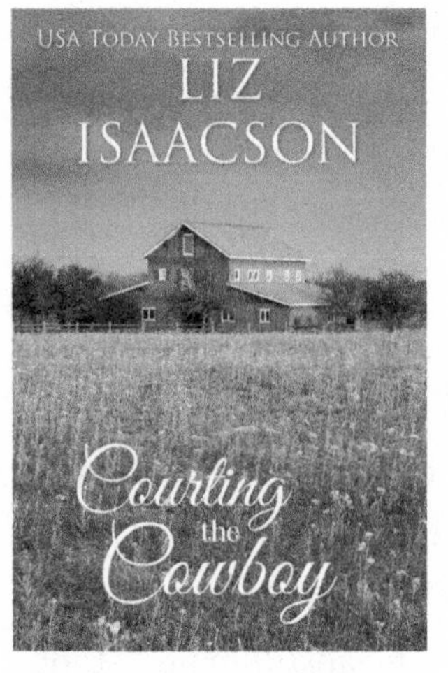


**Courting the Cowboy (Book 3):** Frustrated with the cowboy-only dating scene in Grape Seed Falls, May Sotheby joins TexasFaithful.com, hoping to find her soul mate without having to relocate--or deal with cowboy hats and boots. She has no idea that Kurt Pemberton, foreman at Grape Seed Ranch, is the man she starts communicating with... Will May be able to follow her heart and get Kurt to forgive her so they can be together?

**Claiming the Cowboy, Royal Brothers Book 1 (Grape Seed Falls Romance Book 4):** Unwilling to be tied down, farrier Robin Cook has managed to pack her entire life into a two-hundred-and-eighty square-foot house, and that includes her Yorkie. Cowboy and co-foreman, Shane Royal has had his heart set on Robin for three years, even though she flat-out turned him down the last time he asked her to dinner. But she's back at Grape Seed Ranch for five weeks as she works her horse-shoeing magic, and he's still interested, despite a bitter life lesson that left a bad taste for marriage in his mouth.

Robin's interested in him too. But can she find room for Shane in her tiny house--and can he take a chance on her with his tired heart?

**Catching the Cowboy, Royal Brothers Book 2 (Grape Seed Falls Romance Book 5):** Dylan Royal is good at two things: whistling and caring for cattle. When his cows are being attacked by an unknown wild animal, he calls Texas Parks & Wildlife for help. He wasn't expecting a beautiful mammologist to show up, all flirty and fun and everything Dylan didn't know he wanted in his life.

Hazel Brewster has gone on more first dates than anyone in Grape Seed Falls, and she thinks maybe Dylan deserves a second... Can they find their way through wild animals, huge life changes, and their emotional pasts to find their forever future?

**Cheering the Cowboy, Royal Brothers Book 3 (Grape Seed Falls Romance Book 6):** Austin Royal loves his life on his new ranch with his brothers. But he doesn't love that Shayleigh Hatch came with the property, nor that he has to take the blame for the fact that he now owns her childhood ranch. They rarely have a conversation that doesn't leave him furious and frustrated--and yet he's still attracted to Shay in a strange, new way.

Shay inexplicably likes him too, which utterly confuses and angers her. As they work to make this Christmas the best the Triple Towers Ranch has ever seen, can they also navigate through their rocky relationship to smoother waters?

Praise for Liz Isaacson

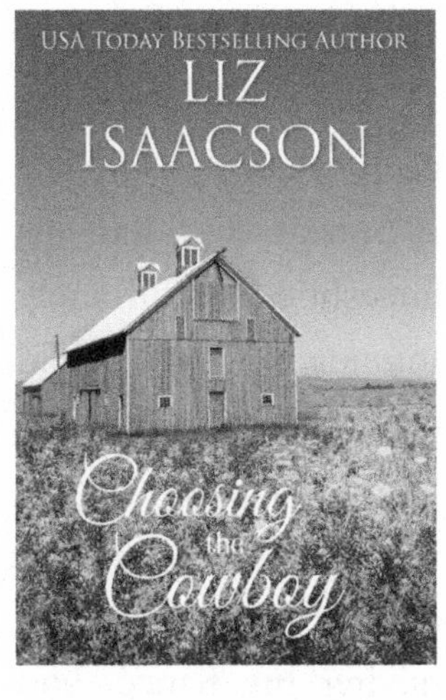


**Choosing the Cowboy (Book 7):** With financial trouble and personal issues around every corner, can Maggie Duffin and Chase Carver rely on their faith to find their happily-ever-after?

A spinoff from the #1 bestselling Three Rivers Ranch Romance novels, also by USA Today bestselling author Liz Isaacson.

Books in the Horseshoe Home Ranch Romance Series:

**The Redesigned Ranch (Book 1):** Jace Lovell only has one thing left after his fiancé abandons him at the altar: his job at Horseshoe Home Ranch. Belle Edmunds is back in Gold Valley and she's desperate to build a portfolio that she can use to start her own firm in Montana. Jace isn't anywhere near forgiving his fiancé, and he's not sure he's ready for a new relationship with someone as fiery and beautiful as Belle. Can she employ her patience while he figures out how to forgive so they can find their own brand of happily-ever-after?

**The Snowstorm in Gold Valley (Book 2):** Professional snowboarder Sterling Maughan has sequestered himself in his family's cabin in the exclusive mountain community above Gold Valley, Montana after a devastating fall that ended his career. Norah Watson cleans Sterling's cabin and the more time they spend together, the more Sterling is interested in all things Norah. As his body heals, so does his faith. Will Norah be able to trust Sterling so they can have a chance at true love?

**The Cabin on Bear Mountain (Book 3):** Landon Edmunds has been a cowboy his whole life. An accident five years ago ended his successful rodeo career, and now he's looking to start a horse ranch--and he's looking outside of Montana. Which would be great if God hadn't brought Megan Palmer back to Gold Valley right when Landon is looking to leave. Megan and Landon work together well, and as sparks fly, she's sure God brought her back to Gold Valley so she could find her happily ever after. Through serious discussion and prayer, can Landon and Megan find their future together?

Be sure to check out the spinoff series, the Brush Creek Brides romances after you read FALLING FOR HIS BEST FRIEND. Start with A WEDDING FOR THE WIDOWER.

**The Cowboy at the Creek (Book 4):** Twelve years ago, Owen Carr left Gold Valley—and his long-time girlfriend—in favor of a country music career in Nashville. Married and divorced, Natalie teaches ballet at the dance studio in Gold Valley, but she never auditioned for the professional company the way she dreamed of doing. With Owen back, she realizes all the opportunities she missed out on when he left all those years ago—including a future with him. Can they mend broken bridges in order to have a second chance at love?

**The Wedding in the Winter (Book 5):** Caleb Chamberlain has spent the last five years recovering from a horrible breakup, his alcoholism that stemmed from it, and the car accident that left him hospitalized. He's finally on the right track in his life—until Holly Gray, his twin brother's ex-fiance mistakes him for Nathan. Holly's back in Gold Valley to get the required veterinarian hours to apply for her graduate program. When the herd at Horseshoe Home comes down with pneumonia, Caleb and Holly are forced to work together in close quarters. Holly's over Nathan, but she hasn't forgiven him—or the woman she believes broke up their relationship. Can Caleb and Holly navigate such a rough past to find their happily-ever-after?

**The Long Way Home (Book 6):** Ty Barker has been dancing through the last thirty years of his life--and he's suddenly realized he's alone. River Lee Whitely is back in Gold Valley with her two little girls after a divorce that's left deep scars. She has a job at Silver Creek that requires her to be able to ride a horse, and she nearly tramples Ty at her first lesson. That's just fine by him, because River Lee is the girl Ty has never gotten over. Ty realizes River Lee needs time to settle into her new job, her new home, her new life as a single parent, but going slow has never been his style. But for River Lee, can Ty take the necessary steps to keep her in his life?

**Christmas at the Ranch (Book 7):** Archer Bailey has already lost one job to Emersyn Enders, so he deliberately doesn't tell her about the cowhand job up at Horseshoe Home Ranch. Emery's temporary job is ending, but her obligations to her physically disabled sister aren't. As Archer and Emery work together, its clear that the sparks flying between them aren't all from their friendly competition over a job. Will Emery and Archer be able to navigate the ranch, their close quarters, and their individual circumstances to find love this holiday season?

**The Love of a Cowboy (Book 8):** Cowboy Elliott Hawthorne has just lost his best friend and cabin mate to the worst thing imaginable—marriage. When his brother calls about an accident with their father, Elliott rushes down to Gold Valley from the ranch only to be met with the most beautiful woman he's ever seen. His father's new physical therapist, London Marsh, likes the handsome face and gentle spirit she sees in Elliott too. Can Elliott and London navigate difficult family situations to find a happily-ever-after?

Books in the Brush Creek Brides Romance Series:

**Brush Creek Cowboy: Brush Creek Cowboys Romance (Book 1):** Former rodeo champion and cowboy Walker Thompson trains horses at Brush Creek Horse Ranch, where he lives a simple life in his cabin with his ten-year-old son. A widower of six years, he's worked with Tess Wagner, a widow who came to Brush Creek to escape the turmoil of her life to give her seven-year-old son a slower pace of life. But Tess's breast cancer is back...

Walker will have to decide if he'd rather spend even a short time with Tess than not have her in his life at all. Tess wants to feel God's love and power, but can she discover and accept God's will in order to find her happy ending?

**The Cowboy's Challenge: Brush Creek Brides Romance (Book 2):** Cowboy and professional roper Justin Jackman has found solitude at Brush Creek Horse Ranch, preferring his time with the animals he trains over dating. With two failed engagements in his past, he's not really interested in getting his heart stomped on again. But when flirty and fun Renee Martin picks him up at a church ice cream bar--on a bet, no less--he finds himself more than just a little interested. His Gen-X attitudes are attractive to her; her Millennial behaviors drive him nuts. Can Justin look past their differences and take a chance on another engagement?

**A Cowboy Proposal: Brush Creek Brides Romance (Book 3):** Ted Caldwell has been a retired bronc rider for years, and he thought he was perfectly happy training horses to buck at Brush Creek Ranch. He was wrong. When he meets April Nox, who comes to the ranch to hide her pregnancy from all her friends back in Jackson Hole, Ted realizes he has a huge family-shaped hole in his life. April is embarrassed, heartbroken, and trying to find her extinguished faith. She's never ridden a horse and wants nothing to do with a cowboy ever again. Can Ted and April create a family of happiness and love from a tragedy?

**A New Family for the Cowboy: Brush Creek Brides Romance (Book 4):** Blake Gibbons oversees all the agriculture at Brush Creek Horse Ranch, sometimes moonlighting as a general contractor. When he meets Erin Shields, new in town, at her aunt's bakery, he's instantly smitten. Erin moved to Brush Creek after a divorce that left her penniless, homeless, and a single mother of three children under age eight. She's nowhere near ready to start dating again, but the longer Blake hangs around the bakery, the more she starts to like him. Can Blake and Erin find a way to blend their lifestyles and become a family?

**The Cowboy and the Champion: Brush Creek Brides Romance (Book 5):** Emmett Graves has always had a positive outlook on life. He adores training horses to become barrel racing champions during the day and cuddling with his cat at night. Fresh off her professional rodeo retirement, Molly Brady comes to Brush Creek Horse Ranch as Emmett's protege. He's not thrilled, and she's allergic to cats. Oh, and she'd like to stay cowboy-free, thank you very much. But Emmett's about as cowboy as they come.... Can Emmett and Molly work together without falling in love?

**Schooled by the Cowboy: Brush Creek Brides Romance (Book 6):** Grant Ford spends his days training cattle—when he's not camped out at the elementary school hoping to catch a glimpse of his ex-girlfriend. When principal Shannon Sharpe confronts him and asks him to stay away from the school, the spark between them is instant and hot. Shannon's expecting a transfer very soon, but she also needs a summer outdoor coordinator—and Grant fits the bill. Just because he's handsome and everything Shannon's ever wanted in a cowboy husband means nothing. Will Grant and Shannon be able to survive the summer or will the Utah heat be too much for them to handle?

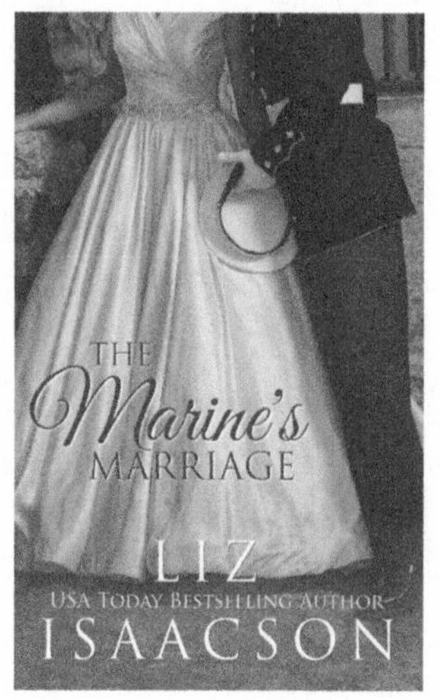


**The Marine's Marriage: A Fuller Family Novel - Brush Creek Brides Romance (Book 1):** Tate Benson can't believe he's come to Nowhere, Utah, to fix up a house that hasn't been inhabited in years. But he has. Because he's retired from the Marines and looking to start a life as a police officer in small-town Brush Creek. Wren Fuller has her hands full most days running her family's company. When Tate calls and demands a maid for that morning, she decides to have the calls forwarded to her cell and go help him out. She didn't know he was moving in next door, and she's completely unprepared for his handsomeness, his kind heart, and his wounded soul.Can Tate and Wren weather a relationship when they're also next-door neighbors?

**The Firefighter's Fiancé: A Fuller Family Novel - Brush Creek Brides Romance (Book 2):** Cora Wesley comes to Brush Creek, hoping to get some in-the-wild firefighting training as she prepares to put in her application to be a hotshot. When she meets Brennan Fuller, the spark between them is hot and instant. As they get to know each other, her deadline is constantly looming over them, and Brennan starts to wonder if he can break ranks in the family business. He's okay mowing lawns and hanging out with his brothers, but he dreams of being able to go to college and become a landscape architect, but he's just not sure it can be done. Will Cora and Brennan be able to endure their trials to find true love?

**The Trooper's Treasure: A Fuller Family Novel - Brush Creek Brides Romance (Book 3):** Dawn Fuller has made some mistakes in her life, and she's not proud of the way McDermott Boyd found her off the road one day last year. She's spent a hard year wrestling with her choices and trying to fix them, glad for McDermott's acceptance and friendship. He lost his wife years ago, done his best with his daughter, and now he's ready to move on. Can McDermott help Dawn find a way past her former mistakes and down a path that leads to love, family, and happiness?

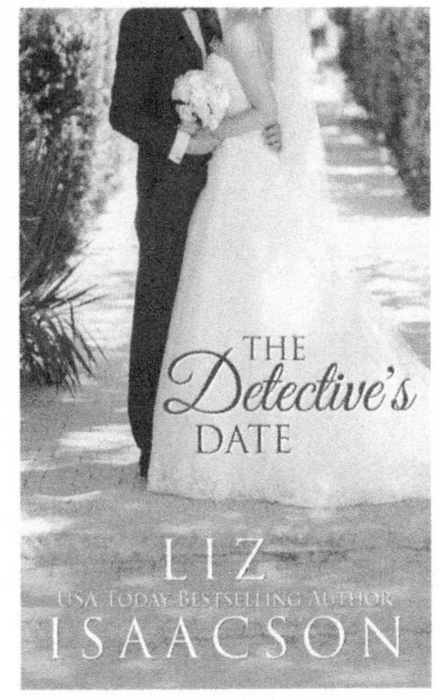


**The Detective's Date: A Fuller Family Novel - Brush Creek Brides Romance (Book 4):** Dahlia Reid is one of the best detectives Brush Creek and the surrounding towns has ever had. She's given up on the idea of marriage—and pleasing her mother—and has dedicated herself fully to her job. Which is great, since one of the most perplexing cases of her career has come to town. Kyler Fuller thinks he's finally ready to move past the woman who ghosted him years ago. He's cut his hair, and he's ready to start dating. Too bad every woman he's been out with is about as interesting as a lamppost—until Dahlia. He finds her beautiful, her quick wit a breath of fresh air, and her intelligence sexy. Can Kyler and Dahlia use their faith to find a way through the obstacles threatening to keep them apart?

**The Paramedic's Partner: A Fuller Family Novel - Brush Creek Brides Romance (Book 5):** Jazzy Fuller has always been overshadowed by her prettier, more popular twin, Fabiana. Fabi meets paramedic Max Robinson at the park and sets a date with him only to come down with the flu. So she convinces Jazzy to cut her hair and take her place on the date. And the spark between Jazzy and Max is hot and instant...if only he knew she wasn't her sister, Fabi.

Max drives the ambulance for the town of Brush Creek with is partner Ed Moon, and neither of them have been all that lucky in love. Until Max suggests to who he thinks is Fabi that they should double with Ed and Jazzy. They do, and Fabi is smitten with the steady, strong Ed Moon. As each twin falls further and further in love with their respective paramedic, it becomes obvious they'll need to come clean about the switcheroo sooner rather than later...or risk losing their hearts.

**The Chief's Catch: A Fuller Family Novel - Brush Creek Brides Romance (Book 6):** Berlin Fuller has struck out with the dating scene in Brush Creek more times than she cares to admit. When she makes a deal with her friends that they can choose the next man she goes out with, she didn't dream they'd pick surly Cole Fairbanks, the new Chief of Police.

His friends call him the Beast and challenge him to complete ten dates that summer or give up his bonus check. When Berlin approaches him, stuttering about the deal with her friends and claiming they don't actually have to go out, he's intrigued. As the summer passes, Cole finds himself burning both ends of the candle to keep up with his job and his new relationship. When he unleashes the Beast one time too many, Berlin will have to decide if she can tame him or if she should walk away.

## About Liz

Liz Isaacson writes inspirational romance, usually set in Texas, or Montana, or anywhere else horses and cowboys exist. She lives in Utah, where she writes full-time, walks her two dogs daily, and eats a lot of peanut butter M&Ms while writing. Find her on her website at lizisaacson.com.

Made in the USA
Las Vegas, NV
03 March 2021

18945306R00340